HUNTING DAYBREAK

HUNTING DAYBREAK

Shattered Sunlight Series Book II

E.A. CHANCE

Darlington
Publishing

eBook ISBN: 978-1-951870-07-2
Paperback ISBN: 978-1-951870-09-6
Hardcover ISBN: 978-1-951870-08-9

Cover Design by Dissect Designs, London

❀ Created with Vellum

ALSO BY E.A. CHANCE

Shattered Sunlight Series

SOLAR FURY

HOPE IGNITES

Omnibus Edition

SHATTERED SUNLIGHT SERIES COLLECTION: BOOKS 1-3

E.A. Chance also writes as Eleanor Chance

ACKNOWLEDGMENTS

Thank you to Joseph Nassise, my mentor/editor/*Sensei* and prolific NYT bestselling author, for his invaluable guidance and encouragement, and to my award-winning cover designer, Timothy Barber, for his immense talent and ability to see into my mind and create the covers I envision.

I'm grateful to my supportive and loving mom and sister who give their time, encouragement, and love in a never ending supply. Thank to all of the rest of my family, too, who are always so supportive and patient. Love you!

A special thanks to my husband for going with very little sleep for an entire weekend to help me meet my deadline! You're the best and I couldn't have done it without you!

Last, and most importantly, thank you to all of you, my readers. None of this would matter without you. Your kind and enthusiastic support means the world to me.

To my sons Jake, Jim, Jeff & Joe. You are my life.

CHAPTER ONE

DR. RILEY POOLE climbed out of the saddle and dropped to the muddy ground. Ignoring her soggy boots and drenched clothing, she sprinted through the sheet of rain and ducked under a shallow rock outcropping. She pulled her raincoat tighter and pressed her back against the stone, hoping it would provide cover from the downpour.

She and her new husband, Coop, had faced nothing but pouring rain and mud from the moment they hit the road three days earlier. It felt more like a month had passed. Was this harebrained trek from the hills of western Virginia to Colorado just one more in a string of her disastrous ideas since the Coronal Mass Ejection destroyed modern civilization and caused millions of deaths?

In the four months since the CME struck, daily life had grown unrecognizable. After the immediate deaths when the global power grid was destroyed and natural gas explosions erupted, the elderly, defenseless, and ill-prepared were wiped out from lack of food, loss of health care and a myriad of conveniences humans took for granted. Life had become a matter of surviving from one day to the next. This was the world

Riley had thrust them back into by leaving the comfort and safety of the ranch, driven by her obsession to get to her two youngest children in Colorado.

Coop ran up and crouched beside her, wrapping his arms around her to shield her from the deluge. "I'm not loving that look on your face," he said loud enough for her to hear him over the rain.

"I can't do this," Riley cried. "Leaving the ranch, leaving my own daughter, was an insane idea. Why didn't you stop me?"

Coop shook his head and laughed. "Since when have I been able to stop you from doing anything you set your mind to? And the point of this adventure is for you to find out what happened to your other kids. We can't lose sight of that because of a little rain. Jared and Emily are waiting for you at the end of this asinine field trip."

"That doesn't change the fact that I abandoned Julia."

"You didn't dump a newborn on someone's doorstep. She's your thirteen-year-old Warrior Princess, recovering from a gunshot wound. Bringing her along *would* have been insane. She's safe with your aunt and uncle on the ranch, and we'll be back for her as soon as humanly possible."

"You're right, as always. I'm just soaked, missing Julia, and questioning my sanity. Let's wait for the rain to taper, then find cover for the night."

"No argument from me. I'm going to check the horses. Biscuit was agitated when I left him."

"When is Biscuit not agitated?" she called as he ran back to the horses.

Riley shivered as she watched him pat the horses' necks, speaking comforting words to them. Her horse, Aurora, was an even-tempered chestnut mare who almost seemed able to read her mind. Coop's horse, Echo, was a proud black stallion, always in a rush to get everywhere, making it a challenge for the other horses to keep pace. He and Coop were made for each other.

Biscuit, the pack horse, was a small dapple-gray gelding; slow, timid, and utterly annoyed at being dragged away from his cozy stall. Riley was sure if he could talk, he'd be complaining as much as she was.

Seeing Coop's patience with the horses made her grateful again that she'd met him in the days before the world was torn apart. Not only had he been vital in helping her and Julia survive their exodus from Washington, DC, but he'd brought love into her life again, something she never expected after the death of her first husband four years earlier.

She marveled that she could love two men who were so drastically different. Zach had been a fearless US Air Force pilot who'd died when his helicopter was shot down on the Afghan border four years earlier. It was a devastating blow that had given her PTSD and had taken years to recover from.

Dr. Neal Xavier Cooper III, who insisted on being called Coop, was a brilliant, but quirky and impulsive cardiologist who could make a joke out of any situation. Zach had been John Wayne. Coop was the friendly and jovial boy-next-door with his sandy brown hair that perpetually stuck out in all directions. Brilliant though he was, Coop never put on airs or looked down on those less gifted intellectually. He was kind, funny, and talented, but no less brave or adventurous than her first husband. She had given Coop her whole heart and looked forward to sharing the rest of her life with him, however long that might be.

The sweet memory of her wedding with Coop three days earlier was the only thing bringing her comfort in the miserable beginning to their journey. She still felt pangs of guilt for sneaking away in the middle of their reception under the guise of going to honeymoon at her Uncle Mitch's fishing lodge. She'd hated leaving without saying goodbye to Julia, but she wouldn't have been able to tear herself away otherwise. Only the burning drive to find out what happened to her two other children had given her the strength to go. Julia was undoubtedly furious with her, but Riley could only pray she'd forgive her in time.

She tucked her thoughts away as Coop hurried back towards her.

"The rain is slowing," he said. "Let's get on the trail and find shelter while there's still light. There may be a forest station or camp nearby where we can rest and dry off for a few days. And I wouldn't mind having an actual honeymoon instead of just a fictional one."

He held out a hand to help her up, then scooped her into his arms. She gave him a lingering kiss, and said, "Let's get this marriage started."

Julia opened her eyes to the dawn light and sighed in contentment at the memory of the wedding reception for her mom and Coop four days earlier. Her mom had made the most beautiful bride, like a little red-haired model in her elegant wedding dress. After all the suffering over the past few months, she was thrilled that Coop was her new dad and her mom had someone to love.

Julia wondered if she'd ever get the chance to be a bride. The only people around were family. She thought of Dane, the boy she'd met during the short stay at a converted senior center and decided to ask her mom if they could take a trip to Blue Ridge Meadows to visit him when she got back.

The smell of bacon drifted into the room, so she threw back the covers to get up and dress for breakfast. As she was pulling her socks on, she spotted white paper poking out from under the bed. She reached for it and saw it was an envelope with her name scribbled in her mother's messy handwriting. She smiled, remembering how her dad used to say her terrible penmanship made her the perfect doctor. She tore the envelope open and began to read.

My dearest Julia,

This is the hardest letter I've ever had to write. For reasons I hope you'll understand, I've had to keep a secret from you. By the time you read this, Coop and I will be many miles away on our journey to Colorado Springs. I've had the plan to get home almost since the day of the CME. I need to find out what has happened to Jared and Emily and let them know we're alive. After seeing everyone alive and well at the ranch, I believe they are, too.

Leaving you is tearing my heart in two and is the hardest thing I've ever had to do. If you don't believe me, ask Coop when you see him again. And you will *see him again.*

We've shared so many extraordinary experiences, my sweetheart. I couldn't have survived many of them without you. You've been my spirit guide and warrior princess. Please believe it when I say you are one of the most remarkable young women in the world.

As soon as I get to Colorado, I'll start making plans to return to you. (Please tell Uncle Mitch I'm sorry for taking his horses and that I promise to bring them back.)

Be brave! Be happy! You are my heart and my life. I love you more than you'll ever know.

With deepest love and devotion,

Mom

Julia's hands shook as tears dripped onto the paper. Her mom and Coop had betrayed her. They'd abandoned her after everything they'd survived together. How could her mom say she loved her, then ditch her at the ranch without saying goodbye?

She grabbed her robe and stormed down the stairs, calling out to Uncle Mitch and Aunt Beth.

Her aunt stepped out of the kitchen and caught Julia just before she barreled into her. "Calm down, dear. What's wrong?"

Julia handed her the letter "Read that. Mom and Coop are gone. They tricked us all and took off after the reception."

Beth's lips tightened into a straight line as she read. She thrust the letter at Mitch and said, "Look at this," then guided Julia to a kitchen chair. She leaned against the counter and rubbed her temples.

Mitch slammed the letter on the table. "Stubborn girl. I told her this foolhardy idea was suicide." Beth cocked her head at Julia just as she looked up and stared. "Sorry, I didn't mean that."

Julia jumped to her feet. "We have to go after them. Trucks go faster than horses. We can catch them and make them come back."

Mitch put his hands on her shoulders. "We can't, Julia. They've had a three-day head start. We have no way of knowing which route they took. They could be anywhere in the wilderness. We have to accept it. They're gone."

Julia rushed at him and pounded her fists on his chest. "No," she cried, "you have to find them! Why would they leave me like this? How could she do this to me?"

Beth took Julia's hand and led her toward the stairs. "Your mother loves you more than her own life. She'll sacrifice whatever it takes to come for you. Just give her time. We love you and we'll protect you. You're like our own granddaughter now."

Julia broke free of Aunt Beth and tore out of the house. She raced down the quarter mile of gravel drive as fast as her gimpy leg would carry her but slowed as she neared the gate. The exertion of running had cooled her anger, but not her feelings of abandonment and worry for her mom and Coop. She limped to the fence and rested her arms on the top rail, wondering where the hell she thought she was going to go. The ranch was in the middle of nowhere.

She turned her gaze toward the road leading the five miles to Wytheville. She'd never make it that far with her bum leg but was determined to find another way. If Uncle Mitch wouldn't go after her mom and Coop, she'd have to go alone, but she couldn't take off half-cocked. Her dad had taught her to always have a solid plan before going on any journey.

She turned toward the house, wondering if she'd ever see her mother's face again or hear her voice. As she slowly made her way up the drive, she resolved to do whatever it took to find her mom and Coop or die trying.

Riley and Coop rose just before dawn after spending a damp night in a partially collapsed shed. The rotted-out roof offered little cover. It was better than being out in the drizzly air, but hardly the honeymoon night they'd hoped for.

After packing in a rush, they mounted the horses in the dark and got back on the trail. As the clouds cleared and the sun rose behind them, they crested a ridge and dismounted to take in the view. Row upon row of the Appalachian Mountains stretched as far as they could see. Beyond that, she imagined the rolling hills and eventually the western plains that spread to the base of the Rockies.

The sight hammered home to Riley that they faced months of travel on dangerous and lonely roads masked in shadow and mystery. Filled with fear, but determined to carry on at all costs, she reached for Coop's hand. With one of her children left behind and the other two waiting ahead, she'd do whatever it took to reach them.

"Magnificent view," she said, "but it makes it painfully obvious how far we have to go. I've never even driven across the country. I don't know what to expect."

"Too bad we don't have my Range Rover. I've made several cross-country trips. Once we cross the Appalachian Mountains, the terrain becomes much easier, but we'll have to push hard to reach the base of the Rockies before the end of June or the heat on the plains will become unbearable. Traveling in snow was a challenge, but traveling in scorching heat is worse, especially if water is scarce. If that scientist, Adrian Landry was right about the aftereffects of the CME, the weather could turn even more unpredictable than usual."

Riley turned and lifted her face to the sunlight. "A little heat sounds glorious to me right now." After absorbing the rays for a moment, she faced west and was disheartened to see a bank of black billowing clouds heading towards them. She groaned and pulled her hood over her knotted mess of red curls. "We'd better get as far as we can before that next storm hits."

They remounted and coaxed their weary horses forward. Riley struggled to keep her eyes open as they moved along. The oncoming thunderstorm had dampened her mood and hopes of a rain-free day. She clung loosely to the reins and rocked with the movement of the plodding horse. Within an hour, blowing rain was stinging her face. Coop motioned for her to stop, but she shook her head and kept moving. It made no difference to her if she was drenched on horseback or under a rock. If they kept going, they'd at least be closer to their goal.

By the third hour, she hardly noticed the passing landscape. Every mile looked like the one before, with nothing but trees, rocks, and mud. At some point, she started crying but couldn't distinguish her tears from the raindrops. She became consumed by her sorrows and gave no heed to the trail in front of her.

As she considered dismounting and curling up in a puddle until the rain stopped, Coop gave a loud whistle. She sat up and turned toward him in a daze. He was stopped and pointing to something directly in front of her. She looked forward in time to see that Aurora's front hooves were resting on the edge of a cliff above a river gorge. The shock jolted her numbed senses, and she reined Aurora away from the ledge. Coop nudged Echo beside her, and they watched in horror as the mud gave way and plunged into the river from the spot where she'd stopped.

Riley gripped his arm. "That could have been me!"

"The weight of the horse must have dislodged the saturated soil." A flash of lightning shredded the sky seconds later and was followed by a deafening clap of thunder. "That's it. We're taking cover until the storm passes. Look for anything that will work as shelter."

Riley nodded and scanned their surroundings, ready to hide anywhere after her brush with death. All she saw were trees and more trees. When another lightning strike illuminated the sky, she spotted a glint of metal about fifty feet into the forest. She tapped Coop's shoulder and gestured for him to follow. She wove the horse through the thick stand of trunks until she came to a small structure with an aluminum roof.

"What is that?" she called to Coop over the wind.

He shrugged and dismounted after handing her Echo's reins. "One way to find out." Mud sucked at his boots as he trudged the five feet to the shed. He yanked on the latch a few times before it broke free and the door swung open. When he waved for her to join him, she climbed off her horse and slogged over to him. "Looks like a well shed. There's just enough room for the two of us."

"It'll protect us from the lightning. That's all that matters."

They grabbed just what they needed and huddled together in the tiny shed. It felt strange to be under a solid roof for the first time in days. Even though they were still cold, it was dry, and the shed would offer protection against the storm.

They removed their drenched rain gear and wrapped themselves in their mylar blankets, then huddled together for warmth. Riley rested her head on Coop's chest and dosed off to the sound of the raindrops pattering on the aluminum roof. The next thing she knew, Coop was shaking her shoulder to wake her.

He pointed to the roof and said, "Listen."

Riley sat up and tilted her head. "To what? I don't hear anything."

Coop's lips curved into a smile. She jumped up and threw the door open to see dissipating clouds and sunlight illuminating steam rising from the saturated ground.

Coop came up behind her and looked over her shoulder. "Stunning. Wish I had a camera," he said, then turned and rummaged through his pack. "We might need to break my rule about avoiding populated areas if these storms keep hitting. I'll check the map to see how far we are from civilization."

"Civilization? Does that still exist?"

Coop spread the map on top of the well pump. "Such as it is. We can't be too far from people. Someone built this well." He stroked his beard as he studied the map. "If that's the New River you almost plunged into, we're off course. My guess is we're headed toward Peterson, West Virginia."

Riley crossed her arms and slumped against the wall. "How far off course?"

"About twenty miles. Less than a day's ride. The bad news is we're nowhere near a town. We need to turn due west to get back on track toward Charleston."

"I don't care which way we go as long as it's dry and we're headed toward Colorado."

Coop folded the map and held it out to her. "Our first job is figuring out a way to cross that river. I'm not a fan of your method."

"Me either," Riley said under her breath and shivered as she threw her pack on her shoulder, then followed him out of the shed.

———

The clear weather didn't hold, and another storm overtook them within two hours. Riley concentrated on staying clear-headed and focusing on the path in front of her. They came on a raised clearing with good drainage at sunset. The rain had become too heavy for them to continue, so they made camp. While they set up the tent in the middle of a downpour, Riley wondered if they should have stayed in the shed. Once they were settled in the tent and changed into their driest clothes, Riley downed a protein bar and slid into the sleeping bag.

Coop pulled her close and after giving her a halfhearted kiss, said, "Even I'm too exhausted to care that we haven't officially consummated this marriage."

"Same. That will have to wait until this rain stops. I promise to make it worth the wait."

"Can't wait," Coop mumbled and was asleep in seconds.

Riley woke eight hours later from her first full night's sleep since leaving the ranch. She had a fading memory of dreaming she was back in her OR in Colorado Springs, operating on a teenage boy who'd broken his leg snowboarding. Instead of her usual surgical team, Coop was assisting her, which was odd since he was a thoracic surgeon and not an orthopedist, but it felt right to work with him at her side.

The dream stirred up a darker memory of the two of them operating on Julia in the woods after she'd been shot by the thugs who took them hostage. Coop had assisted her again when they operated on Julia in the camp where they were being held. It was a miracle her daughter had survived and been able to walk after a prolonged recovery. The visions made her miss Julia even more. She wondered what she was doing at that moment.

She shook the dark thoughts from her mind and focused on the sunlight streaming in under the tent flap. Coop was snoring away beside her with his hair sticking up as usual. She had to fight the urge to lick her fingers and smooth it down. She gave him a soft peck on the cheek instead, then climbed out of the sleeping bag, careful not to wake him.

She'd slept in her jeans and flannel shirt, so after pulling on her boots, she unzipped the tent and went out to soak up sunlight before it disappeared. Thirty minutes later, she'd constructed a decent firepit and had a smoky but serviceable fire going with the driest kindling she could find.

While collecting the wood, she'd found a stream twenty yards from the tent. She had filled their water containers, then hung a pot on a branch she rigged above the fire. She fed the horses while she waited for the water to boil. They seemed as happy about the clear skies and sunlight as she was.

After fixing herself a comforting mug of chamomile tea, she sat on a log by the fire to enjoy it. If not for the upheaval and trauma she'd endured for the past three months, she could almost convince herself she was on a relaxing camping getaway. But there was no ignoring the trauma they'd experienced. In their new unpredictable world, any situation could become life threatening in an instant.

She finished her tea and ate another power bar before deciding it was time to wake her groom and make their marriage official. After tossing another log on the fire, she went into the tent and removed her jeans and shirt before sliding into the sleeping bag.

She moved her lips close to Coop's ear and whispered, "Time to wake up, babe. I'm ready for some quality alone time."

Without opening his eyes, he said, "Fine, but we better hurry before my grouchy wife gets back."

Riley gave him a playful slap, then hungrily pressed her lips to his. He responded with an urgency to match hers. The days of frustration and irritation gave way to intense release. Their lovemaking was over as quickly as it started, and they lay panting in contentment in each other's arms.

When Riley caught her breath, she said, "I told you it would be worth the wait."

Coop kissed the end of her nose. "With some to spare."

She propped up on her elbow and gazed down at him. "Can we stay here for a few days? The ground has good drainage in case the rains return. I've already built a firepit and there's a stream nearby. I'm in a hurry to get to Colorado, but I don't think I can face climbing into that saddle today."

"It wouldn't hurt to get our strength back before the next disaster smacks us in the face. We could do some hunting, and fishing."

"Fresh meat would be nice after days of jerky and MREs."

Coop sat up and rubbed his face. "I think my stomach will close up shop out of protest if I eat another protein bar. Hand me my clothes and we'll get started."

Riley pushed him back down and wrapped her arm around his waist. "We don't have to start this second. I'm not finished with you yet."

Coop reached up and wove his fingers into her hair. "I surrender. Have your way with me."

After what Coop called their honeymoon frolic and a refreshing nap, they were ready to work on setting up their temporary home. Coop gathered and chopped wood while Riley inventoried their supplies. Their food stores were running lower than she'd expected, which wasn't surprising since they hadn't been able to gather supplies or cook because of the rain. Stopping for a few days to replenish wasn't just convenient, it was crucial.

Once Coop had enough wood to last three days, he took the air rifle and went off in search of small game. Riley took the fishing tackle and headed for the stream. She'd loved the outdoors since she was a child, but never learned to fish until Zach taught her early in their marriage. She was hooked from the start. She loved the periods of peaceful contemplation interspersed with the excitement of reeling in a catch. She couldn't have known then that one day, her survival would depend on her fishing skills.

She found a flat boulder near an eddy and set her supplies

down to get ready. The quick flowing stream was so clear she could see the fish darting in the shadows. She knew nothing about freshwater species populating Virginia waterways, but she recognized the Brook Trout and Smallmouth Bass. She took one of the Nightcrawlers she'd dug up on her way to the stream and wove it onto her hook. She knew trout preferred smaller worms but found none in the dark moist soil. Smallmouth Bass usually snapped up Nightcrawlers, so Riley hoped she'd have luck with them.

She cast her hook, and it wasn't long before she had her first bite. It was a Bluegill. She re-baited the hook and cast her line again, figuring it would take longer the second time. She leaned against the boulder and was just taking in her surroundings when there was another tug on her line. It was a Rainbow Trout

She dropped her line in again and immediately had another Trout. A Bluegill followed next, then what she guessed to be a Bream. She was looking forward to the fresh fish for dinner but catching them so fast wasn't allowing much time for peaceful contemplation. She pulled the stringer out of the tackle bag and hooked the fish to it to keep fresh in the stream.

When all the loops on the stringer were occupied with unhappy fish, she decided it was time to quit. If Coop didn't know how to preserve what they didn't eat that night, they'd have to toss out the leftovers and didn't want to be wasteful. She could fish again in the morning.

Riley put her rod away and stretched out on a grassy patch in the sun. With all the rain and constant moving, she hadn't given attention to the environment they'd traveled through. Ignoring the dampness seeping through her clothes, she looked over the idyllic scene and was surprised to find thick greenery surrounding her on all sides and wondered how she could have missed it.

All she'd known of Virginia since the CME was cold, barrenness, and death. Though the world had started to bloom before they left the ranch, what she witnessed that day was an explosion of life. Leaves were so thick on the trees that sunlight couldn't penetrate the foliage in some areas. The grass was lush and aromatic, and ferns waved in the gentle breeze near the stream. Mother Nature was going on in her normal rhythm as if the CME had never happened.

If Riley hadn't been on a journey to reunite with her children, she could imagine stopping there with Coop and starting a life with him. She wondered if that was how the first inhabitants had felt when they arrived on that land. She sat up and wrapped her arms around her knees, contemplating the fact that in some ways, they weren't so different from those early settlers. Modern humans had significant advantages, like medical knowledge and more efficient tools, but in one way they were equal. They didn't have the benefit of electricity or electronic technology

Despite the challenges they faced, Riley was encouraged to see nature springing to life and hoped it also signaled a renewal for humanity. There had been enough darkness and death. It was time to stop looking back at what they'd lost and build a new life.

Riley got to her feet and gathered the gear and fish to walk back to camp. For the first time since the world turned upside down, she had hoped that with time, they would not only survive but thrive.

CHAPTER TWO

RILEY FROWNED at the plant hanging from her fork on their third evening in the camp. "This is disgusting. I don't know how you thought I'd like eating grass."

Coop had proudly prepared a meal of fish, dove breast and salad of fiddlehead ferns, dandelion leaves, and green onions. She didn't mind the onions or dandelions, but the ferns tasted like freshly mown grass.

Coop jabbed a stick at the fire. "It's not grass. Fiddlehead ferns are a delicacy in some places. They even sell it at farmer's markets."

"That may be, and I appreciate all the work you went to, but I just can't seem to get it down my throat. Maybe the horses will like it." When he frowned and folded his arms, she said, "Please, don't pout. We don't have to love all the same things. The fish and dove were delicious."

He gave her a half grin. "Fair enough but get used to eating what we can gather along the way. If we keep our distance from populated areas, we'll have to live off the land."

"I'll do my best. It might be easier when I'm hungrier."

Coop tossed his stick into the fire and swallowed his last bite of fish. "Speaking of the journey ahead, we should get back on the road in the morning. We need to reach Colorado before the worst of the summer weather hits."

Riley's gaze swept over their temporary little haven. "I know you're right, but as anxious as I am to get to my family, it'll be hard to leave. I haven't been this relaxed in months, maybe even since last year." She glanced at her trusty digital watch, the only technology to survive the CME. "It's hard to grasp that today is April 9." She grew quiet and kicked at the dirt with the toe of her boot. "Tomorrow is Emily's birthday." Her voice cracked as she said, "She'll be ten. I should be there."

"Come here," Coop said and held out his arms. Riley climbed onto his lap and rested her head on his shoulder. "You'll just have to celebrate with her two months late. From what you told me of your mom, she'll move heaven and earth to make the day special for Emily."

Riley sat forward and wiped her cheeks. "You're right. Enough of this blubbering. Remembering Emily's birthday is the motivation I need to get it in gear. I don't want to miss Jared's birthday too. The sooner we're on the road, the sooner we're home." She stood and extended her hand. "Let's get packed."

The rain started during the night, and Riley woke at dawn with a groan. They'd have to decide between waiting it out or trudging on in the nasty weather.

"I heard that," Coop said without opening his eyes. "What should we do?"

"This could be one of those thirty-minute storms or a three-day deluge. What I wouldn't give for a weather forecast. It's amazing how we took those things for granted before the apocalypse. Most of me wants to stay, snuggled up in this bag, but a small part wants to go. We're packed except for the sleeping bags and tent. I don't relish the thought of unpacking and then having to redo it."

"It's early. We can afford to wait an hour and see what happens. That will give us time to eat and tend to the horses."

Riley scooted lower into her bag. "Just give me fifteen more minutes."

Coop kissed her cheek, then climbed out of the bag and started dressing. "I'm going to see how bad it is."

Riley stuck her arm out and gave a halfhearted wave. She'd hoped to doze for a few minutes, but she couldn't tune out thoughts of Emily or the sound of the rain splashing on the tent. She gave up after ten minutes and got up to dress. By the time she'd used the makeshift toilet and eaten a power bar and smoked fish, the rain had slowed to a tolerable drizzle.

"Let's saddle the horses," she told Coop when he came in from policing the area and making sure they hadn't left anything. "We can't afford to stop every time there's a storm, which seems to be most of the time around here. Screw the rain. Let's go."

"Just what I'd hoped to hear."

They were on their way fifteen minutes later. The drizzle turned to a fine mist, and the temperature rose to the seventies. They were damp but not miserable, so Riley was glad they'd decided not to postpone their departure.

They'd avoided the major highways to that point in their journey, but Coop told Riley it might be worth the risk to head toward civilization to replenish their provisions. He navigated them to a frontage road that hugged I-64. Riley watched with envy as the occasional car filled with dry people passed, but they'd agreed horses were the better way to travel. It saved them from having to search for gas, dodge debris clogged roads with unsavory characters.

They passed a sign welcoming them to West Virginia at around ten. Their starting point of Wytheville wasn't far from the state border, but to Riley, crossing into another state felt like progress. It was also comforting to see the increasing signs of civilization, such as they were. She caught sight of the occasional group of people walking alongside the interstate and had to fight the urge to ride over and talk to them. Most looked harmless, but she and Coop had learned from bitter experience that anyone could be dangerous.

The sky gave way to black clouds an hour later, and the deluge returned. They made slow progress, but Riley was determined to push on. She'd convinced herself to stop being a grumpy weakling and be the Wonder Woman Julia told her she was. She sat taller in the saddle and pulled her hood lower to keep the rain off her face. When Coop looked back to check on her, she smiled and gave a thumbs up.

Pretending to be positive lifted her spirits, and she felt like she could take on the world, until they rounded a bend at noon and faced tons of mud and trees covering the road, leaving no way around.

Coop dismounted and walked back to her. "This was bound to happen with the soil so saturated. It's like what happened at the river gorge."

Riley stared at the house-tall pile of mud. "Where are the *Mines of Moria* when you need them? What do you want to do?"

Coop stroked his beard. "Seems our only option is to make a u-turn." He remounted and brought Echo next to her. "Let's find cover and check the map. We may not have to detour too far out of the way."

Riley nodded and pulled on Aurora's rein. Biscuit naturally resisted turning back, but after a few tugs on his lead, he got into step behind them. Coop steered Echo to a side road and went under a thick stand of trees that offered some protection from the rain. Riley followed and got down to take their laminated map out of a saddlebag.

She studied it for a minute before handing it to Coop. "Not

many good options. This road curves in the wrong direction and eventually dead ends."

Coop moved closer and pointed to a line on the map. "I hate to say it, but our only choice is this route about fifteen miles back the way we came."

Riley sighed. "That'll add a few hours in this rain, but I don't see what else we can do."

"We might as well eat lunch before we turn around."

Riley munched on her jerky and their last crumbs of trail mix, trying to not let their latest obstacle ruin her mood. It was a minor setback compared to other challenges they'd faced.

When she'd finished, she gave Coop a warm kiss and got back on Aurora. "I love you, Dr. Cooper. Let's do this."

Coop raised his eyebrows, then grinned. "Love you, too, Dr. Cooper. Nice to see you back to your old self."

"Making us both miserable is a waste of time and energy. I'm trying enthusiasm on for size."

"Hope it fits," he said, as he climbed onto Echo. "Onward and upward. Charleston awaits. Snap to, Echo."

They headed back to the frontage road and only made half a mile when they heard popping trees and low rumbling sounds. Coop reined Echo to a halt, and Riley stopped beside him.

"You hear that?" she asked.

Coop gave a quick nod. "What is it?"

"Could be someone cutting trees or moving earth, but I don't know why they'd be doing it in this downpour."

"Could be another mudslide."

"Hope not. We'd be trapped."

Coop coaxed Echo forward, but before Aurora took a step, the hillside fifty yards ahead went into motion and poured across the road in front of them. Trees exploded and car-sized boulders rumbled onto the asphalt. Echo reared up and threw Coop, then took off at a run in the opposite direction. Aurora followed, pulling Biscuit behind her. No matter how hard Riley pulled on the reins, she refused to stop until they neared the other landslide.

Riley jumped down as soon as she could and grabbed the med pack before sprinting back to Coop. To her great relief, he was on his feet and heading toward her by the time she spotted him. When they reached each other, she threw her arms around him and held him for a moment before snapping into doctor mode.

"Where are you hurt?"

"I'm fine, Riley. Just bumps and bruises."

She unzipped the med pack and took out her pen light. "Show me," she ordered.

Coop put his hands on her shoulders. "Take a breath. I'm fine. I landed on my butt and rolled. I'm going to have a nasty bruise and road rash, but that's it. Nothing's broken."

He had a way of downplaying pain and injuries, so she said, "Show me." He reluctantly unbuttoned his jeans and pulled them down. He had an angry red mark on his right buttock but clearly wasn't in pain. Riley gave his other cheek a light slap. "You can pull your pants up. You'll live, but that's going to smart tomorrow after hours in the saddle." While he buttoned his fly, she turned and watched the hillside continue to slide across the road. "We dodged that bullet, but we're just as trapped."

"Let's get to the horses and figure a way out of this mess."

They made their way back to the frightened horses and did their best to reassure them. Echo and Aurora responded quickly, but Biscuit was rearing his head and stamping on the asphalt. Riley tightened her hold on his lead to keep him still and stroked his neck, trying to get him to eat pieces of dried apple. His love for the treat won out over his fear and soon he was happily munching away.

Coop was studying the map when Riley walked over to him. "Whatever we do, it needs to be fast. The rest of this hillside could come crashing down on us any second."

"The side road we turned off onto is higher than the frontage road," he said. "No roads lead around the landslide, but we could go overland to pass it. No way of knowing what the terrain is like, but we've got to risk it if we want to get out of here."

"We could climb over the landslide." Coop stared at her like she was insane. *He might be right*, she thought.

"Are you serious? That ranks as the worst idea you've had yet."

Riley turned her back to him and strode back to the massive mudslide looming between them and Charleston. Coop dismissing her plan out of hand had stung. Her Wonder Woman side was convinced they could cross that mountain of mud, but he hadn't even been willing to listen. She was an experienced climber and had covered more than her share of difficult terrain. The heavy rain would make it a challenge, but the toughest part would entail moving the horses across the barrier of earth. The saturated soil and instability created the chance of them sinking and breaking a leg.

Coop jogged up behind her as she studied the mound of earth coated with splintered trees and chunks of rock. "That was uncalled for, Riley, and I'm sorry, but crossing the slide with the horses is too dangerous. If it were just the two of us, I wouldn't hesitate. We should take the side road and make our way overland."

With her back to him, she said, "That route could add days if it's even possible. I agree taking the horses over the mud won't be easy, but it looks like this landslide isn't fresh like the one that we just dodged." She turned and took his arm to pull him forward, then pointed to the lowest part of the slope on the north side. "There's a natural path on that edge. Trust me. I know what I'm doing."

He eyed her with skepticism, but said, "Fine, we'll do it your way. I surrender my life into your expert hands. Take the lead."

"I'll go first with Echo, then we'll tether Biscuit between him and Aurora. You bring up the rear."

Coop nodded and got to work following her instructions.

When they were ready, Riley guided Echo to the edge of the landslide and gently coaxed him to follow her into the mud. Her boot sunk in less than a foot. That would be manageable for the horses. Echo only hesitated an instant before doing what she wanted.

"Good job, boy," she said. "Let's keep going and show the others it's safe."

She hoped crossing the slide would be simpler than they'd expected. She started moving faster and her confidence soared until she took a step and sank to her thigh. The change threw her off balance and she toppled face first into the mud.

Coop rushed to her as she struggled to her feet. She was doing her best to scrape the mud off her face by the time he reached her. He came to a halt in front of her and burst out laughing.

"Stop that, Coop. I could have been hurt. You didn't even ask."

He forced himself to stop laughing enough to talk. "I'm sorry, but I watched you climb out and saw you weren't injured. There's not an inch of you not covered in brown goo. Good thing it's raining so hard." When she glared at him, he said, "Are you hurt?"

She gave a slight shake of her head. "Just my pride. I got overconfident." She scanned the debris around her and found a break that would work as a walking stick. "I'll use this to test the depth before I take a step. Get back to Biscuit."

He gave her a sloppy kiss on her muddy mouth. "Sorry I laughed, babe. See you on the other side."

Riley dipped the end of the stick to the left of where she fell, but it went in three feet. She yanked it out and moved it to the right. It sank ten inches. She turned and gave Coop a smile, then stepped to the spot. She repeated the process and after another ten yards, crested a gentle ridge and saw the clear asphalt thirty yards ahead. She sped up but remained cautious and reached the other side in twenty minutes. When her boot touched pavement, she gave a loud whoop but wasn't sure if Coop heard.

She guided the horses onto the cleared road, then waited for

Coop to cover the last ten yards. As she turned to face him, she heard a low rumble, and the mud started to move, taking Coop with it into the gully. He cried, "Help!" as the mud buried his head.

When the slide came to a rest thirty seconds later, Riley slid down the wet grass to the base of the gully, then climbed to where she'd seen Coop go under. Dropping to her knees, she frantically dug with her hands until she hit something soft but solid, hoping it was Coop's baseball cap. The flash of red fabric confirmed her hope. She lifted the cap and was elated to see Coop's hair sticking out underneath it. She dug the mud away from his mouth until she heard him gasp for breath. It was the most glorious sound she'd ever heard.

She got his head clear, and said, "Can you breathe well enough for me to get the shovel? Getting you out will go much quicker with it."

"I can," he gasped, "but hurry."

She ran across the mud as quickly as she dared and scrambled out of the gully before sprinting to the saddlebag on Aurora to get the folding shovel and hand trowel. The return trip was faster, but at least ten minutes had passed, and Riley was terrified at what she'd find.

Coop's eyes were closed when she reached him, but she could hear him taking breaths. "Coop," she called, "open your eyes. Talk to me."

"Seen any good movies lately?" he mumbled.

She dropped the trowel and unfolded the shovel. Shoving it into the mud near his shoulder, she said, "It's always a joke with you."

"And why not? I'm just thrilled to be alive."

She had his arms free within minutes and handed him the trowel. "Are you injured, or can you help?" In answer, he buried the trowel in the mud and tossed a shovel full of mud past her head. "Guess I deserved that."

"Just get me out of here."

It took another twenty minutes to free him. As he struggled to climb out of the hole, Riley put her hands under his arms and pulled until he lay gasping on top of the mud. They both rolled onto their backs to catch their breath.

When Coop could speak, he said, "We'd better not stay here too long. The mud could start moving again and I'm *not* going back in that hole."

Riley got to her knees and began checking him for breaks. "Where does it hurt?"

He shivered and shook his head. "I'm too cold to tell, but I don't think anything is broken."

She finished her exam and got to her feet. "As long as there are no internal injuries, you're fine." She held her hand out to him. "Can you stand?"

He took her hand and got up slowly, then put his arm around her shoulder for support as they trudged across the landslide to the horses. When they cleared it, they clung to each other, thrilled to feel asphalt beneath their feet and know that, once again, they'd cheated death.

The sun was setting by the time they were on their way. Riley glanced at Coop every few minutes to make sure he was conscious and breathing.

"Please get us on high, flat ground where there's no chance of a mudslide. I wouldn't mind a sturdy roof either," he said when they'd put the mudslide behind them.

"Sure you can trust me to navigate?" Riley said, avoiding his eyes. "If we'd followed that side road like you wanted, we'd be camped by now and I wouldn't have almost gotten you killed."

Coop pulled Echo up beside her. "Stop blaming yourself,

Riley. I agreed to your plan, and like I said, I'm just happy to be alive."

Riley reined Aurora to a stop. "We should go back to the ranch. We've been traveling for days and have hardly made any progress, and each of us has already nearly died at least once. I'll just have to be patient and wait until the world is more stable before I go to Colorado."

He cocked his thumb over his shoulder. "If you're serious about turning back, I know a great path through that landslide back there." When Riley glared at him, he said, "We've been through a treacherous ordeal. We're exhausted, wet and hungry. After a meal and a good night's rest, we'll revisit this, but I'm in this for the long haul. In the meantime, hand me the map and I'll find us somewhere to camp tonight."

She took the map out of her saddlebag and gave it to him. He studied it for a minute, then put it away and headed up the frontage road toward Charleston. Riley got in behind him and followed when he turned left onto a side road after half an hour. The road climbed to level ground and seemed to lead toward a small town. Just as it was growing too dark to see more than a few yards ahead, Coop gave a loud whistle. When Riley raised her eyes, he motioned for her to follow. He led them into a park with two large pavilions with mulch covered ground. She wanted to cry for joy at the sight.

They'd be able to pitch the tent on dry land and the horses would be protected under the other pavilion. Biscuit gleefully trotted under the roof before coming to an abrupt stop, as if he never intended to take another step. Riley and Coop dismounted and coaxed their horses to join him. The horses huddled together for warmth and hung their heads in exhaustion.

Coop and Riley quickly removed the saddles and gear and carried them to the other pavilion. They set up the tent and changed into dry clothes. Riley was as exhausted as the horses and every muscle ached, but she was so thrilled to be out of the rain that she didn't complain.

After toweling off her mess of curls and pulling it into a ponytail, she joined Coop at the picnic table just outside the tent. He'd set out two MREs and dried fish. She was starving after so much exertion on a power bar and trail mix lunch, so she sat across from him and ate with relish.

As Coop watched her wolf her food down, he said, "We'll stay here as long as you want. The horses need rest, and we need to dry out the gear."

She stopped chewing and looked up at him. "Whatever you think is best, Coop."

"I'm going to take care of the horses, then curl up in the sleeping bag. We'll scout the area in the morning if it's not raining too hard."

Riley got up and kissed him before he could walk away. "I'm so grateful for you and that nothing happened to you today. I hate to think of what could have happened. I'll be in the tent. Don't keep me waiting."

CHAPTER THREE

RILEY QUIETLY CRAWLED to the mesh window the next morning and savored the feel of the sunlight on her face. She gazed upward, never so delighted to see a cloudless blue sky in her life. She left Coop sleeping while she went to the picnic table and downed a cold breakfast of squirrel meat and fruit leather. Needing to wash it down, she went to the outdoor faucet and was thrilled to discover it still worked. She took a long drink, then refilled the canteens.

She hadn't heard a sound out of Coop by the time she finished, so she went back to the tent and climbed into the sleeping bag with him.

When she rolled over to kiss him, he whispered, "Quiet," and put his finger to his lips.

She raised an eyebrow. "Why? Afraid the horses will overhear our amorous activities?"

He shook his head and put his lips to her ear. "There's someone in the camp."

"It was probably just the horses," she said, keeping her voice low.

He shook his head. "Talking? Listen."

Riley cocked her head toward the tent opening and heard faint voices but couldn't make out what they were saying. Coop silently put his clothes on, then crept to the back of the tent for his rifle.

One of the intruders whispered, "Someone's in the tent," but it was loud enough for Coop and Riley to hear.

Coop motioned for Riley to get behind him. "Who's there? You're trespassing in our camp."

A male voice barked a laugh. "Unless you can prove you own this land, it's fair game. Get out here and claim it to my face."

"You know the new rules. We were here first, and you won't like it if I come out. Move on before something happens that you'll regret."

"Trust me, mister, you'll be the one with regrets, if you live long enough."

The voice sounded familiar to Riley, but the odds of it being someone she knew were minute. "This is sounding like a cheesy Western," she whispered. "We should go out before they steal the horses."

"We don't know how many there are or what weapons they have. We can't just rush out, guns blazing."

"He's not alone," Riley called out. Coop sighed in exasperation.

"Riley?" the voice said.

Recognition flooded over her. It was Brooks, who'd had a part in taking them captive two months earlier. He was the man she'd injected with Midazolam to escape from him and who cut his head when he passed out. Riley was probably the last person he wanted to see.

"Is that you, Riley Poole?" a woman said.

Riley recognized that voice immediately. "Dashay?"

Her friend shrieked in delight and rushed into the tent but froze when she saw Coop kneeling with the rifle aimed at her. He slowly lowered the weapon and laid it on his sleeping bag, then raised his hands. Dashay brushed past him and threw her arms around Riley.

"What's happening in there?" Brooks shouted. "All of you get out here, now!"

"Shut it, Brooks," Dashay said, before getting up and ducking out of the tent. "You're not in charge. And put that gun away. It's Riley and Coop."

Riley saw Coop pick up the rifle as they followed Dashay out of the tent. When she shook her head, he whispered, "Just in case."

Brooks was between their tent and the other pavilion with his rifle resting on his shoulder. Nico Mendez, the medic from the compound, stood behind him.

Riley bypassed Brooks and pulled Nico into a hug before stepping back and giving all of them a good look. "I can't believe my eyes. What are you doing here? How did you escape the compound?" She cocked her thumb at Brooks. "And what are you two doing with that snake?"

"Snake's a bit harsh don't you think?" Brooks said. "If I remember right, you're the one who attacked me at the warehouse and left me for dead."

Riley squared her shoulders. "I didn't attack you or leave you for dead. I medicated you in self-defense and stitched your head. I left you with food and water, didn't I? You're the one who took us hostage with that psychopath Jepson, by the way, who shot my daughter!"

Brooks lowered his weapon and rubbed his forehead. "Got me there. Honestly, I'm relieved to see you both survived."

Dashay put her hand on Riley's arm. "Where's Julia? Please don't tell me she didn't make it."

Riley smiled. "She's alive and safe with my aunt and uncle at their ranch."

Brooks squinted at her. "You left Julia? How could you abandon your own kid?"

Coop stepped closer to him. "That's quite a question coming from a man who took part in getting Julia shot before taking her hostage."

Brooks raised his hands and backed away. "It wasn't me, man. That was Jepson. It wasn't supposed to happen."

"It's all right, Coop," Riley said. "I'll answer his question with a question. What if one of your three boys was safe in Virginia, and the other two were in Colorado, and you had no idea if they were even alive? What would you do, Brooks?"

Brooks gave her a pained look, and she knew she'd struck a nerve.

"Before we say anything else, tell us how you got away from Branson. That psychopath had the compound sealed tighter than a drum."

"And what about Angie?" Riley said. "I'll never forget the look of terror in her eyes as we sped away from the compound gate, leaving her behind. If she's dead, I'll never be able to live with myself."

The newcomers glanced at each other before Dashay said, "Angie's the reason we got out of the camp. She was alive and well the last time we saw her. We'll give you the full scoop, but first, do you have any food to spare? We haven't eaten for two days."

"We have plenty," Riley said and went into the tent for the food pack.

"I wouldn't call it plenty," Coop said under his breath as she passed him.

Riley ignored him. She was so happy to see Dashay and Nico alive and free of Branson that she would have given them her last morsel. As she carried the food out of the tent, she spotted the shadow of a fourth person inching his way out of the woods behind the pavilion.

Coop saw him, too, and raised his rifle. "Don't come any

closer," he said, keeping his voice even, but Riley sensed the threat in his words.

The man stopped at the treeline and raised his hands in surrender. "No need for the gun, Coop," he said. "It's just me, Adrian Landry."

"Knowing that doesn't make me want to lower this rifle," Coop said.

Nico gestured for Coop to lower the gun. "It's okay, Coop. He's harmless."

When Coop reluctantly rested the rifle on his shoulder, Adrian slowly crept toward them. Riley hardly recognized him from the man they last saw, emaciated from hunger and recovering from a severe beating at the hands of their captors. He was still thin and pasty, but he'd gained fifteen pounds and his hair had thickened. As his former physician, Riley was relieved to see he'd recovered, but as one of millions who'd suffered because of his actions, she wasn't thrilled to have him reappear in their lives.

"If it isn't Dr. Adrian Landry, world-renowned astrophysicist responsible for the devastation caused by refusing to stand up to Vice President Kearns."

Riley had suppressed her feelings of anger and loathing for him when she treated his injuries at the compound, but he was no longer her patient and the sight of him sickened her.

"Riley, I mean Dr. Poole," Adrian sputtered. "I'm sure you're less than pleased to see me. Not that I blame you."

Coop waved to silence him. "Explain how the four of you escaped that camp before I *kindly* ask you to leave."

"There was a coup after you escaped. Branson's dead," Brooks said. "After his death, we seized control of the compound and left it up to the hostages to stay or go. Thirty percent left immediately, including Angie. We don't know what happened to her after that. The rest of us stayed and waited out the snow. When the weather cleared, we hit the road."

Coop gave a soft whistle. "I never could have predicted this, but I'm glad to hear it."

Riley watched Brooks for a moment, then said, "There's more to that story. What are you not telling us?"

Dashay hooked her arm in Riley's. "It's ancient history. Seems you have a story of your own. What are you two doing out here?"

Riley squeezed Dashay's hand. "We'll get to that later. You're welcome to stay with us." She felt Coop glaring behind her as soon as the words left her mouth. "You can use our extra tent. Do you have any supplies?"

Nico stood and pointed to the treeline behind him. "They're stowed in the woods. We have two tents and a few odds and ends, just no food. Running into you may have saved our lives. We'll work in exchange for food. Whatever you need."

Brooks held his hand out to Coop. "You have no reason to trust me, but I promise I'm a reformed man. Can we join you?"

Coop gave a slight nod and reluctantly shook Brooks' hand. "For now. We'll figure out the rest later."

Riley hugged Brooks, and said, "Forgive me for knocking you out at the warehouse. I was just doing what I needed to protect my family." She turned to the others and smiled. "Seeing you alive and hearing that Angie survived is a tremendous weight off my shoulders. Rest now. You're safe with us."

While the others ate, Coop pulled Riley aside under the guise of needing to check the horses. When they were alone, he said, "I'm not comfortable with this arrangement, Riley. Dashay's great. I have no problem with her, and Nico seems like a good guy, but we know nothing about him. And Brooks and Adrian? Are we supposed to just welcome them with open arms?"

Riley patted Aurora's neck while she sorted through her thoughts. Echo whinnied at not getting attention, so she gave him a piece of dried apple from her pocket. As usual, Biscuit was lost in his own world and didn't notice what was happening right next to him. Riley gave him a piece of apple and he reacted with utter delight, like it was the first one he'd ever had.

With her animal friends satisfied, she considered Coop's question. Her tendency to trust too quickly had gotten them in enough trouble for five lifetimes, but she'd learned her lesson and her gut told her they'd be safe joining up with the others.

"I get your hesitation, but these aren't just any strangers. We have a history with them, and Nico and Dashay's medical skills will be a bonus. You know my feelings toward Adrian, but Nico was right. He's harmless. I'm shocked they let him tag along, but you saw how he cowered in the woods until it was safe."

Coop leaned against Echo and hooked his thumbs in his pockets. "We could allow Nico, Dashay, and possibly Brooks to stay on the condition they part ways with Adrian."

"I can't believe I'm about to defend Adrian Landry, but that could mean sending him off to die. Dashay would never go for that. Adrian may be a brilliant scientist, but I have a feeling his survival skills are nil. He wouldn't last a day on his own."

"Another reason to ditch him. The last thing we need is to be hauling dead weight across the country."

"The others would have ditched him if he was that much trouble. He may have hidden skills we're not aware of, and his scientific knowledge could come in handy down the road."

"And Brooks?"

Riley rubbed her temples as she thought about how to answer. "That's a bigger question mark. He was being chummy when we went on that supply run to the medical supply warehouse. At least, right until I knocked him out."

"How did you know he has three sons?"

"He told me that day. He spent as much time with them as he could before the disaster. Did you see his face when I asked about them?"

"Doesn't matter. He's part of the reason Julia was shot."

"I'm not excusing that, but he's also the one who made it possible for us to do surgery to save her life. Brooks was afraid of Branson and hated the way he treated the hostages. Bottom line, I trust Dashay's judgment. She wouldn't travel with him if he were a threat."

Coop stroked his beard as he considered her argument. "Why do you always have to make so much sense?"

She folded her arms and grinned at him. "Someone has to. Look, aside from whatever happened in the compound, there's safety in numbers and having more people will make it easier to get resources we need."

"They can travel with us as far as Charleston. Then, we'll reassess. This field trip across is going to be tough enough. We don't need to be piling new drama on top."

She wrapped her arms around his waist and gazed up at him. "Since none of us knows what we'll face in Charleston, there's no point to planning beyond that. We'd better ration the food until we can replenish since we have more mouths to feed."

"Another reason I'm not on board with this."

"Don't be so negative. You might end up glad of the help. Trust me."

Coop took a deep breath and let it out slowly. "You said that about crossing the mudslide."

Not exactly the vote of confidence she'd hoped for, but she didn't blame him. "We survived, didn't we?"

He gave her a hard kiss, then turned and headed back to the others without a word. She reminded herself that his first thought was always for her safety, but she wasn't concerned about letting the others join them. If the arrangement didn't work, it would be easy enough to split after Charleston and strike out on their own. She hoped that wouldn't be the case. Traveling with a bigger group was comforting to her, even if one of them was Adrian Landry.

The rain was held off for the rest of the day. After the newcomers had eaten and had time to rest, they searched the park and Nico discovered a stack of wood covered with a tarp behind a nearby abandoned house. They each carried an armload to the horses' pavilion and stacked it in a neat pile, then Brooks and Nico built a firepit while Coop went off to shoot squirrels for dinner.

"He's become quite the squirrel slayer," Riley said to Dashay when they heard the pop of the air rifle. "We should scrounge up something to go with them."

Dashay cocked her thumb at Adrian, who was at the faucet filling anything that would hold water. "He's kind of a plant savant. If there's anything edible around here, he'll find it."

As they started toward him, Riley said, "I told Coop that Adrian's brains would come in handy. Let's take over collecting the water and send him out to search."

"Trying to get rid of him?"

Riley gave her a half-grin and kept walking. After sending an eager Adrian on his mission, she said, "Tell me what really happened at the compound and how you ended with Adrian."

"That's a story for some other day. It was a dark time, best left in the past." Dashay grew quiet for a moment, then said, "We've been through so much since then. The compound seems like another lifetime."

"I can relate, but what have you been through?"

Dashay flashed her brilliant smile Riley loved and said, "You first."

Riley chuckled and said, "Fair enough. I'll tell you one good thing that happened." She lifted her left hand to show Dashay the elegant diamond gracing her finger.

Dashay's eyes widened. "You got married? I didn't know anyone did that these days."

"We even had a preacher, cake, and dress. It was just over a week ago."

She gave Riley a warm hug. "Congratulations, friend! Nice to hear good news for a change. Tell me, how did you tear yourself away from our little Warrior Princess Julia?"

"It was one of the hardest things I've ever done, but I have two other children I love just as much. I knew Julia would be safe, and I hated not knowing what happened to Emily and Jared, or the rest of my family, so I left her. Why didn't you go back to your parents' house? Didn't they live near the compound?"

A cloud passed over Dashay's face. "We traveled to my parents' house and found it a burned-out shell. Thankfully, we didn't find any bodies. I asked around with the neighbors still in the area, but they had no idea if my family made it out in time. I'll never know if they're still alive."

Riley squeezed her hand. "What a nightmare. I'm so sorry."

Dashay wiped a tear from her cheek. "With nowhere else to go, I left with my three boys over there. Traveling with them has kept my mind off what I've lost."

"I'm grateful you did. It's nice to have another woman and friend on this journey. Let's carry the water to the tables and see if Coop and Adrian are back with our dinner, such as it is."

Riley walked back to the pavilion with her in silence, caught up in memories of loved ones lost and hoping there wouldn't be more before their journey's end.

After a meal of squirrel, the last of the dried fish, dandelion and fiddlehead salad, and acorn mush, they enjoyed cups of black birch tea around the fire. Though Riley picked the fiddleheads from her salad, she found it satisfying to be learning how to eat off the land. Adrian regaled them for a good thirty minutes about edible and nutritious plants in the area. Riley hadn't heard him say so much in the entire time she'd known him.

When she'd learned more about local flora than she ever wanted to know, she steered the conversation to a different topic. After taking a sip of Adrian's tea concoction, she said, "I can't believe we crossed paths. What are the odds?"

"I could do the math," Adrian said, "but the short answer is, astronomical."

"You would know," Coop said.

Riley shot him a glance, then said, "We've told you where we're going, and Dashay filled me in on what happened to her family. Where are you headed, Nico?"

"I'm going home. Farmington, New Mexico," he said.

Riley smiled. "I've been through there. It's only six hours from Colorado Springs. And you, Adrian?"

"My wife left a note saying she was taking our two girls and going to her parents' in St. Louis. That's my destination. They left before the CME hit, so I hope they may have made it in time. If not, they should have reached St. Louis long before now. After I find them, we'll start a new life in a new place."

Riley caught Coop watching him. It was going to take time for him to trust Adrian. Admitting he'd warned his family about the CME but no one else didn't earn him any points. She wasn't thrilled about that herself.

To deflect Coop's attention, she said, "What about you, Brooks? You're from Virginia. Why didn't you go home?"

"There's nothing there for me. I went looking for my boys, but only found a note from my oldest son. He said my ex-wife died. Her parents had been visiting for the holidays when the CME hit, so they took the boys with them to Atlanta. I'm also on an adventure to make a new life. Anything to put distance between me and that camp and stay ahead of President Kearns' Reconstruction Troops, as she calls them."

"You mean Vice President Kearns," Coop said, "and what troops?"

The four of them glanced at each other, then Nico said, "You haven't heard? You really must have been hiding in the woods."

Riley leaned forward and said, "What are you talking about?"

"As I told you in the compound, President Carlisle was flying over the Atlantic when the CME hit and there's been no word from him since," Adrian said. "Our lovely former vice president has promoted herself to president and declared martial law. She's ruling from Philadelphia and has taken over whatever is left of the military. She has them herding her citizens into these Residential Zones in the larger towns and cities."

"We haven't heard a word of this," Coop said. "Kearns took over the entire country without resistance?"

"How can she do that and live with herself after withholding life-saving information?" Riley asked. "She has blood on her hands."

Adrian shook his head. "She's keeping a handful of people from her inner circle who know the truth under her all-seeing eye. The rest probably didn't survive. No one else knows, except me."

Riley locked her eyes on him. "Then, you have a responsibility to tell people. You owe this country for keeping your mouth shut when you had the chance to save lives."

Adrian rubbed the scars on his ribs. "You're a witness to the consequences when I told the truth in that camp. I've kept my mouth shut since."

If she and Coop hadn't treated his wounds in Branson's compound, he would have died. She couldn't blame him for his reluctance to share the truth about Kearns, but he had an obligation to get the truth out.

Dashay said, "We've heard rumors that people who defy Kearns' troops get beaten or just disappear."

"Seems far-fetched," Coop said. "This is still the United States, not some lawless banana republic."

Brooks shook his head. "That's exactly what we've become. Would you put it past Kearns to order her troops to force people in internment camps? Have you forgotten Branson and his goons?"

Coop grunted. "Branson was a sociopath."

"But he's a perfect example of what can happen when the wrong person gets into power."

Riley leaned back and crossed her arms. "I don't believe it. I wouldn't put it past Kearns to issue the order, but these troops are former US military. They're honorable people willing to die for their country like my first husband. You were Army, Nico. You'd never carry out such orders."

He eyed her for a moment, then said, "I wouldn't but I've known plenty who would."

Riley struggled to make sense of what they were saying. She thought of Zach's friend Bryce, who had rescued her and Julia from freezing to death. She couldn't discard the hope that there were thousands more like them who hadn't turned to the dark side. If not, what was the point of trying to rebuild their world?

"Whether or not the rumors are true," Brooks said, "we need to stay ahead of Kearns forces. They haven't made it this far west, but it won't be long before they catch up with us."

Coop stood and stretched. "Then, we start for Charleston at dawn. It'll be a long day. We'd better get some sleep."

The others got to their feet and gathered their belongings. Riley gave Dashay a hug, then watched in surprise as she followed Nico into his tent. Riley had assumed the three men shared one tent and Dashay had the other to herself.

Riley joined Coop in their tent and watched as he sat and pulled off his socks. She gasped at the sight of his feet. The skin was dotted with blister bubbles and strips of raw, peeling skin.

She knelt to examine him more closely, and said, "Why didn't you tell me?"

"Because I didn't want you to make a fuss, like you're doing now. Days of wearing wet socks will do this to you. Water leaked into my boots. I haven't had time to dry them. It doesn't hurt."

Riley grabbed the med pack from the corner of the tent and pulled out supplies she'd need to treat his feet. She picked up a pair of scissors and started trimming the dead skin.

While she worked, she said, "You'll never guess what I just saw. Dashay went into Nico's tent with him."

Coop said, "And?"

Riley stopped and looked up at him. "What do you mean *and*? She didn't come back out. I think they're together."

Coop raised his eyebrows. "This surprises you?"

"I never would have pictured Dashay with him. He seems so young and inexperienced compared to her."

She started working again, and he flinched when she cut the skin too close.

"Easy there, Doctor. How did you miss the vibes they've been giving off all day?"

She sat back on her heels and stared at him. "They have? I must have been so shocked at running into them I didn't notice."

"They were thrown together in that camp for weeks, and they've been on the trail just as long. It was bound to happen, like with us."

"What happened with us was different. We were already together when the CME hit." She finished clearing off the dead skin, then rubbed antifungal cream on his feet before wrapping them in gauze. "Put this cream on twice a day and wear your tennis shoes until your boots dry. We can't have you getting gangrene."

He winked and took the tube. "Yes, Doctor. My advice is to keep your nose out of Dashay and Nico's business."

Riley shrugged and started stashing the supplies back in the pack. She had no intention of keeping her nose out. If they were going to be traveling companions, she had a right to ask Dashay about her relationship. She climbed into her sleeping bag, eager for morning so she could get the juicy details.

Riley woke in the gray light of dawn to catch Coop staring at his boots. "Don't you dare," she whispered. "Let those boots dry before you wear them. Where are your shoes?"

He scratched his head. "In my other pack with the horses. I can't go out in my socks."

Riley climbed out of the sleeping bag and put on the flip-flops she only used inside the tent. "I'll get them."

She reached for the flap but froze at hearing a low growl. The horses began neighing wildly a second later, then Nico let out an ear-piercing scream. Coop grabbed the rifle as he and Riley darted out of the tent. They ran to Nico, with the others following close behind. They found him on his back in the horseshoe pit with the rebar post sticking through his lower-left abdomen.

As Coop and Riley rushed to his side, there was another growl and Aurora let out a shriek. Riley looked up from Nico to see a large black bear take a swipe at Aurora's ribs with his enormous claws. She tried to get free as he clamped his jaws on her neck, but she was tethered to the rail.

Coop jumped up and shouted, "Hey, bear, over here!"

The bear let go of Aurora and turned toward the sound before getting ready to charge. Coop raised the rifle and shot him in the chest. He wobbled from side to side, then charged Coop. He calmly fired again and hit the bear between the eyes. It rolled over dead without making a sound. Coop raised his eyebrows at Riley, looking as surprised as she was that he'd made the shot. He dropped the rifle and knelt next to Nico.

"Dashay, there's a med pack by the horses and another in our tent," Riley said. "Get them and hurry. He's hemorrhaging."

Brooks paced nervously behind them and said, "What can I do?"

Coop glanced up at him. "Check Aurora. That was a nasty bite."

Brooks nodded without a word and picked up the rifle before going to see to the wounded horse.

Adrian stared down at Nico in shock. "How did this happen?"

Nico cried out in pain and thrashed his arms and legs. "Get that out of me."

"You," Riley said, pointing to Adrian, "hold him still. He's aggravating his injury."

Adrian hesitated for a second before dropping to his knees and grabbing Nico's legs.

"Nico," Coop said, "I know you're in pain, but you know we can't remove the post until we examine you. Hold still and let us do that." Nico eyed Coop wildly but became still. "Can you tell us what happened?"

Between gasps, he said, "I was taking my turn standing guard when the bear wandered into camp. I was backing up, hoping he wouldn't see me and move off. Biscuit panicked and startled the bear. He was between me and the horses. I think it felt threatened because it lunged for Biscuit, but Aurora stepped in the way." He stopped and took a few gasps for air. "I was keeping my eye on the animals and not watching where I was going. I tripped over the edge of the pit and fell on the post."

Adrian jumped to his feet and frantically scanned the area. "Do you think there are more bears? Are we safe?"

Coop stared at Adrian in exasperation. "Black bears are solitary animals and only attack if they're cornered. They usually keep their distance from humans and take off at any sign of trouble. It's strange this one attacked Aurora. It must have been injured or old."

Nico let out a cry when Riley pressed the skin next to where the rebar was poking out of his body. "I'm sorry. I won't do that again," she said. Seconds later, she heard a single shot and jumped, then slowly raised her eyes to where Brooks stood over

Aurora. He caught her eye and gave a quick shake of his head. Riley fought back her tears as she continued examining Nico. There would be time to mourn her faithful friend later.

Dashay came back with the med packs, and said, "What do you want me to do with these?"

Riley stood and started for the closest picnic table. "Let's empty them onto the table and see what we have."

Dashay's lip trembled as she dumped out the supplies, and Riley remembered her conversation with Coop the previous night.

"We'll do whatever it takes to save him, Dashay. Let's sort these supplies." Riley frowned when they finished going through the pitiful pile.

"What have we got?" Coop called out to them.

"Two bags of IV Vancomycin and two courses of oral antibiotics. Hope that'll be enough to fight off infection. We have just enough morphine to get him through the surgery if the damage isn't too severe. We'd better start before he loses too much blood for it to matter. Dashay, put blankets down on the other table and do your best to create a sterile field."

Riley went back to the horseshoe pit with a pack of QuikClot powder and gauze while Dashay prepared the table. Nico was white as a sheet and unconscious. Brooks had left the poor horses and rejoined them.

"Thank you," Riley whispered to him.

Coop took a deep breath and rubbed his hands together. "We've got to do this now. Brooks, help me lift him off the post. Be ready with that powder, Riley."

She nodded and tore the QuikClot pack open before pouring alcohol over her hands. She let them dry for a moment, then pulled on her gloves. Brooks put his hands behind Nico's knees and Coop tucked his under his armpits. On the count of three, they slowly lifted upward until the post was out, then they laid Nico on the grass. Riley poured the powder into the wound on

Nico's stomach. She did the same when Coop and Brooks carefully rolled him onto his side and let out her breath when the bleeding slowed.

"It will take all of us to get him to the table. Lay him on his right side," Riley said. "Where's Adrian?"

Dashay cocked her thumb over her shoulder to where Adrian was vomiting on the grass.

"Seriously," Coop said. "After all you've seen these past months, you still can't handle the sight of blood."

Adrian straightened and wiped his mouth on his sleeve. "I haven't witnessed anything like that."

Coop glared at him. "Get over here."

Adrian scurried over and took gulping swallows while they carried Nico to the table. Once they had him situated, Dashay checked his blood pressure, oxygen level and pulse.

She eyed Coop knowingly. "Pressure's dropping. Pulse is thready,"

"Get fluids started and keep monitoring his vitals."

Dashay did as Coop asked, while Riley and Coop scrubbed their hands as best they could. Dashay helped them glove up and put on their masks, then she retook Nico's pressure. Coop raised his eyebrows in question, and she gave him a thumbs up.

Riley injected the morphine and local anesthetic. "Hope he stays out until we're done. You take lead, Coop. This is closer to your area than mine."

Coop studied her for a moment, then nodded. While they worked, he said, "That bear shouldn't have attacked. Losing Aurora is an enormous blow. I don't know how we'll all get to Charleston with one fewer horse and Nico in this condition."

"Worry about that, later, Doc," Dashay said. "Saving him is all that matters now."

Riley smiled at Dashay behind her mask and swabbed the blood to clear the field. "What are you seeing, Coop?"

"The post missed the kidney and bowels. It's mostly damaged

vascular and muscle tissue. He's damned lucky. If he had fallen two inches to his right, he wouldn't have a prayer. Fortunately, he's young and healthy. If we can raise his blood count and stave off infection, he might have a chance."

Riley found his assessment overly optimistic but kept that to herself. They had used up most of their medical supplies and Nico had lost too much blood. She couldn't imagine how they'd get him to Charleston when he was strong enough to move. If he ever was.

"Riley," Coop said sharply. She flinched and looked up at him sheepishly. "Swab, please."

"Sorry. Got distracted," she said as she dabbed at the trickle of blood flowing into the surgical field.

He asked Dashay for more sutures. She opened the pack and dropped the threads onto a sterile pad. "Last ones."

"Should be enough. I've tied off all the bleeders. Want to close, Riley?"

Coop moved to the side, and she stepped into his place. "How are his vitals?" she asked Dashay.

"Weaker than I'd like, but stable. He came through like a trooper."

"How many more saline bags do we have?" Riley asked.

"Five," Coop said. "Should be enough to get his fluids up, but we have to figure out a liquid diet for him for the next twenty-four hours. I don't think bear meat will cut it."

"Put Adrian in charge of Nico's diet," Dashay said.

Coop glanced at her. "At least he'll be useful for something. Hope he lives up to all his bluster about being a plant expert."

"Don't be so hard on him. Adrian's knowledge has come in handy for us more than once along the way."

Coop pulled off his gloves and tossed them in the garbage can next to the table. "We'll see. He still needs to earn my trust."

Riley glanced at Coop, then finished closing. Dashay bandaged the wound and took Nico's vitals while Riley and Coop went to their tent to get their sleeping pads to put under Nico so he would be more comfortable. The five of them then carefully carried Nico to his tent and laid him on the makeshift bed. Riley hung the IV bag from a tie near the top of the tent and checked the flow.

Dashay brushed the hair out of Nico's eyes, then kissed his forehead. "I'll stay with him."

Riley patted her shoulder as she went out with the others. "Let us know if his vitals change."

After they left the tent, Coop and Brooks dragged Aurora's body and the bear to the woods, away from the horses. Biscuit was still agitated, so Riley did her best to soothe him. Once he was calmly munching on the last of the dried apple slices, she joined the others at the firepit. Brooks threw a log on the fire and sat between Coop and Adrian, but Riley was too anxious to stay still, so she paced in circles around them.

Brooks rested his elbows on his knees and stared at the ground. "This was not how I imagined this day starting."

Coop nodded. "Times of predictable, uneventful days are long gone."

"Even pre-CME, the concept that life was predictable was an illusion," Adrian said. "It's a lie people tell themselves for comfort. The only certainty is chaos."

"How comforting," Riley mumbled. "That bear's behavior was definitely not normal. I've seen enough black bears in the wild to know they'll scamper up a tree or bolt when people are around. Why did that bear stay when he saw Nico? And why did he attack the horses? Very odd."

Adrian scratched his head. "I've been thinking about that. The winter was far more severe than usual. That might have impacted flora and fauna in the area. People that survived the CME are competing with the bears for the diminished amount of small game and plants available. It might make the bears more aggressive."

"Whatever his reason, that guy caused us a boatload of trouble," Coop said. "Riley and I won't know Nico's prognosis until he's survived the next twenty-four hours. I'd guess a minimum of five days until he's well enough to move. His wound wasn't as severe as it could have been, but he's lost a great deal of blood. His recovery will be difficult and unpredictable in these conditions."

Riley stopped pacing and faced the group. "Five days seems optimistic. With our med supplies depleted, his situation is even more critical."

"We can eat that lump of bear, so that solves our food shortage. Same with poor Aurora. Riley might not like it, but that horse meat is about as good as anything on the market," Brooks said. "The medical supplies are a different story. From what we saw, pickings in the nearest village are sparse. The trip to Charleston on horseback would have been a breeze, but with only two horses now and a critically injured man, it'll take three times longer. That's if the weather holds."

Adrian fidgeted in his log seat. "What medications does Nico need most?"

"Antibiotics," Coop and Riley said in unison. "IV saline and iron supplements, too," Riley added.

"I keep a stash of various herbs and spices that could help, but they won't be as potent or work as quickly as chemically produced medications."

Riley dropped next to him on the log and said, "Which herbs and spices?"

"The usual standards. Garlic, ginger, thyme, and sage work as antimicrobials for intestinal and upper respiratory bacteria. I have others for viral and fungal infections. My supply is running low but could help until we find antibiotics. I can gather dark leafy greens to help boost his iron until he can consume meat."

Riley turned toward Coop. "It's worth a shot. None of those plants will hurt him."

Coop studied Adrian for a moment. "You actually know how to administer those herbs?"

He smiled and nodded. "I do. I've successfully treated my own children with them."

Riley stood and held out her hand to him. "Teach me how to prepare them."

Adrian grasped her hand and got to his feet. "Let me get them. Boil some water."

Coop's gaze followed him as he went to his tent. "I don't care if Adrian's trying to be helpful, that guy rubs me the wrong way."

"Because you see him as a coward for what he did before the CME hit?" Brooks asked.

Coop shrugged. "It's more than that."

"He's not my favorite person, but he's done his part to help get us here."

"You know my opinion of him, Coop," Riley said, "but maybe Dashay is right, and we shouldn't judge him too harshly. Before the CME, he was just a geeky scientist locked up in his lab all day, and he was the only person on the planet to spot that first CME, even if he refused to defy Kearns' back and tell the rest of the world."

Brooks sat back and folded his arms. "Give him time. He grows on you."

"Fine, so Adrian is our plant guy for food and meds," Coop said. "I can dress the bear and Aurora. We'll dry what meat we can and cook the rest to eat while we're in camp."

Riley stared at him in disbelief. "You expect me to eat Aurora? Never. She was my friend."

Brooks rubbed his face. "I hated having to put her down, but she was suffering. She was a beautiful animal."

Coop put his hand on Brooks' shoulder. "You had no choice. It was the right thing."

Riley lowered her eyes and kicked at the dirt with her boot. "I appreciate you doing that. I couldn't have."

Brooks gave her a weak smile. "You're welcome, Riley."

They sat in silence for a few minutes until Coop said, "I don't care how good Adrian's herbs are, they won't do the job to treat Nico."

Brooks stood and stirred the fire. "Dashay and I could go on a scouting trip. It wouldn't hurt to see what we'll be facing between here and Charleston. We can search for the supplies you need at the same time."

"I hear you're good at medical supply runs," Riley said, and gave him a half-grin. Brooks smiled and rubbed the scar on his scalp. "Good luck tearing Dashay away from Nico. I can go."

Coop stood and shook his head. "No, Riley. I need you here to help with Nico. Brooks, take Adrian."

Riley knew that was just an excuse to keep her close and out of danger and get rid of Adrian for a few days. She found it touching but knew that wouldn't work either. "Adrian's the only one who knows how to prepare and administer the herb concoctions. He can't go either."

"I'll go alone," Brooks said. "I can handle myself and I wouldn't mind a few days on my own. It'll save putting another person or horse at risk, and you'll have more hands to pitch in here."

Coop rubbed his chin while he considered Brooks' offer. "Take Echo and the rest of the packaged food. We'll wait here for you but don't take too long. Nico needs those meds. I'll make a list."

Brooks got up and headed for his tent. "I'll be ready in ten."

Riley followed him and stopped him before he went inside. "Please, watch yourself. Now that we've found you, we don't want to lose you."

Brooks put out his hand. "I'll do my best."

Riley ignored his hand and pulled him into a hug. "We're counting on that."

CHAPTER FOUR

PRESIDENT AILEEN KEARNS sat in her office in the Governor's Council Chamber of Independence Hall and tapped the stack of papers on her desk to straighten them. She'd had the massive antique desk and chair moved to the office from a different abandoned historic building in Philadelphia. She slipped the stack of papers into a folder and smiled as she ran her hand over the rich grain of the wood. Her citizens and even some of her advisors had balked at her choosing the historic room as the new "Oval Office," but she found that it fit her station as the new President of the United States.

It had taken weeks to reestablish the government before she and the other surviving VIPs emerged from their bunker under the Pennsylvania hills. She'd been reluctant to leave the comparative luxury of the shelter, but her country was suffering and needed a leader. She ordered her generals to gather troops to clear the streets and get communications restored. Only then did she dare leave her haven.

Kearns' executive assistant had located a gorgeous, abandoned home befitting a US president's family just minutes from Independence Hall. They hooked up a working generator, built a security fence around the property's perimeter, and brought in fresh provisions. Her husband and daughters gave it their stamp of approval and quickly settled in. Though Kearns loved her new home, she spent little time there. Restarting the country took all her time and energy.

That morning, she was waiting for a private meeting with the leader of her band of former special forces operatives whose identities she'd kept off the books. He'd sent word that he had news about the number one name on her most wanted list, Dr. Adrian Landry, code named, *Daybreak*. Her team had successfully hunted down the others on the list, but Daybreak had continued to elude them. She'd hoped he was dead until her team got intel that Daybreak was holed up in a compound for the winter. Though she was disappointed he was still alive, it seemed like a promising lead.

A tap on the door drew her from her thoughts. "Come," she said.

Colonel Orson Yeager walked to her desk and gave a slight nod. "Morning, Madam President."

She studied him for a moment before speaking. Yeager was just about average height but held himself ramrod straight and appeared taller than he was. He was attractive but didn't seem to notice or care. He was especially skilled at disguising his thoughts and emotions, which was a primary reason she'd chosen him for the vital clandestine role. More crucial, however, was the fact that he followed orders to the letter and without question. He tended to adopt the moral compass of his immediate supervisor, which was exactly what Kearns was looking for.

She'd gotten to know him when he'd helped get her family out of DC after the CME. She admired his confident but not arrogant manner. He respected her authority without question from the beginning and was wise enough to know how to play the game.

She put her pen down and pressed her fingertips together. "You have news?"

"Yes, Ma'am. My men located the compound where *Daybreak* was held hostage for over two months until the hostages mutinied and killed the ringleader. They overthrew their remaining jailers and took over the compound. *Daybreak* left the camp when the snows melted. My men got solid intel on the group he's traveling with and are pursuing them. I'm confident it won't be long before he's captured."

President Kearns gave a hint of a smile. "Excellent news. Is the intel credible?"

"The informant, a Darcy Meade, was a guard on the dead leader's staff. When the camp was overthrown, she surrendered and pretended to switch sides, so they'd allow her to stay. She ditched the place as soon as the weather cleared. She's requesting permission to join your forces. All she asks is three hots and a cot."

"Can we trust her? She switched sides once. She could do it again."

"My man says she was eager to spill on *Daybreak*. Word is that he was not well liked in the camp."

"*Daybreak* is a dangerous and unstable man with information he could use to upset the stability of this country. I won't let up until he's captured."

"Mind sharing this information, Ma'am? It might help in his capture."

"That information is need-to-know. You have my permission to enlist this woman but keep a close eye on her. Join your team in the field and take charge of the operation yourself."

"Very well, Ma'am. I'll leave immediately after this meeting. I can reach Charleston by tomorrow night, latest."

"What of this compound *Daybreak* escaped from?"

"Your Reconstruction Troops have peacefully commandeered the facility and annexed it into the nearest Residential Zone."

"Perfect. The reconstruction is progressing faster than I'd hoped. My citizens are desperate for the help and leadership we can provide. It's my privilege to return them to a semblance of their former lives."

Yeager eyed her for a moment, then said, "I'm sure they're deeply indebted to you, Ma'am. I'll leave you to get back to business."

"Thank you for the fine work you're doing, Yeager. Your country owes you a debt as well. I won't forget that. Keep me apprised of your progress."

"Ma'am," Yeager said, then gave a quick bow before turning on his heels and leaving as quickly as he came.

Julia sat on the front porch swing, nervously tapping her feet as she waited for Great Uncle Mitch. Her uncles, Jesse and Russell, had caught her hiding vacuum-packed pouches of venison jerky in her secret stash. She'd been stowing provisions there for days, getting ready to make her big escape. This was the second time she'd been caught preparing to leave and knew Uncle Mitch was going to be furious.

She'd promised not to run away again but had only said it to get him off her back. She missed her mom and the rest of her family, and she wanted to go home. Aunt Beth and Uncle Mitch had been amazing, and she didn't want to seem ungrateful. It wasn't their fault that Mom and Coop ran off without her, but the ranch wasn't where she belonged.

She heard Uncle Mitch's old red truck rumbling up the gravel drive and her stomach twisted into a knot. He wasn't mean, but he could be stern when he wanted to be. She just hoped he wouldn't lock her in her room for the rest of her life.

Uncle Mitch pulled up to the porch and turned off the truck, but he didn't get out for a minute. He was staring at Julia through the windshield, but she couldn't tell what he was thinking. He finally pushed the squeaky door open and climbed the steps to the porch.

After dropping into the swing facing her, he said, "I'm out of ideas, Julia. Your Aunt Beth and I have done our best to make a home for you here, but clearly, we've failed. I don't know what else to do."

Julia felt her cheeks flush with shame. Her aunt and uncle loved her and were trying to make the best of the situation, but she'd repaid them by trying to run away. They didn't deserve to be treated that way.

"It's not your fault, Uncle Mitch. I love you and Aunt Beth, and you've all been awesome, but I want to be with Mom and Coop. I miss Nana and Papa and my friends. I even miss Jared and Emily. I want to know what happened to them. Can't you find someone to take me to Colorado? You have lots of horses and guys who work for you. Can't you spare a few? They can come back once they get me home or we find Mom."

Uncle Mitch watched her for a moment before answering. The look on his face told her he thought her idea was stupid.

"Before I respond to that," he said, "I want you to remember your trip here from DC. Do you know how many miles that was?"

It was a trick question. "Mom said it would have been 300 miles if we'd come straight here," she said, knowing what was coming.

He nodded and leaned back in the swing. "But you didn't come straight here?"

He knew they didn't. She couldn't stand it when grownups did that. "No, we couldn't. Coop said it was more like 400 miles."

"Why, Julia?"

She sat straighter and crossed her arms. "You know the stories."

"I want to hear it from you."

"Because dead people and crashed cars were all over the road, and I got shot and we were taken to that awful camp. Hannah died and a gigantic tree got in our way. Then it snowed a lot and Coop got lost. Don't make me talk about this."

"But can't you see that all those reasons are why you shouldn't leave? You've been here for over two months and I'm worried that you're forgetting how terrible it was out there."

Julia rubbed the scar on her thigh where she was shot. "My leg reminds me every day. I won't ever forget." She considered the point he was making but rejected it. "But things are better now. The bodies and bad guys and snow are gone. We got here in a few hours from Blue Ridge Meadows with no trouble."

Uncle Mitch stood and looked down at her. "A three-hour drive in an armored Humvee is not the same as crossing the country on horseback. It could take a year to reach home if you didn't die first. I don't agree with your mom leaving, but I understand why she did. She and Coop left you here for good reason. If you're determined to run away, I won't stop you, but I won't help you either. No horses. No men to take you. You're on your own. If you decide to leave, I hope you'll at least bother to say goodbye before going."

He went into the house without another word. Julia stared after him, not knowing what to do next. She'd made a promise to herself to find her mom and make it home, but what Uncle Mitch said had gotten to her. Trying to go alone *was* stupid. More than that, it was suicide.

She slowly swung back and forth, trying to figure out her next steps. She'd thrown all her energy into planning her escape. If she stayed, she'd have to find a new focus.

She got up with a sigh and went into the house to find Uncle Mitch. He was in his study messing with his ham radio. She pulled a chair next to him and dropped into it.

"I'll stay," she mumbled. "I mean it this time. I'm sorry for making you and Aunt Beth worry."

He put his arm around her. "I'm relieved to hear it. I'm sure your mom will come back for you one day, but until then, I hope this will come to feel like your home."

She couldn't imagine that ever happening, but she just nodded. "Will you teach me how to use the radio like you did with Mom?"

"I thought you'd never ask. Here, scoot closer and let me show you what to do."

Riley removed the thermometer from under Nico's tongue and frowned when she read 102.5 degrees. She and Coop had been so relieved when he survived the first twenty-four hours and had progressed well after, but he'd started going downhill on the third day. The skin around his incision was swollen, red, and painful, a sure sign of infection. His fever had been creeping up during the day and he vomited up the antimicrobial broth Dashay spoon fed him for dinner.

Riley had been giving him alternating doses of ibuprofen and acetaminophen, but they weren't having much effect and the supply was running low. Adrian had nothing in his bag of tricks to treat fever. They'd kept Nico's arms and legs covered with cool, damp towels out of desperation, but if Brooks didn't show up with antibiotics soon, Riley feared Nico wouldn't last more than a day.

She stepped out of the tent to stretch and get some air. Coop spotted her from where he was drying bear meat and waved her over. Riley went to him, and Coop kissed her cheek before she lowered herself onto the grass.

"Any improvement?" he asked.

Riley picked at a patch of weeds. "The opposite. He's up to 102 degrees and is showing signs of delirium. What about opening him up and inserting a drain? We could clean things out while we're in there."

Coop shook his head. "He's too weak and we're out of morphine. The pain alone could put him into shock. What about Adrian? I'm ready to try any of his ridiculous concoctions at this point."

Riley turned and looked around the camp. "Where is he? I haven't seen him since dinner."

"He's out searching for more plants. I told him not to go alone, but he wouldn't listen. He feels responsible for Nico."

"That's not like him to go off alone. How hard did you try to stop him?" Coop looked away sheepishly without answering. "Should we go after him?"

"He's a grown man who made his choice, and the last thing we need is anyone else getting hurt. What would Nico do if something happened to us?"

Riley knew he was right, but her anxiety ratcheted up a notch. "Adrian mentioned making a poultice but didn't know if he could locate all the ingredients. It might draw out the infection and it couldn't hurt."

"If Adrian comes back in one piece, we'll give it a shot." He cut off a piece of meat and handed it to her. "Eat this. I noticed you hardly touched your dinner. You're losing weight."

She smelled the meat and wrinkled her nose. "My body is rebelling against all this natural, healthy food. I've been queasy all day."

"Sure it's not more than that? You haven't been sleeping well either." He pressed the back of his hand to her forehead. "You don't feel warm."

"I'm not sick. It's just the food. I never thought I'd miss MREs." Coop dropped onto the grass next to her and lifted her onto his lap. She laid her head against his chest and wrapped his hand in hers. "Do you think Brooks is okay? It's been three days."

"Brooks knows his stuff. He's probably just trying to figure out how to get all the loot he scored back to camp. I expect him to come riding up in glory any minute."

Riley appreciated Coop's show of optimism for her sake, but she knew him well enough to sense he was just as worried. "As much as I want to believe you're right, what are we going to do if you're not?"

"We'll jump off that bridge when we come to it."

Riley gave him a quick kiss before getting to her feet. "Do you know how much I love you?"

He looked up at her and winked. "Couldn't be half as much as I love you."

"I'm going to say goodnight to Biscuit and go read some of Adrian's plant notes in the tent. Don't stay out here too long and let me know if Adrian shows up."

He blew her a kiss before she turned to go cheer up Biscuit. He'd been despondent since Brooks left with Echo. She would have brought him inside their tent if he could fit. As it was, she was giving him as much affection as she could spare, which wasn't much.

Riley woke from a dream about eating ice cream out of a mini helmet at a baseball game to hear someone softly calling her name. At first, she thought it was Coop, but he was quietly snoring beside her. She lay still for a moment, wondering if she'd dreamed that, too, when she heard it again.

"Riley, it's Brooks."

She opened her eyes, trying to focus on Brooks, then shook Coop awake before climbing out of her sleeping bag. She grabbed her hoodie and ducked out of the tent to find Brooks standing just outside the door, stamping his feet to keep warm. Riley was relieved to see Adrian hovering behind him.

She gave Brooks a hug, and said, "Am I happy to see you.

When did you get back?"

Coop crawled out of the tent and held his hand out to Brooks. "Good to see you, man."

"Good to be seen, believe me. I just got here. Dashay's with Nico. She says she needs you."

When he turned and headed for Nico's tent, Riley got into step behind him, wondering what new catastrophe awaited her. When she stepped into the tent, she was thrilled to see Dashay connecting a bag of Vancomycin and saline to Nico's IV.

Riley felt Nico's forehead. He was on fire.

Dashay pointed her flashlight at the thermometer for Riley. "It's 104." She handed Riley a syringe. "That's Caldor. I wanted you to approve the dosage before I injected him."

Riley checked the amount of liquid in the syringe before handing it back to Dashay. "Let's hope this takes effect in a hurry. If Brooks hadn't shown up when he did, Nico probably wouldn't have survived the night. Have you slept?" Dashay looked away, which told Riley all she needed to know. "You haven't had a good sleep for days. You can't keep this up or we'll lose you, too."

"I'll watch him to see how he does with the meds. If he improves, I'll let Adrian take over for me."

Brooks cocked his head toward the tent door. "Let's talk outside, Riley."

Coop and Adrian were waiting at the firepit and waved them over.

Riley glanced at her watch, then glared at Adrian. "When did you get back?"

"Hours ago. Coop told me not to wake you."

Riley shifted her glare to Coop. "I told you to tell me when he got back."

He shrugged, and said, "I was going to, but you were out cold, and you haven't been sleeping. I decided it could wait until morning."

Brooks looked at Adrian. "Where did you go?"

"Just out searching for herbs and plants. I got absorbed in what I was doing and lost track of time and the trail. It took a while to find my way back."

"You went out alone? In the dark? After your fit from the bear attack, I didn't think you'd set foot out of camp."

"Nico needed me."

"Very touching," Coop said and turned to Brooks. "What do you have to report?"

"Let's sit," Riley said. She took a seat on the log bench next to Coop. He put an arm around her and handed her a mug of tea. She took a sip and raised her eyebrows. "That's delicious. Did you make this, Adrian?" He nodded and grinned at her. "What is it?"

Coop held up his hand to stop him before he could answer. "Discuss herbal tea recipes later. We need to hear what Brooks and Dashay have to say."

Adrian slumped in his chair and gestured for Brooks to speak.

Brooks cradled his mug and stared at the flames. In the firelight, Riley noticed he had an angry bruise on his cheek.

"It's worse than we thought out there," he said. "Between massive mudslides blocking the major roads and people trying to stay ahead of Kearns' troops, it's hard to travel in the shadows. I didn't even reach Charleston before deciding to turn back. I got the meds from some kind people at a barely functioning pharmacy in a small town. It's not much, but hopefully will be enough to save Nico."

Coop said, "Not what I was hoping to hear. What happened to your face?"

As Brooks rubbed his cheek, he said, "Three men came at me and tried to take Echo. I fought them off."

"With your gun?" Riley asked.

"No, I ran out and left it in the tent, but fortunately, they didn't know how to fight very well. It wasn't much of a battle, but I got this bruise for my trouble."

"Thank god that's all it was," Coop said. "It would have been disastrous to lose you and be left with just Biscuit."

"Sounds like it'll be pretty tough with both horses," Adrian said. "Maybe we should wait it out here until Nico is recovered."

Brooks shook his head. "We can't afford to. With so many streaming into Charleston, supplies will be at a premium and we have to get there before they turn the city into one of those residential zones. I heard that once people are inside the zones, they aren't allowed to leave without permission. We need to get out of here as soon as possible and beat the hoards heading to the city. I found a back route on the return trip that was quicker and easier to navigate."

"We can't move Nico for two days minimum without risking a relapse, even if he responds well to the drugs," Riley said. "He wouldn't survive."

Coop rubbed his face as he got to his feet. "The two days will give us time to construct a litter that Biscuit can pull. Adrian, draw up a design in the morning. Brooks, give him whatever help he needs. For now, let's get back to bed. We're all going to need our sleep."

Riley gulped down the rest of her tea and went to check on Nico once more before going to her tent. "How is he?" she asked Dashay.

"Between the Caldor and cold saline, his temp has already dropped to 101 degrees."

Nico opened his eyes and gave Riley a weak smile. It was the first time he'd recognized her for two days.

"What time is it?" he asked in a hoarse croak.

Riley pressed her fingers to his wrist to take his pulse. It was weak but steady. "Three-thirty. How are you feeling?"

"Alive. Barely. What day is it?"

"Early Saturday morning."

"When was the bear attack?"

"Tuesday, I think. It's all been a blur."

Dashay nodded to confirm her guess.

"I've been lying here for four days? Seems like hours to me. Give me the truth, doc. What's my prognosis?"

"Looking better," she said as she wrapped the blood pressure cuff around his arm. "Dashay hasn't left your side this whole time, and Brooks went on a supply run. He just got back with those delicious fluids pouring into you. If not for that, we might not be having this conversation."

"If I'm remembering right, it was a group effort," he said. Riley nodded and gestured for him to remain quiet while she listened to his pressure. When she finished, he said, "How's Aurora?"

Riley sighed as she removed the cuff. "Didn't make it. Biscuit's devastated but having Echo back will help. Coop killed the bear. Nailed him right between the eyes. You would have been proud. Hurry and recover so you can dine on the delectable meat. You need the iron and B12."

"I'll do my best."

He closed his eyes and drifted back to sleep.

Riley motioned for Dashay to follow her out of the tent. "I'm sending Coop to sleep in Nico's tent. You and I can share for the rest of the night. Nico's improving and he'll be in expert hands."

Dashay yawned and said, "I'll get my sleeping bag."

Riley was glad she didn't argue. She went to her tent and told Coop the plan. He grabbed his bag and stumbled outside without a word. Dashay came as he went out and got settled. She was asleep two minutes later.

Riley was sure she'd sleep well now that everyone was back safely, and Nico was improving, but as she nestled into the sleeping bag, her queasiness returned with a vengeance. A sense of dread washed over her as she forced herself to take slow, even breaths. She hoped the nausea was nothing more than her body being unaccustomed to the foods she'd been eating, but instinct told her it was something more. She dozed off, hoping that for once, her instincts were wrong.

Julia rested her elbow on the desk and propped her chin in her hand as she tried to figure out why Uncle Mitch had been on edge since his trip into Wytheville three days earlier. She'd tried to get it out of him twice at breakfast, but he'd brushed her questions aside or changed the subject. Wytheville was such a small, boring town that she couldn't imagine what could have happened to upset him.

"Julia are you listening?" her Aunt Kathryn asked.

Julia and her cousins were in the middle of a lesson on the history of Europe, and aside from being distracted about Uncle Mitch, all Julia could think was who cared about the French Revolution with the world going to hell?

She sat up and said, "Sorry, Aunt Kathryn. I'm just worried about Uncle Mitch. He's been acting weird the past few days. Do you know what's wrong?"

Aunt Kathryn studied her for a second, then said, "We'll talk about it at lunch. After class."

Julia stared down at her textbook and thought, *another brushoff.* When Aunt Kathryn went on with the lesson, Julia glanced at Holly and rolled her eyes. Holly stifled a giggle and pretended to listen to her mom. Maybe between the two of them they could get some answers at lunch. Julia was tired of the family treating them like babies. They were both almost fourteen and would be in high school that fall if the world hadn't fallen apart.

"Julia, please read the first paragraph on page seventy-two," Aunt Kathryn said.

Julia flipped to the page, but when she opened her mouth to read, there was a roar of trucks coming up the driveway. Julia got up and went to the window but couldn't see the front drive from there.

She was about to ask if she could go see who it was when she heard Aunt Beth say, "Mitch, you'd better get out here, now."

Julia and her cousins ran for the hallway in unison, despite Aunt Kathryn's attempt to stop them. Julia got to the front door just behind Uncle Mitch and followed as he bounded down the steps. She stood on the bottom step and stared uneasily at the soldiers in camouflage uniforms climbing out of four green Jeeps.

"Julia, in the house, now," Uncle Mitch said as he approached the man who looked like he was in charge.

As Julia turned to obey her uncle, she heard him say, "What can I do for you, sir?"

Aunt Beth was waiting in the doorway and herded Julia and Holly into the kitchen as Kathryn ushered the rest of the kids back to the den.

Aunt Beth glared at Julia, and said, "It was reckless to barge outside like that. You don't know who those men could have been. Haven't you learned anything after what you went through? You were shot for goodness' sake!"

Julia knew her aunt was right. It was nothing her mother hadn't told her a hundred times. She didn't mean to be reckless, but her curiosity always seemed to take over before her good sense.

"I'm sorry, Auntie. I just feel so safe here that sometimes I forget how dangerous the world is."

Beth gave her a quick hug. "You're forgiven, but you have to do better or one day your luck will run out."

"I promise to try," Julia said.

Holly snickered behind her. "I've heard that before."

Julia ignored her and said, "When is anyone going to tell us what's going on? We're old enough to take it."

Aunt Beth cocked her head toward the pile of breakfast dishes that Julia was supposed to have washed after breakfast. As she reluctantly walked to the sink, Aunt Beth dropped into a chair and began taking green beans from a big bowl to snap off the ends.

"You're going to find out soon enough, so I might as well tell you. No one heard from President Carlisle after the CME, so he's presumed dead. Vice President Kearns took over as president and she's ordering the army to organize communities into zones. We've heard they're confiscating land from our neighbors without authorization. Your uncle and I believe what they're doing is unconstitutional and we plan to fight it."

Holly turned and stared at her. "You're going to fight the army?"

"Not with guns, honey. We're going to fight through the law, and not against the entire army. Just the troops stationed in Blacksburg."

Julia finished cleaning a plate and absentmindedly handed it to Holly, who was still shocked by what Aunt Beth had said. Julia was glad the government was trying to put the country back together, but she was afraid of what would happen if they were forced off the ranch. She'd learned enough in school to know landowners had rights.

She picked a plate out of the warm water, and said, "What happens to us if Uncle Mitch loses? Where would we go?"

"That won't happen, but in the slight chance it does, I think they'd allow us to live here. We just won't have control of the ranch."

Julia threw the dishcloth in the sink, then turned and crossed her arms. "That's not fair. You and Uncle Mitch have worked so hard to make the ranch what it is. They can't just take it. We should stop them with guns, like they do in westerns. Uncle Russ is teaching me to shoot. I'll fight."

"Even if the world feels like the Wild West now, Julia, this isn't a movie. Uncle Mitch has a plan to handle them. We have to trust him."

"We do, Grandma," Holly said. "He's kept us all alive and safe so far."

The front door slammed, rattling the walls and windows. Mitch stomped into the kitchen seconds later. He was about to say something to Beth but stopped when he noticed the girls.

"Don't worry," she said. "I told them. What happened out there?"

Mitch banged his fist on the table. "It's unbelievable. They say that since Kearns declared martial law, her military forces have the right to confiscate our land, like in times of war. I say that's bull. They're giving us a week to arrange for the troops to take over the ranch. The boys and I are driving into Blacksburg tomorrow with some of our neighbors to see what we can do. I'm not giving up this land to our own army. This is a blatant land grab by the government."

He turned and stalked out of the room, leaving the women staring after him.

"You're right that this isn't the Wild West, Aunt Beth," Julia said. "It's the start of a revolution."

Riley checked the ties holding Nico in place on the litter that they'd harnessed to Biscuit. Adrian and Brooks had done an excellent job constructing the contraption out of tree branches, cut up blankets, and sections of rope. It wouldn't be the most comfortable ride for Nico, but it would be easier than trying to ride Echo.

She knelt next to him and grasped his hand. "Comfy?"

He gave her a weak smile. "It'll have to do. Sorry for being a pain in the ass. I've made so much extra work for everyone."

She straightened and stretched her back. "Enough of that. It was an accident. We're all just thrilled to see you making excellent progress. It was dicey there for a minute."

Coop threw a saddlebag over Biscuit, then walked beside

Riley. "How's our most excellent patient?"

"Ready to go," Nico said. "The sooner we leave, the sooner I get to sleep in an actual bed in Charleston."

"From your mouth to God's ear. We're just about packed and will be out of here in ten. Riley, can you come help me finish with the tent?"

Riley eyed him for a second before nodding. They had packed the tent and loaded it on Echo an hour earlier. She followed him to where their tent had stood, supposing he wanted to tell her something about Nico without him hearing. He walked past their former tent site and headed toward the farthest picnic table.

She dropped onto the bench and folded her arms. "What's the big secret?"

He propped his foot next to her on the bench, and said, "You tell me. You've been moody and quiet for days, which makes no sense. Nico's recovering, you have your friend Dashay, and we're finally getting back on the road. You should be doing your victory dance. This isn't about Julia again, is it?"

She lowered her eyes and played with a thread on her sleeve. "It's always about Julia, but this is something else. I didn't plan to say anything until I was sure, but I'm tired of hiding it from you. Here goes. I'm pregnant."

Coop stepped away and ran his hand through his hair. "You're sure? You can't have taken a test."

"This is my fourth time. I'm familiar with the signs. I don't need a test, but I'll take one to confirm when we get to Charleston."

"How far along?"

"I estimate two months."

Coop squinted at her while he calculated. "Sure you didn't miscalculate? Wouldn't that have been while we were separated after I left the cabin?"

"I'm guessing it happened the night before you left in search of food and didn't come back."

A smile crept up his face. "That was a great night." He picked her up off the bench and spun her around. "This is incredible! I'm so happy, Riley."

She pounded on his chest, and said, "Put me down. It's not incredible. It's the worst thing that could have happened. It's bad enough we're crossing the country under these awful conditions, but now I have to travel in this condition. I don't do pregnant well, and I've never told you, but all three of my kids were delivered by C-Section."

He put her down but kept his arms around her. "We'll be in Colorado long before you're due. I'll do what it takes to get both of you there in time, then I can deliver our baby." He kissed the top of her head. "I'm going to be a father. I never thought it would happen."

Riley pulled free of his arms, then bent over and vomited in the grass, just missing his boot. "Sorry, but it's going to be like that for roughly the next month," she whispered. She wiped her mouth on her neckerchief and gave him a weak smile. "I've been consumed with thinking how this will affect me. I'm scared, but I'm also happy that we'll share this. I love you. Congratulations, Daddy."

"You two newlyweds coming?" Dashay called from across the park. "We're packed and ready to head out."

Coop reached for Riley's hand as they walked back to the others. "Are we going to tell them?"

"Let's wait until I've had the test. We need to be sure this isn't from one of Adrian's concoctions."

"It might be hard to keep secret with you tossing your cookies every ten minutes."

"It's not quite that bad. Maybe Adrian has a remedy for nausea." She glanced up at Coop and chuckled. "That ridiculous grin is a dead giveaway, though."

"Give me five minutes to bask. It's amazing to have something to grin about."

"Then, grin away, babe."

Nico's litter worked like a charm, which was fortunate since they'd had to detour around three mudslides by late afternoon. None of the detours took them too far off course, so they didn't lose as much time as Riley thought they would. They'd packed the bulk of the gear onto the horses and were all on foot, which slowed their progress. Riley estimated that it would take five days to reach Charleston at that pace and hoped their provisions would hold out.

What surprised Riley most was how few people they saw on the roads. From what Brooks told them after his scouting trip, Riley expected the route to be packed with lines of vagabonds marching toward Charleston like them. Instead, the roads were empty, and she feared everyone else knew something they didn't. The few groups they saw kept their distance, which was fine with her.

In the late afternoon, Brooks went ahead to scout a place to camp for the night. He returned less than an hour later to tell them he'd found a burned-out house with a big yard and a pond. It wasn't far off their route and would provide more than enough room for the tents and horses. With news of a good place to stop, they picked up the pace and made it an hour before sundown.

After a relaxing dinner of bear meat and assorted plants Adrian had collected along the way, all except Nico visited until eight when the sun set, then went to their tents.

Once Coop and Riley were zipped into their sleeping bag, he said, "You were a champ today. How are you holding up?"

"Fine, just like I was when you asked me thirty minutes ago. Pregnancies are long, Coop, so you'd better pace yourself. If you ask me how I am every five minutes, I'll lose my mind. I promise to tell you if I'm not fine."

He rolled toward her and rested his head on her shoulder. "This is all new and exciting to me, so be patient. I noticed that you hardly touched dinner. Until we can find prenatal vitamins, you need to make sure you get sufficient nutrients from your food."

"I'm tired of bear meat. The flavor is too strong and gamey. I'd prefer venison or even squirrel."

"I can try to bag a few squirrels along the way, but don't have time to stop for a deer hunt."

"Then squirrels it is."

He gave her a tender kiss, then said, "We'll be in Charleston soon and you can have real food."

"I'm counting the seconds," she said, then scurried out of the sleeping bag and made it outside of the tent just in time to be sick on the lawn.

The next day followed like the one before, and the next. By the fifth day, as they neared the city and passed more travelers, Riley relaxed and grew excited at the prospect of seeing actual civilization. Her reaction was the opposite of what she'd expected. They'd spent months on the road avoiding crowds. Now, she couldn't wait to join them.

She was also eager to get to Charleston and get her hands on a pregnancy test to confirm her diagnosis. The nausea hadn't abated and was comparable to when she was pregnant with Jared. The long miles of walking wore her out, but she felt healthy and fit. Pregnancy was the only diagnosis that made sense.

It still hadn't sunk in that she was going to have another child. Coop thought he'd never be a father, but after Zach's death, she never dreamed she'd remarry and add another member to the family. If it had happened before the CME, she would have been ecstatic, but bringing a life into their chaotic world filled her with dread. She hoped Coop was right that she was overreacting, but after what they'd already survived, how could she not?

As they crested a hill above Charleston, Brooks said, "Riley," in a sharp voice. She jumped and turned to face him. "You planning to roll down that slope into the city?"

She stopped and looked around. Without realizing, she'd walked off the road to the edge of the hill. She backed away and turned toward the others.

Dashay grinned at her, and said, "Where's your head, girl?"

Riley blushed, and said, "Just in a hurry to get to Charleston."

"Bull," Brooks said. "What's been up with you these past few days?"

She glanced at Coop, then cocked her head toward the group. "Might as well tell them."

Coop stood taller and straightened his shirt. "I'm going to be a dad. Riley's pregnant."

They turned their eyes on Riley and stared in stunned silence. She fidgeted and said, "Aren't you going to say anything?"

"Reckless," Adrian mumbled. "Mark my words. This will be problematic."

Coop glared at him, so Adrian clamped his lips and bowed his head.

Brooks made a sweep of his arm toward the city. "Are you two crazy? How could you think bringing a baby into this insanity was a good idea?"

Dashay smacked him on the shoulder, then threw her arms around Riley. "Ignore Brooks. Congratulations!"

Coop beamed at her. "This wasn't exactly on our to-do list, Brooks, but we're thrilled and scared out of our wits."

Dashay stepped away and studied Riley. "I wouldn't call that face thrilled."

"Morning sickness," Coop said.

"Get me out of this thing," Nico called from the litter. While

Brooks and Adrian unstrapped him, he said, "Congratulations, man. This world needs new life. I'm happy for you two."

Brooks helped him off the litter and supported him while he walked to a low concrete wall. Nico lowered himself onto it with a groan.

"Thanks, Nico," Riley said. "You're walking better. You won't need that litter once we reach the city."

"*Gracias a Dios*. I can't stand that thing for one more day. I feel like the inside of a burrito."

Brooks put a hand on his shoulder. "If we hoof it, we might make it by sundown. Can you handle that, Riley?"

She squared her shoulders and raised her chin. "I'm pregnant, not fragile. The next person who treats me like a delicate flower will get my boot."

Brooks held his hands up in surrender. "Deal. I know better than to cross you. I'm sorry for what I said about the baby. Great news."

Riley eyed him coolly but nodded her thanks. Their reaction to her news was what she'd expected. It would make life easier for them to know, but it also made it feel more real for Riley. The last thing she'd been planning on for their cross-country trek was to carry an additional little passenger, especially in the heat of summer.

Coop walked to the edge of the hill where Riley had stood moments earlier and gave a low whistle. "Look at that."

Riley moved closer and gazed at the scene below in wonder. Rays of the setting sun glowed in the gold-plated dome of the West Virginia capitol building, which rose above the Kanawha River. The picturesque city lay nestled between the river and the hills and fanned out through tree-lined streets. The sight was so enticing that Riley was tempted to run all the way to Charleston.

Dashay stepped beside Riley and squeezed her hand. "Why haven't I heard of this place? It looks gorgeous from here."

Brooks pointed toward the highway entrance just east of the

city. "It may not look it from here, but what's happening on that road isn't so pretty."

Riley shifted her gaze in the direction Brooks pointed. Men and women in a hodgepodge of uniforms were constructing a barricade, while others wielding a variety of weapons stood guard. Riley surveyed the valley and saw similar barriers at every visible entrance into Charleston.

"That's trouble," Coop said.

"What are you seeing?" Nico asked. "Help me over there, Brooks."

Brooks and Adrian helped Nico to the edge, where he silently surveyed the view. "Are they keeping people in or out?"

"Both, most likely," Adrian said.

Coop turned his back to the city and patted Echo. "Only one way to know. Let's get down there."

Dashay followed him and shouldered her pack. "Is that safe? Should we wait until morning?"

"Could be worse by then, and we all need a break," Brooks said. "I say we risk it."

Dashay followed him to help get Nico strapped into the litter while Riley anxiously stared at the scene unfolding below them, recalling another barricade early in their journey. That had gone horribly wrong and almost resulted in her losing Coop and Julia. She hoped this time would bring a better ending. Coop gave her a quick glance as he passed and guided Echo toward a trail leading down the hill. His look told her he was recalling the same memory.

She got into step behind him and started whistling *Heigh Ho* from *Snow White*. Another shared memory. Coop winked, then whistled along with her. The others joined in except for Adrian, who clearly considered himself above such childish things. When she realized he hadn't bothered to congratulate them or apologize for his thoughtless comment, she linked her arm in his and sang all the louder.

CHAPTER FIVE

Riley and her companions reached the base of the hill an hour later, along with a massive road-worn throng of humanity. A line of people desperate to enter Charleston stretched for more than a mile from the barricade. Riley's anxiety reached a fever pitch at being hemmed in by the massive crowd. Though she'd looked forward to getting back to civilization, this was far more than she'd expected. Biscuit wasn't any happier with the jostling crowd and nervously shifted his weight on his hooves as the line crawled ahead at a snail's pace. Riley was relieved they'd strapped Nico's litter to Echo to give Biscuit a break.

Coop tapped Riley's shoulder, making her flinch. "Stand still. You're making me antsy."

"Should we find another way to get in?" she asked. "There might be a less crowded entrance."

He took his pack off and handed it to her. "I'll climb on Echo's back to get a better look. Hold him still."

Riley took Echo's rein and watched nervously as Coop climbed to his knees in the saddle. Echo didn't like it either and took a step forward. The movement threw Coop off balance, but he caught himself before tumbling to the ground.

"Whoa, boy," Riley whispered in Echo's ear as Coop righted himself. She patted his neck until he settled.

"What do you see?" Brooks called to Coop.

He jumped down without answering and shook his head. "Looks like a thousand others had the same idea. Going around would be a waste of time. We're better off trying to get in through this gate. Adrian, make yourself useful and break out something for us to eat while we wait."

Adrian reluctantly obeyed and handed Riley some Bear jerky and wild strawberries before giving the others their food.

When she wrinkled her nose, he said, "I know you're tired of this food, but you need to increase your caloric and nutrient intake for the baby, especially if you're having morning sickness."

She studied him for a moment, then took a bite of the jerky, supposing that was his way of apologizing. She swallowed the meat with a gulp of water, and said, "I'm the medical doctor and this is my fourth pregnancy, but I appreciate the thought."

"I just want to ensure you stay healthy. We need you."

"Thanks for your concern," she mumbled as he walked toward Dashay and handed her some food.

While Riley ate, she worked to calm her mind and accept their situation. Getting worked into a panic wouldn't help anyone. She went to Biscuit and fed him some berries, then stroked him between his eyes. He immediately quieted and tilted his head for her to scratch behind his ear. Petting him relaxed her, too. She turned her thoughts to wondering what awaited them once they passed that mysterious barrier.

They were close enough after three hours for Riley to see the five men manning the gateway to Charleston. They wore army fatigues but didn't appear to be active-duty military. Two of them held clipboards, and the other three stood guard with rifles. Riley wondered how many more guards watched from inside the barricade.

When they finally reached the entrance, Riley stepped

between Coop and Brooks as they approached the men with the clipboards.

Coop put out his hand and flashed his friendliest grin. "Evening, gentlemen. I'm Coop. This is Riley and Brooks. We'd like to enter your fine city."

The man closest to Coop ignored his offer of a handshake and looked at him over the top of his glasses. "We'll be glad to have you if you meet our requirements."

Riley felt a chill on the back of her neck as Coop shot her a quick glance. They'd been through that scenario more than once. Never with favorable results.

Brooks stepped closer to the man. "What requirements?"

"We can't accept every person who wants in, unfortunately. Charleston can't support it. To be admitted, you must exchange something of value. By the looks of your group, other than the horses, you don't have much to offer."

"Looks can deceive," Coop said, still grinning. "What is it you need most?"

"Food or similar commodities are always at the top of the list. I can see you don't have those. After that, what we require most now is military knowhow, engineering skills, and medical knowledge and supplies."

Brooks opened his mouth to speak, but Coop held up his hand to stop him. "We're traveling to the west and don't plan to stay. We just need to restock our provisions. My wife is pregnant, and we have an injured man with us. Will you help us? We'll give what we can, then move on."

"I'm sorry, but if you can't offer something of specific value, we can't let you enter. Since it's after dark, there's a refugee camp on the far side of the city. You can get a meal and a safe night's sleep. Nothing more."

Brooks pulled the rifle off his shoulder, but held it lowered in front of him. "Not good enough. We've traveled a long way and need your help."

"Brooks," Coop barked, "put that gun back on your shoulder." He held his hands up in surrender. "I apologize for my companion. He's just exhausted and hungry. I'm sure we can negotiate."

"These two are surgeons," Brooks blurted before Coop could stop him. Riley cringed and glared at him. Brooks cocked his thumb over his shoulder at Dashay. "That woman is an experienced nurse, and the man on the litter is an army medic. The mousey one there is an astrophysicist and I have good mechanical skills. All of us are good shots except for the mousey one. Good enough for you?"

The man with the glasses studied Coop for a moment. "Is what he says true?" Coop hesitated for a second before nodding. "Why didn't you just say that? Come in and move to that table to the left. Maggie will take your information. You can tie the horses to the tree by that bench. Welcome to Charleston."

The other men opened the barrier and waved them through.

Once they were inside, Riley grabbed the front of Brooks' jacket and pulled his face close to hers. "Why did you tell them that? Now, they won't let us leave. I've been a hostage once before, if you recall. I'm not in a hurry to do it again."

Brooks gently removed her hand from his jacket and stepped back. "First, I had no choice. I've been the one on the other side of the barrier. They would never have let us in unless we had something of worth to offer. Second, I don't think we're hostages. We'll stay until Nico recovers and give them what they want. Then, we'll take what we need and go."

Riley crossed her arms and didn't back down. "It wasn't your place to reveal information about us. Tell them whatever you want about yourself. I won't be forced to stay here and run their hospital. I just want to go home."

Her voice broke, and Coop put his arms around her.

Dashay stepped in front of Brooks. "Riley's right. You should have asked before speaking up, but it's done. We're inside. We might as well make the best of it. Nico's deteriorating. We need to get him off that litter and somewhere where he can rest. I know you aren't fragile, Riley, but you need to take extra care of yourself."

Riley pulled away from Coop and said, "Let's get signed in."

They found a middle-aged woman with soft features but sharp eyes, wearing a pinned-on name tag that read Maggie, seated at a six-foot folding table. She handed each of them forms and pens, then gestured to another table for them to fill out the forms. Riley found an empty clipboard and fastened Nico's form to it before handing it to him. She sat down next to Coop to fill out her form in the light of a solar powered spotlight.

Adrian was inspecting his form instead of filling it out. "What are you looking for?" Dashay asked him.

"These were created on a typewriter and copied on a mimeograph machine. Where on earth did they find those machines?"

"In a museum?" Coop said.

"But where did they get the fluid or the typewriter ribbon?"

Riley rubbed her forehead where a headache was starting. "What does it matter? Just fill it out so we can find out what they're going to do with us. You can spend all day investigating tomorrow."

Adrian frowned at her. "Testy, are we? I found it remarkable. They're adapting well here."

Riley started reading her form without responding to him. She'd had about as much of Dr. Adrian Landry as she could stand and hoped they could ditch him in Charleston. The thought of crossing the country with him made her jaw clench.

The top of the form asked the usual questions she expected, such as her name, age and where she'd come from. As she moved down the sheet, the questions became more pointed and personal. They asked about her mental and physical status, loved ones she'd lost and her opinion of their new president's Residential Zone Initiative.

Brooks raised his form and shook it in the air. "What the hell is this? I'm not answering these questions."

Riley raised an eyebrow. "You were the one all fired up to get in here. How does it feel to be on the other side of the clipboard?"

"Just answer the questions," Dashay said, calmly. "What will it matter once we're gone in a few days? It's not like your info will show up on the dark web."

"Good point," Brooks said, and finished answering the questions.

Coop collected all their forms and handed them to Maggie. She flipped through the papers, thanked them and pointed to two men waiting behind another table piled with pillows and olive-green blankets.

"Tim and Dennis there will give you your allotted provisions and take you to your assigned quarters. There is a mandatory orientation tomorrow morning at eight in front of the capitol. A basic breakfast will be provided. Have a good night," she said, then turned to the next group coming up behind them.

Coop smiled at Riley, and sang, "*Heigh ho,* it's off to Tim and Dennis we go."

Riley couldn't help but chuckle despite her irritation and exhaustion. She followed him to the table and waited for instructions, deciding it wasn't so bad having others tell her what to do for once.

The man with the Tim nametag stepped toward her. He was about six-seven and as thin as a beanpole with short curly hair. He reminded her of a waving balloon man in front of a car dealership. Dennis was a foot shorter and round as a basketball. Riley had to bite her cheek to keep from giggling at the sight of them. *I need sleep,* she thought as she stepped to the table.

"Do you need pillows and blankets, or do you have your own?" he asked.

"We have our own, but they're filthy. Can we still have clean ones?"

He handed her two blankets and a pillow with a faint smell of bleach. "Of course. What about toiletries?"

"Do you have toothpaste and deodorant?"

He bent down and pulled a gallon-sized bag filled with every kind of toiletry she could imagine. She took it, restraining herself from kissing the bag in front of him.

With their supplies in hand, Coop retrieved the horses, and they followed Tim and Dennis a good half-mile to a quiet, tree-lined street. A block further down, the men turned and led them up the steps to a plain, two-story house.

As Tim unlocked the front door, he said, "There's a fence and room for the horses out back. In the morning, we'll locate some hay, but there's a creek they can drink from at the edge of the property. It's outside the fence, so you'll have to lead them."

Coop and Riley tied them to a tree in the front yard for the time being, and after helping Nico out of the litter, went in with the others. They got Nico to the living room sofa, then waited for more instructions.

"We hope you don't mind sharing the house," Dennis said. "There are four bedrooms. The master is on the first floor, so your sick friend won't have to climb stairs. The house has a working generator, but use is restricted to scheduled times. Your assigned time slots will be in the welcome information you'll receive at orientation."

"What about water?" Adrian asked.

"The pumps run on solar power, so you'll have running water, but it will be cold."

"Good," Coop said. "Is it drinkable?"

"No, but it's for bathing. There's bottled water in the kitchen."

Tim waved his hand to get Dennis' attention. "Don't forget to tell them about the food."

"Right. It's too late for a hot meal, but there are light snacks in the kitchen to get you through until morning. You'll be able to shop tomorrow. Questions?"

The six of them stared at Tim and Dennis in disbelief.

"No questions," Riley whispered. "Thank you for your generosity. It's the first we've seen since the CME."

Tim shook her hand. "Our pleasure, Dr. Poole."

"Dr. Cooper," Coop said.

Tim glanced at Riley's form. "My apologies. She listed her name as Poole."

Dashay smiled at him. "They just got married."

Riley blushed. "Force of habit, but you can call me Riley to avoid confusion with two Doctor Coopers."

"And I'm Coop," he said and held out his hand.

Tim and Dennis each shook his hand, then left them alone.

As soon as the door closed behind them, Riley and Dashay ran to the kitchen and started rifling through the boxes of food on the table. There were packets of cheese and crackers, cans of beans and tuna, and fruit leather, just for a start. They carried the boxes into the living room and sat around them on the floor, stuffing their faces.

Dashay reached into a box, then shrieked in delight. She pulled out a box of glazed donuts and held it up for the others to see. "There are six, one for each of us."

"I'll pass," Adrian said, and picked up a box of raisins.

Dashay tore the box open and sniffed. "Suit yourself. Riley and I will split yours."

She handed Riley a donut before shoving hers into her mouth whole. Riley took a bite, savoring the delightful taste on her tongue, then covered her mouth and got to make a dash for the front door. She made it onto the porch just in time to deposit everything she'd just eaten into the shrubs. She vomited until there was nothing left, then rested her forehead on the railing with a groan.

Coop came up behind her and rested his hand on her back.

"Remember when I got to the ranch after not eating for days? You told me not to eat too fast because my body wasn't used to so much food."

"Yes," she croaked. "You ignored me and tossed your entire meal. I should have listened to my own advice."

"Let your stomach settle, then try taking nibbles instead of chunks."

She straightened and nodded as he guided her toward the door. "We should unload the gear and get the horses settled. They're as exhausted as we are."

"I'll get Brooks. Dashay and Adrian can help Nico. You find a bed and climb into it. I'll be up soon."

Riley headed for the door with no argument. She squeezed his hand as she passed and waved goodnight to the others before dragging herself up the stairs. She wasn't happy that she'd lost the best food she'd eaten in weeks, but she'd learned her lesson, and it had been worth it.

She found the bathroom at the top of the stairs, and after using the flush toilet, dropped into the queen-sized bed in the room across the hall. She was out before Coop made it upstairs.

———

Riley opened her eyes to the dark room, in the strange house, in another unfamiliar city. Her only comfort was the feel of Coop sleeping soundly beside her. A glance at her watch told her it was 3:17. She leaned against the headboard and wrapped her hands around her knees. It was their first night under a real roof since leaving the ranch. She should have been out cold like Coop, not sleeplessly awaiting the dawn.

Coop stirred beside her, and whispered, "What's wrong, babe? Did you hear something?"

She shook her head and reached for his hand. "I can't shake the feeling that trouble's coming."

"Trouble's always coming these days. You haven't figured that out yet? Come here." She laid next to him, and he pulled her to his chest. "You're exhausted and overwhelmed after everything that's happened the past week, especially finding out you're pregnant. That's huge in any circumstance. More so in this insane world, but you're not alone. We're in this together. I'll do whatever it takes to protect you and get you home."

"Thank you, Coop. That means everything to me."

"Close your eyes and let your mind rest. Tomorrow will be a better day."

She snuggled against him and took a few relaxing breaths, then fell into a restful sleep.

She woke to Coop shaking her shoulder after what felt like five minutes.

"Wake up, Riley. It's Nico," he said, then climbed off the bed.

She rolled over and looked up at him, trying to force herself awake. "What time is it?"

"Six-thirty," Dashay said from the doorway. "I'm sorry to wake you, but he's in bad shape."

Riley swung her feet to the floor. "We'll be right down."

She and Coop dressed in a hurry, then raced downstairs to Nico's room. Riley could tell from the doorway he'd take a turn for the worse. His complexion was gray, and beads of perspiration dotted his forehead. He didn't even respond when Dashay slid the thermometer under his tongue. Riley took his pulse while Coop checked his blood pressure.

Dashay held the thermometer for Riley to read. The digital reading flashed 103.7 degrees.

"His infection's back with a vengeance," Riley said. "We've got to find the hospital. Dashay, wake Brooks so he can help us get Nico in the litter. I'll tell Adrian what's happening."

They jumped into action, and Coop and Riley were soon mounted on Echo with Nico trailing behind on the litter. They had no idea where they were headed, so Coop guided Echo toward the gate where they'd entered the night before.

The first person they passed was a woman holding the hand of a young girl. Riley leaned toward them, and said, "Can you point us to a hospital?"

The woman shrugged. "Sorry, we've only been here for a day."

Riley thanked her, and Coop snapped Echo's reins. They didn't pass anyone else until they were half a mile from the gate when they saw two men in fatigues coming toward them, holding rifles across their chests.

When they reached them, the man on the left held up his hand to stop them. "What are you doing out? Curfew doesn't lift for another thirty minutes."

"We just got here last night," Coop said. "We're surgeons. We need to get this man medical help immediately."

The other man eyed Riley, the doubt obvious on his face. "You're a surgeon?"

"Yes, I'm Dr. Riley Poole. Orthopedic Surgeon. Ask Maggie if you don't believe me. Where's the hospital?"

The other man elbowed his companion. "Quiet, Barnes." Turning to Coop, he said, "Turn around and go back five-hundred yards, then turn left. You can't miss the hospital a quarter mile down the road."

Coop dipped his head in thanks, then got Echo moving. When they reached the hospital, Riley dismounted and ran to find a gurney and someone to help them lift Nico onto it. She was shocked when the doors slid open as she approached. She marched inside and introduced herself, then started barking orders like she owned the place. She didn't have time to stop and explain.

A man in scrubs came towards her, pushing a gurney. "I'm Flynn Jamison, OR nurse. We weren't expecting you until after orientation, Dr. Poole. What do you need?"

She studied him for a second, then nodded. "We have a

dangerously ill man with us. Help me get him inside. Tell someone to have saline and Vancomycin ready if you have it."

Flynn called out her orders to a passing woman in a nurse's uniform. She ran through a set of double doors as Riley and Flynn headed outside. Nico's color was worse, and he was moaning and incoherent. Flynn helped Coop lift him onto the gurney, then guided them to a trauma room.

A man wearing a white coat with Dr. Powell stitched above the pocket was waiting for them. "What have we got, Dr. Poole?"

"One-week post-surgical infection," she said in a rush. "Possible peritonitis or sepsis."

"We operated in the field and have had limited meds. We've been on the road the past several days," Coop said.

Dr. Powell pried Nico's eyelids open and shined his penlight at his pupils. While he continued working, he said, "You're in luck. I'm an infectious disease specialist. Leave him with me. We'll take care of him. What's his name?"

"Nico Mendez," Riley said, "but we'd rather not leave him."

Dr. Powell glanced up at her. "Orientation is mandatory. You can check on him after you've registered."

Coop wrapped his hand in her elbow and nudged her toward the door. "Thank you, Doctor," he said.

"Call me Hank. Why did you perform surgery on Nico?" Riley explained the bear attack and Nico's accident. Hank gave a low whistle. "You people have been through it."

Coop shook his head. "I'm Coop. This is Riley, and we've just scratched the surface."

"I look forward to hearing about your adventures," Hank said and went back to work.

Riley looked around in disbelief as they walked out of the hospital. The lights worked, and she heard monitors as they passed some rooms. How could this place be so far ahead of everyone else in having functioning electricity? It reminded her of the senior community she and Julia had stayed in briefly, but that was just one facility. It looked like the entire city had power.

"We should just bring Julia here and wait for the baby to come," Riley mumbled as they unstrapped the litter and stashed it inside the hospital entrance.

Coop stopped and stared at her. "Not a terrible idea. She might not be happy about leaving Holly and the rest of the family, but she'd love this place, and I know she'd rather be with us."

Coop helped her onto Echo's back, then climbed up behind her.

Riley settled into place and said, "Once we're satisfied it's safe here, let's go get Julia. If the rains stay away, the return trip will be much faster now that we know the route."

Coop flicked the reins and pointed Echo toward the capitol which was easy to spot from any point in Charleston. "Let's keep that option tucked in our hats and go find out what the deal is with this place."

Coop directed Echo to the main street instead of traveling along the river. As they plodded along at a steady pace, the pedestrian crowd thickened around them, all heading in the same direction. Riley wasn't surprised to see so many newcomers after the throng trying to get in from the day before. What she hadn't expected were the rows of armed and uniformed men and women lining the road. It reminded her of footage she'd seen showing soldiers going off to fight during the world wars, but these soldiers weren't parading. They were mustering for battle.

When they reached the green space across from the capitol, they dismounted, and Coop tied Echo to a tree behind the waiting throng. People who Riley assumed were volunteers sat at six-foot tables lining the outer edge of the open area. They

stepped in front of a middle-aged, balding man at the closest
table.

He was looking down, reading something in a file folder.
When Riley cleared her throat, he said, "Name?" without raising
his head.

She sighed and said, "Drs. Riley Poole and Neal Cooper."

That got his attention, and he glanced up. "It's about time you
got here." He leaned back in his chair and waved to get the
attention of a tall, thin woman seated at the opposite end of the
table. "Your doctors are here."

The woman picked up a thicker folder, then got up and walked
toward Riley and Coop. She held her hand out and smiled. "I'm Mrs.
Samuels, Vice-chair of the hospital board. You may call me Natalie."

Riley's eyes widened as she shook Natalie's hand. "Your
hospital has a board?"

"Certainly," she said, then turned and walked briskly toward
the capitol building without another word.

Natalie crossed several yards before she realized they weren't
behind her. When she did, she spun around and marched back.
She stopped a few steps from them and put her hands on her
hips. "I meant for you to come with me."

Riley stood taller and crossed her arms. "We refuse to follow
anyone who doesn't tell us where we're going."

Natalie cocked her thumb at the bald man. "Didn't Brian
explain?" Riley shook her head. "I apologize. We have a separate
orientation for medical personnel twice a week in one of the
capitol conference rooms. We're running late, so please come."

Riley gestured for Natalie to show the way, then she and
Coop fell into step beside her.

As they worked their way through the mass of humanity,
Riley said, "I have a million questions about this place. We've seen
nothing that comes close to what you've accomplished. How is
this possible without communications or power?"

"Most of the residents had hardened generators, and we've relied on our coal reserves and solar power to keep functioning. Once we were up and running, Governor Mitchell sent representatives to surrounding communities, asking them to migrate to the city. Many of the survivors came, but some, especially those with land or their own fuel sources, stayed where they were. We continue to exchange materials and provisions with them."

"Remarkable," Coop said. "It's encouraging to know this can be done but brings up another question. A scientist told us that power generation is based on huge transformers, and those were destroyed by the CME. If I understood him, no matter the fuel source, it's useless without transformers. So, what good is your coal?"

"Simple. Power companies in the state began hardening the transformers after 9/11. Not all of them were finished, so parts of the state have to rely on solar and natural gas generators."

Every word Natalie said convinced Riley even more that they needed to get Julia to Charleston. Though the city hadn't entirely escaped the destructive effects of the CME, they'd survived remarkably unscathed. She understood why they were so reluctant to allow entry to everyone who wanted in. Even with their infrastructure relatively intact, their resources would still be severely limited.

Natalie paused to let a column of soldiers pass. When they reached the entrance to the capitol building, Riley said, "One more question. What's with the heavy military presence? It looks like you're prepping for war."

Natalie studied her for a moment, then handed Coop and Riley their folders and opened the door for them to enter the capitol. As they passed, Natalie said, "We are."

"What?" Riley said, but Natalie had moved away to speak to a guard. They tried to catch up with Natalie and make her explain the cryptic comment, but she entered a conference room and took her seat at a front table with four others.

"Riley," Dashay called from behind her.

She spun to see her grinning from where she sat at a long table. Riley let the matter with Natalie drop for the moment and followed Coop to their seats. She lowered herself into the chair between Coop and Dashay and dropped her folder on the table.

Dashay squeezed her hand. "What's wrong, Riley?"

"We need to talk," Riley whispered as a distinguished-looking man with salt and pepper hair stood at the front table and cleared his throat.

When the buzz of conversation in the room quieted, he said. "My name is Dr. Nigel Prichard, chair of the hospital board. Welcome to Charleston. We know many of you have been through harrowing journeys to get here, but we're glad you made it this far, and we're grateful for your willingness to contribute your talents and expertise to the wellbeing of our city. Before we begin the orientation, please enjoy breakfast on us."

Dr. Prichard stepped out of the room, and Riley heard him mumble something to someone in the hallway. He came back in, followed by four people pushing trolleys piled with covered plates. The servers handed each person a plate, utensils rolled in a cloth napkin, and a bottle of water.

Riley set her plate on the table, and before she could get the cover off, a violent wave of nausea washed over her. She covered her mouth and ducked out a back door into a deserted hallway. She made it just in time to vomit into a large garbage can.

Coop came up behind her and stroked her back until she finished. "I can't believe you have anything left in your stomach to bring up. You haven't kept anything down since yesterday afternoon. We need to treat this before you get dehydrated."

She straightened and he handed her his napkin to wipe her mouth. "It's because I waited too long to eat. We'll deal with it later."

Dashay peeked her head out the door. "You two all right out here? Natalie is asking about you."

Coop smiled and said, "On our way." Dashay gave a small wave and closed the door. "Let's get back in there before we arouse suspicion. Feel up to trying breakfast?"

"I'll do my best," she said and headed to the conference room.

She felt the stares as she took her seat but ignored them and uncovered her plate. There was an omelet with actual cheese, two pieces of whole-grain bread, and a bowl of fruit cocktail. She would have preferred oatmeal, but the food was far better than anything she'd eaten in weeks.

She took a small bite of bread and followed it with a sip of water. Her stomach cooperated, so she tried the omelet. It was lukewarm and rubbery, but she couldn't remember tasting anything so delicious. She ate at a sensible pace, and by the time she finished, her head had cleared, and she felt her strength returning.

As she pushed her empty plate away, Dr. Prichard stood and tapped the table. The room quieted and everyone turned their eyes on him.

"Let's move on with the orientation so all of you can settle in and begin your duties. Our other staff is eager for you to get to work. You'll find information in your packets about housing, use of your generators, shopping, and currency, but it's all self-explanatory, so you can read that on your own time. The purpose of this meeting is to cover hospital protocols and operations. These are perilous times. We have much to prepare for and little time to do it." He held up a packet of stapled papers. "Please take out your handbooks that look like this and scan through them. We'll cover each section in detail during your breakout sessions."

Riley pulled her packet from the folder as visions of mind-numbing HR intake meetings flashed into her mind. She would have sacrificed anything to be sitting in one of those at her home hospital in Colorado Springs. She flipped through the pages, but what she saw wasn't anything like HR. handbooks of the past. It read more like a frontline field-hospital instruction manual.

"What is this?" she heard a man at the adjacent table ask.

People seated around him started nodding, and a chorus of mumbling broke out.

Natalie stood and raised her hands to quiet the crowd. "We're aware this information may not be what you expected, but it's what will be the most useful to you in the coming days."

A hulking brute of a man with arms as thick as tree trunks jumped up and said, "I was an OR nurse in Afghanistan. This information could have been taken straight from our training manuals. What's this about? You're not at war."

Natalie bent down and whispered to Dr. Prichard. A man on the other side of Natalie leaned over and joined the conversation. The three of them whispered back and forth until Dr. Prichard said, "You might as well tell them."

Natalie hesitated a moment before saying, "As I'm sure you are all aware, President Kearns is ordering her troops across the country to create her residential zones. When reports reached us of the terrible conditions in these zones and atrocities being committed, Governor Mitchell sent his officers out to investigate. What they discovered was shocking. After meeting with his advisors, Governor Mitchell called for a vote to see if his citizens would stand with him against Kearns' forces. The overwhelming response was yes."

The OR nurse took a step toward Natalie. "You're telling us that West Virginia is declaring war on the United States?"

Dr. Prichard got to his feet. "No, we're simply defending our constitutional rights and preparing to repulse Kearns' forces. We refuse to be forced into one of these Residential Zones."

The room became dead silent. Coop and Riley stared at each other in disbelief, and Dashay grabbed Riley's hand.

"I want no part of this," the OR nurse said and headed for the exit.

Several people rose to follow him, but a guard who equaled him in height stepped in his path. They faced each other with their arms crossed until another man came up behind the guard and ordered him to step away.

The guard said, "Yes, sir," and backed into the hallway.

The nurse didn't budge until the five at the front table stood in unison, and Dr. Prichard said, "Welcome, Mr. Governor."

Riley studied Governor Mitchell as he strode in and stopped in the center of the room. He was tall and gray-haired, reminding Riley of her grandfather, who had been a gentle man with inner strength. The governor's expressive bright eyes slowly swept the room, then he gestured for everyone to sit. The group obeyed without hesitation.

"I heard a bit of your conversation from the hallway as I passed," he said, just loud enough for them to hear. "As outsiders, I understand your reluctance to become a party to our battles but trust me when I say the alternative is far worse. We're not asking any of you to fight. We simply need you to help care for our sick and wounded. You'll be protected and generously compensated."

A young, dark-haired woman at the far end of Riley's table raised her hand. When the governor acknowledged her, she said, "What if we refuse to help? Are we prisoners?"

He gave her a benevolent smile. "We won't force you to work, but those who don't contribute to the community cannot access our provisions. You aren't prisoners, but we can't allow you to leave for security reasons. Kearns' troops are only a day or so from Charleston. For our safety and yours, you must stay until after the battle. We're hopeful it won't last more than a day." He let that sink in, then said, "Any more questions?"

Riley had questions. As she raised her hand, Coop grabbed it and tucked it under his leg. He gave a quick shake of his head and a look that told her to keep quiet. She relented under protest, trusting his judgment.

When there were no raised hands, Governor Mitchell said, "I appreciate your service. I'll let you get back to your orientation."

Riley was numb as she went through the motions of paying attention to the rest of the ninety-minute meeting. She'd been so hopeful about moving Julia to Charleston, but she couldn't bring her daughter into the middle of what may become a war zone. She also knew that she and Coop had to get out of there before the fighting started, no matter what it took.

The minute the orientation ended, Riley, Coop, and Dashay hurried to where Echo was tethered under a tree. The area in front of the capitol had cleared, except for the troops.

Dashay said, "I want to check on Nico. We'll talk on the way."

As soon as they were out of earshot of anyone they didn't want to overhear, Riley said, "We didn't have time to tell you this morning, but we're heading back to Wytheville. We'd hoped to get Julia and bring her here, then stay until the baby's old enough to travel, but that plan's shot with the governor declaring war on Kearns. I just want you to know you're welcome to come with us."

Dashay stopped in the middle of the street. "I can't believe what I'm hearing. You've been all fired up to get to Colorado, and now you're turning tail? How do you plan to get past Kearns' troops? You heard what they said in that meeting."

Riley tugged on Dashay's arm to get her moving. "I'm not turning tail. Brooks and Adrian are right. Trying to cross the continent pregnant is a bad idea. We'll wait it out at the ranch until we can travel with Julia and the baby."

"We'll travel back to the ranch overland, just the way we got here," Coop said. "Most of the trail we took is isolated. Kearns' troops can't have the resources to cover every piece of land in the country. You and Nico should join us. It'll make us all the stronger when we start out for Colorado in a year or two."

Dashay shook her head. "Nico won't be strong enough to travel for weeks, and he's almost as determined to get home as you are. He's from a close family. He wants to get back to them, and I have no objection to settling in New Mexico."

"We could wait until Nico can go with us," Riley said. "He'd just have to wait a little longer to get home. Maybe the world will be more settled by then."

"There's another glaring flaw in your plan," Dashay said, as they approached the hospital. "You have to escape from Charleston first. They're not just going to let two surgeons walk out the door."

Riley had thought of that. She was quiet as she watched Coop tie Echo's reins to a bike rack, trying to figure out how to answer. As he walked back toward them, she said, "I don't care what it takes, I'm getting out of here. We escaped Branson's compound. Leaving Charleston will be a cakewalk compared to that."

"Give it a minute," Dashay said. "We haven't even been here for twenty-four hours and you're planning your exit strategy. Waiting out a one-day battle might be better than heading into the thick of it."

Riley shrugged, then walked into the hospital. She smiled as Dashay looked wide-eyed around the hospital entrance. "What do you think of your new workspace?"

"Feels like waking from a nightmare into reality. Like the CME never happened."

"My exact thoughts at first sight," Coop said.

Riley led the way to the reception to find out Nico's room number. She rested her arms on the counter and was about to ask the gray-haired woman seated behind the desk when Flynn, the nurse who'd helped them earlier, ran up behind them.

"I'm so glad you're here," he said in a rush. "Come with me, now."

"We're going to check on Nico first," Coop said.

Flynn waved for them to follow. "I'll fill you in on the way." He noticed Dashay and paused for a second. "You a doctor, too?"

"Surgical nurse," she said.

"Excellent. You come, too."

When she hesitated, Coop cocked his head for her to join them, so she got into step behind him. Flynn led them toward the trauma unit. As they followed him, Riley was puzzled to see maimed and broken patients on gurneys lining the walls. The hallways had been clear when they'd passed that way in the morning.

"Was there an explosion?" she asked Flynn, as she hurried to keep up with him. "Wouldn't we have heard it?"

"No explosion," was all he said as he opened the curtain to one cubicle.

A young man in blood-stained clothes lay on the bed, groaning as what looked to be two nurses worked to staunch the bleeding.

"What happened to this man?" Coop asked, as he pulled on a pair of gloves. "What's going on here?"

Flynn eyed him for a moment, then ran a hand through his hair. "These people were all wounded fleeing Kearns' forces in a town called Beckley, about fifty miles southeast of here." Turning to the nurses, he said, "These are two of our new surgeons, Drs. Cooper and Poole."

Riley stepped toward the patient and the nurses moved out of her way. Coop went to the other side of the gurney. As Riley began examining the patient, she said, "Fifty miles? These wounds are fresh."

"The governor has sent out buses to gather up survivors," one nurse said. "It's getting rough out there."

Coop lifted a square of gauze to reveal a gaping abdominal wound, and the patient cried out in agony. "Do you have morphine or other pain killers?"

Flynn gave one nurse a quick nod. She rushed out and returned with a vial and syringe moments later. As she handed them to Coop, Flynn said, "Dilaudid."

"Ah, the good stuff," he said, as he injected the drug into the patient's IV. The man immediately relaxed.

"What's your name?" Riley asked.

He gave her a drug-addled grin, and said, "Doug."

"Good, Doug," Riley went on. "Can you tell us what happened to you?"

"Sure. The army showed up and took over our town. There were too many of them for us to fight, so some of us bided our time, then made a run for it. They caught up and shot us with big guns. They killed my brother."

Doug had just confirmed what they'd heard in their orientation. Riley glanced at Coop, then went back to work on Doug.

"We need to operate on you, Doug," Coop said. "Have you eaten anything recently?"

Before Doug could answer, his eyes rolled back in his head, and he went limp. Alarms blared on the monitors.

"He's in arrest. Crash cart!" Riley ordered.

Dashay helped Coop and her work to resuscitate him for five minutes before Riley stepped back and shook her head. "He's gone."

Flynn turned to the two nurses standing near the door. "Please, take care of him and clean this room. We need it. The rest of you, next patient."

As the three of them followed Flynn to another cubicle, Dashay touched his arm to stop him, and said, "I know these people are critical, but how's Nico?"

Flynn shook his head. "Right, sorry. He was doing much better when I left him. Fever was down and he was more coherent. I don't know his prognosis, but he has a chance now."

"Thank you," she said, as they started moving.

"This reminds me of the early days after the CME," Riley said. "How long has it been this way?"

"Hours," Flynn said. "We've seen nothing like this in months. Proves Kearns' forces are closing in. You got here at just the right time."

Riley passed him on her way to the next patient, and said, "We're not staying."

Flynn stared at her like she was mad. "How can you say that when you've seen what we're up against? What kind of doctor would you be? And why would you leave? You see what's waiting for you outside the city."

Riley folded her arms. "We've survived worse."

Coop stepped between them. "We'll stay and do what we can for the critically wounded. Who's next?"

Flynn introduced them to their next patient, then took Dashay to give her a quick tour of the hospital. Flynn's words echoed in Riley's head while she helped Coop clean and stitch a woman with a gunshot wound through the fleshy part of her upper arm. For all her bravado, she was terrified of what awaited them outside the city.

They'd passed through the edges of Beckley on their way to Charleston. It had been a quiet little hamlet only days earlier before Kearns' forces arrived. How much more of the countryside had changed since they'd traveled there? Was there any hope of returning the way they'd come?

She pondered their situation as she treated the never-ending stream of patients but came no closer to a solution. Each patient coherent enough to speak came with a harrowing story of barely escaping soldiers determined to stop them. What chance did she and Coop stand against such forces?

When she was about to drop from exhaustion that evening, she found an empty room and propped herself on the bed to eat her snack of cheese and crackers, fruit cup, and a protein bar. She'd eaten every few hours to stave off nausea. Her plan had worked but had done nothing for the fatigue. The only thing that would cure that was a good night's sleep.

After her meal, she took out the blood draw kit she'd swiped from a supply cabinet. After sanitizing her skin with an alcohol wipe, she wrapped the tourniquet around her upper arm and slid the needle into a vein in the crook of her elbow. Before she finished drawing the blood, Coop burst in and glared at her.

"I've been searching all over for you." He strode up to her and wrapped his fingers around the syringe before pushing her hand away. "What are we doing with your blood?"

He slid the needle out when the vial was full and motioned for her to press a piece of gauze to her arm while he looked for tape.

While holding the white square in place, she said, "Pregnancy test. This is more accurate than over-the-counter tests. Before we decide our course of action, we need to be certain. Let's carry that to the lab and ask for a rush. We'll wait for the results, then get out of here."

He held out his hand to help her off the bed. "No argument from me."

After dropping her sample with the lab technician, they found a bench in a quiet courtyard to wait. Sitting there in the gentle evening air, watching the sun dip below the hills, she could almost persuade herself that the day had been a bad dream.

Coop wrapped his arm around her, and she rested her head against his chest. "What are we going to do, Coop?"

"Whether or not you're pregnant, I see three choices. We stay and ride out the war and your pregnancy, we try to make our way back to the ranch and stay there until we can travel safely to Colorado, or we head west as planned."

She looked up at him, and said, "Is there a choice D?"

Coop brushed a tear from the end of her nose. "Give me a minute to come up with one. We'll know which path is the right one when the time comes."

"I'll have to trust you on that."

"Wise choice. Have you seen Nico today?" She shook her head, so he stood and helped her to her feet. "We have time before your results are ready and he could probably use some friendly faces."

No one paid attention to them as they made their way to Nico's room. Riley peeked through the door, then went in when she saw he was propped up eating dinner. After giving his hand an encouraging squeeze, she dragged a chair next to the bed while Coop went to the nurses' station to ask for his notes.

"You're making a miraculous recovery," she said.

"Hardly," he answered weakly, then held up his arm to show her the IV tube. "It's the good juices they're pumping into me. Dr. Powell says I wouldn't have survived the day if you and Coop hadn't gotten me here when you did. Severe sepsis. Looks like I'm going to be here for several days."

"Glad we made it to Charleston in time." Coop came in with Nico's chart and handed it to Riley.

While she read, Nico said, "What's it like out there? No one tells me anything. What have you been doing all day? Kicking up your heels, I bet."

Riley glanced at Coop, unsure of how much they should tell Nico in his weakened state. Knowing the truth wouldn't change anything.

Coop leaned against the arm of Riley's chair and said, "We've just been settling in and helping around here. This place is incredible. Almost like before the CME, except no Wi-Fi or cell phones."

"I've noticed," Nico said. "How'd they get so lucky?"

"Bunch of smart and tough people working together. It's heartening to see it can be done," Riley said. "Have you seen

Brooks or Adrian today? Dashay told us she stopped in to see you."

"Haven't seen either of them. Tell them hey for me."

"Will do," Coop said, and motioned to Riley that it was time to go. "I need to get her home. She's been on her feet all day. We'll come tomorrow."

Riley kissed his cheek. "Get some rest so you can get out of here. It's not the same without you." She gave a small wave as she turned into the hallway and leaned against the wall. "Did you see his numbers? It's a miracle he survived. Hopefully, he'll continue to respond to the treatment. The next few days will be critical."

"Even if he does, he won't be going anywhere for at least two weeks. If we decide to leave, we'll be doing it without Nico."

She started down the corridor toward the stairs, and said, "As much as I hate to admit it, we can't base our choice on Nico's recovery, even if it means leaving Dashay behind, too. This decision has to be about what's best for our family. My blood test should be done. Ready to find out the results?"

He took her hand and pulled her toward the stairwell so fast she could hardly keep up. She followed along, wishing she shared his excitement, but after the day they'd had, all she felt was a renewed sense of dread.

When they reached the lab, Riley leaned on the counter and smiled at the technician. "Do you have the results for Dr. Poole?"

"Right here, Doctor," he said, and slid the paper with the handwritten results across to her.

She nonchalantly picked up the paper and folded it without looking. She gave his nametag a quick glance, then said, "Thank you for taking care of this so quickly, Paul. Have a nice evening."

She and Coop strolled nonchalantly out of the lab, then ran to an empty room as soon as they turned a corner.

Riley's hands shook as she unfolded the paper. She thrust it at Coop and looked away with her arms folded. "I'm too nervous. You read it."

She heard the paper rustle, then nothing. Thinking Coop's silence meant the test was negative, she slowly turned to find him beaming.

"Hot damn!" he said and slapped his thigh. "I'm going to be a dad."

He held the paper out to her, and she shook even harder as she reached for it. Her tears dripped onto the paper as she read. A part of her had hoped she'd been wrong about the pregnancy and just contracted some parasite, but as the reality sunk in, she realized a bigger part was thrilled to be creating a new life with Coop. Of one thing she was certain, their lives had just become much more complicated than ever and would never be the same.

CHAPTER SIX

JULIA LOOKED out the living room window for the twentieth time, hoping to see Uncle Mitch's old red truck coming up the drive. He and her uncles Russell and Jesse had gone to Blacksburg three days earlier, and no one had heard a word from them since.

"A watched pot never boils," Aunt Beth said, as she came up behind her.

"That's just a myth," Julia replied, as she continued to stare out the window.

"Maybe so but looking out every five minutes won't bring them home any faster. They'll get here when they get here." When Julia still didn't move, Beth said, "Come away from the window and help me get lunch ready."

Julia climbed off the couch in a huff and followed her aunt to the kitchen. "Why am I the only one who's worried? Don't you care what's happening to them?"

Beth dropped a fresh loaf of bread on the cutting board and began slicing. "You're asking if I care about the safety of my husband and sons? You know that answer to that. I just understand that working myself into a state of panic won't bring them home faster. I choose to keep busy and focus on work that needs to be done. We're all trying to pick up the slack, even Holly. It wouldn't hurt for you to pitch in more."

"I'm sorry, Auntie, but first Mom and Coop left, and now my uncles are gone. After what we saw on our trip here, I'm scared for them. But I'll try it your way."

Julia walked to the refrigerator to get the sliced ham and cheese for their sandwiches, but Beth stopped her and tenderly pressed her hand to her cheek. "Sometimes I forget you haven't been safe here with us since the CME. Your uncles are smart and tough. They know how to take care of themselves."

"Thanks, Aunt Beth. You're right. I'll try not to worry so much."

Julia hugged her, then went back to pulling containers from the fridge. As they assembled the sandwiches, they heard trucks rumbling up the drive and rushed to the door to see who it was. Julia almost ran out without looking to see who it was, but then remembered Uncle Mitch's warning to always check first. She peeked through the curtain over the window next to the door.

"It's the soldiers," she whispered, as Aunt Kathryn and her cousins came up behind Beth. "Two are coming up the stairs."

"You kids get in the kitchen and stay there," Kathryn said and glared at Julia.

"Yes, ma'am," Julia replied, as she steered her younger cousins out of the room.

She and Holly got the other kids eating, then they leaned out of the kitchen doorway just far enough to hear without being seen.

"What are you doing here?" Kathryn snapped. "Our week isn't up."

"We're just checking on your preparations," one of the men said. "It doesn't look like you've done anything."

"We're not sure exactly what we're supposed to do," Beth said.

"Then, I'll make it clear. Pack up your family and vacate this house," another man said.

"We were told we could stay," Kathryn said. "You can't just take our home."

"Yes, we can. We apologize for the misunderstanding," the first man said. "You may stay on the property, but the United States government *will* take possession of this house."

Holly stared at Julia and gasped. Julia put her finger to her lips to shush her.

"We may remain here in the cottages to run the ranch as usual," the second man said. "Where is your husband, ma'am?"

"Out on ranch business," Beth said. "We expect him back this evening."

"Tell him to find me when he returns. We're camped in the north field. We expect you out of this house in two days, so you'd better get to work."

Julia ran to the living room the instant she heard the door close, with her cousins not far behind. "We heard the whole thing. What are we going to do, Aunt Beth?"

Beth looked into the anxious eyes of her daughter, great-niece, and grandchildren. "We're going to make a show of packing just in case they come back. Then, we'll wait for the men to come back and report. As a precaution, all of you pack a bag you can grab if we have to leave in a hurry. Only bring what's absolutely necessary. That means no toys, Jason."

Kathryn took the kids who were already living in the guest houses and the rest scattered to their rooms. Julia pulled out her pack and shoved a pair of sweatpants into it, but Holly fell onto her bed and started to cry. Julia stopped what she was doing and dropped next to her.

She rubbed Holly's back and said, "Don't give up yet. You said you trust Uncle Mitch and your dad. They'll come back with a way out of this."

Holly sat up and wiped her face with a corner of the bedspread. "But what if they don't? The guest houses aren't big enough to fit all of us, and I can't imagine Grandpa will just lie down and let the soldiers take his land. This property has been in the family for almost 200 years. It's our legacy. What if he wants to fight?"

"Guessing won't do any good. Let's just wait for him to get back, then he'll tell us what to do."

Holly flopped back onto her pillows and mumbled, "If he comes back."

Julia got up and pulled armfuls of clothes out of her drawers and tossed them on the bed. As she sorted, she said, "Now you sound like me. I must be rubbing off on you. Just get up and pack. We'll figure out the rest later."

Holly reluctantly stood and dug her pack out of the closet. Julia watched her for a moment, then turned to her own packing, wishing she felt half as confident as she sounded.

───

Julia woke to someone shaking her by the shoulders. She bolted upright and frantically looked around in confusion. Holly was standing next to her bed with her pack on her shoulder, quietly weeping.

"It's just me," Aunt Kathryn whispered.

"What's going on? What time is it?"

"Three-thirty. Get dressed and grab your pack, then come with me."

Julia got up and did as she was told without question for once. She dressed in two minutes, then nodded to Aunt Kathryn that she was ready. She followed her into the dark hallway with Holly close on her heels.

"Stop that blubbering, Holly," Aunt Kathryn said. "Don't waste your energy on crying."

Julia reached back and squeezed Holly's hand to reassure her. "You can do this. Coop always made everything into an adventure," she whispered. "That's all this is. A new adventure."

Holly sniffled, then straightened her shoulders and quickened her step. They made their way down the stairs by light of the battery-powered lantern Kathryn carried. When they got to the front room, the entire family was there waiting, including all her uncles.

"I'll make this quick and explain the details later," Uncle Mitch said. "We're leaving the ranch." Holly let out a sob, so Julia put her arm around her. "We'll make our way to the fishing lodge tonight. We should reach it around dawn, then we'll rest for a few hours. It'll be a tight fit, but we'll manage. Then, we'll take the south exit, away from the troops, and head west."

"But where are we going, Uncle Mitch?" Julia whispered.

"You'll be happy to hear that if all goes well, to Colorado Springs."

Julia tossed and turned on the lumpy and musty cot for three hours before finally giving up. Aside from being uncomfortable, she was too excited to sleep. Soon, she'd see her mom, Coop, and the rest of her family. She thought of her friends in Colorado, wondering how many survived the CME. What would they think when she suddenly appeared after being gone for so long?

She got up and grabbed her boots, then tiptoed out to the stoop to put them on. She was surprised to see Uncle Mitch leaning against a tree ten feet away. She laced her boots as quickly as she could and went to join him.

"What are you doing out here?" she asked when she reached him.

He winked, and said, "I could ask you the same thing."

She folded her arms and smiled. "I asked first."

"Let's sit over there," he said, and led Julia to a log bench under the next tree over. "It's too stuffy in the cabin to sleep, and I needed to think."

"Please tell me what happened. Why do we have to leave? You can tell me the truth. Nothing shocks me after what I've seen."

He studied her for a moment, then said, "All right, the truth. President Kearns' forces have taken over this entire region. I wasn't prepared for that. I just expected a few troops fanning out to the farms and ranches. The courts and the government agencies are controlled by Kearns supporters. No one in Blacksburg will help us fight them legally. There are too many for us to fight them. I refuse to stay here and watch them take over my land, so we're leaving. That's why we loaded as much as we could take on the carts and horses. They're welcome to the rest."

Julia wrapped her arms around him, and he patted her back. "I'm so sorry. I know this is torture for you to abandon the ranch. I'll do whatever you need."

"Thanks, Warrior Princess," he said, using her radio call sign. "What you've learned will come in handy on the road."

She sat up and looked at him. "What if my mom and Coop come back for me?"

"Don't worry about that. They couldn't get back it they wanted to. We heard the troops stretch from Maine to Florida and are moving west. The only hope is to head towards Colorado and stay one step ahead of the line. We're going the southerly route since the terrain will make for easier travel. It's longer in miles but should be quicker."

"Do you think that's how Mom and Coop went? Maybe we'll catch up to them."

"With just the two of them on horseback, they can travel lighter and faster. Your mom and Coop are probably almost to Missouri by now."

"Maybe they'll be waiting for us at Nana and Papa's."

"I pray they will, WP. Then, we'll be one big happy family."

Riley sank into the couch cushions, waiting for Coop to start the meeting he'd called so together the five of them could figure out their next course of action. She wanted to be alert but was struggling to keep her eyes open after downing the stew Adrian had whipped up with canned meat and his magic herbs.

Coop whistled to signal he was ready to start, and when everyone quieted, said, "The horror stories we heard at the hospital today made it clear we need to reconsider our options. Before we get to that, Riley has news to share."

She sat forward and slowly let out her breath. "It's official. My pregnancy test was positive, so that will factor into whatever Coop and I decide."

Dashay flashed her a smile. "Not news to me. Your reaction to that breakfast plate this morning was all the proof I needed."

"I'm happy if you're happy," Adrian said, unconvincingly, "but you have to admit this complicates our situation."

"It complicates *our* situation," Coop said. "You three aren't bound by what Riley and I decide."

Brooks turned his chair backward to straddle it and rested his arms on the backrest. "Since I'm just tagging along for the ride, I'm open to suggestion, but my preference is to continue west. Last thing I want is to stay here and get caught up in a fight that has nothing to do with us. I'm ready to put land between me and the East Coast."

"And if we go back to the ranch?" Riley asked.

Brooks hesitated before saying, "Is that still an option?"

"By all reports, the towns east of here are crawling with Kearns' forces," Coop said, "but that doesn't mean we can't avoid them if we stick to the forests. Having the horses makes that trickier, but not impossible."

"You're willing to take that risk?" Adrian asked. "Word at the university today was that the entire eastern seaboard has been colonized by Kearns' military. Chances are your uncle's ranch already falls within one of these 'zones.'"

"My daughter is there, Adrian," Riley said. "Trust me, that has occurred to me."

Dashay raised her hand, and said, "But how could they have covered the whole East Coast in so short a time?"

Brooks opened his mouth to answer, but Adrian cut him off. In his annoying, know-it-all way, he said, "Kearns' has control of every military base in the country. Think of the labor force that implies. Those bases are constructed to withstand nuclear attack, so many of the troops may have survived the CME. If she has communication capabilities, she controls an immense military machine."

As irritating as Adrian was, Riley couldn't deny his point, but his reasoning overlooked one important factor. "I have it from a reliable source that there have been massive desertions since the CME struck."

"Then there's military personnel who got separated from their units like Nico," Dashay said. "His unit was on a field exercise when the CME hit, and he got lost when communications went down. He was trying to find his unit when Branson's people captured him."

Riley nodded. "There were probably thousands more like him in the immediate aftermath. If the forces are stretched so thin, why would they bother with my uncle's ranch in such a remote area?"

"For the resources. Horses, generators, crops," Brooks said. "From what you told us, they have a nice setup. That would make it an attractive target."

Riley stood and walked to the window. As she peered into the darkness, she said, "Our plan this morning was to bring Julia here and stay until the baby was old enough to travel. It seemed like the perfect answer, but with war looming, that option's out. If we made it back to Wytheville, we'd be forced to stay indefinitely."

"Charleston doesn't stand a chance against Kearns' army," Brooks said. "Her forces have massive supply reserves and equipment. That's not the case for Charleston or even the state. Resources and personnel numbers are pitiful in comparison."

"Such a shame," Adrian said. "This would have been the perfect place for my family to start a new life."

"So, returning to the ranch is too risky and staying put is out," Coop said. "Choice number three, then. We travel to Colorado as planned."

Their plans had swung a hundred and eighty degrees in the hours since Riley woke in the night, overwhelmed at the thought of continuing west. Those feelings had receded, only to be replaced with confusion and hesitation. She felt trapped in the center of a no-win situation.

If the ranch had been incorporated into a Residential Zone, she and Coop would be prohibited from leaving if they went there. She'd be with Julia and the baby, but Emily and Jared might be lost to her, possibly forever. If she pressed on to Colorado, she'd have three of her children, her parents, her home, but she wouldn't see Julia for years, if ever again. That risk had existed when she left her behind, so in that respect, nothing had changed. The only difference was the real chance Julia was in danger, and Riley was powerless to protect her. Her only choice was to trust in Mitch and Beth to keep her safe.

Riley turned from the window and faced the others. "Choice three presents new obstacles. We're under a time crunch of less than two days to gather supplies and plan our escape. That means leaving Nico behind. You've been quiet, Dashay. What are you thinking?"

Dashay stared down at her hands clasped in her lap. "I won't leave him, no matter what everyone else decides. We're a package deal."

"It breaks my heart to be forced to separate from you, but I don't blame you. Problem two, how the hell do we get out of here?"

Coop glanced at her, then stroked his scruffy chin. "Sneaking out with two horses and so little knowledge of the city won't be easy."

"Getting out of Charleston won't be like escaping Branson's compound," Brooks said, "That place was small and sealed up tight. As one trying to keep you in, I can say it's a miracle you two got out."

Coop gave him a half-grin. "I can vouch for that."

"Good times," Dashay said and shook her head.

"They do have patrols on the city's perimeter, and the major roads are barricaded, but I guarantee they've left gaps. If we all agree that we're leaving, I'll ride out on Echo tomorrow and scope it out."

"So, do we vote on this now or what?" Adrian asked.

Riley stepped next to Coop. "Decision's made. Come to Colorado with us or don't. It's your choice."

Coop put his arm around her waist. "We should leave tomorrow night. Riley and I need to put in a full day at the hospital to avoid arousing suspicion. That leaves it to the two of you to map our route and gather supplies."

"They'll have their heaviest patrols out when it's dark," Brooks said. "We should leave early the following morning after daybreak."

Adrian got to his feet and cocked his thumb at Brooks. "He makes a good point."

Dashay stood and stretched. "That's only a delay of a few hours and it will be safer for you to travel in daylight. I'll do whatever it takes to make sure Nico and I catch up as soon as he's recovered." She gave Riley a hug, then took her hand to lead her to the stairs. "You need sleep, mama. You look like hell."

Riley laughed and said, "Which is exactly how I feel." She gave a slight wave to the others. "Goodnight."

After dragging herself up the stairs with Dashay, she went to her room and got ready for bed while Coop tended to the horses.

By the time he came in, her thoughts were a whirling kaleidoscope of confusion.

He climbed into bed and pulled her into his arms. "I don't even need to ask how you're feeling," he said. "One look at your face told me all I needed to know."

"In the weeks immediately after the CME, we were in defensive mode and would go off half-cocked, taking little thought before we acted. That got us into more trouble than I care to remember. I did the same at the mudslide when I nearly got you killed. This time, we only have one choice, and it's the most difficult one. I'm devastated we can't go back for Julia. We're jumping off into the unknown with a baby on the way. Is there any chance of a positive outcome?"

"I have every hope of that. We can do this, Riley. We've survived far worse, and we won't be alone this time. The terrain is gently rolling hills and flat plains from here on. If we stay ahead of Kearns' forces and the weather cooperates, we're home free."

She gave him a quick kiss before saying, "Thanks, I needed to hear that, but I want it in writing for when everything goes horribly wrong."

He rolled onto his stomach and punched his pillow into submission. "I'll get on that first thing in the morning."

"I'm holding you to that," she said, then closed her eyes and let sleep come.

Riley enjoyed her first uninterrupted night in days and woke energetic and in a more positive frame of mind. Coop left to get an early start at the hospital while she took a few moments to collect her thoughts and nibble crackers to ward off morning sickness. It was a promising sign when she got to her feet without feeling nauseated. Her stomach continued to cooperate while she dressed and packed whatever she wouldn't need for the next twenty-four hours.

She went downstairs and put the kettle on to heat before fixing her breakfast and packing a lunch. Dashay came in carrying her shoes and gave Riley a good looking-over. "Now, that's the Riley I remember. Glad to see you looking like your old self."

Riley leaned against the counter and crossed her arms. "It's amazing what a good meal and sleep can do. I'm ready to brave the wild. How are you feeling today? Still determined to stay?"

Dashay dropped into a chair and slipped on her shoes. "No other choice. Nico and I will be fine."

As Riley spread a heaping spoonful of peanut butter on a cracker, she said, "It'll be hard to leave you. I was looking forward to us making this journey together, and aside from your friendship, I'll miss your nursing skills. Coop may be a doctor, but he knows nothing about pregnant women."

"Prenatal care isn't exactly my area of expertise, but I *am* a woman. That counts for something. We'll see each other down the road, my friend. You have my word."

"I'm holding you to that," Riley said, then popped the cracker in her mouth.

Dashay gave her a weak smile. "Come with me to see Nico. You need to say goodbye."

"I feel guilty for abandoning both of you, but I'm relieved you have each other. Promise not to take any unnecessary risks."

Dashay got up and laid her hand on Riley's arm. "My plan is to work during the day and crash in Adrian's room at night. The hospital will be the safest place during the battle, and I don't want to be alone in this house. They can give it to someone who needs it."

Riley wondered how the city leaders would react when they realized she and the others were gone. She hoped they wouldn't take it out on Dashay and Nico, but there wasn't anything she could do to prevent that.

Riley reached over to drop a fruit cup into her canvas lunch bag when someone pounded on the front door.

"Who in God's name is that?" Dashay asked, as she walked to the living room.

Riley followed close behind, and whispered, "Check the peephole first."

Dashay raised an eyebrow at her before stepping toward the door. "I'm not one of your kids."

She peeked through the hole, then shrugged. "Looks like two harmless country boys."

"Who is it?" Riley called.

"Dr. Poole live here?" one of them said.

Dashay pulled aside the curtain next to the door. "Who wants to know?"

After a moment's silence, he said, "I'm Clive. This is Steve. Dr. Prichard asked us to deliver these boxes of food and supplies. You going to open the door? Cause if not, I'm happy to take this stuff home to my wife and kids."

Dashay glanced at Riley, who gave a quick nod. She swung the door open and gestured for them to enter. "Come in, boys. Put the boxes in the kitchen."

Riley followed them and opened the first box. It was filled with packages of pasta, jars of sauce, cans of vegetables, and vital medical supplies.

Turning to Dashay, she said, "Where are they getting all this stuff?"

Steve dropped a box on the floor, straightened, and then said, "These are from the doctor's personal stash. Enjoy it. You won't see more like this once it's gone."

He went out, leaving her and Dashay staring at each other.

"Guess we won't need to go scavenging supplies tonight," Riley said. "We'll separate some out for you and Nico. If Brooks can hunt down a cart for Biscuit to pull, we'll have room to carry the rest. Is Brooks still here?"

"No, he saddled Echo and took off at sunrise. He said not to expect him until after dark."

Riley checked out the back window and saw Biscuit contentedly eating oats from a trough. "Adrian's not with him?"

"No, he went to the university but said he'd make some excuse at lunchtime and come back for Biscuit. Leave him a note about the food so he knows they don't need to keep scavenging."

They made the trip to the hospital in record time and hurried to Nico's room. Dr. Pritchard was standing over him reading through his chart, but he looked up when he heard them.

"I'm glad to see you here and looking so well after yesterday, Dr. Poole. I was afraid you'd contracted an infection of your own."

"What she has isn't contagious," Nico said. "She's pregnant."

"Pregnant?" he said, looking like Nico had just told him she had The Plague.

Riley instinctively put her hands over her abdomen. "It wasn't planned." She cocked her head at Nico to change the subject. "Speaking of infections, how's our patient?"

"Marginally better. It might take another day to see significant improvement."

Dashay sat in a chair on the opposite side of the bed and wrapped his hand in hers. "How are you feeling, Babe?"

"Less like I'm on my way out of this crazy world. Still weak, but my appetite is getting stronger."

Riley smiled. "That's an encouraging sign."

Dr. Pritchard turned for the door, and said, "I'll leave you in the capable hands of these ladies."

"Before you go," Riley said, "let me thank you for the boxes of food and supplies. That was very generous of you."

Dr. Pritchard gave a small wave. "I'm sorry it wasn't more. Just a little gift to get you settled and to say thanks. You and Dr.

Cooper have been an enormous help already, and you, Ms. Robinson. You couldn't have come at a better time."

Riley felt another twinge of guilt. Dr. Pritchard had been so kind, and they were going to repay him by running off with his gift. Under different circumstances, Riley would have been willing to stay and serve in the hospital. She just hoped the day would come when she could pay that forward.

She shook his hand, and said, "We were honored to help."

He gave her a look that made her feel like he'd read her thoughts, then he left without another word. Riley shut the door behind him and took the chair on the other side of Nico's bed.

Riley glanced at Dashay, who nodded for her to go ahead. "This isn't easy to say, but I have something to tell you."

Nico held up his hand to stop her. "You're leaving. I already know. Adrian came to see me." He studied her for a moment before saying, "Get that look off your face, Riley. I understand and I don't blame you. Hell, you saved my life, so no guilt."

"We wouldn't do this if there was any other way," Riley said. "At least you'll have Dashay."

Nico's eyebrows shot up as he turned to face Dashay. "What? You're not going with them?"

Dashay kissed his cheek. "Of course not. I wouldn't leave you."

Nico slowly shook his head. "I was so relieved when Adrian told me you were all getting out of here. I thought he meant you, too, Dashay. No way I'm letting you stay because of me."

Dashay dropped his hand and crossed her arms. "Letting me stay? That's not your choice to make. Did you honestly think I'd abandon you in a city about to go to war? You're my family. We stay together, no matter what happens."

Nico pushed himself up higher in the bed. "I think of you as family, too, which is why I want you out of town before this damned war starts. I couldn't live with myself if you stayed because of me and got hurt or worse. I want you to go."

Riley stood to leave. "I'll let you talk about this in private."

Nico pointed at her chair. "Stay where you are. This concerns you." He took Dashay's hand and gently stroked it with his thumb. "I'm in the safest place for the coming battle. Even Kearns's troops will know better than to destroy the hospital. They're taking care of me. Riley needs you more than I do. Who will help her with the baby coming? Coop? He's too emotionally invested to be worth a damn."

Riley raised her hand to stop him. "Don't use me to guilt Dashay into going. I agree with what you're saying, Nico, but Dashay needs to make this decision for herself and for the right reasons."

Dashay glanced at Riley, then sniffed and wiped her cheek with her sleeve. "Don't push me away, Nico. I can't take it. I lost my parents. I lost Jerome. I'd rather die here with you than spend the rest of my life wondering what happened to you."

"I refuse to die, woman, but it would kill me to watch you die. I've witnessed enough death to last ten lifetimes. I love you, Dashay, and will move heaven and earth to find you, but I want you gone."

Dashay collapsed onto his chest and sobbed while Nico silently stroked the back of her head. Riley awkwardly shifted on her feet, averting her eyes from the intimate scene. Nico caught her eye and mouthed *help.* She walked to the other side of the bed and nudged Dashay off Nico.

When Dashay looked up at her with red, swollen eyes, Riley said, "You're going to be late for work. Come after your shift and stay until it's time to get back to the house and pack." She took Dashay's hand and encouraged her to stand, then drew a small package of Oreos from her pocket and tucked it under Nico's blanket. "We'll stash the rest of your things and more food in a safe place before we go. Dashay will let you know where. Get well and find us, little brother. We'll be watching for you."

She gave him a quick peck on the cheek and guided a dazed Dashay out before she lost control of her own emotions. She found an empty room down the hall and locked the door. She pulled Dashay into her arms and cried with her.

Dashay finally pulled away and gave a weak smile. "Pull it together, girl. We can't have both of us sniveling all day. I need you to be strong for me."

"It's the hormones," Riley said, then blew her nose on a paper towel. "I'll be fine as soon as I shift into doctor mode. So, are you coming with us?"

Dashay frowned as she handed Riley a box of tissues. "I don't want to ignore Nico's wishes, but how can I walk away from him?"

"You'll do it because it's what's best, not easiest. I left my daughter, Dashay."

Dashay dropped onto the bed and stared at her tattered shoes. "It was a miracle I found love again in this madness. Now, I'm forced to turn my back on it. You know the odds of Nico finding us aren't in my favor."

"Coop found me when we got separated. You found us. The odds in favor of those things happening were practically nonexistent."

"We not so much found you as stumbled on you when we were about to rob you, but I get what you're saying."

Riley wrapped an arm around her shoulder. "I know leaving Nico is torture, but you can do this. In a month when you're reunited, the heartache will be forgotten. Now, get down to the ER. Working will take your mind off it. If you see Adrian, send him to me up in surgical."

Dashay got up and hugged Riley before hurrying out the door. Riley watched her go, wishing they didn't have to wait another twenty-four hours before getting out of Charleston. She took a breath and stepped into the hallway, ready to save as many lives as she could before stepping into the unknown of their next adventure.

CHAPTER SEVEN

RILEY WOKE to the sound of an explosion rattling the walls. She sat up and shook her head to clear it. "What was that?"

Coop got up and went to the window as another blast shook the room. "It's started. We're not waiting for daylight. Get dressed while I tell the others we're bugging out."

Riley jumped up and reached for her jeans but stopped when a surge of nausea roiled in her gut. She'd forgotten the crackers in her hurry to get ready. She pried the window open and leaned out but forgot her morning sickness when she saw the sky lit by fires on the eastern border of the city. She groped for her clothes and dressed between bites of cracker, then shoved the rest of her belongings into her backpack. Coop rushed in as she finished, grabbing his bag before taking her hand.

"How are you holding up?" he asked, as they raced down the stairs.

She stopped on the bottom step and laid her hands on his shoulders. "I'm good, Coop, honestly. Just get all of us out of here in one piece."

He pulled her close and gave her a hurried kiss. "That's my Riley."

Dashay and Adrian were waiting for them in the living room. Dashay squeezed Riley's hand and did her best to look brave. She'd told Riley of her agonizing farewell with Nico the night before. Riley understood more than she knew.

Brooks was in the backyard, harnessing Biscuit to a rickety wooden cart he'd found behind an abandoned feed store.

"He probably needs your help, Coop," Dashay said.

Coop gave a slight nod, then ran through the kitchen to the back door.

Riley picked up a small box and went after him. "Let's carry out the rest of the stuff," she called over the roar of bombs and gunfire.

The cart was strapped to Biscuit and loaded ten minutes later. Coop led Echo to the street, and an agitated Biscuit followed him with little encouragement. He seemed in as much of a hurry to escape the explosions as they were.

"We couldn't have picked a better distraction," Brooks said as they trudged down the vacant streets. "No one is going to notice us with that light show on the opposite border of the city."

"But guards will be protecting the entrances to keep Kearns' forces out," Adrian said. "They might consider us deserters if they catch us trying to leave."

Brooks clicked his tongue. "No need to worry. I found an exit no one will be guarding."

He led them away from the river toward an industrial part of the city. They navigated deserted streets between abandoned warehouses until they reached an old set of train tracks.

Brooks pulled Echo to a stop and pointed. "I discovered these tracks yesterday. A local told me they don't use this line anymore since there's a newer one south of here. There's a high trestle above a gorge that leads to those hills on the city's western edge. The trouble will be to get the horses across it while pulling the cart."

Another explosion boomed in the distance and Biscuit

stamped his hooves. Echo whinnied and tossed his head. Coop tugged on the reins while Riley stroked his nose to calm him.

"No going back," Coop said. "We need to cross that trestle and put Charleston behind us before daybreak."

"Forward it is," Brooks said, as he took Echo's reins and coaxed him onto the tracks.

Echo balked at first but got into a rhythm after a few steps and tentatively moved forward. Getting Biscuit and the cart over the rail was another matter. Whenever Biscuit stepped over the rail onto the ties, he'd veer off at the last second, nearly upending the cart.

After the fifth failed attempt, Riley said, "This is just making him more agitated. Dashay, catch up to Brooks and tell him to bring Echo back and harness the cart to him. Biscuit is more likely to cooperate without the cart rumbling behind him."

Dashay ran to the tracks while Coop and Adrian freed Biscuit from his unwelcome burden. As soon as the straps were off, he gleefully pranced along the edge of the tracks.

Adrian ducked out of the way to avoid getting stepped on. "That horse will never survive the journey. Why didn't we just hook the cart to Echo in the first place?"

"Echo isn't as jittery as Biscuit, but he's more impatient," Riley said. "Biscuit is the workhorse, better at slow and steady, even if he's flighty. He's tougher than he looks."

Adrian scratched his chin. "I'll have to take your word."

Brooks and Dashay came up with Echo and waited for instructions.

Coop stared at the tracks for a minute before saying, "If we can manage it, we should get the cart onto the tracks before we strap it to Echo. It's going to take all of us except Riley. You hold the horses."

Riley threw her shoulders back and took a step toward Coop. "I can tether the horses to that light pole and help with the cart. I'm not an invalid."

"Listen to Coop," Dashay said. "Don't start taking unnecessary risks five minutes out of the gate. We have a long way to go."

Riley frowned and crossed her arms, feeling if anyone took her side, it would be Dashay. Brooks held the reins out to her, trying to hide a smile. She snatched the reins from his hand and yanked on them to move the horses out of the way. As the others pushed and pulled to get the heavy cart onto the tracks, she leaned against the light pole, wondering if they'd been right to stop her.

The baby was the size of a peanut, and she'd had no complications with her other pregnancies. In fact, she'd hiked and run well into her fifth month with Jared and saw no reason for them to coddle her. They were going to need her strengths on this journey, but as she watched them heave and struggle, she admitted to herself that this wasn't her previous pregnancies.

If she had complications in the middle of Nowhere, USA, there would be no 911 to call, no ER to drive to. At least she had her own personal doctor. That was something. The words Dashay had used, *unnecessary risk*, took on new meaning in their world. It was up to her to find the dividing line between what was necessary and what wasn't.

She glanced up as the back wheels of the cart rolled onto the tracks with a final, massive shove. They all cheered with the sounds of war taking place not ten miles behind them. They pivoted the cart to face west. Miraculously, the wheels fit snugly between the rails. Riley walked the horses back to the tracks and handed Echo's reins to Coop. The horse stepped into place and waited patiently while Brooks harnessed him to the cart. Riley held Biscuit back until Echo dug in and got the cart rolling over the ties.

"It's your turn," she whispered in Biscuit's ear. "I trust you, friend. You have the courage to do this, and the sooner we get moving, the sooner we leave that raging battle behind us. Now, let's go, boy."

She climbed over the rail and tugged on his reins. He only hesitated an instant before stepping onto the tracks. The others clapped and patted Biscuit, telling him he was a good boy. He raised his head and got into step behind the cart. First hurdle managed, Riley thought as she walked along beside him. Only a thousand more to go.

They made steady progress along the tracks and had nearly reached the trestle when the sun rose behind them. They hadn't passed a single person since leaving the house, so signs were promising for escaping from Charleston without incident. Riley was pleased the tides of fortune had shifted in their favor for once.

As Brooks led Echo at the head of the group, he looked back over his shoulder and said, "That escape was almost anticlimactic."

Riley cringed and spit on her knuckles three times to ward off evil as her grandmother had taught. "You've jinxed it, Brooks. We're in for trouble now."

Adrian gave her a dismissive wave. "Ha, groundless superstition. You never struck me as someone who believes such nonsense."

"Nonsense?" Coop said. "What about Newton's law, 'for every action, there is an equal and opposite reaction?'"

"Or the theory of Quantum Entanglement," Dashay said.

Coop pointed at her. "Excellent point."

Adrian rolled his eyes. "None of you has the first idea what you're talking about. How do those laws relate to Brooks' comment about our uneventful escape? Life being what it is these days, we're bound to have trouble no matter what any of us says, so that won't prove your theory."

Riley eyed him for a moment, then said, "Believe what you want, Adrian, but Grandma was never wrong."

He rolled his eyes. "Nothing more than coincidence."

"Hush," Brooks said, as he reached the edge of the trestle. "Doesn't look like this has been used for a while. Stay quiet so I can hear the creaks and cracks."

Coop walked past him and stepped onto the first slat. "Let me test it before you bring Echo and the cart across." He stepped gingerly along the ties until he'd covered fifteen feet. "Seems sturdy. Probably wouldn't hold a train, but we should be safe."

Brooks got Echo moving and Coop waited for them to catch up before walking ahead. The group was hushed at first as they crossed the bridge but chatted quietly once they saw it was safe. The ground gradually dropped away into the gorge beneath them until they were suspended by at least a hundred feet. The scenery was breathtaking, but Riley couldn't appreciate it with sounds of the raging battle echoing against the hills.

Riley was leading Biscuit and glanced at Dashay, who was walking on the other side of him. She was frowning down at her feet, oblivious of the scenery.

"Nico's fine," Riley said. "Like he told you last night, he's in the safest place in the city."

Dashay raised her eyes to Riley and shook her head. "But helpless to defend himself."

"The military won't destroy Charleston. They just want to control it. They'll need the hospital intact."

"That makes logical sense, Riley, but things get out of hand in wars. And what if he can't escape once he's recovered?"

"He's smart and he won't let anything stand in the way of finding you. He has his military training to fall back on. I just wish we could tell him how to find these tracks and give him our route."

"He knows. Brooks visited him last night while I was there.

He gave Nico a map he'd drawn with the direction we're headed. If he survives to make it out, he'll know where to go."

"That should give you peace of mind."

"Some, but Nico is a long way from strong enough to escape. If Kearns' forces take the city, they won't make the mistake of leaving this exit unguarded."

That thought had crossed Riley's mind, too, but speculation was pointless, and Nico was on his own. They walked in silence until they reached the halfway point on the trestle. Through the cracks between the ties, Riley could see a river snaking along the gorge below. A brisk wind had kicked up, making the rickety bridge supports groan and sway. She was anxious to reach the other side and get back on solid ground.

She cupped her hands to the sides of her mouth and called for Coop to pick up the pace. As he spun to face her, Echo stepped on a rotted-out tie, and it snapped beneath his weight. His front left leg went in up to his knee. He let out a cry of pain and struggled to free himself. Coop and Brooks ran to his side and worked to get his leg loose and keep him from heaving against the weight of the cart. After several tries, Brooks coaxed Echo to bend his knee and lift his leg. The instant he was free, he reared up on his hind legs, then slammed down, smashing more of the surrounding ties.

Brooks grabbed the bridle and pulled himself onto Echo's back to stop him from galloping off. Echo hesitated for an instant before lurching forward with the cart. The front wheel dropped into the hole where Echo's leg had been, knocking him off balance. Brooks flew off Echo's back from the jolt and slammed into the trestle railing. Echo lost his footing and tumbled into Brooks, pinning him against the rail. The decaying wood bowed under their weight, then shattered like a twig.

Riley froze and watched in horror as Brooks fell through the opening. He locked eyes with her for an instant, as if saying goodbye, then plunged headlong into the gorge. His body splashed down in the river and was swept out of sight in the current. Visions of another river, another death, flooded into Riley's mind and she began to tremble violently before dropping to her knees and vomiting over the edge of the bridge.

Coop wrapped his arms around her waist and carried her to the center of the trestle, away from the fractured barrier. Dashay stared in stunned silence at the gaping hole where Brooks had been only seconds earlier. Coop whistled to snap Dashay out of it, and she slowly shifted her gaze to him.

"Riley's in shock and needs your help," he said. "Find a blanket."

Dashay nodded numbly and headed for the demolished cart. Adrian knelt beside her, surrounded by their scattered belongings.

"I'll get the blanket," he said. "You're in no better shape than Riley."

Dashay crawled to where Riley had lowered herself onto the tracks and threw her arms around her. "Is Brooks really gone?" she asked in a stunned whisper.

Riley gave a muffled cry in answer. As she clung to her friend, Echo bellowed and started struggling to get on his feet. Coop left the women and ran to the horse's side. He released the harness anchoring Echo to the cart. As soon as he was loose, Echo flailed his legs, fighting to stand.

Coop draped himself over Echo, and said, "Adrian, help me hold him down."

Adrian climbed to his feet and dropped a blanket over Riley's shoulder on his way to Coop.

"Riley, Echo's hurt," Coop called to her. "We need you to come examine his leg for breaks before we can let him stand. He's too strong for us to hold him down for long. You need to hurry."

Coop's command brought Riley out of her stupor. She snapped into doctor mode and knelt beside Echo's injured leg.

"I don't know what broken horse bones feel like," she told Coop, as she ran her hands along his leg.

Echo fought against her, so Coop patted his shoulder to calm him. "You're the closest we have to an expert. It shouldn't feel much different from a broken human bone."

Riley closed her eyes and shut out thoughts of the horror she'd just witnessed. Taking a deep breath, she started again. The bones felt whole and steady beneath her palms and fingers. The skin was broken in places, but the abrasions appeared superficial.

She let out her breath and turned to Coop. "It's impossible to tell if the bones have hairline cracks, but I don't feel any large breaks."

If Echo's leg had even hairline breaks, they'd have no choice but to put him down, but they wouldn't know until his full weight was on the bones. Coop's look told her he was thinking the same.

"Once he's up, examine his side, too," Coop said. "He went down hard on his ribs. You *do* have experience with broken ribs."

Riley glanced at him, then gave a slight shake of her head. "If any of our medical supplies survived, I can disinfect these cuts, then bandage and tape his leg. Diagnosing broken ribs is out of my wheelhouse but I'll do my best. If he puts his full weight on the leg without exhibiting signs of pain, that will tell us what we need to know."

Dashay got up and searched through the supplies that hadn't spilled into the gorge with Brooks. "Looks like the main med container is gone, but the emergency pack survived. It has enough of what we need to treat Echo's cuts but not more."

She carried it to Riley, and they tended to Echo while Coop and Adrian emptied and righted the cart. The scene had an otherworldly feel as they went about their tasks, pretending they hadn't just experienced a horrifying tragedy.

"The wheel isn't broken, but that side panel is shattered," she heard Coop say. "If we have enough rope, we can piece something together."

Adrian nodded. "It won't have to hold as much weight since more than half of the contents went over the side."

Coop gave a slight nod and wiped Echo's blood off his hands with a neckerchief. "Let's do what we can. We'll catalog the remaining supplies later."

Riley glanced up and saw Coop hesitate before lifting Brooks' pack off the ground. She was sure he was blaming himself for the accident since he was their leader, but he was no more responsible than the rest of them.

Coincidence or jinx? she wondered, remembering their lighthearted jesting over Brooks' comment that the escape from Charleston had been anticlimactic. Her eyes teared up as she whispered, "Grandma was never wrong."

Echo squirmed, so she stroked his side and comforted him while Dashay finished bandaging his wounds. When they'd done what they could, Dashay shoved the materials into the backpack, and the two of them moved away to see if Echo would stand without help. He tucked his legs and rolled onto his chest, then looked around as if figuring out what to do next. Riley held her breath as he tossed his head from side to side before throwing his front legs out straight and pulling himself to his feet. He turned and stared at the group, looking as surprised as they were that he was upright.

Biscuit was tied to the opposite railing and tugged on his tether to get to Echo. Riley untied the reins and led him to his friend. They greeted each other joyfully for a moment, then Echo took off running until he reached the far side of the trestle. He stepped off the tracks onto a grassy mound and stuck his muzzle into a patch of clover.

"Guess the leg's good," Coop said as he walked back to their pile of provisions. "Let's load the cart and get off this cursed bridge."

Adrian picked up a twelve-pack of toilet paper and tossed it on top of a stack of boxes.

"Don't overexert yourself," Riley said under her breath as she lifted a case of canned goods into the cart.

Adrian straightened and glared at her but let her comment pass. "What if Biscuit won't pull the cart?"

"Biscuit will do what he needs to because he knows we're counting on him," she said.

Adrian huffed. "How can he know that? He's a horse. He's done nothing to earn your confidence that I've seen. He's just a silly horse."

Riley dropped the box she was holding and grabbed the front of Adrian's shirt. "More than you," she shouted in his face. "Your friend just died, and you want to argue about Biscuit? I'm sick of your constant bickering and negativity. What did your wife ever see in you?"

Coop rushed over and peeled Riley's fingers from Adrian's shirt before dragging her away from him. Dashay nudged Adrian to the opposite side of the bridge.

Coop grasped her by the wrists, and said, "Look at me. This isn't about Adrian. You're just lashing out."

While struggling to free herself, she said, "No, it's about Adrian."

"We don't have time for this, Riley."

She glanced up at him and caught his grief-stricken look. She wasn't the only one in shock from Brooks' death. She pulled Coop into her arms and whispered, "I'm sorry, babe." She held him for a moment, then walked to Adrian. Holding out her hand, she said, "That was uncalled for. Please, forgive me."

He stared at her hand for a moment, then shook it without a word before going back to loading supplies. She got into place beside him and lifted their tent into the cart. The four of them worked in silence until their remaining supplies were packed.

Riley watched anxiously as Coop strapped Biscuit into the

harness, hoping her faith in him hadn't been misplaced. When Coop urged him forward, Biscuit held his head high and marched along like the most important horse on Earth.

With less weight to pull, they crossed the second length of the trestle in half the time. Adrian had gone ahead to keep Echo from wandering off and to put some distance between himself and Riley. The two of them were waiting next to the tracks as Coop led Biscuit onto a nearby road. They rested when they got across the bridge, then quietly put the cart in order. No one spoke as they worked.

Coop finally gathered the others around him and said, "I get that we're all still reeling from Brooks' death, but it was nothing more than a freak accident. No one is to blame."

"Except Echo," Adrian mumbled.

Riley clenched her fists and took a step toward him. "Haven't you learned anything? He's a damned horse, you idiot."

Coop put his hands on her shoulders and gently pushed her away from him. "Enough, Riley. Let it go. Let's get camp set up for the night. Tomorrow is soon enough to gather our wits and put this tragic day behind us."

Adrian and Dashay walked to the cart to unload it. Riley silently watched as Dashay ignored the tears streaming down her face while she stacked boxes on the grass.

Coop wrapped his arm around Riley's waist. "We'll find time to mourn later, but we've got to put Charleston behind us first."

She put her hand over his, more grateful than ever to have him at her side. "Let's see if our jackets survived. It's going to be a chilly night."

Riley scanned the terrain below the trestle, searching for their scattered supplies, searching for Brooks, searching for peace. She'd been trying and failing all morning to keep her mind focused on the job at hand. There was no time to inspect the gorge. The round trip and accompanying search would take most of the day. From what they could see, Brooks and the supplies were carried away by the river. They would just have to hope they had enough supplies to get to the next weigh station and they could scrounge what they needed along the way.

Riley watched the swollen river rushing past, conjuring up older memories she'd been fighting to suppress since the accident. Hannah's drowning felt like another lifetime, but in reality had only been months earlier. Riley had descended into a dark void in the aftermath of that tragedy, believing it was the worst possible thing that could happen. She'd had no way of knowing what was still to come.

With the love and help of Coop and Julia, she'd pulled herself together and moved on. Her experiences since had strengthened her, and she refused to descend into that dark place of vulnerability and self-pity. The others needed her strength. Her baby depended on her.

Still, it wasn't healthy to pretend the emotions churning beneath the surface didn't exist. Her resistance to facing those dark thoughts was draining energy she didn't have to spare. She closed her eyes and allowed herself to mourn Brooks' death and pay homage to the memory of Hannah. Coop came up behind her and laid his hand on her shoulder, waiting in silence as she poured out her grief.

"Are you going to make it through this?" he finally asked.

Riley dried her face on her sleeve, then looked up at him with gratitude. Coop helped her to her feet, and she brushed the mud from her knees. "I am. Brooks' death and being here are dragging up memories of Hannah, and I tumbled down that rabbit hole. Why does it always have to be a river?"

"I've been having the same struggle, but as I told you last night, there will be time to mourn."

"Will there?" When Coop raised an eyebrow, she said, "Strike that. I just wish we could find Brooks' body and have a burial. It would give us closure, which is in short supply lately."

"He's miles downstream by now, Riley, but we can hold a memorial before we leave for Huntington."

She wrapped her arms around him and rested her head on his chest. "That would help. How's Dashay? I haven't seen her since breakfast."

"I think she headed downriver to see if she could spot Brooks. I didn't stop her. This must be rough on her so soon after leaving Nico. She lost the two most important people in her life in two days."

Riley pulled away and looked up at him. "Her real family is gone, and now her surrogate one, too. She was much closer to Brooks than we were. We'll need to help fill that void."

"A task I'll willingly take on. Let's find her and take another load up top. Come away from the edge. Looking down here gives me the creeps. Feels like an enormous grave."

Riley shivered as she took hold of his hand. "Now who's down the rabbit hole?"

———

Riley held her hands over the fire in their camp that was only a half mile from the end of the trestle. As Riley waited for the others to join her to start the memorial, she considered what she could say about her brief acquaintance with Brooks. She'd come to consider him a friend after moving past their tumultuous beginning and had even grown to respect him. She regretted never taking the time to tell him and hoped he'd known.

"I'd like to go first," she told the others once they were gathered around the fire. "Brooks is the first person in my life who started as an enemy and later grew to be my friend. On the night Julia was shot, and Branson's thugs took us hostage, Brooks was the only one who helped us get what we needed to save

Julia's life. If it hadn't been for his quick actions, she wouldn't have survived."

"That's how he was," Dashay said. "Especially toward the end before the coup. He did a hundred acts of kindness in secret to make up for Branson's treatment of the hostages. Many more would have died without his help."

Tears glistened in Riley's eyes as she said, "I was too angry and consumed in my own troubles to notice. I'm grateful I got the chance to know him for the man he truly was."

"There was more to Brooks than his little kind acts," Adrian said. "Something he didn't want us to tell you. Brooks was a bonafide hero."

Coop eyed him in confusion. "Seriously? Brooks was nothing more than one of Branson's puppets to me during our time in the compound."

Adrian glanced at Dashay before saying, "After you two escaped from the camp with Julia, Branson locked Angie up in his jail. The next morning, he sent his goons around the compound to announce a mandatory gathering at the firepit for noon the following day. He wanted to make an example of Angie and show us the consequences for attempting to escape."

"Make an example. How?" Coop asked.

"Public execution."

Riley shivered. "What a monster. Branson cutting off Jepson's finger for shooting Julia and those poor souls in that church was one thing. But execution? I didn't think even Branson was capable of that, especially to an innocent like Angie. It's sickening."

Coop took off his cap and ran his hand through his hair. "How did Angie escape that?"

"Brooks rounded up a few guys he could trust to help overthrow Branson," Adrian continued. "On the day of the scheduled execution, Branson had his people armed and surrounding the hostages. They brought Angie out with her hands tied behind her back and forced her to kneel near the firepit. When the crowd figured out what was happening, they went crazy and started shouting at Branson. Then, all hell broke loose."

Dashay shook her head at the memory. "Several of the hostages suddenly rushed out in all directions. Branson's idiots started firing, so Nico and I hit the deck to avoid the crossfire. I was terrified out of my mind. They killed a few of the hostages, but Branson's people were outnumbered. The hostages overpowered them and took their guns. Brooks spotted Branson sneaking off in the chaos. He captured and killed him. When Branson's people realized the boss was dead, most of them bailed, and we never saw them again. The rest surrendered. Brooks took charge and organized the camp. You know the rest."

Riley's respect for Brooks rose to new heights after hearing of his courageous actions. "It breaks my heart his sons will never know their father died a hero."

Dashay smiled sadly. "Brooks hated it when anyone called him a hero. He said his actions that day didn't make up for the pain he'd caused others. He never forgave himself for Julia getting shot or for the carnage at the church."

"Branson was the first and last person he ever killed," Adrian said. "He was haunted by the memory for months. That was what drove him to get as far away from the compound as he could."

Coop gave a low whistle. "Wish you had told us when you first ran into us at the park. It took me a while to trust Brooks considering our history. Would have been different if I'd known."

"He understood, but those were his wishes," Dashay said. "He was grateful you allowed him to tag along and wanted to gain your trust without you knowing."

Coop blinked and swiped a tear from his cheek. "He did."

Riley lifted her canteen and waited for the others to join her. "To Brooks, a genuine hero. You will not be soon forgotten."

Riley was up early the next morning, eager to make what happened on the trestle and in Charleston a distant memory.

"Morning," Adrian said as he walked up, drawing her from her thoughts. She wasn't happy to see him. Aside from his help in gathering a few edible plants and berries, he'd become a useless appendage to the group.

Coop came up next to Riley and whispered, "I can read your thoughts."

She turned her back to Adrian and, lowering her voice, said, "I vote we ditch him in Huntington and let him find his own way to St. Louis."

Coop studied her for a moment before saying, "Is this regret I'm hearing? Weren't you the one convincing me to let Adrian travel with us when we were in the park?"

"Maybe. Yes. I don't know. I didn't want to abandon him to die in the woods. Why couldn't it have been Adrian instead of Brooks?"

Coop gestured for her to stop talking, but she missed the cue until it was too late.

Adrian walked up behind her, and said, "Why don't you say how you really feel, Riley? Guess I should be grateful you weren't willing to leave me to die."

She sighed and slowly turned to face him. "I'm sorry, Adrian, that was an appalling thing to say. I didn't mean it."

Adrian looked her in the eye for once. "Didn't you? Look, I understand that I've given you cause to hate me, but I thought we were past that."

"I don't hate you, Adrian, and this isn't about what happened before the CME."

"Then what? Is it that I don't fit in with your cool little clique? I thought you had accepted me as a member of this group."

Coop opened his mouth to speak, but Riley held up her hand

to stop him. "I can tolerate your eccentricities, but not your arrogance and laziness. We're all working ourselves to the bone, but you act as if you're above menial labor like some Lord of the Manor. I get that you're a genius physicist and not used to getting your hands dirty, but Coop and I are surgeons, and you don't see us slacking. I'm suffering from morning sickness, but I'm still doing more than my share."

Dashay came up carrying a bike she'd found in the ravine. She dropped it and dusted off her hands. "What's with the raised voices? I thought you two had settled your issues."

When Riley looked away, Adrian said, "Riley was just pointing out that she wishes I were dead."

Coop leaned closer to him. "That's what you took from what Riley just said? Do you ever listen to anything besides the sound of your own voice?" He stopped and took a deep breath before turning to Dashay. "Riley was trying to get Adrian to understand that he needs to do his fair share like the rest of us."

Dashay folded her arms and glared at Adrian. "We had that exact conversation this morning."

He raised his hands in surrender. "You're acting like I never lift a finger. I've foraged for fruits and vegetables to augment our food supply, and I do most of the cooking."

Riley had to give him that. She didn't like to cook and most of Adrian's meals had been delicious, given the ingredients and tools at his disposal.

"We *do* appreciate those contributions," she said, "but that doesn't mean you're not expected to help in other ways, and it wouldn't hurt to lose the negative attitude. No one in the world is thrilled that our lives have been torn apart, but we're making the best of it. Given your role in what we're dealing with, you're the last person who should be complaining. The constant griping won't improve our situation or get the work done. It only drags us down with you."

Adrian's face reddened and he shifted his feet. "It's just my way. I'll work on it."

"So, a bike," Coop said, breaking the tension. "What do you expect us to do with just one of these?"

"I know it needs repairing and parts, but the frame is sturdy, and the chain is intact. It could come in handy when one of us needs to move around in a populated area unnoticed," Dashay said. "The horses draw too much attention and bikes don't need food or rest."

Riley ran her fingers over dinged up handlebars. "Maybe we should look for more as we go. Riding would cut our travel time in half and save my poor feet."

Dashay pointed to a hole in the toe of her boot. "No argument from me."

Coop shrugged and lifted the bike into the empty cart.

Adrian walked to the edge of the gorge and stared into the depths. "Wonder how it got there. Think someone went over the side like Brooks?"

Riley shivered at the memory of Brooks plummeting to his death that she'd been trying to suppress. *Leave it to Adrian to bring out the dark side*, she thought. "Let's load the cart and get out of here."

Adrian caught Riley's eye as he deliberately lifted a heavy box into the cart. She stared him down and tossed her pack in after it. Once they were packed, Adrian grabbed hold of Biscuit's reins to get him moving. The two of them had formed an unexpected bond over the past two days. Riley recalled Adrian's earlier doubts that Biscuit would be of any help to them or survive the journey, but her trusty friend had won him over. *Two misfits together*, she thought.

Dashay pulled the map out of her pack and measured a distance with her fingers. "Huntington is just under fifty miles from this spot. Think we can make that in three days?"

Coop glanced at the map over her shoulder. "Two and a half if we hook back up with the interstate and don't run into trouble."

"When have we not run into trouble?" Adrian asked.

Riley snapped her fingers at him. "Attitude, Adrian." He flinched and nodded. "But this time, you might be right," she said.

She brought up the rear, hoping that for once, they'd reach their destination without disaster dogging their every step.

Nico grabbed the side of his bed when an explosion shook the hospital, startling him out of sleep. It was the closest one yet. The bombing had stopped for more than an hour, and he'd dared to hope the three-day pounding Charleston had endured at the hands of Kearns' troops was over. He was disappointed to be wrong.

A young night-shift nurse was changing his antibiotic bag. She stopped and stared at him, wide-eyed after the explosion. "That was too close. Will they bomb the hospital?"

Nico did his best to smile and reassure her. "Not a chance. They've made their way into the city and were probably aiming for the capitol building."

"Hope you're right. It's hard enough being overrun with casualties. The governor should surrender and get it over with. We all know it's inevitable." She finished what she was doing and pressed the back of her hand to his forehead to feel his temperature. Nodding in satisfaction, she said, "Think you can move to the chair so I can change your bedding?"

In answer, he rolled onto his side and swung his feet to the floor. She helped him stand and walk to the chair. Even though he was improving by the hour, he was still shocked at how weak he was. He was used to being fit and agile. It was hard adjusting to being helpless. He settled into the chair and closed his eyes.

He'd have to regain his strength much faster to have any hope of catching up with Dashay.

As he opened his eyes, the lights flickered, then went out. The nurse gasped in the darkness. The only light came from the fires burning in the city.

"They probably broke a line feeding the generator," he said. "Do you have a flashlight?"

She pulled a penlight from her pocket. "Just this one. I need to find out what's happening, but I'll finish making the bed and get you back into it first." She handed him the light. "Please hold this so I can see what I'm doing."

He shined the beam toward the bed and watched her tuck the sheets and straighten the blankets. "Would you mind letting me know what you find out?" he asked as she helped him back to bed.

She nodded. "As soon as I can." She took a bedpan off a cart in the corner and held it out to him. "Don't get out of bed for any reason. I'd hate for you to fall and break your neck in the dark."

Me, too, he thought as he watched her hurry out of the room. He tore off the tape keeping his IV in place and slid the needle out of his arm. To staunch the blood, he pressed the wad of tissues he'd pulled from a box on his tray to the puncture, then covered them with the tape. Without electricity, the IV wouldn't do him any good. He'd need oral meds if power weren't restored in a hurry.

He closed his eyes, hoping to sleep, but the sound of the war raging outside his windows made that impossible. With no light and being stuck in bed, he had nothing else to do but stare at the dark ceiling. He would have given anything to be on his feet, treating the wounded. Instead, he lay there utterly useless.

By the end of the first hour, he thought he'd go out of his mind with boredom and lack of information. The nurse hadn't come back. He considered defying her orders to get up and open the blinds. His window didn't afford him much of a view, but it was enough to see a patch of the street beyond the hospital complex.

He lay back with a sigh and pictured Dashay sleeping in a cozy, abandoned house on the outskirts of some small town, miles west of Charleston. He estimated that if they'd stayed on the train tracks, they could have made over fifty miles since leaving. The instant his legs were strong enough, he would scrounge a few supplies and hoof it out of the city. He'd be able to move fast on his own and could catch up to them in a matter of days. If he got his hands on a horse or bike, all the better.

After the second hour, the world grew still. Nico figured that was because they couldn't fight a war in the dark. He took advantage of the quiet and gave sleep another try. Just as he was drifting off, he saw a flash of light through his eyelids and heard footsteps on the tile floor. He opened his eyes and squinted into a flashlight beam, unable to tell who was holding it.

Covering his eyes with his hands, he said, "Could you please point that somewhere else? You're blinding me."

The beam shifted slightly to the left of his head, and the man holding the light said, "Just making sure it was you. Is your name Nico Mendez?"

Nico pushed himself higher in the bed and tried to focus on the face staring down at him. "I'll answer that after you tell me who you are and why you want to know."

The man pulled a gun from a holster at his hip and pointed it at Nico's face. "I suggest you answer the question, son."

Nico held his hands up in surrender and did his best to fake a smile. "Just trying to be careful. You can't know who to trust these days, as you're proving by aiming a gun at an injured man. Since you already know the answer, yes, I'm Nico Mendez. May I ask your name?"

The man ignored him and gestured to someone waiting in the doorway. The nurse came in pushing a wheelchair. She glanced at him with a look of apology as she helped him into it. Once he was seated, she gathered his few belongings and set them in his lap. The man started for the doorway and motioned for her to follow with Nico.

The hallways were empty as they made their way to the stairwell, and he wondered what had become of the other patients and their caregivers. Were he and the nurse the only people left in the building?

When they reached the stairs, three men appeared out of the shadows and lifted Nico's chair to carry it down. As the stairwell door closed behind them, he heard the nurse say, "Take care of yourself, Nico. We'll miss you."

His heart pounded, and he shook uncontrollably as the men carried him down the two flights of stairs. He was sure they were planning to take him to some deserted field and kill him, although he couldn't imagine why anyone would want to do that or how they even knew who he was. On the ground floor, one of the men pushed him toward the entrance while two others ran ahead to pry open the sliding doors. The man holding the gun walked a few steps behind. Medical staff and patients scattered into the shadows at the sight of them.

They wheeled him outside to a black Humvee waiting at the curb and lifted him into the back seat. The man who'd pushed his chair wrapped a blindfold over his eyes and tied it behind his head. They shouldn't have bothered. It was too dark to see a thing out of the tinted windows, and he didn't have the first clue where they were.

They rode for about twenty minutes in silence, during which Nico decided maybe they weren't going to kill him because they would have had plenty of opportunities by that point. The vehicle finally came to a stop, and someone lifted him back into the wheelchair and pushed him through what sounded like a parking garage. Even with the blindfold, he could tell it was well lit.

After an endless maze of twists and turns and an elevator

ride, his chair came to a stop. Another person removed his blindfold. He squinted in the bright light to see a room with whitewashed concrete walls and sparse furnishings, including a hospital bed. The men who brought him there faded away to be replaced by a middle-aged nurse, a wiry, dark-complected doctor who couldn't seem to stop fidgeting, and a tall, smartly dressed man with a pleasant but guarded face.

The nurse helped Nico to the bed and hooked him to an IV while the others looked on without a word. The nurse took his vitals, then left as soon as her duties were completed. The doctor came forward and extended his hand. Nico shook it without taking his eyes off the doctor's face.

"I'm Dr. Antony Matti. We won't hurt you, so you can relax. I've read through your charts. Since you're responding so well, I'll continue Dr. Pritchard's prescribed course of treatment. When you're rested, Colonel Yeager here will have a discussion with you about why you're here, but for now, you need rest. Is there anything we can get you?"

Let me the hell out of here, he thought, but said, "Please, tell me where I am and why I'm here?"

"The Colonel will explain everything in the morning. We'll leave you to sleep now. Your nurse call button is there on the side of the bed if you need anything in the night."

Nico glanced at the button, then watched the two men leave the room, more confused than ever.

He slept so soundly in the silent room and comfortable bed that he was convinced the doctor had drugged him. A functioning wall clock read 12:37. Nico wasn't sure if that meant AM or PM. He pressed his call button to have the nurse help him to the bathroom. While he waited, his stomach growled ferociously, and he realized how ravenous he was. He couldn't remember the last time he'd eaten.

He heard the door unlock and a different nurse came in who looked to be about his age of twenty-five. She had spiky, multicolored hair and looked like she'd just stepped out of a high-end salon. It made Nico wonder if these people knew they were living in an apocalypse.

"Hi, Nico. I'm Candace," she said, in a lighthearted, singsong way. "I bet you're about to burst. Let's get you to the toilet."

As she reached out to help him up, he saw the tattoos covering her arms. He'd never seen or worked with a nurse like her.

As he shuffled along beside her toward the bathroom, she said, "Do you need me to come with or can you manage?"

"I've got this," he said, closing the door behind him.

"Such a big boy," she said, and snickered at her joke.

While she walked him back to the bed and helped him get settled, he said, "Are you allowed to tell me where I am or are you sworn to secrecy, too?"

"You'll get your answers when the Colonel comes in after breakfast. It's not as cloak and dagger as you think. I can tell you that as soon as you've recovered, they're shipping you back to your unit. I bet you'll be happy to be back with your own people instead of those strangers you've been stuck with. I'm going to get your breakfast. The food's excellent here."

She breezed out before he could say another word. What she'd said had creeped him out even more than he was before. He couldn't figure out how these people knew so much about him without computers or internet, and the last thing he wanted was to be sent back to Kearns' Army. Dashay, Coop, and the others weren't just some strangers he was tagging along with for company. They had become his family. Thinking of them made him want to get home to his real family, but they were 1500 miles in the opposite direction.

Candace danced in carrying a plate piled with Belgian waffles, poached eggs, and real bacon. Nico wondered if he'd either died in the night or was dreaming, but the incredible aroma was a dead giveaway that it was real. He couldn't remember ever having a dream with smells.

She put the tray on his rolling table "Enjoy, sweetie. Buzz me when you're finished, and I'll inform the Colonel you're ready for him."

He caught her wrist as she brushed past the bed to go. "Can't you stay and talk to me while I eat? I'm tired of being alone. I promise not to ask questions about this place."

"Sorry, cuteness. I have other work to do. I'll sit with you after my shift. I got nowhere else to be tonight."

She went out, locking the door behind her, and he pinched himself to make sure he was awake. Convinced he was, he wolfed down his food, then immediately regretted eating so fast. He kept it down but made a mental note to pace himself at his next meal.

He pressed the call button to let Candace know he was finished. She came in five minutes later, followed by Colonel Yeager, who was again dressed in civilian clothes. Candace winked as she picked up Nico's tray and flittered out.

"There'd never be another war if more people were like her," Colonel Yeager said, as he watched her go. "Good morning, Corporal Mendez. I trust you slept well."

Nico straightened as much as he could. "Yes, sir. Thank you for asking, sir."

The Colonel lowered himself into a leather recliner in the corner. "At ease, Corporal. You can relax. I'm here to help you."

Nico let out his breath and relaxed against the mattress. "May I ask which branch of the service you serve in, Colonel?"

"Used to be in the Marine Corps. I guess you haven't heard that we're all one force now. We're simply the Military Forces of the United States. With all five branches decimated after the CME, President Kearns' pressed what remains of Congress to combine our country's armed forces. You're no longer in the Army. You're in the US Military."

"It'll take time to decide how I feel about that," Nico said. "Sir, may I ask what's happening here? Where am I?"

"Certainly. This is a secure underground government facility. Several of these facilities exist throughout the country. We were fortunate to have one close to Charleston."

Nico leaned closer to him. "I'd heard rumors about these places, but I wasn't sure I believed they existed."

"We keep knowledge of them from the public, which I'm sure you can understand given conditions in the world."

Nico nodded. "Makes sense. Why am I here, sir? Do you need a medic? Candace said you're returning me to my unit once I'm healed."

"You won't be staying. You're here for another reason."

He reached into his pocket and took out a piece of paper. He slowly unfolded it and held it up for Nico to see. It was a sketch of Adrian. In an instant, everything that happened the past day made sense.

The Colonel studied him for a moment. "I can read from your reaction that you recognize this man."

Nico understood that there was no point in denying it, and he couldn't lie to an officer, even if he worked for that snake, Kearns.

"That's Dr. Adrian Landry. I was held hostage with him at a camp in Virginia. We've been traveling together since we left the camp. At least we were until my group had to leave without me."

Nico sensed he hadn't told Colonel Yeager anything he didn't already know.

He watched Nico stoically for several moments, then said, "Yes, we were aware of that. I appreciate your honesty."

"Even if you hadn't known, I'd have no reason to hide it, sir. He's just a person I met and traveled with, nothing more."

"Not that simple, Corporal. You may not be aware that Dr.

Landry is a dangerous, unstable man who has committed crimes against our country and needs to be brought to answer for those crimes. He's skilled at hiding his true persona."

Nico struggled to keep from laughing. The idea of Adrian being anything more than a wimpy, absentminded scientist was ridiculous, but the Colonel was portraying him as some evil genius mastermind. Nico had no doubt the Colonel believed what he'd been told about Adrian by Kearns, but if he'd spent five minutes with him, he'd figure out none of it was true. Nico didn't dare contradict an officer, though, so he tried to act shocked.

"Are you sure we're talking about the same person? Adrian seems so mild-mannered and geeky. He's smart, but his favorite thing to do is collect plants."

The Colonel leaned back and crossed his arms. "All an act. If you knew the truth about him, you'd realize how dangerous he really is. We intend to capture him before he hurts anyone else. What can you tell me about his current whereabouts?"

"I honestly have no idea where he is, sir. He left with my other friends to travel west four or five days ago. They wanted out of Charleston before the war started. I was too sick to go with them."

"What's his eventual destination, Corporal?"

"I'm sorry, sir, but I don't know. He may have said Oklahoma or Texas. I didn't pay much attention to Adrian when he talked. He's kind of annoying."

The Colonel reached into his other pocket and took out another piece of paper. Nico recognized it before he unfolded it. It was the map Brooks had drawn for him. Fortunately, it only showed the route as far as Lexington, Kentucky, since Nico knew they were going to St. Louis. Nico tried to keep his face neutral while the Colonel studied him with a strange grin but laser-focused eyes. Nico sensed something unnatural about the man and realized this was not a man to be trifled with. Even so, he instinctively knew that he should keep to himself the group's plans to go to St. Louis.

Nico nonchalantly reached for the paper. "Is that my map? I wondered what happened to that." Colonel Yeager held it just beyond his reach. Nico gave what he hoped was a lighthearted smile and withdrew his hand. "Guess I won't need it now since I'm going back to my unit."

The Colonel continued to study him, then said, "You told me you don't know where they are."

"I don't. That's the way they planned to go, but we both know how those kinds of plans go these days. They could be anywhere along that route by now, but it shouldn't be too hard to find them. I hope you do so he won't hurt my friends, though he never seemed like he wanted to hurt anyone."

Nico realized he was rambling, so he closed his mouth and waited for the Colonel to speak. He watched Nico for several more moments. He sensed the Colonel hadn't bought his act. Nico's only choice was to be quiet and force himself to relax.

"Before I go, Corporal, are you sure there's nothing else you want to tell me?"

Nico shrugged. "Like what, sir?"

"Things Dr. Landry told you about the CME, his history, or what he plans to do when he gets where he's going. We're aware that he told the other hostages in that compound about his role in the CME disaster."

"All I know is that he said he knew the CME was coming earlier than everyone was told, and he kept his mouth shut. He was beaten nearly to death for confessing that in the camp. I ran the clinic and didn't spend much time with Adrian until we left the compound months later. Then all he talked about were planets and plants. Like I told you, he was annoying, so I didn't pay much attention. If you want more information, you've got the wrong guy."

The Colonel stood and stepped next to Nico's bed in one fluid motion. As he moved his face close to Nico's, all pretense of compassion faded. "This isn't a game, Corporal. I'm here at the request of your Commander-in-Chief. If I find out you've withheld crucial information, the consequences will be severe. Is that clear?"

Nico's heart pounded as he slowly nodded, and he hoped the beats weren't visible through the blankets. The Colonel straightened, and a smile crept up his face but never reached his eyes. "Good. Get well soon. We need you back in the field, son."

Colonel Yeager left without another word. Nico prayed he'd seen him for the last time but feared that wouldn't be the case. The Colonel made that psychopath Branson look like an amateur. As Nico struggled to calm himself, he was sure of one thing. He wouldn't see his home or Dashay anytime soon, if ever again.

CHAPTER EIGHT

RILEY IGNORED HER SWOLLEN FEET, her back muscles spasming into knots, and the tiny blisters that had bubbled up on her sunburned cheeks as she trudged along on their fourth day to Huntington. Her complete focus was on Echo's labored breathing, the way he hung his head as he walked, and his worsening limp. It was the outcome she'd feared when she'd changed his bandages that morning before leaving camp. The skin around his wounds had been swollen and warm, despite her efforts to fight the infection festering in his abrasions. Their first order of business in Huntington would be to locate a vet, which would be no small feat.

It was a clear sunny morning in May when they approached Huntington, West Virginia. As they made a turn in a valley, Riley could see the entrance down into the city with the Ohio River meandering slowly north of the city. She scanned the area to get a sense of where they were. Just ahead of her was a busy street surrounded by office and retail buildings. She scanned the area for signs of a checkpoint or military presence and was relieved to find none.

The scene that greeted them was the opposite of what they'd

encountered in Charleston. Residents rushed along the debris and garbage-strewn streets in panic-stricken groups. No one seemed in charge. It reminded Riley of cities she and Coop had passed through in the first weeks after the CME.

Adrian pulled Biscuit to a stop and turned to Coop. "Which way, Boss?"

Before Coop could answer, a middle-aged woman with a mass of tangled curls sticking out of an olive-green helmet sped by on a bike. She wore a yellow flowered skirt, a cherry red tank top, and cowboy boots. As she passed, she lifted a megaphone to her lips and bellowed, "Get out while you can. The troops are on their way. They'll make you prisoners in your own homes or worse. Get out now!"

Dashay chuckled as the woman pedaled off, then said, "What in the hell was that?"

"Her helmet's probably lined with tin foil," Adrian said, shaking his head.

Riley watched people scurrying past her, carrying their belongings stuffed in packs or bulging boxes. She walked Echo to a patch of grass off the side of the street, and said, "Crazy or not, it looks like everyone else has the same idea. What if she's right? Kearns' people could have had time to take over Charleston and be on their way here by now."

The roar of an engine behind them interrupted her. She spun around as an ancient, dilapidated Ford truck with smoke pouring out of the exhaust pipe came barreling towards them. Dashay dove into the patch of grass beside Echo to avoid getting run down. The driver didn't bother taking his eyes off the road to see if he'd struck her.

Riley helped Dashay to her feet and helped her dust the grass off her legs. She checked to make sure she wasn't hurt, then said, "We need to get off the major streets and find out what's going on around here." She ran her hand along Echo's neck. His skin was hot to the touch. "And Echo is in bad shape. We have to find a vet immediately or we could lose him."

Adrian, who had come to care more about the welfare of the horses than his other traveling companions it seemed, walked back to her and patted Echo's forehead. "Isn't there anything you can do?"

She shook her head. They had a small stock of antibiotics, but she had no idea if any of them would work on a horse or what the dosage should be. Mammals metabolized drugs at different rates. The wrong drug could be useless or lethal. She regretted not spending more time learning from her cousin Jessie, the ranch veterinarian.

"This is out of my wheelhouse. Echo needs expert care," she said.

As Coop rubbed his sunburned neck, he said, "Let's split up. Dashay, why don't you and Adrian take Biscuit and find a place for the night on the west side of town? Riley and I will search for a vet and get info on the situation here. We'll start at the medical college hospital and tell them we're doctors. Grab the map, Dashay, and we'll pick somewhere to hook back up in three hours."

After choosing to meet in a park near the center of the city, Coop and Riley headed toward the university hospital, hoping someone there could give them news of what was happening and point them to a vet. Adrian and Dashay turned Biscuit toward the western edge of the city so they could make a quick getaway in the morning.

As Riley and Coop headed toward the hospital with Echo, she watched the evening sunlight glitter on the Ohio River, wishing she had time to enjoy the view and wondering if dousing Echo in the river might bring his fever down if they couldn't find a vet.

It took ninety minutes to reach the hospital, and after tethering Echo in the shade of a large oak tree, they hurried inside and were met with silence and deserted hallways. They searched for ten minutes before spotting what looked like two young doctors conversing near the nurses' station on the surgery ward. They both looked like they were fresh out of medical school. As they approached, the men stopped talking and stared wide-eyed at Coop and Riley.

The young, tall and thin doctor with thick, jet-black hair stepped toward them and held up his hands to stop them from coming closer. "This area is restricted to medical staff. You can't be here."

As the other doctor, who reminded Riley of a younger version of Coop except for the hipster glasses, came up behind the first to offer moral support. He was going to cross his arms, but stopped when he got a look at Coop.

He extended his hand, and said, "Dr. Cooper?"

Coop raised an eyebrow and studied the man's face for a moment before saying, "Should I know you?"

"You wouldn't remember me. Name's Brent Holverson. I did my residency in Chicago and attended some of your seminars. You're a legend."

Coop turned to Riley and winked. "Hear that? Legend." Riley rolled her eyes as Coop turned back to Dr. Holverson. "Sorry for not remembering you. Dozens of doctors passed through my seminars over the years, but it's nice to meet you now." He gestured toward Riley. "This is my wife, Dr. Poole. Ortho. Running into you is a stroke of good fortune. We've traveled a long way and stumbled into Huntington a few hours ago. We need your help."

The first doctor moved closer and cleared his throat. "I'm Dr. Walser. It's an honor to meet you, Dr. Cooper, but I'm not sure how much help we can offer. We're closing the hospital today and moving out of the city under orders from Governor Mitchell. Since the fall of Charleston, he's ordered us to empty Huntington and not give Kearns the satisfaction of capturing us. Her people will be here by morning."

"Where will the people go?" Riley asked. "How do you hide an entire city's population?"

Dr. Holverson shifted his feet. "There wasn't much of a population left after the CME," he said, softly. "It was a rough time, especially for the students who had just returned for the new semester. Out of those that survived, most moved to Charleston when the snows came. As word trickled in about the residential zones a few weeks ago, more headed for the hills. The rest traveled west to warn residents of what's coming. I have family in Cincinnati, so I'm going there."

"I'm staying even though we're shutting down the hospital," Dr. Walser said. "My family is in Arizona. I wouldn't make it there on my own, and I figure they'll need doctors in the zone. More so if what we hear of how the troops are treating people is true."

Coop pulled off his cap and ran his hand through his hair. "It is true."

The doctors glanced at each other. Riley recognized the look. She'd seen it in countless faces of the poor souls she'd passed on her journey. These young men had experienced horrors they couldn't have imagined six months earlier. Riley wished for the power to erase their memories and pain but hadn't been able to do that with her own demons.

"What is it you need, Dr. Cooper?" Dr. Holverson asked.

"First, call me Coop. Believe it or not, we need a vet. We have an injured horse whose leg is infected. I think his condition is critical."

Dr. Holverson's face brightened. "You're right, I didn't expect that request, but you're in luck. I have a cousin who's a vet. His name is Dylan Clevenger, and he has a clinic less than a mile from here. He knows his stuff, but I warn you, he's a bit of a character. Harmless, though. He's planning to see this thing out in Huntington, so he should be around."

Riley let out her breath. "That's more than lucky. It's a

miracle. Please, point us in the right direction. We don't have much time."

Dr. Holverson grabbed a legal pad and pen to draw a quick map. When he handed it to Riley, he said, "Come back when you're done with my cousin, and we'll see if we can hook you up with some supplies before we take off."

Riley folded the map and stuffed it in her pocket, then shook each of their hands. "We will if we have time. This may seem impossible now, but we wish both of you long and happy futures. You're doing an incredible service here. Stay safe."

Dr. Walser turned away when his eyes teared up. Dr. Holverson patted him on the shoulder and said, "We'll do our best. Same to you. Tell Cousin Dylan I'll stop by tonight."

Coop gave a quick nod, then took Riley's hand as they hurried to the entrance. "What was that about?" he asked.

"Must be the maternal hormones. They just seem so young and vulnerable to be carrying such responsibility. I couldn't have shouldered what they are so soon out of med school."

Coop pulled her to a stop and kissed her cheek. "I don't believe that for a second. You would have whipped this entire city into shape by now, Red Queen."

Riley gave a weak smile at his use of Julia's call sign for her. "Believe what you want, but the biggest challenge in my life then was to get the other Orthos to accept a five-foot tall woman into their boys' club and respect her. None of us knew what truly mattered in that old life."

Coop shrugged. "It was still kind to give those boys their own dose of hope. My wish is someday you'll see yourself for the remarkable Riley Cooper I know and love."

She gave him a tender kiss before starting for the door. "Don't hold your breath."

Echo let out a whinny of welcome when he saw Coop and Riley. The brief rest in the shade had restored his strength slightly, but his skin was still hot to the touch. Riley was grateful the vet clinic was nearby. When Coop untethered Echo and clicked his tongue to get him moving, Riley was disappointed to see his limp hadn't improved.

"Help is close," she whispered.

The streets grew quieter the closer they got to the river. People were clearly moving out of the city or hunkering down. The sun was setting, and Riley guessed people were locked in their houses for the night or had abandoned the city already. She hoped Dr. Clevenger hadn't left the clinic. They made the last turn and Riley wanted to whoop for joy when she saw lights flickering in the windows.

The clinic was in a large building on a corner with steps leading to the main entrance, but Coop pointed out a sign reading *Large Animal Clinic in the Rear.* He led them around back and past a bank of solar panels to where they found a set of rolling barn-style doors. The doors were closed, but they could hear a generator humming and see light trickling out. They only had to wait a few seconds for the doors to slide open after Coop pounded on the green painted wood.

A young woman with her blond hair pulled into a ponytail and wearing jeans and a tank top stepped through the doorway. She hooked her thumbs in her belt loops and studied them for a moment before saying, "We're closed and not taking new clients."

Riley marched up to her, and said, "Our horse won't survive without emergency treatment. Brent Holverson sent us here. He said Dr. Clevenger would see us."

The woman broke into a smile, exposing the deepest dimples Riley had ever seen. "Uncle Dyl will do anything for friends of Dr. Brent. This way."

"Dyl?" Coop whispered in Riley's ear as the girl led them into the clinic.

"My name's Callie, cause that's where I'm from," she said over her shoulder as they walked. "My mom is Uncle Dyl's sister. She and my Dad sent me out here to train with him and I got stuck here for obvious reasons, but I don't mind. I've always been crazy about animals. Guess it runs in the family. What's wrong with your horse?"

"Chatty," Riley whispered to Coop before raising her voice, and saying, "He injured the skin on his leg about a week ago and it's become infected. We're both doctors and we've been treating the wounds with people meds, but Echo needs more help than we can give."

They entered an open room the size of a basketball court, containing stalls, tables and medical implements. What they didn't see was any animals.

Callie said, "Echo? I love that name. Who are you two?"

As Coop inspected the room, he said, "I'm Coop. This is my wife, Riley."

"Married doctors. Cool. Wait here. I'll get Uncle Dyl."

"Julia would love her," Riley said, as they watched Callie push through a set of swinging doors. She looked at the well-equipped room in wonder. "Cousin Jessie would have loved a room like this."

"He probably trained in a facility like this, just like Callie. I've been thinking the past few days that when we get to Colorado, it might be smart to breed horses and other large animals and learn to treat them. There's going to be an enormous need in the coming years."

Before Riley could respond to Coop's surprising comment, an enormous man of about fifty wearing stained scrubs burst through the doors. He finished gnawing on a chicken wing, then wiped his plate-sized hands on his pants. Riley stifled a giggle at the sight of chicken bits in his gray-streaked beard.

"Evening," he said, grinning. "Call me Dyl. How do you know my cousin?"

Coop shook his hand and said, "He attended a medical seminar of mine in Chicago a couple of years back."

Dyl walked to Echo and pressed his ear to his side. "Well, that's good enough for me. This must be Echo. Fine specimen, but I could tell the instant I walked through the door he's one sick fellow." He straightened and stared down at Riley like it was all her fault. "What happened?"

Riley quietly recounted the accident on the bridge and what they'd done to treat Echo. She was close to tears by the time she finished.

Dyl gripped her shoulder and smiled. "You did your best. Don't worry. I'll fix him."

It sounded like he was going to repair a broken toy, but Riley hoped Dyl was right. He went to work examining Echo and barking orders at Callie, who assisted without hesitation. Coop gestured to some folding chairs behind them. Riley gladly took the suggestion and sank into one with a sigh. Dyl worked for another twenty minutes before walking toward them with his hands on his hips.

"His fever was 104 degrees. Good thing you got here when you did. I dosed him with a drug called Dipyrone even though my supplies are low. It will get the temp right down. That's the simple part. Callie says you're both doctors, so you'll understand this. The deepest laceration is over the fetlock. Infected joint wounds in horses can be dangerous, but this infection looks like it's still localized. It'll take weeks of loving care, but I predict he'll survive. I'll have to keep him here until he's well. Do you live in the area?"

Riley and Coop stared at him in shock. *Weeks?* They were only staying in the city for hours.

"We're just passing through on our way to Colorado," Coop said. "Since we are doctors, Riley's an orthopedist, can't you just tell us how to treat him and give us the meds? We'll trade for them."

"Impossible. This horse has to go easy on that leg, not take a cross-country trip."

Riley had known in her gut that Echo wasn't up to going with them, but hearing her diagnosis confirmed was more than she could take in her exhausted state. She leaned forward and sobbed into her hands while Coop silently rubbed her shoulder.

"Now, there," Dyl said. "None of that. I'll take excellent care of this fella. You can trust me."

"She's pregnant," Coop said. "She cries at the drop of a hat these days."

"Well, I do my own share of blubbering these days," Dyl said.

Riley wiped her face on her shirt and glared at Coop. "You say that like we haven't been through hell the past week. No, these past months. This has nothing to do with me being pregnant. Don't you get it? We have to leave Echo with these strangers."

"Wait a second," Dyl said. "What do you mean, leave Echo? You can't wait for your horse to recover?"

"Trust me, we have good reason for moving on and Kearns' forces are on their way. We saw firsthand what they did to Charleston. Why are you staying?"

He barked out a laugh. "You think I'm going to let those snot-nosed babies order me around? This is my home. It's always been my home, and I won't abandon it. I'm not going anywhere. Stay until Echo's well. I'll put you up with my family."

Coop stood and helped Riley to her feet. "That's a generous offer, but we have to be gone by sunrise. Would you be willing to take Echo in trade? We'd feel better knowing he was in your excellent hands."

Dyl tried to hide his reaction, but Riley caught the slight widening of his eyes. "You're giving me your horse? Do you know how much he'd fetch in trade? I own nothing matching his value I can part with."

Riley half-heartedly searched the room, hoping to find something of value they could take for Echo. She was about to give up when she spotted an item worth its weight in gold on a corner table in Dyl's office. It looked like it was in decent condition, maybe a few years old.

"We'll take that ham radio," she blurted out. "Does it have a backup battery pack?"

Dyl glanced over his shoulder towards his office. "It does, but I'm sorry, Riley. Anything but that. We use the ham to communicate with Callie's parents. She'd be heartbroken if I gave away her only connection to them."

Riley moved closer to him and gently laid her hand on his arm. "I have one daughter in Virginia and another daughter and a son in Colorado. I don't even know if they survived. They don't know I'm alive. Both families they're staying with have ham radios. I'd trade a hundred horses for yours if I had them to give."

"Let her have it, Uncle Dyl," Callie called from where she stood at Echo's side. She gave her new friend a quick scratch behind the ears, then crossed the room in five strides to join them. "I'd miss talking to Mom and Dad, but poor Riley's got kids. They need to know their mom's safe. I would if I was them."

"Think of what you're saying, Callie," Dyl said. "You might not talk to your parents for years or even the rest of their lives."

Callie dismissed his words with a wave of her hand. "Stop being such a hen. I'm young. I'll make it home once this nonsense calms down."

Dyl shook his head. "Your choice." He shifted his gaze to Coop and Riley. "The radio for Echo but give us a chance to reach Callie's parents one last time and let them know."

Riley got up on her toes and kissed his cheek. "You'll never know what this means to me, and thank you, Callie. I understand the sacrifice you're making."

Callie flashed her dimples and gave a quick curtsy.

Riley smiled back, then glanced at her watch. "We need to meet Adrian and Dashay. We'll come back with the cart. That will give Dyl and Callie time to make their call."

Dyl leaned closer to Riley. "Excuse me, did you say Adrian?" When Riley nodded, he asked, "Dr. Adrian Landry?"

Coop and Riley eyed him in confusion.

"How can you know that?" Coop asked.

"I'll show you," Dyl said. He hurried to his office and came back clutching a piece of paper. Holding it out for Coop and Riley to read, he said, "This is how. Adrian's an uncommon name. When I heard Riley say it, I wondered if it was the same person."

Staring back at Riley from the page was a disturbingly accurate sketch of Adrian under the words *#1 Most Wanted*. Below the picture was a list of Adrian's alleged crimes, including treason and murder, with instructions on how to contact Kearns' people if he was spotted. Riley's throat tightened and she couldn't take a breath. As her legs gave way, Coop caught her and lowered her into the chair.

"Put your head between your knees and take deep breaths," he ordered before turning to Dyl with the poster in his fist. "Tell me about this."

"They started showing up around the city a few days ago. Callie brought that copy home this morning."

Riley took a deep breath and jumped to her feet. "It's all lies. Believe me. Kearns is the offender, not Adrian. I can't believe she's making him the scapegoat to cover her crimes."

Coop looked at the paper. "Can we have this?"

"It's of no use to me." Dyl watched as Coop folded it and shoved it in his pocket. "Now I understand your hurry to get out of town by dawn. Are you sure this Adrian character hasn't manipulated you into believing he's innocent?"

"We never said he was innocent, but he's not guilty of these crimes," Riley said, as she started for the door. "We'll be back in one hour for the radio."

Coop rushed to catch up with her as she headed for the street. "Riley, stop. We need to discuss this."

She ignored him and kept going. "We shouldn't leave Adrian

and Dashay exposed out in the open in the park. Talk while we walk."

Coop got into step beside her. "You know what we have to do, right?"

"Yes, we've got to get Adrian far away from here, then hide and protect him."

Coop put a hand on her shoulder and pulled her to a stop. "No, Riley, that's not what we're going to do. We'll warn him, get him situated, and then we part ways. He'll have to make his own way from here."

"Ditching him now is worse than leaving him alone to die in the woods. He's coming with us."

"A week ago, you were ready to strangle the man. Now you're willing to risk your safety for him? I was willing to tolerate him tagging along for the ride, but that was before his very presence put my wife and child in danger. He's being hunted by the most powerful authority in the country. You know what Kearns is capable of. If we're caught with Adrian, who knows what they'll do to us."

Riley paused for a moment to clear her thoughts. Coop's argument made logical sense, but that didn't make it right. Adrian was the last man in the world she thought she'd defend, but she felt obligated to do it.

"You know how I feel about Adrian," she said. "That man gets on my last nerve, but that doesn't mean I'm willing to leave him at the mercy of Kearns' brutes any more than I could leave him at Branson's mercy in the compound. You helped me save his life then. Do the same now."

"The compound was different. We just gave him medical treatment. We weren't at risk."

"They'll torture and kill him, Coop. You know that. Adrian's the only person in the world who knows that Kearns kept her mouth shut about the CME. She stood by and watched millions die and millions more suffer rather than risk her own ass. We could have been most of the way to Colorado if we'd known the truth. Kearns may not have been able to predict the extent of the damage the CME would cause, but I believe her choice was a calculated power grab. Look what she's doing with that power. Destroying more lives."

"You're making *my* point, Riley. She's powerful and dangerous and will stop at nothing to consolidate her chokehold on this country. You want to bring down her wrath on us? Yes, Adrian's at risk, but he's just some guy we crossed paths with. We've saved his life more than once. We don't owe him anything."

"I can't justify my argument rationally, but my gut is telling me we have an obligation to protect him and keep him alive. This may be one of those turning points in history where someone made a choice with long-term ramifications that put them at risk. Or maybe it's just the doctor in me not wanting to send Adrian like a lamb to slaughter. Either way, I'm determined to do this."

As Coop studied her, the frustration and fear were etched in his face. Riley hated going against his wishes for the sake of a man she could barely tolerate, but Adrian's life had value and she felt he had an important role to play.

Coop put his cap on and took a deep breath. "Everything in me is screaming that this is wrong, but I made a promise to go along with whatever you said. You've made that a hard promise to keep more than once, Riley, but I'll trust you. Don't make me regret it."

Riley threw her arms around him and held him tight. "I appreciate your trust in me. I'm right. You'll see." She released him, then tugged on his hand to get him moving. "I feel like we're characters on a vital mission in an espionage novel. Let's get to Adrian before Kearns' people capture him."

"Feels more like a Greek tragedy to me," Coop said, as he reluctantly got into step with her.

Riley spit on her knuckles three times to ward off evil as she ran along the dark, deserted street toward the park. Only time would tell which of them was right or if they both were.

———

Riley ran to Dashay and Adrian as soon as she spotted them and waved for them to follow her to a dark stand of trees where Coop was waiting. He handed the most-wanted flier to Adrian and shined his flashlight on it while Dashay read over his shoulder.

Adrian stared at the paper in stunned silence. After several moments, he whispered, "What are you going to do with me? They're offering a reward."

Riley grabbed the flier and tore it to pieces, then let them blow away on the wind. "Do you actually believe we'd trade your life for shelter and supplies? Give us some credit."

He raised his frightened eyes to her. "You were wishing me dead last week."

She linked her arm in his and started walking, pulling him along. "Haven't you gotten it through your thick head yet that I didn't mean it? I was just distraught over Brooks. Coop and I are committed to getting you to safety, wherever that means. Dashay, it's your choice to stay with us or not. Just be advised this little field trip of ours could get a lot dicier."

Dashay took Adrian's other arm. "You say that like it isn't already. We knew Kearns could be after Adrian from the beginning. What's the plan?"

As Coop led Biscuit toward Dyl's clinic, he explained to them about Echo. "Once we have the ham radio and say goodbye to Echo, we'll get a few hours of sleep, then be on the road before sunrise. I'll ask Dyl to help us reroute our way out of here. We can trust him. Avoiding population centers will slow our progress, but we have no choice if we're going to protect Adrian and dodge Kearns' army."

Dashay let go of Adrian and came to a halt. "How will Nico find us if we do that?"

The others avoided her gaze. The thought had crossed Riley's mind, but she'd held out little hope of Nico finding them since they left Charleston.

"I'm going to stay in Huntington and wait for him. We'll catch up with you together."

"If you stay, you'll be trapped here," Riley said. "That's exactly what Nico was trying to protect you from."

Dashay shook her head. "He was trying to keep me from getting caught in the middle of a war. That won't happen here. Maybe this Dyl will let me stay and work for him until Nico gets here."

"It didn't look like he had much business and he had Callie," Coop said over his shoulder. "I refuse to leave you behind, Dashay. Nico would never forgive me. We'll help you find him once we reach safety."

Adrian crossed his arms and said, "No. Leave me."

Riley glared at him. "Are you insane? You wouldn't last a day."

"I got myself into this situation. I won't be responsible for putting your lives in jeopardy, and you're under a time crunch with the baby coming, Riley. I could find a hollow up in the nearby hills and hunker down until the danger passes. My education and knowledge of plants will get me by. I'll live off the land until this blows over. I'm not helpless."

Dashay waved her hand at Coop to get moving and retook Adrian's arm. "Don't be ridiculous. We'll go together and figure the rest out later. You can help me figure out a way to leave clues for Nico. If that fails, I have his family's address in New Mexico."

Riley watched Dashay out of the corner of her eye, knowing it was breaking her heart to sever all chances of reconnecting with Nico. When Riley insisted to Coop that Adrian come with them, she hadn't stopped to think how much of a sacrifice protecting him would be for all of them. *Long-term ramifications,* she thought as her determination wavered until she reminded herself that Adrian was under immediate threat. Kearns' people were the ones distributing the fliers. That meant they were already in Huntington.

"This is a discussion for later," she said. "Pick it up, Coop. We need to get off this street."

When they reached the clinic, Dyl eyed Adrian with suspicion as he worked with Coop to find an alternate route out of the region. Riley enlisted Adrian to help carry the radio rig out to the cart, then she and Dashay gave a much-improved Echo a tearful goodbye.

Riley hugged Callie, then surprised Dyl with a hug, too. "Take care of my boy," she said. "Maybe we'll be back this way to say hello someday."

Dyl stepped away and blew his nose loudly on a huge paisley handkerchief. "You have my word that I'll do my best. Safe travels, my friends."

Riley hurried out and took hold of Biscuit's reins. "It's down to you now, friend. Take us where we need to go."

After what felt like five minutes, Coop was shaking Riley awake. "Time to ditch this popsicle stand, babe. Don't forget to nibble your crackers before you get out of bed."

She sat up and wrapped her unruly mop of hair into a knot. "Thanks for the reminder. I'll meet you outside in ten minutes."

Coop kissed her, then threw his backpack over his shoulder on the way out. Riley looked around and frowned while she munched a cracker, wondering how long it would be before she'd sleep under a roof in a proper bed. "This will be our life now, always on the run," she said to the empty room, hoping Kearns would give up at some point and trouble wouldn't dog them all the way to Colorado.

After throwing on her last clean set of clothes and brushing her teeth with bottled water, she went out the front door to join the others. They were gathered around the opposite side of the cart, chatting enthusiastically over something Riley couldn't see. She quickened her pace and was delighted when she came around the cart to find four bikes gleaming in the first rays of dawn.

"Look," Dashay said, excitedly waving her over.

She patted the seat of the smallest bike, and said, "Where did these come from?"

In answer, Coop held a card out to her. She raised her eyebrows in question, then read it.

Dear Drs. Riley and Coop,

When cousin Dyl told me your story, I knew I had to help, so we rounded up these bikes. We hope they'll get you to safety long before the new arrival makes an appearance. As an OB/GYN, Riley, I recommend you ride in the cart after your second trimester. I hope you don't mind I took your old bike to fix up and pay forward to someone else.

We also left a few packs of medical supplies and food for humans and horses (with instructions). Use them well.

Our best to all of you and Godspeed.

Dr. Brent

Riley's eyes teared up, so she bit the side of her cheek to ward off a crying jag. "Glad to know there's goodness left in this world," she whispered.

Coop put his arm around her shoulders. "Hopefully, much more than we know. We're going to need it more than ever."

Dashay tossed her pack into the cart and got on the neon purple bike. "Enough of this mush. Let's get out before the cavalry descends. Riley, that tiny pink bike must be for you."

"Funny," Riley said, as she shoved her pack in the bike's flowered basket and climbed on the glittery seat. Emily had a bike just like and made her feel closer to her. She hadn't ridden a bike in seven or eight months, so she took a few loops around the yard to get the feel. Adrian stood next to his bike, silently watching her.

"What's the holdup?" Dashay asked as she rode past him. "Mount that thing and let's go."

Adrian gingerly threw his leg over the bike. "I haven't ridden since I was a child, and I wasn't much good at it then. I'm apprehensive."

"We'll need to ride slowly to keep pace with Biscuit," she said, as she circled around him. "You've got this."

Coop walked his bike next to Biscuit and wrapped the reins around his hand before climbing on. "Your choices are the bike or stay and die. Walking's not an option."

"I might die on the bike," Adrian mumbled.

"Bike it is," Coop said as he started pedaling and got Biscuit moving.

Dashay let out a whoop and took the lead. Riley got behind the cart, leaving Adrian staring after them.

Riley glanced back and smiled to encourage him. "You know the saying, 'it's like riding a bike.'"

Adrian pushed off and wobbled a few times before stabilizing and getting into rhythm. He grinned proudly and moved next to Riley. "You're right. It's coming back to me. I think I'll prefer this to walking."

"My feet agree," Riley said.

"I haven't thanked you, Riley," he mumbled. "Your feelings are no secret, but you didn't have to stick your neck out for me. I've done nothing to deserve your kindness. That changes from this point on. I'll make sure you don't regret it."

Riley glanced at him and gave him a half-grin. "I appreciate that, and I'll hold you to it. The information you possess about Kearns could destroy her. My gut tells me the time will come when you'll be forced to divulge what you know. Will you be prepared to do that?"

He grew quiet while he mulled over her question. Riley was

anxious for his answer. Courage wasn't a characteristic Adrian had demonstrated in the time she'd known him. She wouldn't go so far as to brand him a coward, but he'd shown more than once he cared more for his own self-interest than the wellbeing of those around him. She hoped he'd learned enough that when given a second chance, he'd make the honorable choice.

"My honest answer right now is I hope it doesn't come to that, but if it does, I want to do what's right. I'm ashamed of my past failures and don't want to repeat them. I may need you to keep me in line."

"You can count on that," she said, pleased to see a glimmer of progress. "And it's all we can ask."

They rode in silence for a time, each lost in thought and doing their best to keep pace with Coop and Dashay. Riley was grateful for the time to consider if she'd judged Adrian too harshly and held him to too high a standard. He'd made mistakes, no question, but she knew little of his life before that moment. Did she owe it to him to find out? If she was going to risk her life, the least she could do was find out who the man was. She had nothing but time to dig a little deeper.

CHAPTER NINE

JULIA PAUSED from hammering in a tent stake to watch the incredible colors spread across the sky as the sun slipped below the horizon. They'd spent the late afternoon getting drenched by rain, but the storm had blown east and left behind a stunning sunset.

They'd wound their way south for the past few days from Knoxville, Tennessee to just north of Birmingham, Alabama. Uncle Mitch had plotted a more southerly route, hoping it would keep Kearns' troops off their trail if they were still following them. It had worked so far. They'd seen no signs of the military in the small towns they'd passed.

None of the group was happy about having to go so far south since that route meant a longer trip. Unlike the others, Julia had spent most of the year on the road and was past ready to get home and stop running. If they didn't run into trouble, Uncle Mitch estimated they'd reach Colorado Springs in ten weeks. That put their arrival in August. Julia thought that was optimistic since they always ran into trouble. In her opinion, they wouldn't see Colorado until October. What she cared about most was that they got there before the snows started.

She'd had enough of getting stuck in the snow to last the rest of her life.

As the sky darkened, she finished pounding the stake in, then dropped onto the ground to munch on a protein bar. Aunt Beth said it was too late to bother with a hot meal. It had been the same for the past three days since Uncle Mitch was pushing them pretty hard. He'd promised that morning before they left the camp that if it was safe, they'd spend two nights outside Birmingham. They needed to replenish their stores and rest the horses.

As much as Julia was in a hurry to get home, she was all for taking a break. Their camp was in a beautiful spot near a lake, and she was enjoying getting to see the southern part of the country. Her family had usually flown when they'd taken vacations, but all she saw was the view from her plane window. If life ever got back to normal, she hoped to take some road trips to get to know more of the country.

"Julia," Uncle Mitch called, startling her out of her thoughts.

When she looked up, he waved her over to where he was sitting on a hunting stool at a small table with the ham radio and dual band VHF/UHF antenna set up and hooked to the solar battery. It had become their ritual each morning and evening to get on the radio and communicate with people around the country, and sometimes, even around the world. Reports from the east had become sporadic, probably because the military had taken the radios away from civilians, but she and Uncle Mitch had still connected with people in surrounding areas and further west. Julia continued to hope that one day, they'd reach Grandma and Grandpa in Colorado.

She hurried over to Uncle Mitch and watched quietly as he gave his call sign and said, "Monitoring." Next came the part Julia didn't like, waiting for someone to respond. It could take several minutes for someone to answer. They got lucky that day. The radio crackled right away and a woman in San Antonio, Texas, answered. They'd communicated with her before, so they exchanged information on their situations and Mitch updated her on the progress of the western movement of the military.

They interacted with five or six other people over the following thirty minutes until Julia yawned. Uncle Mitch was about to stop broadcasting for the night when the radio crackled again, and a voice Julia hadn't heard for a month came across the receiver.

Her mom's voice trembled as she gave her call sign, and said, "Uncle Mitch? Is that you? It's me, Riley."

"Yes, it's me, Riley Kate," he answered in a hoarse voice, trying to control his emotions. "I have someone else here with me."

Julie grabbed the handset and cried, "It's me, Mom! It's Julia! Where are you? Are you okay? Is Coop there?"

Her mom laughed and cried at the same time in answer. "I'm perfectly fine and so is Coop."

"Hey, WP," Coop said. "How's the leg, Champ?"

"I'm great, Coop. It's awesome to hear your voice. Where are you? We're in Birmingham, Alabama."

There was a moment's silence before her mom said, "Why in the world are you in Alabama?"

Uncle Mitch took the handset back from Julia. "President Kearns' troops took over the ranch. We escaped just in time. There are fifty of us here, plus the horses."

"That's horrible, Uncle Mitch. I'm sorry you lost the ranch but relieved you all got out safely."

"Me, too. We're heading to you. Should be in Colorado Springs by August. How far have you gotten?"

"You're headed to Colorado? I didn't think I'd see you for years, if ever. That's incredible news. We have news of our own. You're going to have another brother or sister, Julia."

Julia jumped up and squealed in delight. "Seriously?" she said over Mitch's shoulder. "When?"

"Not exactly sure, but we estimate mid-November. It's more

than I could have dreamed that you'll be there in time for the birth. There's someone else here who wants to say hi."

Julia couldn't imagine who it was, but hoped it was Angie. She held her breath until a voice came on, and said, "Is that my Julia? How're you doing, girl?"

It took Julia a second to put the voice with a face. "Dashay? What are you doing with Mom and Coop?"

"That's a story I'll save for when I see you."

"Is Angie there, too?"

"She's not, but don't worry. She's fine, Julia. She went home to her kids."

"That's so great. I've worried about her every day. Where are you guys?"

The others in the camp heard Julia's squeal and had gathered around the radio. Aunt Beth gave Julia's hand a squeeze and Holly fist bumped her.

Her mom came back on, and said, "We're in a small town, southwest of Louisville, Kentucky. We have Biscuit with us. He's been a trooper. I'm sorry to tell you, Uncle Mitch, but Aurora was killed by a bear. It was so awful. Echo's alive, but we had to leave him with this amazing vet in Huntington, West Virginia. His leg got injured but he'll recover. I'm hoping to go back for him someday. He's the reason we got the ham rig. We traded Echo for it."

"That's fine, Pumpkin," Uncle Mitch said. "Don't worry about the horses. Sounds like you've had quite the adventure."

The line was quiet again, until her mom said, "We have but we're good. The rains slowed us down at first, but we got some bikes, and we're making good time. I'm sorry for running off without saying goodbye but was afraid I wouldn't have been able to tear myself away. Guess it wasn't necessary since you're on the road now, too. I'm sorry I took your horses and provisions, Uncle Mitch. I needed to get to Jared and Emily. I'm deeply indebted to you for taking care of Julia."

"All is forgiven, and Julia is like another granddaughter to us. We won't let anything happen to her!" Uncle Mitch said.

Julia leaned closer to the handset. "Are you really fine, Mom? I remember how sick you get when you're pregnant."

"I really am, sweetheart. I was sick at first, but I'm past that and feeling strong. You know how much I enjoy biking."

"I do," Julia whispered, trying not to cry.

Aunt Beth took the handset and pressed the button to speak. "Hello, dear. It's Beth. Congratulations on your news."

"Let's connect every night around this time, when possible," Mitch said. "Maybe we can meet farther down the road and travel together."

"We'd love that, but it may not be possible. I'll explain later. We need to sign off now. Battery's running low. We'll try to reach you tomorrow. We have so much to tell you."

"We all love and miss you, Pumpkin. Take care of yourself and that little one."

"I will. We love you all, too, especially you, Julia. I miss my Warrior Princess."

"And I miss my Red Queen," Julia said. "Love you, Mom."

After they signed off, Julia lowered herself onto a log and sobbed into her hands. Holly dropped next to her and threw her arms around her. "Riley and Coop are alive!" she said. "It's the best ever, and a new baby, too. Just think, Julia, we'll be there when it's born. How cool is that?"

Julia hugged her back and the two of them laughed and cried until Mitch told them that was enough sniveling, and it was time for bed. They moved to their tent but stayed up talking for hours until Holly finally drifted off. Julia was too excited to sleep and lay awake till dawn imagining the reunion with her mom, Coop, and the rest of the family in Colorado. She realized it was the first time since the CME she believed deep down they'd make it home. It was almost more happiness than she could handle.

She grabbed her flashlight and the journal Aunt Beth had

given her to record their journey. She poured her feelings onto the page as fast as the pen could move, looking forward to the day when she'd share her feelings with her new brother or sister. Satisfied, she returned the journal to its hiding place in her pack and closed her eyes for two hours of sleep before it was time to get back on the road and do it all over again.

Colonel Yeager leaned against a corner table in the missing mayor's office and watched as Dr. Walser gave a description of Adrian Landry's companions to the sketch artist. Yeager already had descriptions of Dashay Robinson and Brooks Dunbar from his informant, Darcy Meade, but Dr. Walser had been far less obliging than she was, at first.

Yeager didn't bother threatening to lock him up if he didn't cooperate. He'd learned through his long years of service that the best way to get results was to give people what they thought they wanted, so he offered the good doctor a ride to Cincinnati if he spilled. Yeager had expected some resistance, but Walser couldn't share information fast enough once he was promised a free ticket home.

It had been a struggle for Yeager to hide his disgust at how easily the man caved. Where was the courage and loyalty that odd veterinarian, Dylan Clevenger, had shown? Yeager knew he could have bribed, threatened, and tortured that man all day and gotten nothing. The world needed more people like him, even if he was an eccentric. Yeager depended on people like Walser to get what he needed and knew better than most how to exploit and manipulate weaknesses.

When the artist finished the sketches, Yeager ordered his assistant to drop them at the science museum where they had an old crank mimeograph machine waiting, then get Walser to Cincinnati. Kearns wouldn't have approved if she'd known he was letting people through her net, but all he cared about was fulfilling his mission. Yeager didn't care in the least about *President* Kearns' ridiculous zones. He viewed her actions as a waste of resources. It was his opinion that instead of fighting useless battles with residents and herding them like cattle, she should utilize her forces to rebuild infrastructure and reestablish society.

He'd almost let his thoughts on the matter slip in his last meeting with her, but she was the type of leader who cared little for the opinions of her underlings, and he didn't want to jeopardize his position. It was all he had left in the world.

It had been nothing more than a stroke of luck that he'd been the one to get Kearns' family and her cronies out of DC after the CME. He'd just gotten word that he'd lost his wife and daughter to a natural gas explosion in their home and was planning to find a hole to crawl into and die when his commanding officer ordered him to make his way to the Vice President at the White House. He'd allowed events to sweep him along since. At least it gave him a reason to get up each morning.

That was harder some days than others, especially when he had to commit distasteful or questionable acts in the name of his Commander-in-Chief. He'd always been an obedient, hardworking soldier who followed orders without question and believed in his mission. It was how he'd risen through the ranks, but that all changed the day the CME struck and thrust him into the new hellish world.

He didn't believe in Kearns' mission or respect her as a person or a leader, but he'd learned how to numb himself to his emotions and get the job done. He wasn't sure what he'd do once *Daybreak* was in custody, but he was getting close to capturing him and was more determined than ever to get the job done.

Once the hundreds of fliers with the sketches of Landry and his companions were distributed, all he had to do was follow the breadcrumbs. He expected that there would be others as easy to manipulate as Dr. Walser. Operation Daybreak would be tied up in a matter of days, and he'd be free to ponder his next course of action. He could stay in Kearns' service or melt into the countryside where she'd never find him. Both options had merits worth considering.

———

Riley listened to the drops pelting the tent, bemoaning the fact that the rains were back. They'd spent the past four days dodging ever deepening puddles and rivers while trying to stay dry and keep out of sight. Every piece of clothing she owned was drenched and she had no way to dry them.

She rolled on her side facing Coop and said, "I know we're far behind schedule and running low on food, but we should hole up here for a few days to let the rains pass. I feel like I have mushrooms growing between my toes.'"

Coop turned onto his back and tucked his hand behind his head. "You may be right. If the water gets any deeper on the roads, it won't be safe on the bikes, not to mention how hard it makes Biscuit work. I suppose it can't keep raining forever."

"Not according to Adrian, who droned on about the drastic atmospheric conditions all day. Fortunately, it was raining hard enough to drown out most of what he said."

"I'll let you take charge of Biscuit when we get back on the road. I'll take a turn babysitting Adrian. From what you have heard, is any of what he says relevant to our situation?"

"He admits most of it is speculation since Earth hasn't been hit by a solar storm of this magnitude in modern times, but he thinks the weather changes are tied to the CME. It makes sense. Almost ninety-nine percent of artificial emissions stopped in an instant. Suddenly turning off those emissions might well create these climatic changes. Adrian says no one has ever predicted that a massive CME would change weather patterns, but no one alive has ever lived through one." Riley yanked her damp sock off and tossed it across the tent. "Whatever the reason, if this keeps up, we're in for a long, soggy journey."

"Adrian says the weather is definitely impacting your ability to connect with Mitch on the ham radio."

Riley sighed, then scooted closer to Coop and laid her head on his chest. She'd been overjoyed at finally connecting with them the previous week. They'd made contact two more times but hadn't been able to reach them since the rain started.

"I just hope they aren't worried something happened to us," she mumbled.

"From what Mitch says of the direction they're taking, they're on a parallel route about three-hundred miles south. Maybe they're experiencing the same storms." He reached up and rubbed her back. "We'll get in touch with them soon. Let's try again in the morning. We should get some sleep."

Riley looked up at him. "Why? If we're not going anywhere tomorrow, we can sleep all day."

"Because we need supplies, babe. I know you hate it when I say this, but you're eating for two, remember? I'll ride out on Biscuit in the morning. A city called Evansville is just north of the Ohio River, only about fifteen miles from here."

Riley sat up and wrapped her arms around her knees. "Only fifteen miles? You say that like you're just making a quick trip to the convenience store. It will take the entire day just to travel there and back, even if you push it and the roads aren't flooded. And what about the two of us sticking together? You're just going to go off and leave me? Why don't you just grab me a diet soda and some chocolate peanuts while you're at it?"

Coop stared at the top of the tent while he fished up an answer. No matter what he said, it wouldn't be good enough for Riley. He'd gone off alone once against her wishes and they got separated for weeks without her knowing if he was alive or dead. She was determined to not to live through that heartache again.

Coop blew out a breath and said, "I made a promise to never leave your side, but you know as well as I do that's just not practical anymore. You need rest, and we need food and medicines. I'll take every precaution and you have my word that if I see the slightest risk, I'll turn back." When she looked away and didn't respond, he gently put his finger under her chin and turned her to face him. "Admit it, Riley, I have to do this."

Riley wrapped his hand in hers and lifted it to her lips. "Fine, but at least take Dashay. Biscuit can carry both of you. It's not safe for any of us to go out alone."

"I can move faster on my own, but it is safer to go in pairs. I'll ask her in the morning. Satisfied?"

She shrugged, then gave a quick nod, glad that he was open to compromise. "I'd rather be the one going, but you're right that I need rest. I'd forgotten how much energy carrying an extra passenger takes."

He gave her a tender kiss, then pulled her down next to him. "That's just what Biscuit is going to think tomorrow, but I appreciate that. It's not my first choice either, but we haven't seen signs of the military for two days. Maybe the rain is hindering their progress, too."

She settled next to him in the sleeping bag. "I suppose I could be overreacting."

He yawned and said, "Understandable after what we've been through. Love you, babe. Go to sleep."

He closed his eyes and was asleep in seconds. Riley watched his chest rising and falling in a slow, steady rhythm, wondering what forces had been at play for her to have stumbled upon such a remarkable man to have at her side, not only their cross-country trek, but for the rest of her life. She brushed her lips on his cheek, then snuggled into the crook of his arm, counting herself as the most fortunate woman alive.

Riley basked in the welcome sight of the sun shining into the tent. She felt for Coop to awaken him, but his side of the sleeping bag was empty. She jumped up and pulled on her boots before rushing out of the tent. She threw her arms out and lifted her face to the sun, then twirled in the mud at the luscious feel of it.

Dashay, who was watching her from a camp chair, laughed, and said, "Feels incredible, don't it?"

Riley went over and took her hands to pull her out of the chair. She spun her around but had to stop when her stomach did a somersault. She doubled over and grabbed her belly.

"Forgot about this guy," she gasped. "He's clearly not fond of spinning."

Dashay laughed harder and went back to the chair. "So, you've decided it's a he?"

Riley shrugged. "Fifty-fifty shot. I'd like for it to be a boy. Then, I'll have two of each, but I'll love it no matter what."

"I didn't doubt that. It's good to see you smile. You've been a bear the past few days."

Riley dropped into the chair next to her and took a few slow breaths to calm her queasiness. "Sorry about that. I have an aversion to monsoons. I'm thrilled to see we're getting a reprieve." She scanned the camp and frowned when she didn't see Biscuit or Coop. "Please, don't tell me my husband left without you."

"He didn't. He found a creek down the hill and took Biscuit to water him and give him a good feed before we go. You sure you wouldn't rather I stay? I'm not sure how comfortable I feel leaving you alone with Adrian."

Riley chuckled. "I promise not to strangle him."

"Not what I meant. I'm talking about how much help he'll be if you have any trouble."

"Surprising as this may sound, I think he'll step up if it comes to it. He just hasn't had to, yet. Besides, I'm more than man enough for both of us."

Dashay barked out a laugh at that just as Adrian walked up to them. He put his hands on his hips and cocked his head. "What's so funny? Not laughing at my expense, are you?"

Dashay snorted as she tried to stop laughing, but Riley said, "Wouldn't dream of it. Are you aware of the plan for the day?"

He set the plants he'd harvested on the small folding table and sat on the ice chest. "Coop informed me. Guess it's just us today." Dashay broke into a fresh round of laughter, and Riley had to bite her cheek to keep from joining her. Adrian nodded toward Dashay. "What's with her this morning? She's not usually the giggly type."

"Just a joke I made that's not appropriate for mixed company." She gestured at the plants. "What have you got there?"

Riley hardly heard the answer as he droned on about the foliage he'd found surrounding the camp. It was a never-ending mystery to Riley how anyone could be so enamored with plants. She reminded herself she should be grateful since the nutrients and medicinal properties they provided had been useful. She just couldn't get as excited about it as Adrian did.

"Is Coop still planning to go on his run now that the sun is out?" Adrian asked. "If the clear skies hold out, we could get going in the afternoon."

"He is going," Coop called as he came over the hill with Biscuit. He tethered him to a small tree, then walked over and kissed Riley's cheek. "Morning. Glad to see you had a good sleep." He pulled an energy bar from his pocket and took a bite before turning to Adrian. "Riley needs rest, and we need to dry out and replenish. I'm hoping to get some info on what we can expect coming up ahead of us, too."

"We'll do laundry and get our gear dried out and repacked," Riley said.

"Watch yourself around that creek. It's flooded and swift. There's an eddy about a hundred yards to the west of the trail that leads to it."

Coop gave her a look full of meaning. She nodded and said, "We'll be careful."

"I'll fix a hot meal for tonight," Adrian said. "I'm sick of bars and cold canned food."

"Perfect. Keep the Glock and an extra magazine close to you to keep the bears and other unfriendlies away," Coop said. "Ready, Dashay? We should get going."

In answer, she stood and kissed Riley's other cheek. "Take good care of Adrian."

Dashay laughed all the way to Biscuit. Riley watched as she secured the .243 Savage rifle and a box of ammo in case of trouble. Riley could still hear the echo of Biscuit's hoofs long after they rode out of sight.

───────────

Riley groaned, then glanced at her watch when she felt the first drop of rain on her head. It was already six-thirty. The day had passed in a rush without her stopping to notice. She and Adrian had been busy cleaning their gear and inventorying the supplies. The clouds had blown in around four, but she'd hoped the rain would hold off until Coop and Dashay returned. She crossed her fingers and prayed that they'd just get a light drizzle.

"Food's ready," Adrian called to her from the campfire. "Better eat while it's hot. Don't know how long before the rain douses the fire."

Riley stood and stretched her back before pulling the clean clothes from the line. They were still damp and would dry by morning in the tent. The downside of the sunshine returning was that it brought the humidity with it. She was used to the dry climate of Colorado and wasn't prepared for the steamy vapors rising in waves from the ground as the temperature climbed. She was drenched in sweat minutes after scrubbing the clothes. If

Adrian hadn't been nearby, she would have stripped down and worked in her underwear.

After hanging the clothes in the tent, she joined him at the fire. He handed her a bowl of delicious smelling soup made from rabbit meat, canned vegetables, and plants Adrian had found that day. She had to resist the urge to gulp it in one swallow.

"You're in the wrong vocation," she told him between bites. "If life ever gets back to normal, you should open a restaurant. You'd kill it."

He stopped eating and eyed her over the top of his glasses. "That may not be a bad idea. Even if life gets back to normal, as you call it, I won't be reading solar data from satellites for decades, if I live that long."

Riley got up and refilled her bowl, then said, "Is it possible we'll see a return of electrical grids and technology in our lifetimes? Humankind has invented those things before. Why can't we do it again?"

"It's a matter of numbers. So many of the minds capable of recreating our world perished. The few of us that survived will have to pass that knowledge down to the next generations and rely on them as the population grows. As you well know, humankind's primary focus will be mere survival for years to come. Once we remaster food and tool production, sanitation, and medical care, we can turn our minds to technology."

"Humans are adaptable and innovative, so I choose to have a rosier outlook. I'm counting on existing know-how to speed up the process."

Adrian finished his soup, then rinsed the bowl in a bucket of clean water. "Tell yourself what you want. Like I told you when we met, we're looking at a mid-nineteenth century existence for a generation at least." The rain started falling in a steady stream. "We'd better get the gear in the cart and covered."

The two of them rushed around in the downpour, repacking and replacing the tarp over their supplies. Riley was in her tent setting up the ham radio thirty minutes later. She attempted to reach Uncle Mitch on and off for an hour with no luck and finally gave up in frustration.

She turned the radio off and grabbed the novel out of her pack she'd taken from the house in Huntington. She'd been too exhausted each night to read, but now she needed the distraction that night to keep her mind off Coop and Dashay. She flicked on her solar-powered flashlight and leaned against the rolled sleeping bags and pillows. The story drew her in and held her attention for an hour, but as the rain grew heavier, it became more difficult to stay focused.

She set the book aside and crossed her legs to meditate. It reminded her of doing the same in her DC hotel room on the day the CME struck as she waited for Coop to return with news. Her thoughts shifted from the horrors of that night to events a day earlier. Coop had kissed her for the first time in the hotel lounge, then she returned to her room and fantasized about him sharing her luxurious king-sized bed. That had been her last night, knowing peace and contentment. None of them could have predicted the waking nightmare that awaited them less than twenty-four hours later.

She shook her head to clear it and started again. Ignoring the howling wind and pelting rain, she focused on her breathing and starting with her feet, relaxed her muscles and imagined herself resting on a cloud of cotton. When she reached her abdomen, she pictured her growing baby floating inside, and smiled. She was about to shift her thoughts to her torso when she felt a gentle tap of movement from the baby for the first time. She opened her eyes and gazed down at her belly.

"Well, hello there. Thank you for reminding me I'm not alone."

She closed her eyes and relaxed her muscles. She was rewarded with another kick. With her mood lifted, she made up her bed, then climbed inside and wrapped her arms around herself. No matter what lay ahead, she had a duty to get herself home alive and safe to bring her child into the world. With renewed determination, she closed her eyes and drifted off to sleep, despite the storm raging just beyond her walls.

The steady downpour continued throughout the following day with no sign of Coop and Dashay. Riley invited Adrian to join her in her tent and keep her company. They played cards and Adrian instructed her on the uses of plants they'd find in the areas they'd travel through. She didn't remember half of what he said, but it helped the time pass.

When it was time for bed, she asked if he'd be uncomfortable sleeping in her tent. "Not in the least," he'd said. "I think of you as a little sister."

She wasn't sure how she felt about that, but she was grateful when he brought his sleeping bag and gear from his tent, and they chatted just loud enough to hear each other over the wind and rain. Adrian eventually fell asleep mid-sentence. Riley gave meditation another shot, hoping to feel the baby move. She'd told Adrian about her experience the previous night and was surprised when he showed interest. It reminded her he hadn't just sprung into life in a vacuum. He had a wife and two daughters out in the world somewhere. She made a mental note to ask about them in the morning, then laid down, hoping to sleep.

The second night didn't go as well as the first. She'd spent hours tossing and turning, only dozing off for sporadic moments.

She'd been asleep for an hour when she woke at dawn and realized the rain had stopped. She poked her head out of the tent to find the camp under six inches of water. She was grateful they'd thought to pitch the tent on the highest ground in the area. Adrian was still sleeping, so she quietly put her boots on and went out to use the toilet bucket. The clouds still lingered, but they were high and thin. Riley hoped that meant they'd dissipate once the sun rose.

She sloshed through the water and pulled the bucket off the cart to carry to Dashay's tent. A wave of sadness washed over her at seeing her friend's belongings tossed around in a jumbled mess. Dashay had an abundance of amazing qualities, but neatness wasn't one of them. Riley closed her eyes and tried to call up the sound of Dashay's laughter as she and Coop had ridden away from camp, but all she heard was silence.

After relieving herself, she emptied the bucket downhill from the camp and went to get something to eat. She and Adrian were almost out of food and had made a rationing plan before going to sleep. If Coop and Dashay didn't return within the next four days, they'd have no choice but to go in search of supplies. Riley loathed the idea of leaving, even if only for a few hours, but they couldn't just sit still and starve to death.

She took her pack to Dashay's tent and dug out a roll of fruit leather and a baggie of squirrel jerky. As she chewed on the tough, dry food, she let her mind wander into territory she'd avoided since Coop had become overdue. She had to admit that she might be forced to make gut-wrenching choices. She looked around and remembered that Dashay had made a similar choice when she left Nico. Riley chided herself for not being more sensitive to what Dashay had done. Would she be as strong if it came to that?

She heard Adrian call her, so she stood with a sigh and went to see what he wanted.

"This isn't a great way to greet the day," he said, as she walked toward him. He scratched his head and gazed up at the sky. "Hopefully, these clouds will burn off."

Riley looked down at her boots buried in six inches of water. "Just what I was thinking. Adrian, we need to discuss how long we'll wait before moving on. I hate the idea, but we can't just stay here in the middle of nowhere forever."

"No, we can't. My vote is we give them another two days. We have enough food to subsist on for that long. Then, we try to find out what happened to them."

Tears pooled in Riley's eyes at the thought, but Adrian was right. She couldn't start heading west without answers. She nodded and wiped her eyes. "We're not there yet, so let's make the most of today. Is it worth trying to start a fire on higher ground?"

"Possibly, if we can find dry kindling. Even the wood under the cart is soaked."

They searched the area and found enough dry wood under a thick strand of trees to make a fire. They carried rocks to a knoll behind Riley's tent and made a ring of stones to keep the wood out of the mud. Riley watched silently as Adrian worked for half an hour to get the kindling to light. She gave a cheer when the flames took, then carried their chairs to the fire. The clouds parted the instant they sat down and the temperature rose rapidly.

Adrian fished two cans of beans out of the cart and poured them into a pan to heat. Riley had never been a fan of beans, but they were an excellent source of nutrition and the best they had on hand. She finished the entire can in order to keep her strength up. She was sweating by the time they'd finished their meager meal.

When she removed her hoodie and wiped her forehead with it, Adrian said, "At least the ground will dry in a hurry."

"Is this weather typical for early June here? We're not too far from Saint Louis. You must have traveled there in summer to visit your wife's family."

"We did a few times. It might be slightly warmer than I remember, but they get heavy rains and flooding this time of year, occasionally."

Riley poked a stick at the fire as she said, "Tell me about them."

Adrian raised his eyebrows when he looked up at her. "Who?"

"Your family."

"You're really interested in hearing about them?"

Riley chuckled. "More than hearing about plants."

He smiled. "Fair enough. Where do I start?"

"Tell me how you met your wife."

Adrian rubbed his chin while he thought, then stopped and his eyes widened. "Did you hear that?"

"Hear what?" Riley asked as she heard a horse whinny. She jumped up and faced the direction the sound came from. A second later, she caught sight of Biscuit lumbering toward them with Coop and Dashay on his back. She headed for them at a full run. As she got closer, she could see Coop was slumped over the saddle.

When she reached them, Dashay jumped down with a splash, and said, "Hurry, Riley. Coop's sick. We've got to get him to your tent."

As if on cue, Coop let go of the reins and toppled over. Adrian showed up just in time to help Dashay and her catch him. The three of them carried him to the tent and laid him on the sleeping bag.

Riley could feel his skin burning with fever as she removed his clothes to examine him. "Adrian, hand me the med pack."

"I'll get it," Dashay said, but as she tried to stand, her legs gave way and she slumped against Riley.

Adrian dropped to his knees next to her and laid his hand on her forehead. "Are you sick too? You don't feel warm."

"Adrian, pack," Riley barked as she removed Coop's sock and eyed Dashay. "Answer him."

"No, not sick," Dashay whispered. "Just exhausted. I wanted to stop at a village we passed, but Coop insisted on getting back here to you. He saved my life, Riley, so I didn't argue."

Riley took a few deep breaths and shook her head to clear it. "You can tell me the details later. Go to your tent and rest."

She sat up and crossed her arms. "I'm not going anywhere until you tell me what's wrong with him."

Adrian handed her the med pack, and as she tore it open, she said, "That will take time. You got Coop here alive. You've done well and you're safe now." Dashay held her gaze for a moment before gesturing for Adrian to help her to her feet. "Just one question. How long has Coop been sick?"

As Dashay ducked out of the tent, she said, "He woke up that way this morning."

Riley pushed the thermometer under Coop's tongue and took his blood pressure while she waited for it to beep. She was distressed to see his pressure was seriously elevated. The thermometer beeped, so she slid it out of his mouth and was stunned to see it read 104.5 degrees. She jumped up and ran to Dashay's tent.

She pulled open the flap and said, "Have you given him any medication?"

Dashay nodded and propped herself on her elbow. "I gave him 800 milligrams of ibuprofen about five hours ago."

Riley grabbed hold of Adrian's arm and pulled him out of the tent. "Get me as much cold water as you can carry and as many towels as you can find."

Adrian ran off to do her bidding while she returned to Coop. She opened a packet with the highest safe dose of acetaminophen she could find, then tapped his cheek to rouse him. His eyelids opened half-way, and he studied her face for a moment before closing his eyes.

"Dying, Riley," he croaked. "I'm breaking my promise not to leave you alone. I'm sorry, love of my life. Tell my son I loved him."

"Don't be so melodramatic," she said, doing her best to

conceal her fear. "You're not dying. I need to sit you up so you can swallow these tablets. Can you help?"

"Can't move. Too weak. Too much pain."

Adrian rushed in with a full bucket of water.

"Put that down and help me sit him up so I can give him these meds," Riley said. Adrian did as she asked, then helped her lift Coop against a pile of packs and boxes. He let out a groan as they moved him.

"Sorry, Coop, but we have to reduce your fever and you can't swallow lying down. Be a good boy and take your medicine." She lifted a canteen to his lips and poured water into his mouth. "Swallow," she ordered. He grimaced as he gulped the water, but most of it went down. "Excellent. Now we're going to do that again, along with the tablets. Open your mouth."

He lowered his jaw and stuck his tongue out like a baby bird. She placed the tablets in his mouth, followed by more water. It took a few gulps, but he got them down.

Adrian clapped and said, "Excellent job."

Coop attempted a thumbs-up but couldn't quite manage it. The fact he'd tried gave Riley hope that he was still in there.

She turned to Adrian and said, "Start soaking those towels while I get his clothes off. We've got to keep wrapping him and replacing the towels when they get warm. We can't wait for the acetaminophen to work."

Adrian reached outside of the tent for the towels and dunked three into the bucket. Riley took the top one and wrung it out before wrapping it around Coop's leg. He flinched and tried to push it off, but Riley held his hand to stop him.

"I know it's uncomfortable, babe, but this will save your life."

Coop relaxed his hand and let her finish covering him.

While she worked, she said, "I have wonderful news. I felt the baby move while you were gone, and he's getting stronger every day. He gave me a good kick this morning."

"He?" Coop croaked.

"I've decided it's a boy. We'll take bets once you're recovered and see who's right when he's born."

"Deal," he whispered.

"Keep that fire going all day to boil water and keep me supplied with cold water, too." She handed Adrian the empty canteen. "Fill this please."

She turned her attention back to Coop, hoping to diagnose his illness. As she removed the towel covering his chest to replace it, she noticed a cluster of bumps near his shoulder. She leaned closer to examine them. She found several more on his arms and legs and recognized what they were. Mosquito bites. Her mind shuffled through the diseases carried in that part of the country and couldn't come up with any that would cause severe illness so rapidly, but epidemiology was hardly her specialty.

Riley was sure of one thing, Coop would need specialized care, and fast. She finished covering him with the cold towels, then went to Dashay for more information. Her friend was out cold on top of her sleeping bag. Riley gently reached for her arm to examine her for bites. Her skin was warm, and she had bites on her upper arm, but not as many as Coop.

Dashay swatted at Riley's hand, and without opening her eyes, said, "Leave me alone. I need sleep."

Riley patted her cheek. "Wake up. I know you're exhausted, but you need to answer my questions. What are your symptoms right now?"

"Headache. Muscle aches. Joints hurt."

"Can you tell what happened out there? How did Coop save your life? Where did you go? What did you see?"

Adrian slipped into the tent and leaned over Dashay. "Her, too?" he asked. Riley looked him in the eyes without answering, but he got her message. "What do you need me to do?"

"Riley," Dashay whispered. "Help me sit up."

Riley and Adrian propped her against the side of the tent. Dashay rubbed her face, then said, "The Ohio River has flooded.

Henderson, which was our next planned stop, is under five feet of water. Bridges are washed out. It's a nightmare out there. Coop and I helped who we could. I was trying to rescue a woman and her baby and got swept into the current. If Coop hadn't dived in and grabbed me, I would have drowned." She stopped to catch her breath and her face twisted in pain. "The woman and baby didn't make it."

"Were people sick?"

Dashay shook her head without opening her eyes. "Not that we saw, but it was total chaos. Impossible to know."

"I'm guessing you didn't bring back supplies."

"No. Riley, the only way out is south."

"Noted," Riley said. "Adrian, we need to cover her with cold cloths and give her lots of water, just like Coop. If we're out of towels, use whatever you can find. Then, we need to discuss what we're going to do."

While Adrian went to fill another bucket, Riley found some acetaminophen for Dashay. and made her swallow them. She was relieved to see that her blood pressure wasn't elevated like Coop's. After assisting Adrian in covering her with a wet blanket, she went back to Coop and rechecked his temp. It had dropped to 102, which meant the cold towels were working since the acetaminophen hadn't had time to take effect.

With her two patients stable for the moment, she and Adrian went to the firepit. Adrian dropped into a chair while Riley paced in circles around him.

"We have to get them to a town today if we can. They both need more than I can give them. If we can't find a functioning hospital or clinic, I'll need a library to read up on their symptoms and plan a treatment. I suspect this was caused by mosquito bites, but not malaria. The infection is escalating too rapidly. Do we have any repellent?"

"I'll recheck the inventory, but I don't remember seeing any when we went through the supplies."

"Add mosquito repellent to the top of our list. Next step is to plot a course out of here. Do you have the map?"

Adrian pulled the map they'd picked up in Huntington from his back pocket. He opened it across his lap, and they poured over their options, which were limited.

Riley poked her finger at the map, and said, "We're here, just southeast of Henderson. If the valley is flooded and the bridges gone, it looks like our only option is Madisonville, due south. How far do you think that is?"

"Twenty-five miles," Adrian said without hesitation. "If we pack in a hurry, it doesn't rain, and we push Biscuit, we can make it by nightfall."

Riley faced south and did the calculation in her head. The distance was twice what they'd been covering in a day because of the rain slowing them down, but if it stayed dry, they had a chance.

Turning back to Adrian, she said, "I hate to do it, but we have to leave two bikes and half of the gear behind to make room for Coop and Dashay in the cart. Let's get packed."

They loaded the gear as quickly as they could with having to move through the wet, muddy camp but were ready to head out an hour later. Adrian had conceived of a way to lash the bikes and some extra gear to the outside of the cart, so they didn't have to ditch as much as Riley thought they would.

The hardest part had been getting Coop inside. Dashay had recovered enough to climb in most of the way on her own, but Coop was barely conscious. He moaned and cried out in pain as Riley and Adrian lifted him into the cart. Riley was exhausted and nearly in tears by the time they had him resting on his makeshift bed, and they hadn't even started on their trip to Madisonville.

She straddled her bike and rested her head on the handlebars. "Give me a minute," she told Adrian.

She could hear him puffing for air as he laid his hand on her shoulder. "That will be the hardest part of the day, sis."

"From your mouth to God's ear, as Coop likes to say."

After giving themselves five minutes to recover, they got underway just after noon and headed due south. The morning sunshine had helped dry the standing water, and they were far enough from the river that the road was passable with the occasional deep puddle they had to circumvent.

The cloud cover returned with a refreshing breeze two hours into their trip, and miraculously, the rains held off. Riley was grateful since the temperature dropped at least ten degrees. She and Adrian had rigged a tarp canopy to keep Coop and Dashay shaded and dry, but the cooler air was an even bigger help.

Riley got a second wind and pedaled along the frontage road at a steady, sustainable pace. Adrian seemed rejuvenated, too, and talked non-stop about the flora and fauna of the environment they passed through as he rode alongside Biscuit. Riley didn't mind for once as it kept her distracted from obsessing about her gravely ill husband groaning in the cart.

She kept her eye on Biscuit as she listened to Arian. The horse was exhausted after the four-day excursion, but he had brought Dashay and Coop back safely. There had barely been time to tend to him while caring for Coop and Dashay, but he was making a herculean effort to save his master by pulling him to Madisonville. Faithful Biscuit was the unsung hero in the entire ordeal. Riley dared let herself believe they'd reach Madisonville in time because of him. The alternative was too terrifying to consider.

CHAPTER TEN

RILEY FOCUSED on the beam shining out from the light on Adrian's bike, repeating the mantra, *just pedal.* A glance at her watch told her it was almost midnight. Between circumventing washed out roads and having to stop and tend to Coop and Dashay, the journey had taken hours longer than expected, but they'd spotted lights in the distance on cresting the last hill. Adrian assured her the town was only five miles ahead. *Five miles,* she'd told herself. *I can manage five more miles. I must.*

She was so fixated on Adrian's light that she missed the occasional business or house they passed. When she couldn't pedal another inch, Adrian stopped and pointed to a checkpoint fifty yards ahead.

"We made it, Riley," he said, in a hoarse voice. "Help is just beyond that barrier."

She nodded with tears glistening in her eyes. "I wouldn't have made it without you. I'll never forget what you did today."

"Thank me later. Let's get these two to a hospital."

"Adrian, wait," she called out as he resumed pedaling. "What if Kearns' people are here searching for you? What if they've left fliers? Should you wait here until we know it's safe?"

"This place is so out of the way, Riley. I can't imagine they've gotten this far, and we haven't seen a military presence for days. I say we risk it."

"Your call. Lead the way."

She followed him the final distance to the rickety barricade blocking the road into town. A woman in her early twenties wearing a baseball cap jumped up from her lawn chair when she saw them and nudged a young man with long, black hair and multiple nose and ear piercings of about the same age. He rubbed his eyes, then got up and stood beside her.

"We have a medical emergency," Riley blurted out before either could speak. "Do you have a functioning hospital or clinic? I'm a doctor."

"We have a hospital, if you want to call it that," the boy said. "Good thing you're a doctor because we don't have one."

Riley lifted the barrier out of her way and motioned for Adrian to get Biscuit. "Does it have electricity?"

"Yes, the librarian taught us how to use solar panels," he said.

"A librarian taught you how to use solar panels? Is he an electrical engineer, too?" Adrian asked as he pedaled up to them, leading Biscuit along.

"He teaches us how to do everything. He's in charge around here."

"What, like a mayor?" Riley asked.

"We didn't vote him into office or anything. He's just the smartest person around, so we do what he says. If you want anything, you have to go through him, but he shouldn't mind if you use the hospital tonight since it's late and an emergency."

Riley straddled her bike and said, "Show us the way."

"We're not supposed to leave our post," the girl said, "but I'll break the rule if you'll let me borrow one of those bikes."

"Deal," Riley said.

Adrian propped his bike against the cart and went to unstrap Dashay's bike. "You can borrow this, but we need it back."

"No problem," she said, "but if you're staying, you'll have to declare all your belongings to the librarian."

Riley thanked them and rode up next to Adrian as they followed the girl. "They didn't react to seeing you," she whispered. "That's an encouraging sign."

"And if the rest of the town is like those two, we shouldn't have any problems. They're lucky we weren't hostiles."

"Right. I could have taken both of them by myself."

Adrian chuckled. "That paints a delightful picture. The pregnant woman taking out security guards."

"You know what I mean, but, anyway, a town run by the librarian can't be too menacing."

They arrived at the hospital less than fifteen minutes later. The girl did a u-turn, and as she rode by said, "I'll get the bike to you at the end of my shift. Good luck."

The facility resembled the countless small-town hospitals they'd passed on their journey. Riley hoped it would be well stocked and equipped enough for their needs. She was relieved to see lights shining through the lobby windows.

"Electricity is half the battle," she told Adrian as she got off her bike and leaned it against a wall. "Wait here while I find gurneys and help."

Dashay sat up and grabbed the side of the cart. "I can get out by myself. I'm feeling better."

"Glad to hear but stay where you are," Riley ordered. "I don't need you falling over and cracking your head."

Dashay slumped down onto her sleeping bag. "Yes, boss. Might not be a bad idea."

Riley rushed inside and went directly to the large elderly man at the reception desk. "I'm Dr. Riley Poole. I have two critically ill patients in that cart, and I need help to get them inside. Do you have any orderlies?"

The man rubbed his chin and stared at her for a moment.

"No, but we have a nurse and a janitor," he drawled. "Will that do?"

"It'll have to." When he didn't move but just sat watching her, she said, "Get them now."

He shrugged and heaved himself out of the chair as she ran down the hallway to grab some gurneys. By the time she returned to the lobby, a teenage boy and a broad-shouldered nurse in scrubs were waiting for her. The nurse resembled the man at the desk, and Riley assumed they were related.

"I'm Jace," he said, then cocked his thumb at the teenager. "That's my nephew, Kip, and I see you met Grandpa. He volunteers for the night shift. We never get patients after dark, so he usually just sleeps. What do you need, Doctor?"

"My husband and friend woke up critically ill this morning. We've traveled all day from just outside Henderson. They need IV fluids to start and ibuprofen. We'll go from there."

Jace and Kip each took a gurney and ran to the cart without another word. Dashay helped them get her out of the cart, but Coop was semi-conscious and delirious. It took all four of them to lower him onto the gurney. Jace led Riley to the ER and got to work running an IV line in Coop while she took Dashay's vitals.

"Your temp is down to 100 degrees," Riley told her. "Excellent. The fluids and ibuprofen should get you back to normal soon. What about your other symptoms?"

"Still have the headache and my gut's doing somersaults, but the joint pain is gone. See if they have Zofran for the nausea."

Jace heard her, and said, "We might, but our stores are severely depleted. The rains and military restrictions have disrupted our supply network. The librarian is doing his best to solve the problem, but progress is slow. You should know, he'll expect you to check in with him tomorrow."

As Riley rifled through the shelves and drawers in the room, she said, "Not until my husband is stable. Your librarian can wait."

"Fair enough," Jace said as he handed Dashay a dose of Zofran to put under her tongue.

With Dashay settled, Riley went to work on Coop. His fever had spiked back up to 104 degrees and his blood pressure was elevated. "Do you have Toradol? I've got to get his temp down."

Jace nodded and ran out of the room. While Riley waited, she examined Coop's bites. The swelling had gone down, but a rash of flat, red spots was spreading across his torso.

Jace came back and injected the Toradol into Coop's IV line, then leaned closer to his chest next to Riley. "What are you thinking is wrong with him, Dr…?"

"Dr. Poole. Call me Riley," she said, as she covered Coop with the sheet. "My husband is a doctor, too. Neal Cooper. Cardiologist."

"*The* Dr. Cooper? Him I've heard of."

"Yes. *That* Dr. Cooper. I'm speculating this is a mosquito borne illness. I'm an orthopedist, so I haven't studied infectious diseases since medical school. Is there a lab and pathologist in the hospital?"

"Lab, yes. Pathologist, no."

"Then, I need medical books to run the tests and diagnose him myself. What about a community college that teaches medical courses and has even a small library?"

"All the books have been moved to our main town library." He hesitated a moment before saying, "The librarian controls all knowledge in this town. He calls it our currency. He trades books and information for books and information he doesn't have or goods he needs. If you need medical information, that's where you'll find it. But I warn you, he drives a hard bargain."

Dashay had been listening to their conversation. She sat up and swung her legs over the side of the bed. "Why does everyone just let this librarian call the shots? Is he dangerous like a mob boss or something?"

Jace burst out laughing. "Hardly," he said when he got control of himself. "The residents were floundering here after the CME. He got us organized and set up a workable barter system. We're indebted to him, and he distributes food and supplies fairly. You just have to pay for it with something he or the town needs, even if it's labor."

Riley folded her arms and leaned against Dashay's bed. "Like those two manning the checkpoint?"

Jace smiled. "Exactly. You're a doctor, which is a valuable commodity, but he'll charge extra for the medical books. That kind of information is rare and expensive these days."

Dashay hopped to the floor, then grabbed the bed to steady herself. "That's BS. Let's go take what we need, Riley."

Riley rolled her eyes. "Easy there, Dashay. You can barely walk. Let me try bartering with this librarian and see where I get. If he won't cooperate, we'll explore other options. You should know, Jace, Dashay is a nurse, too. A damned good one."

Jace walked over and helped Dashay back onto her bed. "Then rest and recover, Dashay. We need you."

She smiled and dropped back onto her pillow. "I'll do my best."

Coop rolled onto his side and vomited over the edge of the bed. There were spots of blood in the splattered mess. As Riley rushed to his side, the lights flickered, then went out.

"What's going on?" Riley asked in the darkness. "Get me a flashlight."

She heard a drawer open, then Jace shined a beam at her. "This happens. Our electrical system is jerry-rigged, at best. I'll get the battery-operated portable lights until they get the power back on. The monitors and medical equipment are on separate backup systems."

When he handed Riley the flashlight, she said, "Wait. I can't wait until morning to get the information I need. After you get the portable light, take me to the librarian. Dashay can monitor Coop until we get back."

While Jace went for the lights, Riley pulled on a pair of gloves and cleaned the floor with a towel she then tossed in a bin. "Whatever this is, it's bad, Dashay. I don't know why Coop's case is more severe than yours, but Jace is right. I need you well so you can assist us."

"I'm getting stronger by the hour. I'll be at your side in a day, at most."

Riley reached for her hand and gave it a squeeze. "I'm counting on that."

Adrian ran up to meet her as she came through the doors. "What's going on in there? I saw the lights go out."

"Shoddy electrical system," she said. "Jace is taking us to meet the librarian. Unstrap Coop's bike for him."

"Don't bother," Jace said. "It's only a few blocks. You can leave the horse and cart. You have my word they'll be safe."

Adrian tethered Biscuit to a light pole, then said, "Why are we going to see a librarian in the middle of the night? Shouldn't you stay with Coop and Dashay, or are they better?"

Riley glanced at him, reluctant to speak the words she was thinking about Coop. "Dashay is. This librarian pulls the strings in town. We're going to trade for medical books I need to diagnose Coop. It can't wait. I'll need your help to research."

"Whatever I can do, Riley," he said as he got into step beside her.

Jace stopped and gestured to the library sign less than ten minutes later. "Here we are."

Riley's eyebrows went up as she read the sign. "Why are we at the library? I thought we needed to clear it with the librarian to take the books."

Jace shrugged. "He lives here."

"In the library?" Adrian asked. "That's weird. But now that I think of it, I'd love living in a library."

"Why doesn't that surprise me?" Riley said as she bounded up the steps and pounded on the door.

"His quarters are in back, Doctor," Jace said. "This way."

He led them to a walkway that circled around the brick building through the perfectly landscaped grounds. He went to the red painted metal door and rang a doorbell that was clearly a recent addition. When there was no response after a minute, Riley pushed the button several times.

Jace said, "Give it a second. His girlfriend says he sleeps like the dead."

Adrian glanced at him. "Why would his girlfriend tell you that?"

"She's my sister."

The door finally swung open and a thin young man of no more than thirty stood in the doorway, squinting at them. He slipped on a pair of wire-rimmed glasses, then tried to flatten the mess of dark blond curls sticking out in all directions on his head. Riley had imagined him as an authoritative gentlemanly type in his fifties, not this young man wearing a superhero t-shirt, rumpled and stained pajama bottoms, and flip-flops.

His voice cracked as he glared at Jace and said, "What is this? You're only supposed to wake me in a dire emergency."

"It is," Riley said before Jace could answer. "I'm Dr. Poole. I've two critically ill patients at the hospital with infections I can't diagnose. I need medical reference books and I don't have time to stand here explaining this." She pushed past him into what looked like a studio apartment. "Show me where they are."

"Hey, you can't barge in here without permission," he said as he hurried after her. "These are my private quarters."

Riley stopped and turned to face him. "Don't care. My husband is one of the patients and he's dying. Are you going to help me or not?"

"I'd cooperate," Adrian said. "She may be tiny, but she's fierce. Her husband is a doctor, too, and the other patient is a nurse."

"And what are you?" the librarian asked, looking Adrian up and down.

Riley grabbed the librarian's arm and dragged him toward a door that looked like it led to the library. "That can wait. Is it this way, Librarian?"

He jerked his arm free and stopped with his hands on his hips. "My name is Dr. Craig Himes. There's no need for violence. I'll help you. Just give me a second to get the keys."

Riley took a breath and held up her hands in surrender. "Sorry. I've traveled all day, had very little sleep, and we're fighting against the clock."

"And she's pregnant," Adrian blurted out.

Riley let out her breath in exasperation. "He didn't need to know that."

Dr. Himes gave her an odd grin as he turned to get the keys.

"Does your sister live here with him?" Adrian asked as they waited.

"She lives with me. Craig didn't want it to look like he was showing favoritism toward her."

"How romantic," Riley mumbled.

Dr. Himes walked back, dangling the keys in the air. "This way, Dr. Poole."

He unlocked the door and led them into the most crowded library Riley had ever seen. She wondered how he kept track of the books. They wound their way through the racks until they reached an area behind a sign that read *Science and Medicine.*

"Take whatever you need, Dr. Poole." He pulled a clipboard from a hook and handed it to her. "Record the number from the back of whatever you take. Be advised there will be a price to pay, but we'll settle once the crisis is past. Good luck to you. I honestly hope your husband survives. Jace, take them out the front exit. Come see me after your shift."

Jace nodded sheepishly and watched the librarian head back to his apartment. Riley noted that Hime's request to Jace sounded less than friendly.

"I hope we haven't gotten you into trouble," Riley said as she searched through the book titles.

"Don't worry about Craig. He's a grouch when he wakes up. What are we looking for, Dr. Poole?"

"Anything that might contain information on infectious or communicable diseases. Honestly, just grab any medical books that look like they might have information we need. Pile them on the little empty table in the corner."

While the three of them worked, Adrian said, "What did Dr. Himes mean when he said the books will come at a price. What kind of price?"

"I can't answer that. Craig has a system I don't understand, but he always makes it clear how he arrived at the price. He doesn't barter though. What he asks for is the price. No exceptions."

Adrian stopped and eyed him for a moment. "That hardly seems fair."

"People usually know the price up front and can choose to pay or not. This is a unique situation."

"No price is too high to save Coop's life." Riley dropped three books on the table, then said, "I've got to ask. Why do people put up with Craig?"

Jace watched her for a moment, then said, "Not everyone does."

"What does that mean?" Adrian asked.

Jace gave them a cryptic smile before turning back to the shelves.

"This is enough books for now," Riley said. "Let's get back to the hospital."

Dashay was propped against Coop's bed and leaning over the arm with his IV when Riley rushed into the room. "What are you doing out of bed? How is he?" she asked as she pulled on a mask, gown, and gloves.

She looked up at Riley as she finished sticking a piece of tape to his arm. "Coop's been thrashing around and pulled his line out twice."

Riley stepped across from her and felt Coop's forehead. His temperature was elevated. "I've got this. Get back in bed."

"Yes, ma'am. Gladly," Dashay said as she climbed on the gurney and slumped against the pillows.

Riley looked around the brightly lit room. "When did the power come back on?"

"About ten minutes after you left. Some guy in coveralls named Buck came in and told me the power would stay on for the duration. What took you so long? Was there trouble with the mystery librarian?"

Riley glanced at Jace as he walked in. "No trouble. I'll fill you in later. We got the books. Think you'll feel up to helping us research a diagnosis after you've had some sleep?"

"Absolutely." Looking at Jace, she said, "Speaking of sleep, any way I can get my own room with an actual bed? I'll get no rest with Coop as a roommate."

Before he could answer, Riley said, "I'm going to move both of you into private rooms. Jace, get Dashay settled, then come back and help me with Coop."

"Yes, Doctor," Jace said. He unlocked the gurney wheels and rolled her toward the door. "Come, Lady Dashay. Let me escort you to the royal suite."

"Got that right," Dashay said, and tucked her hands under her head.

Riley was glad to have a minute alone with Coop to think. She checked his vitals and was frustrated to see that his temp was 102 degrees, and his BP was elevated. "Wish you could tell me what's wrong with you, Babe."

When Jace returned, she asked him to point her to the pharmacy. "Until we can pin down the best treatment, I'm going to throw everything available at him," she said. After Jace gave her directions, she asked him to monitor Coop until she got back. When a beam of sunlight shined through a crack in the blinds, she stopped halfway out of the doorway. "What time does your shift end?"

He avoided her eyes as he said, "An hour ago."

"Hm. Sorry. Where's your replacement?"

Looking her in the eye, he said, "I told her to take care of our five other patients and that I'd assist you."

"That's unnecessary. Go home and sleep. I'll need you fresh, and Craig expects you."

"I'm not that tired. This is the most exciting thing to happen around here since the early days after the CME, and it's an honor to treat Dr. Cooper. As for Craig, he can just wait until he comes over to have dinner with us tonight."

"I guess he doesn't think eating with your sister is favoritism?"

Jace shook his head. "He has his own ideas about how to run this town and doesn't see dinner as a problem. He and my sister are getting married in a few months and already have a house close to the library picked out. Then it'll just be back to Kip and me. She spends most nights with Craig but no one is supposed to know that."

"Kip doesn't live with his parents?"

"My brother and his wife were killed in the CME. Kip's been with me since."

"I'm sorry. That's horrible. I'm glad he has you. Do you mind me asking about your parents?"

"No, Grandpa lives with them. Grandma died five years ago. I'm glad she didn't have to live through this, but Grandpa's been a trooper."

"I can see that. I'm grateful for the help if you insist on staying."

He stood taller and raised his chin. "I do."

She nodded and left for the pharmacy, not bothering to talk him out of staying. She'd been awake for twenty-four hours and needed all the help she could get.

She found the pharmacy easily and after greeting the pharmacist wearing a nametag that read Sadie Whitlock, rattled off a list of meds she wanted to try on Coop. Sadie scribbled them down as quickly as she could, then finally held up her hand and asked Riley to slow down.

When Riley finished, Sadie said, "We have maybe a third of these drugs. Which are most important?"

Riley ticked off on her fingers as she said, "The antivirals, antibiotics, IV antipyretics to get his fever down, and sedatives."

Sadie glanced at her notepad. "That covers every drug on your list."

"Let's go at this the other way round," Riley said. "What do you have back there?"

"Give me a sec."

Riley paced in front of the pharmacy window as she waited for Sadie to search her stock of drugs. Riley was surprised and grateful the hospital had even a third of what she'd requested and wondered where they were getting supplies. It wasn't as if drug manufacturing plants were functioning. At some point, warehoused stocks would be depleted or expire.

Sadie interrupted her thoughts when she came out from behind the counter carrying a bin filled with IV bags and pill bottles. "I found more than I expected, but I'm required to report this to the librarian. You'll have to trade for them, probably with your time in treating other patients."

"Easy enough, and I've met Dr. Himes. Why does everyone refer to him as The Librarian instead of using his name?"

Sadie shrugged as she handed Riley the bin. "He asked us to."

What an odd town, Riley thought as she went out shaking her head. Jace was waiting for her when she got back to the trauma room, but Coop was gone.

"I took him to our one and only isolation room," Jace said. "It's on the second floor, so we have to climb the stairs. The elevators got fried by the CME."

He took the bin from her and led her to Coop's room. It was a much better setup than the ER. Jace set the bin down on the counter and the two of them started unpacking the contents onto a rolling table. Riley picked the drugs Coop needed most urgently, and the two of them began dosing him.

"I'm giving him the sedative since he's delirious and keeps pulling out his line. Monitor his O_2 sat, blood pressure, and heart rate closely. Once his fever comes down and stays down, I'll take him off it. I suspect this is a mosquito borne illness that won't respond to antivirals, but I'm going to administer them in case I'm wrong, along with Cipro, which will cover most bacteria. If none of those treatments work, we'll try the parasitic route. Take another blood sample to the lab and ask them to prepare slides for me and grow cultures."

A wave of dizziness washed over Riley. She grabbed the counter to steady herself.

"When was the last time you ate or slept, Riley?"

She took a few deep breaths and rubbed her forehead. "I don't remember. Too long ago."

Jace put his arm around her shoulder and guided her toward the door. "I made up the adjacent room for you, and I'll find you something to eat, then you need to sleep."

She grabbed the door frame and hung on with an iron grip. "No. I want to stay with Coop."

"Trust us to care for him. You won't sleep if you're in the room with him, but you'll be right next door if we need you. You've got your baby to think about, too."

Riley let go and moved her hands to her belly. She'd forgotten about the baby in her rush to save Coop. "Bring my meal here. I promise I'll go to my room after I eat. That should allow enough time for Coop's fever to come down."

Jace helped her to the recliner in the corner. "I have your word that you'll rest as soon as you're done eating? Adrian and Dashay are both already sleeping."

"You have my word."

She watched Jace leave to get her food, then closed her eyes to rest them and the world went dark.

Yeager swore when his driver slowed the truck to a stop in front of the sentry blocking the road. He was out the door when the truck had stopped moving. "What is this, Sergeant?" he demanded.

The sergeant put his hands on his hips and scowled at him. "Why should I tell you?"

Yeager was about to berate him when he remembered he was dressed in jeans and a t-shirt. He drew his wallet from his pocket and flashed his new military ID. "Does that answer your question?"

The sergeant came to attention and saluted. "My apologies, sir. I didn't recognize you."

"At ease, son. You acted according to protocol. I could have been an enemy. Now, answer my question."

"The bridges are washed out ahead due to the flooding. The floodwaters have receded in the valley, so you can get into Henderson, but to cross the Ohio River, you'll need to backtrack or travel south."

Yeager swore again. Another delay. "How long have the bridges been out?"

"Nearly a week, sir. Lots of deaths and destruction, too. There was also what doctors think was a typhoid fever outbreak. Teams have been scouring the area, trying to get their hands on drugs to treat it. It's been a mess, sir."

"Bad news but good intel, Sergeant." Yeager reached into the truck and pulled the wanted posters off the seat. "It's a long shot, but have you seen these people?"

The sergeant studied the papers for a moment, then shook his head. "Sorry, sir."

"That's fine. Keep your eyes out for them. Notify your superiors if you spot them."

"Yes, sir."

Yeager got back in the truck and lowered his window. "You're doing a fine job. Keep it up."

The sergeant saluted again and moved out of the way for them to pass.

"Where to, sir?" the driver asked.

"Henderson. We need to refuel and replenish our supplies, and I need to assess the situation."

"Yes, sir," he said.

Yeager studied the map and read off instructions. "Should take about two hours. Wake me when we arrive."

"Yes, sir."

Yeager pulled his baseball cap over his eyes and slumped down in the seat. His last thought before drifting off was that Daybreak and his companions would face the same delays and obstacles. He hoped that they'd gotten laid up in Henderson and would be there for the taking. He was sick of this never-ending game of cat and mouse, unable to figure out how they'd eluded capture for so long.

After what seemed like moments, he heard the driver calling his name. "Far as we can go, sir."

Yeager slid his cap off his eyes and sat up to get a look at his surroundings. The devastation spreading out before them left him speechless. He climbed out of the truck to get a clearer view. Mounds of mud were piled where streets should have been.

Wooden structures had been reduced to matchsticks and cars lay flipped like turtles on their shells or stacked in mangled piles. It was worse than the destruction he witnessed in DC after the CME.

He swept his gaze over the area, looking for where to turn next, and spotted a cluster of olive-green military tents to the south. The road between the truck and the camp was clear. Yeager pointed it out to the driver and climbed back into the truck. As they moved toward the camp, Yeager avoided making eye contact with the souls wandering the streets like the lost sheep he'd seen countless times since the CME.

Another sentry stopped them at the entrance to the camp, but Yeager remembered to have his ID ready. The sentry pointed them to the base commander, a major still wet behind the ears who must have had multiple field promotions. Yeager explained his mission and asked for the VIP tent.

"The VIP quarters are occupied," Major Collier said, "but I'll arrange the best I can for you, sir."

"Occupied? By whom?" Yeager asked, unable to imagine who could be more of a VIP than him in the area.

"Admiral Barker. Down from Crane Naval Warfare Center. He was traveling to Nashville when the storms hit and trapped him here."

Yeager couldn't expect to displace an admiral. "Just find a dry, quiet corner for me and a place for my driver." Before turning to go, he said, "I'll need some soldiers to distribute fliers for me in the morning."

"I'll make them available to you but don't expect much help. Most of these people have lost loved ones and are just trying to stay alive. They won't care much to help you locate some fugitives."

"I'm aware," Yeager said. "Where's the mess? We haven't eaten since yesterday."

Yeager was lost in his head while he and his driver tramped

through the mud to the mess tent. If Daybreak and crew had been killed by flood or disease, he'd have no way to verify their deaths and would have no choice but to keep searching. Counting on his targets being too smart to die, he sat down to his meal of rations, planning his next move.

Julia's gut twisted into a knot while she watched Uncle Mitch tune the radio. They hadn't been able to reach her mom and Coop for days. She was mad and scared at the same time. It felt like someone had played a dirty cosmic cruel trick on her by letting her find her mom, then taking her away just as quickly. It wasn't fair after all the trouble they'd been through.

"Getting anything?" she asked, crossing her fingers.

Uncle Mitch's look told her all she needed to know. When she stuck out her bottom lip, he gave her a weak smile.

"Don't get discouraged, Julia. I'm having trouble contacting anyone. If your mom is having this same terrible weather, it's no wonder we can't reach her. The storms will pass as we get farther west, then we'll be able to talk to her and Coop every day."

"Promise?"

"I can't promise, but you know I'll do whatever I can to make it happen. Go pack up. We need to get moving."

Julia slogged across the muddy camp to her tent, discouraged and not even pretending to exude a positive attitude. She'd assigned herself as morale officer earlier in the week when she was sick of all the grumbling and gloomy faces, but even she was having a hard time maintaining her cheerful attitude. It was bad enough she couldn't talk to her mom. Having to travel day after day in waterlogged clothes, eating soggy food made it worse. As she slowly rolled her sleeping bag, she wondered what she wouldn't give for an hour of sunshine.

Holly came in and grabbed her backpack, then stopped and watched Julia for a moment. "What's with the face?"

Without looking up, Julia said, "Couldn't reach Mom on the ham."

Holly sat next to her and wrapped an arm around her. "That stinks. I'd hate it if I wasn't with Mom and Dad and couldn't talk to them."

Julia kicked her sleeping bag away and crossed her arms. "Every time I think life is getting better, something else bad happens. It's been dragging on for so long. I'm sick of it."

"We all are, but I know you've been going through it longer than us. Life wasn't so bad on the ranch. There were days I almost forgot about the CME. I didn't stop to think what it was like outside of our little bubble."

Julia cringed at the memory of those months on the road. "It was hell. You have no idea. This is easy compared to what that was like."

Holly lowered her arm and clasped her hands around her knees. "This is going to make you mad, but I'm going to say it, anyway. We all think it was stupid for your mom and Coop to run off like they did. Or if they had only waited a few weeks, they'd be with us now."

Julia turned and looked at her. "I'm not mad. I've thought the same thing a hundred times, but they didn't know the Army was going to swoop in and take over the ranch. None of us did. She just wanted to get to my brother and sister. She thought I was safe. I don't blame her anymore."

"You're more forgiving than I'd be. If my parents did that, I'd never speak to them again."

"Yes, you would, but it doesn't matter. They won't leave you. Uncle Mitch says as soon as we're out of the bad weather, I'll be able to talk to Mom."

Holly climbed to her feet and threw her pack over her shoulder. "You can believe him. Grandpa's always right."

He wasn't right about saving the ranch, Julia thought, but kept her thought to herself.

"You better hurry," Holly said. "Everyone's ready and just waiting for us to pack the tent."

"Be there in a minute," Julia said, as she watched her cousin hurry out of the tent. She had no choice but to trust her uncle and hope he was right this time. She got up and threw her rain poncho over her head to go help Holly take down their tent. Before ducking out of the tent, she pasted on a smile, determined to take her morale officer duties more seriously, hoping that pretending to be happy would make it true.

CHAPTER ELEVEN

RILEY'S EYELIDS felt like lead when she opened her eyes. She looked around the dark room, confused at how she got into the bed. Last thing she remembered it had been early morning. When she sat up and swung her legs over the end of the bed, the room spun for a second before she got her bearings. She lifted her arms to rub her face, but something tugged on the left one. She glanced down and was surprised to see an IV line in the crook of her elbow.

She reached over to pull it out, but a voice said, "Don't you dare. We've had a hard enough time keeping those in your disobedient husband."

Riley shifted her gaze toward the sound and found Dashay in a recliner, watching her. Dashay got up and lifted Riley's legs back onto the bed, then gently pushed her against the pillows.

Riley cooperated for the moment but had no intention of staying in that bed. "Tell me what's going on right now," she said, "and why are you out of bed taking care of me?"

"You sort of passed out in Coop's room, which wasn't surprising since you hadn't slept in more than a day or eaten in almost as long. I don't care what Julia says, you aren't Wonder Woman. Are you trying to hurt your baby?"

Riley glared at her. "Don't be ridiculous. I feel better after my nap."

"Nap? You've been asleep for twelve hours."

She sat up again and tried to climb off the bed. "I have to get to Coop. How could you let me sleep for so long?"

Dashay pushed her back onto the pillows a little less gently than the first time. "Don't worry about Coop for the moment. He's in excellent hands. A Nurse Practitioner named Loraine came in to check on you after Jace moved you in here. You were severely dehydrated, and your electrolytes were out of balance. She's been pumping you full of that wonder juice all day. Guess what? I got to hear your baby's heartbeat. It's nice and strong despite what a neglectful mother you've been."

Riley was speechless for once and felt tears spring up in her eyes. "Can I hear it?" she whispered.

"Later. First, you need actual food. I'll go order it if you promise not to leave this bed. Then, I'll fill you in on Coop while you eat."

Riley sank into the pillows and crossed her arms. "I won't move until you get back."

Dashay flashed her best smile. "About time you did as you're told. Be right back."

Riley watched her go, then rested her hands on her belly. The baby responded by flipping and turning inside her. She closed her eyes and imagined getting to hear the heartbeat and maybe even seeing an ultrasound. Every hospital had one.

Dashay came in carrying a small plastic box and set it on the bed. Riley peeked inside and was delighted to find crackers, cheese, a tuna packet, and applesauce. There was even a pack with two cookies in it. Her stomach growled at the sight of the food. She had to admit she was ravenous.

She tore open the tuna packet and said, "Tell me about Coop."

Dashay dropped into the recliner and rubbed her face. "It was rough for a few hours. Severe vomiting and diarrhea, fever spikes, and erratic vitals. But he seems to have turned a corner and is stable now. Loraine's not sure the infection is mosquito borne, but she's not ruling it out. She has Adrian and a few nurses pouring over those books. You and I can help now that you're rested and fed." When Riley started wolfing her food, Dashay put a hand on her arm. "Slow down. Five extra minutes won't matter, and we need that food to stay down."

Riley took a breath and chewed slower. "You're right, Dashay. I'll be no good to Coop or this baby if I don't start taking better care of myself."

Dashay held up her fingers in a victory sign. "Glad to see you're recovered from whatever this is."

Riley finished her second cookie and dusted off her hands "I'm ready to get at it. Am I allowed off this bed?"

Dashay got up and pulled on sterile gloves, then removed Riley's IV. "Get up slowly. We don't need you passing out."

Riley sat up slowly and gave herself a few seconds to equalize before sliding off the bed. She held the bed for a moment but felt perfectly stable. "I'm good. Take me to Coop."

"He's just next door."

She followed Dashay to Coop's room and gasped when she saw him. His skin had a gray hue, and his hair was a matted mess on his head. He slowly turned his head toward them when he heard them come in. Riley rushed to his side and grasped his hand, but he was too weak to squeeze back. Though she was relieved to see him awake, his sunken eyes rimmed by dark circles were a shock. She laid her head on his chest and gently wrapped her arms around him. He lifted an arm and rested it on her back.

"Just the sight of you looking so amazing makes me feel better," he said, in a hoarse voice.

She straightened and looked into his eyes. "Glad to hear it,

Babe. I'm strong and so is our baby. Dashay got to hear his heartbeat. I'll make sure we both get to hear it later, but right now I'm going to figure out what's wrong with you and cure you. You stay here and do whatever they tell you. Promise?"

He raised his hand and made a cross over his chest, then closed his eyes. Riley ran out of the room so he wouldn't see her cry. Dashay followed her out and pulled her into a hug.

When Riley regained control of herself, she stepped away and said, "You're telling me this is better than he was earlier?"

Dashay eyed her for a moment, then nodded slowly.

"I'm glad I was passed out for the worst, then. I've seen dead people look better than he does."

"He *is* improving, Riley, but I have a feeling we're stuck here for the long haul, so get comfortable. Figuring out what he's got would help us zero in on a treatment. Before you go, I forgot to tell you that the librarian dude wants to see you first thing in the morning."

"Who does he think he is? He's not even an elected official. He'll just wait until I'm ready to see him."

"I recommend you don't make waves, Riley. People here seem either in awe or a little afraid of this guy. I'm not sure which, but I'm guessing we need him on our side."

Riley suddenly felt the weight of the world pressing down on her. How many more of these eccentric rulers would she have to deal with before they made it home?

"Fine. I'll ride over to see him after breakfast, and I promise to be on my best behavior."

Dashay turned up her palms and shrugged. "That's all I ask."

Riley sat back in her chair and rubbed her neck. She'd been scanning through medical books for hours between trips to check on Coop and was no closer to finding an answer. She glanced at her watch out of habit, but her wrist was bare.

"What happened to my watch?" she asked Adrian.

He shrugged. "They must have taken it when you passed out. Ask Dashay."

She jumped out of her chair and headed for the door. "She's asleep."

"Where are you going?"

"To find my watch. It's the only thing I have left that came with me from Colorado. It's my good-luck talisman."

Adrian stood and pointed at her chair. "I'll go. You're more valuable here than I am." He pointed at the wall clock on his way out. "Since you were wondering, it's two in the morning."

"I'll give it two more hours, then I need to sleep."

"Me, too," Adrian said as he left.

Riley was glad for a moment alone. She appreciated Adrian's help, but he had little knowledge of medical matters. He was a methodical researcher, but so far hadn't come across a single helpful idea. He was so eager to help that she didn't dare ask him to leave, but he jabbered or asked questions incessantly and made it hard for her to focus.

She got up and went to the whiteboard Jace had found for her. She erased the mess of notes they'd all made for the past twenty-four hours to start fresh. She started by making an updated list of Coop's symptoms, then she wrote down any infectious diseases that even remotely fit his symptoms. Finally, she listed the treatments they'd tried. She drew lines between the symptoms and diseases that matched but didn't come up with anything conclusive. She was missing something.

She stared at her work for several minutes but got no inspiration. She went back to the table and started flipping through one of the books. It opened to a page she'd missed the first time through. A picture on the page gave her the answer to

Coop's illness. She picked up the book and started for the door just as Adrian rushed in, calling her name.

"They need you in Coop's room, stat."

As she ran alongside him down the hallway, she said, "Did they tell you what the emergency is?"

"All I heard was 'anaphylactic shock.' I know what that means because my daughter has severe allergies to nuts."

Riley picked up the pace and raced into Coop's room in time to see Jace giving him an injection.

"What is that?"

Jace held up the vial. "Epinephrine."

"Who prescribed it?" she demanded as she pulled on gloves.

A tall, dark-skinned man with strands of gray in his short, tight curls turned toward her from where he stood by the sink. "I did," he said, raising an eyebrow at her. "Who are you?"

Riley noted the white coat he wore but ignored his question and leaned over Coop. His face was blue, deepening to purple, and his lips were swollen. "When did this start, Jace?"

Jace's eyes widened as he backed away, shaking his head. "Dr. Williams should answer that."

She dropped the book on the bed by Coop's feet and snatched a stethoscope off a tray. "I don't care who answers me. Just tell me what's happening to my husband," she ordered as she pressed the end of the stethoscope to Coop's chest.

Dr. Williams stepped to the opposite side of the bed. "My apologies. You must be Dr. Poole. How are his cardiac and breath sounds?"

"Weak but steady beat. His breath sounds are good. The epinephrine's working." She let out her breath without taking her eyes off Coop. "They told me there wasn't a doctor at this hospital."

"There wasn't. I was in Atlanta when I got stuck after the CME. I'm making my way back to Mayo Clinic in Minnesota. I'm a cardiac surgeon who assisted Dr. Cooper with the development of the Xavier Procedure. What are the odds?"

That got Riley's attention. She ran to his side of the bed and threw her arms around him. He stiffened and left his arms at his sides. She let him go and stepped away. "Pardon me. I'm just so thrilled to have another doctor here, and you knowing Coop makes you like family."

He gave her a warm smile. "He still insists on being called Coop?"

She wiped her eyes and returned his smile. "Of course." She picked up the book and flipped to the page with the picture. "Look at that rash. It matches Coop's." She handed him the book and uncovered Coop's chest. "Jace, do we have a magnifying glass?"

As Jace started for the door, Dr. Williams said, "Don't bother. I recognize that rash. You're right, Dr. Poole. Coop has Typhoid Fever. Excellent catch. Let's just hope he wasn't reacting to the Cipro."

Riley was so relieved that her diagnosis was right, she almost hugged him again. "Please, call me Riley. Coop's never mentioned allergies to any meds, and he would have reacted much sooner if it were the Cipro, but we can't take the chance. We'll have to stop everything and try something else."

"Were you giving him azithromycin?"

"No."

"It's a reliable alternate treatment for Typhoid."

"I'll go to the pharmacy and see if we have it," Jace said and ran out of the room.

Coop's eyes flickered open, and he turned his head toward Riley. "What now?" he whispered.

Riley wrapped his hand in hers and lifted it to her cheek. "Welcome back. Almost lost you again. Dr. Williams saved your life."

"That's a coincidence. I know a Dr. Williams, but this is the last place he'd be."

"Hello, Coop. Glad to hear you remember me."

Coop slowly turned his head to face his old colleague. "Mack!" he croaked and raised his other hand. "What are you doing here, you old dog?"

Mack grasped his hand. "Something told me you'd gotten yourself into trouble again and needed my help."

"He got here just in time," Riley said. "You reacted to one of the meds. You never told me you have drug allergies."

"Didn't know I did. What have you been pumping into me?" Riley rattled off the list and he gave a dry whistle. "I should have asked what you weren't giving me. How are we going to know which it was? You can't allergy test me."

"Ever taken Cipro?" Mack asked.

"Many times."

Riley rubbed her forehead. "It's not likely that then."

"We should go with the azithromycin," Mack said.

Coop tried to sit up but was too weak and fell back onto the bed. He looked up at Riley, and said, "Hold on. Why do I need antibiotics? You said this is viral."

"I was wrong. It's Typhoid Fever." She showed him the picture, and he looked down at his torso to confirm. "The mosquito bites threw me. If I hadn't seen that photo, I never would have guessed that."

"Where could I have contracted Typhoid? We don't even have that in the US anymore."

"When you dove in to save Dashay. She got it too, only a much milder case. The flood waters must have been mixed with sewage."

Jace came in carrying an IV bag. He held it up and grinned at them. "Azithromycin. And there's more where this came from." He hooked it up to Coop's IV, then glanced down at him. "Good to see you're still with us, Dr. Cooper. You gave us a scare. More than once."

"Let's give these two a minute alone," Mack said. He patted Coop's shoulder. "Does my heart good to see you again, old friend."

Coop shook Mack's hand. "Mine, too."

Riley watched them leave before pulling a chair next to the bed. "Are you ever going to stop scaring the hell out of me?"

"If I did, what would we have to talk about?"

"I can think of a few. Let's give it a shot."

"You can start by filling me in on what I've missed the past few days."

"Not much to tell. You and Dashay came back to the camp deathly ill. Adrian and I rushed you here, and I've spent the past day trying to cure you."

Coop looked around the room. "Where's here?"

"Madisonville, Kentucky, I think. The bridges up north are washed out from the flooding. We had to go south. When you're strong enough, we'll go northwest."

"Is it safe to wait with those people after Adrian?"

"First off, you were almost dead just minutes ago and you're far too weak to travel. We'll be here two weeks, minimum. Second, no one here had mentioned Kearns or the military. They haven't recognized Adrian, so I think we're safe."

Coop scooted away from her and patted the bed. "Come here." She climbed up and snuggled against him. "You did a superhuman thing getting Dashay and me here and saving our lives. You never cease to amaze."

"I couldn't have gone on without you. When are you going to learn I'll do anything for you?"

"You are more than I deserve."

She lifted her head and looked up at him. "I won't argue with that, but I can't take all the credit. Adrian was a huge help and poor old Biscuit dragged your butt here."

He smiled, then grew quiet and closed his eyes. Less than a minute later she could feel his slow, rhythmic breathing. She found Jace and asked him to monitor Coop, then dragged herself to the next room and collapsed on her bed, exhausted but too afraid to sleep. She worried Coop wouldn't be there when she woke. Fearing it had all been a dream.

Riley held her breath as she walked into Coop's room at nine after a fitful night's sleep. When she found him propped up sipping broth, she sighed in relief. It hadn't been a dream. His coloring was still bad, and he looked weak, but that was to be expected after his ordeal. She glanced at his monitors and flipped through the chart, then blew him a kiss.

"I'd give you the real thing, but Mack says I should keep my distance for a few more days. He's prescribed prophylactic antibiotics for everyone that had contact with you."

"He came to see me earlier and told me. I agree with that treatment. I wouldn't wish what I just went through on my worst enemy. Will you stay and keep me company?"

"I can later. First, I have to go see the eccentric guy that runs this town."

"The Librarian? Jace told me about him. What do you think he'll ask in payment for all this?"

"Jace said he'll probably ask for my skills as a physician, so I'm not worried. I should be back in an hour. It's incredible to see you awake and talking."

He lifted his mug in a toast. "It's great to be alive."

She blew him another kiss on her way out and went to find Dashay and Adrian, who had offered to go with her to see Dr. Himes. She found them laughing over a breakfast of muffins, mixed nuts, and dried fruit in the deserted cafeteria. Dashay pushed a chair out with her foot for Riley when she saw her in the doorway.

"Good to see you looking halfway human this morning. Sit. Eat."

Riley took two muffins and a packet of fruit. "Where does all of this come from?"

"It just magically appears," Dashay said, and grinned at her.

Adrian shook his head. "Don't listen to her. Jace's sister left this for us. She found a nice stable for Biscuit and the cart, too."

Riley stopped chewing and stared at him. "With all of our stuff?"

He shrugged. "Everyone keeps telling me no one will take it. I don't know how they can be so sure."

"Once I've eaten, we'll go get some answers from Dr. Himes," Riley said.

"Rain's back," Dashay said. "Adrian, why don't you see if you can find us ponchos or umbrellas."

He got up and left without a word. "Where's he been sleeping?" Riley asked between bites.

"Jace tucked him into an empty room. If we're staying until Coop is recovered, we should ask for a place to stay. The hospital's fine, but I'd like a real bed."

"You and Adrian can go. I'm not leaving Coop. I'll get a bed moved into his room. Have you met Mack? I wonder where he's staying?"

"He examined me this morning before prescribing the azithromycin. He says I'm lucky to get off so easy. He's an impressive man, and handsome, too. Distinguished. He hasn't seen or communicated with his wife or family since the CME. He doesn't even know if they survived."

Riley stared down at her plate. She knew how Mack felt. "Is he traveling alone? He's come a long way and has even longer to go."

"He stayed in Atlanta working in a clinic until three weeks

ago when he found a way home. He was with a convoy, traveling by truck until they ran into Kearns' troops. They confiscated their vehicles and all their provisions. He slipped through the cracks and has been traveling alone on foot since."

"That is impressive. I'll have to hear his story when we're through this crisis." Riley took her last bite of muffin, then pushed her plate away and wiped her hands. "Let's get this parley with the librarian out of the way."

Adrian came in with his arms loaded with ponchos and umbrellas.

Dashay's eyes widened when she saw him. "Where did you find all that?"

He dropped them and the table before doling them out. "Grandpa gave them to me."

"Grandpa?" Riley said as she pulled a poncho over her head.

Adrian handed her a flowered umbrella that matched the color of her poncho, and said, "That's what he likes to be called. I'm not sure if we'll need all this. The rain's slowing."

Riley glanced out the window. "It'll be back if I know our luck, but let's make the best of it."

They left the hospital and hurried to the library in the misting rain. The front entrance was open, so they made their way in, discarding their rain gear in the foyer. The first person they saw inside was the girl from the checkpoint.

"Hello again," Riley said. "You never told us your name."

She shoved the book she held onto the shelf, and said, "Kendra."

Riley extended her hand. "Nice to meet you, Kendra. So, you do double duty at the library and as a security guard?"

"I was just filling in with Logan at the checkpoint. How are your patients, Doctor?"

"This is one of them here. Dashay, meet Kendra." Dashay flashed a smile and gave her a chin jut. "My other patient, my husband, will survive, but it was a close one. We're here to meet with the Librarian."

"I know. He told me." Kendra turned and waved for them to follow. "You can wait in the conference room. I'll get him."

She left them in a windowed room with a glass door and round table surrounded by six chairs.

Once the door was closed, Adrian said, "Do you suppose this room is bugged?"

Dashay eyed him for a moment, then said, "What would be the point of that? Are you turning into a conspiracy theorist?"

Adrian crossed his arms. "Have you forgotten that maniac Kearns is after me?"

Riley chuckled at that. "If the room is bugged, you just gave yourself away."

"Good point," he said.

Their conversation was interrupted when Dr. Himes pushed the door open and strode into the room like he was President. The action was pointless since he was wearing a different fanboy shirt, tattered shorts, and his flip-flops. Riley was glad to see he'd bothered to comb his hair. Dashay turned and gave her a look that read, *Seriously, this is the guy everyone kowtows to?*

He dropped into a chair, stretched out his legs before crossing his ankles, and clasped his hands behind his head. Doing his best to look bored, he said, "Morning Drs. Poole and Landry. Morning Dashay. Thanks for coming."

If he was trying to intimidate them, he was going about it all wrong. Riley resisted the urge to send him to the corner for a timeout.

"Did we have a choice?" Adrian asked.

His lips curled into an obnoxious grin. "You always have a choice, Dr. Landry. The question is how willing you are to accept the consequences."

Riley rested her elbows on the table and clasped her hands.

"I'd love to sit here discussing the philosophy of choice, but I'd like to get back to my critically ill husband."

"You can relax, Dr. Poole. Dr. Williams is attending to him."

Riley got to her feet and pressed her palms on the table. "That's it. I don't have time to be condescended to by a puppy. Send my bill to the hospital." She started for the door but came to a halt when she saw the two hulking giants standing on the other side with their arms folded.

"How cliché," Adrian said.

Dashay burst out laughing. "Is this a joke? What are you going to do, have those two beat up a five-foot pregnant woman?"

Dr. Himes gave her the same insufferable grin. "I'm a pacifist. My friends are simply there to keep you from leaving. I'd like to see you get past them."

Dashay beamed at him. "Challenge accepted. Shouldn't be a problem if they won't lay hands on me."

Riley lowered herself into her chair and tugged on Dashay's arm. "Sit," she said, and Dashay reluctantly obeyed but kept her eyes locked on the Librarian. "Fine, Dr. Himes. Tell us what it is you want from us and let me get back to the hospital."

He sat forward and opened the folder in front of him. "I prefer to be addressed as Librarian."

Dashay barked out a laugh. "That's not going to happen."

Riley glared at her as he went on. "We'll come back to that. This meeting isn't only about what I want from you. It's about what we have to offer each other. The medications and equipment you've been using are expensive. It's not unreasonable that you should be expected to pay for them. I've calculated the cost and converted it to time. I expect you and Dashay to work in the hospital until that time is paid."

He slid the paper across the table for them to read.

"Looks reasonable," Dashay said. "That equates to about three weeks."

Riley nodded. "Since Coop won't be well enough to travel for at least that long, I'd be happy to work in your hospital."

"Understand that this only covers until this morning. Costs will continue to accrue, and there's also the matter of room and board. Am I wrong to assume you'd like quarters?"

"Only for Adrian and Dashay. I'll be staying in Coop's room until I can discharge him."

He made a note on his legal pad. "I'll assign quarters large enough for the four of you, so you have somewhere to go at that point."

"I'm doing the math in my head," Adrian said. "If costs continue to accrue and you expect us to pay in labor hours, how will we ever be able to leave?"

Dr. Himes hesitated for a moment before saying, "I also accept payment in goods."

"We have little to offer," Riley said.

"I disagree. You possess several items I consider quite valuable."

Dashay started to stand, but Riley put a hand on her shoulder to keep her in her seat. She took two deep breaths but stayed in her chair. "How do you know what we possess?"

He looked Dashay in the eye, and said matter-of-factly, "Your provisions have been inventoried."

"You went through our stuff?" Adrian asked.

When he nodded, Dashay said, "Have fun rifling through my panties?"

"I didn't take the inventory myself, but I assure you, my assistants used the utmost discretion. Everything has been left just as it was."

Adrian's voice rose with each word as he said, "I assume this is still the United States. That violates our civil rights."

"So, sue me."

Adrian sputtered, then grew quiet, knowing they were at the Librarian's mercy until Coop was well enough to travel. Dr.

Himes was no violent sociopath like Director Branson, but he was far more intelligent and cunning. Riley thought he would have made an excellent member of Kearns' staff.

"What did you see in our belongings that you deem valuable?" she asked. "Before you answer, understand that our horse and cart are nonnegotiable."

"That's no problem. I can easily get my hands on those goods. I only want two items, your solar battery and the ham radio."

Riley rose from her chair and backed away from him, shaking her head. "No, you can't. The radio is the only way I can communicate with my daughter, my family." She pressed her back against the door and struggled to keep her panic at bay. "I'm a skilled orthopedic surgeon. Working in your hospital is enough price to pay."

"Let me make this clear, Doctor. I don't barter. My price is also non-negotiable."

Riley's gut twisted into a knot and she began to tremble. She had traded Echo for that radio. It was her only connection to those she loved most in the world other than Coop. "I won't. I won't do it."

"Then I will have your husband removed from the hospital immediately and you'll leave my town today with nothing."

Dashay rushed to her side and put her arm around Riley's waist. "Proud of yourself, you heartless bully? You've traumatized a pregnant mother who has been through more than you can imagine. Come on, Riley. Let's put Coop in the cart and ditch this madhouse of a town."

"We can't," she whispered. "He's too weak. He'll die without the drugs. We have to give Himes what he wants."

Dr. Himes folded his arms and nodded. "I'll allow you limited use of the radio until you leave. It'll cost extra, but I gather it's worth the price to you."

"What else could we possibly have to give?" Adrian asked.

"We'll work that out as we go. Everyone has something to

offer, and you're conveniently overlooking the fact that I'm providing room and board."

Dashay crossed the room and held her face inches from his. "No, thank you. We'll camp outside your city limits and find our own provisions, as we've always done. We'll work off our time, then we're out of here."

As he leaned away from Dashay, Riley caught the flicker of fear in his eyes. She wondered if they were the first people to defy him but couldn't imagine why that would be.

Himes regained his composure and waved Dashay off. Leaning over to make a note on his pad, he said, "Suit yourself, but I don't understand why you're being so obstinate. It's not an unreasonable exchange. Nothing in life is free."

Riley straightened and squared her shoulders. "Take what you want, Dr. Himes, and justify your actions in any way that helps you sleep at night. Just know there's a name for what you're doing. Extortion. The radio and loss of connection with my daughter for my husband's life. Dashay and Adrian, I won't have you starving and sleeping in a tent. I need you healthy and strong when we get back on the road. Move into the quarters he provides and do whatever he asks. We're finished here. May I go?"

"You've made the reasonable choice, Dr. Poole. I'll send my men to retrieve the ham radio," he said, doing his best to appear in control of the situation.

Riley wasn't buying it. In her mind, he was nothing more than a brainy kid pretending to be a man. In different circumstances, she would have fought back and won the day, but all that mattered was saving Coop's life.

Himes signaled for his henchmen at the door to move aside. Though Riley had lost the battle, she knew she and Dashay had shaken Himes and given him something to mull over. Riley strode out of the room with her head high, followed by Dashay and Adrian.

"What a tool," Dashay said as soon as they were back on the sidewalk in front of the library.

"What I can't understand is why the people put up with him," Adrian said. "Those two behemoths at the door aren't enough to keep an entire town in line."

Riley quickened her pace and opened her umbrella against the increasing rainfall. "It probably started innocently enough when the people needed a leader and Himes stepped into the role. For the residents not planning on going anywhere, it's a fair arrangement. As so often happens, the more power Himes gained, the more he wanted. No one has bothered to deny him if they're getting what they want. The townspeople I've met seem content."

"Until that cretin pushes them too far," Dashay said. "Then they'll realize their mistake too late. I hope we're long gone before that happens."

"Agreed," Adrian said. "I'm going to head to the stables to visit Biscuit and make sure none of our stuff is missing. I'll meet up with you at the hospital later, Dashay, to find out where our quarters are."

Riley watched him hurry off in the opposite direction, amazed at how much her attitude toward him had changed in the past week. He still wasn't a person she'd seek as a friend, but more like the odd cousin with endearing qualities that made you love him despite his eccentricities.

"I'm sorry about the ham radio," Dashay said, drawing her out of her thoughts. "I know you must be devastated."

"I'm just grateful I'll get the chance to tell them what happened and say goodbye until we meet up in Colorado."

Dashay reached for her hand. "Once this rain stops and we're over the river, the going should be faster. If all goes well, we could be there in two months, long before baby makes an appearance."

When has all gone well? Riley thought, but said, "That sounds incredible. Can't come soon enough for me. I want to pop in and update Coop. Then speaking of baby, could you find Loraine to come in and let us hear the heartbeat?"

"Do you even need to ask?"

Dashay kissed her cheek, then ran inside the hospital. Riley propped her umbrella against the wall in the foyer and took off her poncho before tenderly running her hands over the growing bump in her belly. Soon she'd need bigger clothes and it would be impossible to hide her condition. Hopefully, they'd be well on their way home by then.

After four days of battling the mud, Yeager reluctantly ditched his street clothes for cammies. He preferred not to be associated with the military while carrying out his current mission, but practicality won the day since boots and camouflage made much more sense than casual loafers and slacks.

He was slogging back to his tent after dinner in the mess when a Corporal caught up with him and handed him a note. Yeager waved the Corporal off and waited until he reached his tent to read it. The message was from Major Collier informing him that a civilian claiming to have information about Landry was waiting to see him. Yeager tucked the note in his pocket and rushed across the compound to the command tent.

He barged into Collier's office and said, "Where is he?"

Collier jumped to his feet. "I'll take you." He led Yeager to a pup tent fifty yards away. "The sentry brought him to me about thirty minutes ago. His story sounds credible, but he might just be after the reward. I'll leave it to you to decide."

Collier gestured to the tent opening, then headed back to his office. Yeager lifted the tent flap and peered inside. A young man with long black hair, multiple tattoos, and piercings was stretched out on the cot with his hands tucked behind his head. He grinned at Yeager and stayed where he was.

"Come with me," Yeager said, and started for his tent without waiting to see if the boy followed, certain he would.

Yeager smelled the reek of body odor before the kid caught up with him. It was a smell he'd grown accustomed to since the CME. Most people didn't have access to hot, running water. Yeager had always been religious about his hygiene and hadn't let that slide in his new reality. He'd found ways to bathe every day, even if it meant washing in a freezing river. He wished others would do the same. Cleanliness was one of the best ways to stay healthy, and it was a common courtesy.

When they reached his tent, he opened the door and gestured for the filthy boy to enter. He pointed him to a chair, but he remained standing. Yeager crossed his arms and studied his guest, attempting to assess his character. The piercings and tattoos were common enough with someone his age, as was the attitude. Most people squirmed under the scrutiny, but this boy just grinned at him, not intimidated in the least.

"My name is Colonel Yeager. Who are you?"

"Logan Black from a nowhere dead-water town called Madisonville, thirty miles south."

"What are you doing here?"

"The boss sent me to find out why deliveries have stopped. Mystery solved. This place is a mess."

"Who's your boss?" Yeager asked, then leaned against his small writing table and crossed his legs to appear more relaxed. Not that the boy was on edge. It was just one of his reflexive tactics.

"The Librarian. That's what he likes to be called. The guy who runs the town now. He's weird, but all right. Real smart."

Yeager's curiosity was piqued. Even if the information about Daybreak wasn't legitimate, a trip to Madisonville might be warranted.

"Major Collier says you have information for me."

"Yeah."

He reached into the pocket of his torn and mud-covered black jeans and pulled out crumpled copies of the wanted posters. He held them out to Yeager, who gestured for him to put them on the table. The boy stood with an exasperated sigh and dropped the papers on the table. As he returned to his chair, Yeager unfolded and smoothed the papers.

He picked up the one of Daybreak. "Have you seen him?"

"Yeah. First time about five nights ago. I saw him in passing the next day. He was still in town when I left to come here."

Yeager's heartbeat faster. It was the best intel he'd had in weeks, and he didn't detect signs of deception in the boy. His story would be easy enough to verify in Madisonville.

He pointed to the other sketches. "And these others?"

"All there except the one guy. I haven't seen him."

Yeager held up the posters of Dr. Cooper and Brooks Dunbar. "Which?" Logan pointed to Dunbar. "You haven't seen him?" Logan shook his head. "But you're certain you've seen Dr. Cooper?"

"Only the first night. He was sick in the back of a cart. The Librarian says he almost died of Typhoid, whatever that is, and he knows everything that goes on in town. The black woman had it too, but she wasn't as sick. I've seen her a couple of times."

Yeager crumpled up the poster for Dunbar and tossed it in the trash. He'd inform his assistant to stop making copies of his sketch. He wasn't the target, but it would be a bonus to capture the other four and present them to Kearns.

"Is your business finished here?"

"Since all the people I needed to meet with are probably dead, I'd say yes. The boss will need to find new suppliers and not from here."

"Then, you're going to ride back to Madisonville with me in the morning and take me to these people. I'll reward you with whatever you ask that's in my power to deliver, which is just about anything that still exists. Get yourself some dinner in the mess tent, then clean yourself up and get a change of clothes. I won't have you riding in my truck in that condition."

Logan's grin widened. "Sweet. I thought I was going to have to bike home. After you catch these guys, can I come with you?"

"You don't know where I'm going."

"Anywhere is better than where I am."

Yeager walked to the door and held it open for Logan to go. "You wouldn't ask if you'd seen the things I have in getting here, but I'll give it some thought." Logan stepped out of the tent and Yeager pointed out the mess tent. "We leave at eight. Don't keep me waiting."

Logan held up his wrist. "Who has a watch anymore?"

"I'll send someone to wake you at seven, so you have time to dress and eat."

Logan gave him a sloppy salute, then turned on his heel and headed for the mess. *Don't like the piercings, but he might be just the unflappable companion I need. He could get access to places I can't,* Yeager thought as he stepped back into his tent, elated that he was just hours away from the successful completion of his mission.

Julia had stopped waiting with Uncle Mitch in the mornings when he tried to get in contact with her mom. It was too heartbreaking. She'd asked him to come get her if he made a connection, but she couldn't help peeking at him from time to time. He'd told her the night before he was baffled at still having trouble getting in touch with anyone, even though the weather had improved. Julia wondered if it had anything to do with the CME. Uncle Mitch said that made no sense, but nothing did these days in Julia's opinion.

She continued to do her best to appear cheerful as she helped

Aunt Beth clean up from breakfast so they could get on the road. It was hard to hide her disappointment that another day would go by without getting to talk to her mom. The only consolation was that they were traveling north again. It felt good to be heading in the right direction. They were almost to Memphis, and she hoped they'd get to go into the city. Uncle Mitch was still being cautious to avoid the military, even though they'd seen no signs of them for a while, so it was probably safe.

She helped Holly pack and load their tent, then mounted her horse, Peppers. They'd become good friends over the weeks of traveling together. When no one was close enough to hear, Julia would carry on conversations with her, pouring out all her thoughts, feelings, and memories. The diary Aunt Beth had given her was nice, but there were just some things she didn't want to write down in case anyone ever read it. Peppers was a good listener and couldn't spill her secrets.

Julia was lost in a conversation with her that morning when she heard a commotion up ahead. She was riding near the front third of the company and was close enough to see a line of olive-green Jeeps blocking the road. Her heart pounded at the sight of Uncle Mitch and Russell in a heated discussion with some men in military fatigues.

Aunt Beth and Holly rode back to her, the fear clear on their faces.

"What's happening? Have they caught us?" she asked in a rush.

Aunt Beth did her best to look calm as she answered. "Looks that way but we're not in danger. They're demanding that we go with them to Memphis. It doesn't sound like they know who we are, but everyone is required to enter the residential zone."

"Just like that we're giving up? We're just going with them after all we've been through?"

Holly's hands shook as she held her horse's reins. "What else are we supposed to do? There are a lot of them, Julia, and they have big guns."

Julia wanted to swear but didn't dare do it in front of Aunt Beth. She pasted on a smile instead, and said, "You're right. I'm sure it will be fine. Maybe we can trade the horses and some of our stuff to get them to let us go."

Holly's face brightened. "You think they will? I won't mind walking if we can keep going."

"We'll see," Aunt Beth said. "You girls go back with your mom, Holly. I'm going back up with Mitch."

Julia and Holly watched Aunt Beth ride to the front of the company before turning back to find Kathryn. Julia kept her eyes lowered, struggling to fight her tears in the face of their devastating defeat. If they got stuck in the zone and their jailers took the radio away, her mom would never know where she was or what happened to her. The thought of causing her mom that kind of pain was almost more than she could bear.

She leaned close to Peppers' ear and whispered, "Don't worry, girl. I'll make sure they take good care of you. I promise to get us home, no matter what it takes."

The journey to Memphis took five grueling hours. Every part of Julia's body ached by the time they arrived. A man ordered her to dismount, then led Peppers away. As she watched him go with tears stinging her eyes, she wondered who she'd have to tell her secrets to.

Their captors had forced them into a several block enclosures, surrounded by barbed wire on the edge of Memphis. Uncle Mitch called it an internment camp. The soldiers assigned them quarters in a rundown apartment complex and confiscated all their belongings except for clothes and personal items. Uncle Mitch and Aunt Beth took Julia to their apartment, but Holly had to go with her parents. The girls agreed to have sleepovers if they were allowed.

Julia's room had bare walls and no furniture except a dinged-up dresser and a twin bed. They were on the fourth floor, so it was stiflingly hot in the June heat. Opening the windows didn't help until after the sun set and a slight breeze came up. After they'd had a cold dinner of tuna sandwiches and canned fruit, Julia asked if she could go outside for fresh air. Uncle Mitch said he'd join her.

They walked a short distance down the street that ran in front of their apartment building, until they came to a bench under a tree. Uncle Mitch slowly lowered himself onto it and sat back with a sigh. It looked to Julia like he'd aged ten years in one day.

"It's not your fault," she said. "You tried so hard to keep us from getting caught."

"I did, Julia, but here we are. I never thought I'd end up a prisoner in my own country. The commander I spoke with tried to convince me this is for our own good. I knew that he didn't believe it any more than I did."

"I've been through worse, Uncle Mitch. What happens to us now?"

"They'll find work for us. You'll go to school in the fall. Life will go on."

"Don't worry. Mom and Coop will find us and get us out of here."

He nodded and closed his eyes. Julia knew that meant for her to stop talking. She got up and looked up and down the street. It looked like any street in any big city, except for no lights, and burned-out buildings. She walked to a wall of missing signs on the side of an empty store behind them. They'd seen the sketched posters in every city they'd passed. Julia wondered if she'd end up on one.

She walked to the far side of the wall to the wanted posters. Those were scarier. She wished she'd see one for that horrible Jepson that shot her, but he was in Virginia, too far away. She just glanced at the faces until she saw one that made her body go cold. It was Dashay. As she tore it off the wall, she noticed the ones beside it. Her mom and Coop. It said they were wanted for treason and harboring a fugitive.

Her hands shook as she grabbed the sketches and carried them to Uncle Mitch. She stopped when she saw him talking to a man in a uniform. Uncle Mitch stood and called to her. She ran to him as the man turned to leave. She handed Uncle Mitch the posters, trying not to be sick.

"It's Mom!" she cried. "Mom and Coop, and my friend Dashay. It's a lie. I know it. Mom would never do anything wrong. What are we going to do?"

The man who'd been talking to Uncle Mitch stopped and stared at her. She took the papers from Uncle Mitch, then folded them and shoved them in her pocket. Uncle Mitch nudged her toward their apartment building. The man didn't follow but watched until they were in the building. Julia ran up the stairs and threw herself into Aunt Beth's arms. Her life was over. She was in prison and soon her mom and Coop would be, too.

CHAPTER TWELVE

RILEY STUFFED the blood pressure cuff into her pocket after taking Coop's vitals. "If you keep this up, I'll be able to spring you in a few days."

Coop blew out his breath in relief. "Not a second too soon. I'm going mad staring at these walls."

"I have a treat for you. Since the rain *finally* stopped, I'll push you out to the courtyard after lunch for some sunshine."

"Sounds like just what I need, except one thing. Let's hear it again."

Riley went to the counter and picked up the fetal heart monitor. Loraine had agreed to give it to her when they kept bugging her to let them hear their baby's heartbeat. Riley climbed up onto the bed with Coop and lifted her shirt. He turned on the monitor while she spread the lubricating jelly on her belly. Coop gently ran the monitor over her skin until they heard the rapidly pulsing heart of their child.

Coop laid his head on her shoulder. "I'll never get enough of that."

"It is pretty amazing. Now, all we need is to get our hands on an ultrasound."

Mack stuck his head through the doorway. "Am I interrupting?"

Coop waved him in, and said, "Come listen to this."

Mack moved next to the bed and closed his eyes while he listened. "Music to my ears." He opened his eyes and patted Coop's hand. "Sounds like a healthy beat. You've got a fighter there."

Riley clicked off the monitor and lowered her shirt. "It's a miracle, considering what we've been through. Pull up a chair and sit awhile."

"Thanks for the invitation, but I'm here to say goodbye."

Coop sat up and frowned. "You're leaving? So soon?"

"I wouldn't have stayed this long if not for you. I've been separated from Olivia and the family for too long. This was just supposed to be a stopping off place. I've worked off what I owed the Librarian, and I met a family traveling north that has agreed to let me tag along."

Riley got up and gave him a hug. "We understand more than you know, but we'll miss you. Thank you for staying to help me care for Coop. I couldn't have done it without you."

"It's been one of the greatest honors of my life. I owe a great deal to this crazy husband of yours."

Coop held up his hand, and the two gripped forearms. "I'll do whatever I can to get back your way. The world can't stay backward forever."

Mack's eyes glistened as he said, "I'll keep my ears open for news of the great Dr. Neal Xavier Cooper."

"Give my love to the family."

Mack hurried out of the room, and Coop watched after him for several moments. "There goes one of the best men I've ever known. What a gift that I crossed paths with him again, against the odds."

"I hope he makes it home. He's got a long journey ahead."

"Not as long as ours," Coop whispered. "I hate being in this bed, holding up our trip."

"Not for much longer, then we'll be home before you know it."

"Do you know how excited I am to meet Emily and Jared, and the rest of the family?"

"You'll love my sister, Lily. She's quite the character." Riley bent down and kissed his cheek. "I have a meeting with Himes to discuss the use of *my* radio. I won't be gone long, then I'll give you that ride to the courtyard."

"Good luck, Babe. Put that punk librarian in his place."

"I'll give him my best shot," she said as she headed out of the room.

She wished she felt as confident as the act she put on for Coop. It infuriated her to cooperate with Himes, but he'd left her little choice. He'd been generous in supplying them with food and supplies, but no matter how many hours she worked, the charges kept piling up. She hadn't told Coop the half of what they owed, so he wouldn't worry, but if he didn't recover enough to get out of that hospital soon, they'd be stuck in that backward town for months.

She pushed her worries aside as she entered the library. That day, her purpose was to do whatever it took to get time on the ham radio and talk to her daughter. It had been two weeks since she'd last heard her voice.

Himes was in his office and waved her in as soon as he saw her approaching. She took a breath and straightened her shoulders before opening the door.

"Morning, Dr. Himes," she said as she took the chair across from him. "I need to get back and do my rounds, so just tell me the price for the use of the ham radio."

"This should be an easy one for you. You're an orthopedic surgeon. My mother needs a knee replacement. I'd like you to perform the surgery."

Riley let out the breath she'd been holding. That was an easy one. "If you can procure what I need, I'm more than happy to perform the knee replacement. I'll need to run tests and see any records the hospital has."

"She has all the paperwork you need, and I have everything you need already. The surgery was scheduled for a week after the CME hit, but the surgeon died in the same explosion that killed Kip's parents. You're the first person capable of helping her since. She's in a great deal of pain, Dr. Poole."

"Have her schedule an appointment with me for tomorrow, and we'll get the process started. How much time will this get me?"

"This will give you three hours on the ham radio and knock off forty labor-hours."

It was more than Riley expected for a one-to-three-hour procedure and got her wondering if anyone else needed surgeries. She was capable of far more than just orthopedic surgeries. Her hopes of getting out sooner soared.

"That's very generous, Dr. Himes. May I schedule it for tonight?"

"Use it whenever you want. Kendra keeps the sign-up sheet."

He pressed his fingertips together and stared at her over the top of his glasses for a moment. "Is there something more?" Riley asked.

"If you refuse to call me Librarian, you may call me Craig. I consider us equals. Dr. Himes is too formal and reminds me of my father. He's a physicist."

Riley raised her eyebrows. "You've got to introduce him to Adrian. He's a physicist too."

"He is? Wish I'd known that. I have him working in the stables and greenhouse. He seems content with that."

"He would," Riley said, and chuckled. "But he's quite brilliant."

"Dad will be thrilled to have someone on his level to converse with."

"You've never told me your specialty, Craig," Riley said, putting emphasis on his name.

"Doctor of Comparative Literature, what else? Though I have working knowledge in several other fields."

"Like electrical engineering?"

"Dad helps with that."

Riley stood and extended her hand. She still resented being extorted by the man, but knew it made more sense to pretend to cooperate. As he shook her hand, she said, "Bring your mother in tomorrow. I'll schedule with Kendra on my way out."

She signed up to use the radio after dinner at the time she'd arranged with Uncle Mitch, then hurried back to the hospital, relieved the meeting had gone far better than expected. If her plan held up, they'd be out of Madisonville and on the way home within a week.

Riley struggled to concentrate on Craig's mother's knee as she examined her to prepare for the surgery. She'd failed to contact Julia either the night before or that morning after breakfast and was afraid Uncle Mitch's ham radio had gotten damaged. She refused to let her mind wander to more alarming reasons she hadn't been able to reach them. She'd signed up for another session that evening, knowing that each attempt was costing her, but she wouldn't have many more chances to contact them.

After her failed attempt that morning, she'd returned to the hospital to find a document box containing Mrs. Himes' medical records. She'd poured over them while she waited for her patient to arrive. Though Mrs. Himes was a candidate for the surgery, Riley wished she could do one more MRI to determine any changes or deterioration that had occurred during intervening months. The hospital didn't have an MRI suite and had utilized Mobile MRI before the CME. She'd order an x-ray series instead, which was the best she could do.

Riley made a note in the chart, then smiled at Mrs. Himes. "From what I can see, you're healthy other than the knee, so we'll schedule the surgery for Friday. Go to the lab tomorrow morning for pre-op blood work. Fast for twelve hours beforehand. If the lab results are good, be here at seven on Friday. The surgery should take roughly two hours, and I'll have you stay for two nights, just to be safe. You may get dressed. I'll send someone in to help you to the waiting room."

Mrs. Himes put her hand on Riley's arm as she turned to go. "You have no idea how much this means to me. My knee is so painful I can't even move around the house on my own anymore. You coming to Madisonville is a miracle."

Riley patted her hand. "We'll get you fixed and feeling better soon. I've done hundreds of these surgeries."

Riley rushed out of the room as quickly as she could without arousing suspicion. She had no problem doing the surgery for the kind, old woman. She just resented that Craig was forcing her to do so. She went in search of Percy, the nurse anesthetist, who was the closest thing the hospital had to an anesthesiologist. Percy assured her he'd done most of the work during surgeries. The anesthesiologist usually monitored from a distance. He'd assisted Loraine in a few surgeries since the CME with no problem. Mrs. Himes had no underlying conditions to complicate things, so Riley wasn't concerned.

After discussing the surgery with Percy, Riley went to assist Dashay in the ER. They'd had an influx of refugees fleeing the flooding and devastation up north. Most were suffering from typhoid, exposure, or malnutrition, which Dashay could handle alone, but the occasional injury or critical illness required her expertise. Riley was half tempted to warn some of them to keep moving before they got caught in Craig's net, but most wouldn't have survived long enough to escape.

She was casting a man's arm that she'd had to reset and noticed he kept staring at Dashay. When she raised an eyebrow at him, he said, "That woman looks familiar."

Riley glanced at Dashay. "She was in Henderson about a week ago. You may have seen her there?"

He slowly shook his head but kept his eyes on Dashay. "I wasn't in Henderson then. I only spent a night there before heading south. I got injured on the road. She has a unique face."

"Yes, she's beautiful," Riley said to deflect him.

"She is. That's why I would have remembered her."

"You must have crossed paths with her somewhere on the road. You know how it is nowadays." Riley finished casting him and helped him into a sling. After giving him instructions on caring for his arm and how long he'd need the cast, she said, "You're free to go. Just be careful out there."

He nodded and climbed off the gurney to leave but followed Dashay with his eyes as he walked out of the room. Jace came over and started preparing the table for the next patient.

"Be back in a sec," Riley told him and headed for Dashay. Riley led her to a quiet corner. "Did you see that broken arm guy watching you? Said he recognized you from somewhere."

"I wondered what his deal was. I've never seen him as far as I know, but he's average looking. Why should I care if he recognized me?"

Riley shivered. "It made my radar go up. I'm hoping it has nothing to do with Adrian."

Dashay put her hand on her shoulder. "We haven't seen or heard anything about that since Huntington. Honestly, I'd forgotten since no one here pays the least bit of attention to him. I thought we'd thrown Kearns people off his trail."

"We should be careful, just in case. I have a feeling Kearns won't give up that easily."

Dashay shrugged. "You may be right, but what does that have to do with me? They're searching for Adrian."

"I'm probably overreacting, and it was just a fluke. Be careful just in case." Riley looked around the crowded ER at the throng of sick and injured. "I'll be glad to put this town behind us."

Dashay gave a quick nod before heading to her next patient. Riley watched her for a moment, unable to shake the feeling of warning. Until that moment, she'd only worried about Adrian being recognized, but the three of them had been traveling with him for weeks. Someone was bound to have their description. She shook off her thoughts as she went back to work. No sense asking for trouble. They had enough to deal with as it was.

Riley had been too busy in the ER to have lunch with Coop and wasn't able to slip away until dinnertime. She'd been careful to take breaks and to snack throughout the day, but she'd reached her limit and needed to get off her feet. She hurried to his room before someone stopped her and climbed up next to him on the bed.

He put his arm around her and kissed the top of her head. "You look worse than I do. Stop working yourself so hard for these people. It's not worth putting yourself at risk."

She closed her eyes and took a deep breath. "I'm not doing it for Craig. These poor souls need my help." She sat up and put her lips to his ear. "We're not safe here. I want to get out as soon as I finish the replacement on Friday under the guise of me discharging you. That gives us two days. You'll have to travel in the cart until you're stronger, but we're leaving."

"No argument from me. Just tell me what you need."

She kissed him, then rested her head on his chest. "I want to go home."

"Then I'll take you there." He reached for a paper sack sitting on his tray table. "Craig's mother had this delivered for you."

Riley's stomach growled when she opened the bag, and the

smell of roasted chicken filled the room. After removing a whole chicken, Riley pulled out mashed potatoes, seasoned carrots, and sliced tomatoes. At the bottom was a plastic bowl containing berry cobbler. She and Coop feasted on the delectable meal until she thought she'd burst.

Rubbing her hands over her belly, she said, "That was selfish. I should have shared this with Dashay and those people starving in the ER."

Coop took the empty cobbler container and set it on the tray. "There's enough left over for Dashay, and Craig will provide for the rest. This was a gift meant for you, and the baby needs the nutrients. Cut yourself some slack."

"If you insist," she said, as she relaxed against him. "That was the best meal I've had since leaving the ranch." She sat up and glanced at her watch. "Speaking of the ranch, it's my time on the ham radio." She climbed off the bed and gave Coop a quick kiss. "I'll be back in an hour. If that new nurse comes in, have her take the food to Dashay."

She made it onto the street just as the sun set. She'd miss part of her scheduled hour but still had time to reach Uncle Mitch.

When she was a block from the library, Jace called out to her in a loud whisper from an alley between two brick buildings. When she turned toward him, he waved her over. She hesitated, not wanting to lose more of her time on the radio, but he looked frantic.

She looked up and down the deserted street before rushing over to him. "Hurry, I'm scheduled on the ham radio."

He took hold of her hand and pulled her in the opposite direction down the alley. "No time. Come with me now."

She tried to stop and free her hand, but Jace was too strong, so she had no choice but to go with him. He led her toward a nearby house she'd never seen before. After stopping to check the street, he motioned for her to go with him into the house. She trusted Jace, and he'd never behaved that way before, so she nodded and followed him.

The house was only a small, one-bedroom duplex. It was a mess and clearly a bachelor pad. Kip sat on the mattress of an open sofa bed, staring at her, wide-eyed. Jace closed the blinds and locked the door. Riley was about to demand that he tell what was going on when he lifted a finger to his lips to silence her.

Jace reached into his pocket and pulled out some crumpled, folded papers. He handed them to her and waited while she unfolded and read the papers. The top one was Adrian's wanted poster. The other three were uncannily accurate sketches of Dashay, Coop, and her. She let the papers fall from her trembling hands and sank onto a wooden chair. The posters explained the man who had recognized Dashay. If he did, others would.

"It's not true, Jace. None of it," she whispered. "Believe me. Where did you get those?"

Jace retrieved the papers and tossed them into a large glass bowl before igniting them with a lighter. After watching them burn to a mound of ash, he removed a pile of dirty t-shirts from a chair and set it down only inches from her before sinking into it.

Keeping his voice low, he said, "I believe you. One refugee showed these to my sister. He told her there are copies posted all over Henderson. He wanted to know if Patrice had seen you so he could find you and claim the reward. She said she hadn't seen you and asked if she could have them. He said he has your faces memorized and gave her the posters. She came straight to me."

Riley clasped her hands to keep them from shaking. "Craig doesn't know?"

"Not yet, but it's only a matter of time. He finds out everything that goes on around here. You've all got to get out of here tonight. Patrice, Kip, and I will do what we can to help you. Tell me what you need."

Riley jumped to her feet. "I can't let you put yourself at risk. Just get us the horse and cart, Coop's meds, and enough supplies, including oats for Biscuit, to last a few days. They stored our rifle, handgun, airgun, and ammo somewhere. See if you can find those items as well."

"You've done so much for this town. We owe you more than that. Patrice already went to warn Adrian before going home to have dinner with Craig. She's going to stall him there for as long as she can. There are others we trust to help gather supplies. I'm sorry, Riley, but it's too dangerous for you to go to the library. You're going to have to miss your time slot on the ham radio."

"I haven't been able to reach my daughter for days, anyway. I'll find another way to get in touch. For now, let's get to the hospital and rescue my husband."

Kip got off the bed and stepped in front of Riley. "I'll draw an escape route out of the region that will keep you clear of the librarian's supply lines." He picked up a city map showing parks and local trails and pointed to an area in the forest circled with red ink. "That's where we'll meet around midnight."

She took the map, once more grateful and humbled that strangers had come to their aid at the risk of their own safety. "Thank you, Kip. I'm ready. See if the street's clear."

Kip opened the door a crack and peered out. "No one around."

Jace stopped Riley before she stepped onto the porch. "It's better if we act normal. Get Coop into a wheelchair and tell anyone who asks you're taking him for a walk in the summer air. After I fill Dashay in, I'll get Coops' belongings and meds, then meet up with you. No one will pay attention to me."

Riley gave a quick nod. "Good thinking."

"I'll round up some friends I trust to help get supplies," Kip said. "We'll load the cart and come to the spot marked on the map."

Kip sauntered off in the opposite direction with his hands in his pockets while Riley and Jace walked toward the hospital, chatting like they were in a casual conversation. When they reached the lobby, Jace went to find Dashay. Riley snagged a wheelchair and forced herself to walk with it to Coop's room.

He sat up and grinned at her as she came through the doorway. "What's this? Another trip to the courtyard?"

"Better. I'm taking you for a walk in the park," Riley said, hoping Coop caught on to her pretended cheerfulness.

He studied her for a moment before saying, "That sounds delightful."

Riley moved his IV bag from the pole to the hook on the chair, then helped him off the bed. After a quick glance into the hallway, once he was settled, she dropped a few of his belongings and small medical instruments, including the fetal heart monitor, into his lap before covering him with a blanket.

"Cozy?" she asked as she wheeled him out of the room.

A nurse spotted them and waved. Riley kept moving but slowed when the nurse headed toward them. "Evening, Leah. Did you just get here for the night shift?"

"Yes, and I was going to check on my favorite patient first, but I see he's already in excellent hands. Getting out for some air, Dr. Cooper?"

Coop gave her an exaggerated grin. "So my doctor tells me."

"We're heading to the park," Riley said. "Jace tells me it has a nice level path."

Leah waved as she walked away. "Perfect night for it. Enjoy your outing. I'll catch you later, Doctors."

Riley picked up speed in the empty hallway as soon as Leah rounded the corner. They got Coop to the main floor, and headed for the main entrance, where Dashay was waiting for them, holding a backpack.

"Mind if I join you on your walk?" she asked.

"We'd love the company," Coop said. "What's in the backpack?"

Dashay got into step beside Riley, and said, "Jace packed a few snacks and things you might need, Coop. He didn't want us to get stuck empty-handed."

"That was thoughtful," Riley said, as she went through the entrance doors and rolled Coop down the ramp. When the three of them reached the sidewalk, she turned toward the park near the woods.

When they were out of earshot of passing townspeople, Coop said, "Want to tell me what's going on now?"

"Adrian isn't the only *Most Wanted* anymore. A man came into Madisonville from Henderson with posters of all four of us."

Dashay leaned closer to Coop. "And someone else recognized me in the ER earlier. Time to hit the road."

"Jace and his family are helping us. Adrian should be waiting for us at the spot marked on this map." She took it out of her pocket and handed it to Coop. "Kip said for us to wait until he brings Biscuit and the cart around midnight."

Coop turned and looked up at her. "Can we trust him?"

"What choice do we have?" Dashay answered for her. "People were streaming into town from Henderson today. We can't sit around waiting for someone to turn us in."

"We can trust them," Riley said. "Jace doesn't like Craig but wouldn't defy him openly. I've been wondering if his sister only stays with Craig to keep him distracted and to be in his inner circle for information."

Coop ran his hand through his hair, as he always did when he questioned one of her schemes. "Makes some sense, but this sounds like another of our knee jerk plans that always ends in disaster."

"Probably is," Riley said, "but Dashay is right. What choice do we have?"

"True, but I'm going to bring up the elephant in the park. Am I recovered enough for this? I can barely walk to the bathroom."

"You'll have to ride in the cart until you can walk," replied Riley. "You'll have plenty of room now that the infernal librarian confiscated all our stuff. My bigger worry is your meds. You should be on the antibiotics for at least another week."

Dashay reached over to Coop and dropped the backpack in his lap. "Look in there."

Coop unzipped the pack and lifted out IV bags and pill bottles. "Where did he get all of this, and so fast? He just found out we were leaving."

Dashay chuckled. "I didn't stick around to ask."

Riley gave Coop's chair a shove to get it over a bump of dirt, then stopped to catch her breath. When she could talk again, she said, "I have a feeling that Jace has his own secret operations going on that he doesn't let on about."

Coop put the meds back in the pack and zipped it. "We would have called it drug dealing in the old days."

"First, he didn't ask for anything in exchange," Riley said. "Second, we didn't have rogue presidents and lunatic librarians after us in the old days."

"Excellent point," he said.

Dashay gently nudged Riley out of the way and took over pushing the wheelchair. "You don't have to do everything yourself, boss. Coop, point me to the X."

Coop guided her across the park to the woods on the opposite side. The park was deserted, but Riley scanned the area before Dashay pushed Coop's chair off the paved sidewalk onto the rough path. When she saw it was clear, she signaled for Dashay to go, then followed her into the dark forest. It was a cloudy, moonless night, and they couldn't see more than a few feet ahead.

"Any flashlights in the pack?" Dashay asked.

As Coop dug through the backpack, he said, "I guarantee Riley has a penlight in her pocket."

"Right," Riley said, and reached into her pocket. She clicked on the light and shined it down on Coop so he could see into the bag. He pulled out a flashlight and held it up for her to see. "Aren't you glad I do?"

He turned his flashlight on and laughed. "As long as you don't point it at my eyes."

"What's that about?" Dashay asked.

"Sometimes I forget how little you know about us," Riley said. "Tell you later when we're not on the run."

Coop shook his head. "That's a story that will never get told. Trade me lights, so I can use yours to read the map if you can part with it." She gave him a tap on the head with the penlight, then handed it to him and took the flashlight. "We should be close."

Riley shined the flashlight ahead of them and spotted a pinpoint glow just beyond the beam. "Hope that's Adrian."

Coop switched off his light. "Dashay, head toward that glowy little spot."

Riley stepped out in front. "I'll go first."

"Don't get too far ahead," Dashay said. "I can't see more than a foot in front of Coop's chair."

Riley kept her eyes riveted on the dimly lit path as she began walking toward the pinpoint glow. Dashay gave the wheelchair a shove to get it moving and rolled Coop over the bumpy terrain just behind her. The light was much farther away than Riley judged it to be as it played tricks with her perspective in the darkness. At times, she felt it was moving away from her, but it eventually grew brighter.

When they'd traveled what she guessed to be a hundred yards, Riley could make out a person attached to the light and quickened her pace. If they were heading into a trap, she wanted to be the only one her enemy saw. When she was within ten feet, she recognized Adrian's glasses and the shape of his head. She stopped and waited for Dashay to get closer, then waved her forward.

"It's him," she called over her shoulder.

"Riley?" a faint voice cried in the blackness.

"Yes, Adrian. Come help Dashay push Coop's chair."

Adrian ran at her, nearly knocking her over as he threw his arms around her. "I'm so relieved to see you. I've been waiting for over an hour and thought you'd been captured." It was the most affection Riley had ever seen him express, and it caught her off guard. She lifted her arms to pat his back when he released her to hug Dashay and Coop. "I was afraid I'd have to go on alone. What happens now?"

Dashay let go of the wheelchair and bent over with her hands on her side to catch her breath. "You're heavier than you look, Coop," she gasped. She sank down to the base of a tree and leaned against the trunk. "We wait. Kip will bring Biscuit and the cart loaded with supplies."

Adrian's head swiveled from side to side on his scrawny neck as he scanned the area. He was wasting his time. There was nothing but inky blackness beyond their flashlight beams. "Is it safe here? We're not that far from the park."

Dashay rubbed her legs. "Felt like a long way to me."

Riley lowered herself to the ground next to Dashay. The baby began to kick and wiggle enthusiastically. She put her hands on her belly and smiled. "Someone is enjoying our little adventure. Relax, Adrian. Jace and Patrice wouldn't have sent us here just to put us in danger. You might as well get comfortable. We could be here a while."

"Sorry to be a pain," Coop said, "but my IV bag is dry, and I'm about to burst. I don't suppose we have a bucket handy."

"No, but plenty of trees. Give me a minute to catch my breath," Riley said.

Adrian stepped in front of her and stood at attention. She was afraid he was going to salute.

"Put me to use," he said. "I don't know how to change the medicine bag, but I can take Coop to relieve himself."

Riley sucked her cheek between her teeth to keep from laughing at Coop's reaction to Adrian's offer. He gave Riley a look that cried out for help, but she said, "That's kind of you,

Adrian. Take Coop first, then I'll change his IV. Lock the wheels before lifting him out of the chair."

Riley watched as Adrian painstakingly helped Coop to his feet, treating him like a fragile egg.

When the men were out of earshot, Dashay said, "You're going to pay for that later."

Riley leaned her head on Dashay's shoulder. "It was worth it, and honestly, I'm too exhausted to get off the ground."

She patted Riley's hand. "I hear that. What's come over Adrian? I haven't seen him act this way the entire time I've known him. Only time he ever offered to help with anything was if it involved plants."

"Maybe this is what his wife saw in him."

"Whatever the reason, I'll take this Adrian any day." They were quiet for a moment, then Dashay said, "What do you think our chances are, Riley?"

"About as good as they ever are, which means, not very. But I've survived far worse. It's a vast country, my friend, and our odds are far greater without satellites and communications. We just need to stay one step ahead of this ghost that's chasing us until we reach home."

"I'll do everything in my power to make that happen. You sound tired. Close your eyes for a few minutes. I'll see to Coop. Let me get the blanket."

Riley lifted her head and waited for Dashay to spread the blanket over a patch of thick grass. She crawled to it and curled up in a protective ball. "Wake me when Kip gets here," she said, then drifted into sweet oblivion.

Riley woke with a start to the sound of a bird squawking above her head. She sat up and brushed the leaves matted in her hair. Coop was curled in the fetal position on the blanket next to her, breathing deep and steady. Adrian was stretched out in the wheelchair, and Dashay was slumped against a tree, dead asleep. She was supposed to be standing guard. Riley checked the time and was shocked to see it was three in the morning. Jace and Kip hadn't come.

Riley made a flash assessment of their situation. Coop was barely hanging on, too weak to walk more than a few feet. They had little food or other supplies, even water. Their escape was doomed before it had begun. She only had one course of action. She had to liberate Biscuit.

After pulling on her boots and lacing them in a silent rush, she switched on her penlight and hurried back up the path toward the park. She hugged the tree line, then wove her way through deserted streets. She paused at the gate leading into the fields behind the stables on the edge of town. Her courage wavered as she gazed across the tall grass stretching to the buildings beyond.

Here I go off half-cocked again. Without a plan, as usual, she thought. Zach would have been so disappointed. He had pounded it in so many times that the most crucial part of any mission or adventure was a well-ordered plan. But there hadn't been time to plan. Craig and Kearns were on their heels, and they'd get nowhere without Biscuit. He was a vital part of that plan. "Sorry, Zach," she said, as she climbed over the gate. "Having a plan didn't save you in Afghanistan, so you aren't here to help me. I'm doing the best I can. Deal with it."

Her heart pounded as she stole across the moonlit field, afraid someone would spot her in the open, but there was no other way to reach the backdoor to the stables. She made it without incident and was relieved to find the door unlocked. She rolled it open and tiptoed to Biscuit's stall, careful not to wake the stable hand sleeping in his quarters next to the office. As she neared Biscuit's stall, he raised his head and neighed in welcome. Riley moved to him as quickly as she could to quiet him, but he only got louder.

"Hush, you bloody horse," she whispered, as she went to open the stall door. Her heart sank when she saw it was bolted shut with a heavy padlock. No way she could free Biscuit without the key. She scratched Biscuit's ear. "I'll be right back. Stay quiet and you'll get a treat."

As if understanding, he nodded his head twice. Riley crept across the concrete floor, past the stable hand's closed door to the office, hoping that wasn't locked, too. She mouthed *thank you* when she found the door wasn't even closed. A bank of keys hung on the wall behind the desk. *What's the point of locks?* she thought as she started snagging keys from their hooks. She carried them back to Biscuit and began jiggling them in the locks to find the right one. On the ninth try, she heard a click, and the lock fell open.

"Almost home free, old friend," she whispered.

He gave a soft nicker, which reminded her she needed to find him a treat before leaving. As she rolled the door open, she spotted his tack hanging on the back wall. Another stroke of luck. She had him bridled and saddled minutes later, then took the reins to lead him to the field. She cringed with the echo of each hoof step on the hard floor. When they were yards from freedom, she heard a door bang open behind her. She turned to find the stable hand staring at her open-mouthed in his boxers.

"Are you stealing that horse?" he cried as she climbed into the saddle.

"I can't steal something I own," she said with her back to him. "Biscuit's my horse. The Librarian didn't take him from me. He's just allowing me to stable him here."

He ran to the door and spread his arms to block her from leaving. "Prove it."

Riley nudged Biscuit forward until they were inches from him. "Ask him yourself."

"It's three in the morning. Why are you going for a ride in the middle of the night?"

"Insomnia. I'm taking my horse, so get out of my way, or I'll run you down."

"You wouldn't."

Riley snapped the reins and shouted, "Go, Biscuit."

The horse was so surprised that he took off at a run and headed straight for the man. The stable hand dove out of the way just in time but got up immediately and ran out into the field after them.

Riley looked back as Biscuit tore across the field to see the stable hand standing in the tall grass, shaking his fist.

"You're crazy, lady. The Librarian's going to hear about this."

I'm sure he will, she thought as she urged Biscuit onward, not letting him slow until they were out of sight of the field.

She patted his neck and gave him a scratch behind the ear. "Such a good boy. I owe you a big treat for that." She directed him toward the path and hardly dared breathe until she reached the camp. She dismounted and shook Dashay to wake her.

Dashay straightened and rubbed her face. "Kip already came and left? I didn't hear a thing. Some security guard I'd make."

"It's five, Dashay. Kip never showed."

Dashay's eyes narrowed. "Then how'd Biscuit get here?"

Riley picked up Jace's backpack and tied it to the saddle. "I'll explain on the way."

"On the way where? Tell me what's going on right now, girl."

Coop and Adrian heard her, and both said, "What time is it?" in unison.

"Five," Riley said, "Coop, we're in trouble. We've got to get moving."

Coop used the tree to get to his feet. As he shuffled towards them, Adrian jumped out of the wheelchair and helped Coop into it. "Where's the cart?" Coop asked.

"Gone. This is all we have. Think you can ride Biscuit?"

"Before I answer that, tell us what's going on."

Riley sighed and crossed her arms. "We don't have time for this, but I woke at three and saw that Kip and Jace never showed. You three were dead asleep, so I went back into town and got Biscuit. Now can we go?"

Coop tried to lift himself up but was too weak and fell back onto the seat. "You did what, Riley Cooper?"

"It's done. Answer me. Can you ride that horse?"

"I can if Adrian and Dashay boost me up. You're going to ride with me."

She picked up the blanket and shook the debris off, then rolled it up and shoved it in a saddlebag. "Fine. Let's go."

Dashay put her hands on Riley's shoulders to stop her from rushing around. "Go where, Riley? Kip was supposed to draw us a map."

"Hang on," Adrian said, then hurried to a nearby tree and came back holding up a backpack. "I had just enough time to pack my belongings before coming out here. I still have our US map, and the compass is finally working. I'll chart a course to the nearest safe place to hide out until Coop is stronger."

"Great. Do that," Riley said. "We need to be as far away as we can get by dawn."

Adrian opened the map and spread it over Coop's lap. The two of them poured over it while Riley and Dashay packed their pitiful bit of gear. When they were ready, Riley helped Dashay and Adrian push Coop up onto Biscuit's back, then climbed up behind him.

"That's going to get old," Dashay said, rubbing her shoulder.

"Hopefully, you won't have to do it for long," Coop said. "Another few days and I'll be running circles around you."

"Right," Riley said, though she knew he was weeks away from even being able to walk. "Adrian, lead the way."

Adrian ignored her and started wrapping his belt around the wheelchair handles.

Dashay watched him for a few seconds. "What are you doing?"

"Why abandon a perfectly functional wheelchair? We might need this."

"Leave it," Riley snapped, imagining Craig getting closer to them by the second.

Adrian unstrapped his belt in a huff and started walking up the path away from Madisonville. Riley flinched at every flutter of a bird or chatter of a squirrel they passed, fearing it was Craig's people or Kearns' on their tails. Being on constant alert was sapping her energy, but she wouldn't be able to relax until she was sure they'd escaped.

They'd been in more dire circumstances since the CME nightmare began, but their current situation came close. She stood by her decision to move on, knowing it wouldn't be long before the entire town had discovered they were gone. She ran through scenarios of what could have happened to Kip and Jace, but none of them ended well. She prayed their new friends wouldn't pay too high a price for coming to their rescue and forced herself to accept that she would never know their fate.

———

Yeager wanted to bark at the driver to go faster, but he loathed appearing to be anything but dispassionate and in control of any situation. He forced himself to take a few deep breaths and relax into the seat. They'd gotten a late start leaving the compound because the vehicle needed a maintenance check and tune up before launching off. Yeager would have preferred to leave earlier, but he wanted to ensure his vehicle was up to snuff since repairs mid-trip would be next to impossible.

He turned to Logan Black, riding in the back seat and serving as their navigator to Madisonville. "How much farther?" Yeager asked, clipping his words.

Logan sat forward and checked their location through the window. "Thirty minutes if the road's clear. It should be since the rain has stopped."

"Looks safe enough to speed up," Yeager told the driver. Thirty minutes felt like an eternity. He'd have to keep his mind occupied to make the time pass faster. He sat back and mulled over his options once he had Daybreak in custody.

He was much farther from Philly than he'd expected to be when he captured his target. He'd considered handing him over to the military to let them get him back to Kearns, but that could mean leaving a significant asset in the hands of morons. Personnel he'd come across who'd been in the military before the CME were competent enough, but the new recruits were worthless from what he's seen. It wasn't their fault, but the result of poor leadership and lack of proper training.

He could return Daybreak to Kearns himself, but he didn't relish the idea of backtracking to Philly. He enjoyed being out in the open despite the scarcity of resources. It was enticing to imagine just disappearing into the wilderness, staking a piece of land for himself, and staying off the grid for the rest of his days.

He'd always gotten along well with others because he knew how to please people and do what was necessary to be accepted into any group, but he preferred to be on his own. Even in the military, he'd carved out time alone. His wife and children had softened this drive in him, but it had never gone away completely and had returned with a vengeance after the death of his family.

The third option was the least desirable, but perhaps the most practical. He could take care of Kearns' Daybreak problem for her permanently. He'd been in combat in Iraq and Afghanistan and had taken lives before, but these were foreign enemies, who were trying to kill him. There were clear rules of engagement. It would be a totally different matter to kill American civilians. He had no clear-cut orders but these were unprecedented times. If the threat was truly legitimate, he might rationalize eliminating these targets. At this point in his life, the moral code that he had lived by seemed to dissolve in his own despair. For now, that was the option of last resort, and he was resigned to the fact that he'd have to escort Daybreak and his companions to Kearns himself.

They passed a road sign showing Madisonville was five miles ahead. He was almost to his goal. "Take us to this Librarian as soon as we get into town," he told the boy. "If he's on top of what goes on in town, as you say, he'll know where to find these people."

"I'll take you to him," Logan said. "I only saw two of them at the hospital. They know where to find the other two."

"Just take me to the Librarian."

The boy shrugged. "Whatever. Have you decided if you'll take me with you after you find this guy?"

"I'll decide once the mission is complete. If you've led me on a goose chase, I won't have any use for you."

"I haven't," Logan said, looking him directly in the eye. It was a trait Yeager admired.

The driver pulled up to a laughably incompetent barricade guarded by a couple of teenagers.

The girl approached the driver, and he lowered his window. She held a clipboard and pencil. "Name and reason for wanting to enter Madisonville," she said without taking her eyes off the clipboard.

The driver stared at her without answering.

Logan lowered his window and stuck his head out. "Hey, Kendra."

Her eyes widened when she recognized him. "How'd you end up with these people?"

"Long story. They're here to see the Librarian. I'll vouch for them."

Kendra waved for her companion to move the barricade. "I'll take your word for it. You better not get me in trouble."

"No worries," he said as they drove through the checkpoint.

If that was how they were protecting the town, Yeager wasn't concerned about dealing with this person who called himself the Librarian. *What a ridiculous title*, he thought.

Logan directed the driver to the library, and Yeager's heart beat faster when they arrived two minutes later. The driver pulled up to the curb. The other vehicle transporting his team stopped behind them. Yeager jumped out of the Jeep and signaled for his team to stay put, then he strode toward the library entrance.

Logan caught up and stepped in his path to stop him. "Let me go first. His guards will let us in if they see me."

Yeager gestured for him to go ahead but followed close on his heels. Logan waved and winked at a girl shelving books. She rolled her eyes at him, then went back to work. He led them down a short hallway and stopped in front of a closed door, guarded by two mountainous men. *That's more like it*, Yeager thought.

"The Librarian is expecting me," Logan said.

One of the guards glanced at Yeager, who held his gaze, then said, "He's in an emergency meeting. You'll have to wait."

"I don't think you want to keep this guy waiting. What's so important about this meeting?"

"None of your business. I'll tell the boss you're here but wait over there in those chairs."

"Why? You've never stopped me from seeing the Librarian before."

"It's fine, Logan," Yeager said. "These men are just doing their job and following orders. The Librarian must have a good reason for not wanting to be disturbed. We'll wait in the chairs."

"Whatever," Logan said as he followed Yeager. "The Librarian won't be happy when he finds out his bruisers wouldn't let us in."

Yeager quietly lowered himself into a chair, though he was incensed at being delayed by this backwoods upstart. Fortunately, they didn't have to wait long. The guard they'd spoken with stepped out of the office and waved them over. He held the door for them as they stepped inside.

Yeager sauntered into the office and employed great restraint to stop from bursting out laughing at the sight of the scrawny young man in a superhero T-shirt standing behind the desk. He was the last thing Yeager had expected, and he wondered how this punk had kept the townsfolk in line.

There were two other men and a woman with him. They looked like typical small town residents, though the woman was roughly the same age as the Librarian and attractive in a natural country-girl way.

The Librarian sank into his chair and said, "Logan, who is this?"

Yeager stepped closer to the desk and extended his hand before Logan could answer. The Librarian gave his hand a half-hearted shake. "My name is Colonel Yeager. I'm here on a mission of utmost importance on behalf of President Kearns. I'm looking for four fugitives."

The librarian held up a hand to stop him and shuffled through a mess of papers on his desk. He pulled out the wanted posters and spread them on top of the other papers.

"Are these the ones you're trailing?"

Yeager was surprised but pleased to see the posters had made it to Madisonville. "Yes. Logan tells me they're here."

"*Were* here, Colonel. They stole a horse and escaped in the middle of the night. I have my best trackers searching for them."

Yeager did his best to conceal his devastation at the news, but the Librarian's look told him he wasn't fooled. "Your best trackers? I hope they're more skilled than those two at the checkpoint."

"Far more skilled. Trust me. Those two who allowed these people into my town in the first place will be replaced within the hour. We've stepped up security and are questioning any refugees wanting to enter."

Yeager eyed him for a moment, then said, "My team will take over the search. Set up an operations center where I can work. Everyone answers to me from this moment forward. Tell me what I need to know."

"Our best lead is the two people who I thought were my friends that helped the fugitives escape. They're her brother and nephew, actually," the Librarian said, pointing to the pretty country girl. "She's my girlfriend."

Yeager raised an eyebrow and said, "Ouch."

The woman shook her head sadly. "I was totally clueless about what Jace and Kip were doing." She wrapped the Librarian's hand in both of hers. "We were having dinner while my own family was betraying us."

Yeager didn't buy her act for a second, recognizing the ploy to distract the Librarian while her family helped the others escape. The Librarian, however, ate up every word. Yeager caught her eye, and she held his gaze for a moment before looking away with the color rising in her cheeks.

"Would it be possible for us to talk alone?" he asked.

The Librarian gave her a peck on the cheek. "I'll see you tonight, babe," he said before shooing the others out with her.

Yeager waited for the door to close behind them, then said, "Where are the suspects?"

"In a holding cell at the police station, but I couldn't get anything out of them."

Yeager gestured at the guards. "Not even those two?"

"Those are my bodyguards. Some people I do business with are less than trustworthy, but I'm a pacifist."

Not surprising, Yeager thought as he turned on his heels and started for the door. "Take me to the suspects."

"What about my bodyguards?"

Yeager ignored the question and kept walking. The corners of his lips curled up a fraction when he heard the Librarian scurrying to catch up with him. He'd removed the punk pacifist from power in sixty-seconds.

After the Librarian gave Yeager's driver directions to the police station, Yeager said, "You never gave me your name."

He got a smug look, and said, "People address me as the Librarian."

Without shifting his gaze from the windshield, Yeager said, "That's a ridiculous title. Commands no respect. I refuse to call you that. What is your name?"

"Dr. Craig Himes."

"You're a doctor? *That's* a title that commands respect. Why wouldn't you use it after all the work to earn it?"

Yeager could tell Craig was doing his best not to pout. "I grew up in this town and my father is a doctor, too. I wanted to distinguish myself from him."

"You must be intelligent. Librarian is the best you could come up with?" Craig nodded, then turned toward the window. "Are you a medical doctor?"

"No. My doctorate is in literature, hence the Librarian. My father's a physicist."

Yeager detected a hint of daddy issues. If this man were his target, he'd find a way to exploit that. He hesitated a moment before saying, "I'd like to address you as Dr. Himes. Is that acceptable to you?"

Craig looked him in the eyes. "If you won't call me Librarian, just call me Craig. That puts us on friendlier terms."

"If you prefer, Craig it is." The driver stopped in front of the police station and got out to open Yeager's door. As he climbed out, he said, "You see, Craig, that's respect."

He took the steps two at a time with Craig trudging behind. His disappointment at just missing Daybreak hadn't diminished, but toying with Craig had at least distracted him from it for a moment.

The lone police officer on duty led them to the holding cell.

The suspects were sitting on opposite benches facing each other. They got to their feet when the officer unlocked the door for Yeager and Craig.

"Knock this off, Craig," the older one said. "You've held us long enough. Let us out."

Craig leaned against the bars and crossed his arms in a pathetic attempt to regain control of the situation. "That's Dr. Himes to you, and not until you give this man the information he wants. This is Colonel Yeager. He works directly for President Kearns."

Yeager read the concern in the man's eyes. He may not have respected Craig, but he understood genuine power.

Yeager sat on the end of one bench and crossed his legs. "What's your name, son?"

He only hesitated a fraction of a second before saying, "Jace. He's my nephew, Kip."

"Thank you, Jace. Please, you can both sit." They lowered themselves back onto the benches without taking their eyes off him. "I'm tracking four dangerous people that you helped escape last night. I'm not angry with you. You seem like nice guys, and I'm sure they fooled you into believing they're innocent. All I need is for you to tell me where they went."

Kip opened his mouth, but Jace put up his hand to stop him. "We seriously have no idea where they were going. All we can tell you is where we told them to wait for us to bring them supplies. Craig's idiots captured us before we got that far. We don't know what happened to those people after eight last night. That's the truth."

He didn't show any signs of lying. Yeager turned his eyes on Kip. He just nodded enthusiastically.

"They can't have gotten far, Colonel," Craig said. "The redhead is pregnant and one of the men is seriously ill. Plus, they don't have any supplies, just the horse."

"Will you show me where they were supposed to meet you?" Yeager asked Jace.

When Jace hesitated, Kip said, "I will. I've never gotten in trouble in my life. I want to go home."

Jace was clearly disappointed with his nephew but stayed quiet. He rested his elbows on his knees and lowered his head.

"I'll make sure you're released if you cooperate," Yeager said. "Tell me where you where you're supposed to meet."

"I need a city map that shows the park."

Yeager signaled for the police officer to get him what he needed. While they waited, he said, "Can you describe the area?"

Kip described a wooded area beyond a park on the edge of town. Yeager's disappointment lessened, and his hope was rekindled. It had gone much easier than expected. His quarry had a horse, but some in his party were on foot. One was pregnant, another ill, and they had no supplies. He'd have them in custody by the end of the day.

The officer returned with the map, and Kip drew an X on the meeting spot. It looked easy enough to find.

Yeager stood and left the cell with Craig following. When the police officer locked the cell, Kip jumped to his feet. "You said I could go if I helped you."

Yeager turned and gave him a kind smile. "That's up to Dr. Himes, but I'll put in a kind word. Thank you for your cooperation."

Jace joined Kip at the bars as they walked to the door "You suck, Craig," he shouted. "And stay away from my sister."

"Adrian, we need to stop," Riley called out as she grabbed ahold of Coop's shirt before he toppled out of the saddle. "Coop's had it."

Adrian and Dashay rushed over to help lower Coop to the ground. Riley slid off behind him with a groan, then grabbed his blanket to spread it under a tree. They'd traveled for three days since their escape, sleeping on bare ground in the woods, and avoiding towns, just like she and Coop had done after leaving the ranch, but without a tent or provisions. They'd been fresh and healthy then, but their current condition was far from that. Instead of recovering, Coop was growing weaker by the day, and she was getting more pregnant. It was critical they find a place with resources to stop and recuperate.

Riley got Coop settled, then shuffled to the stream running nearby. She lowered herself onto a boulder and ran her tongue over her cracked lips. They'd passed countless bodies of water in the past three days but had to boil whatever they collected. They'd run out of matches and had no success starting a fire the old-fashioned way. It had been twelve hours since their last drink, and temperatures had soared in the afternoon. As Riley watched the crystal stream trickle by, she was tempted to break her rule and risk a sip. She would have traded anything for those earlier days of endless rain.

"How much farther to that town, Adrian?" she asked, in a hoarse voice.

He wiped his sunburned forehead with a neckerchief. "I'd guess only two or three hours."

She raised her eyes to him, wishing she'd heard wrong, not knowing if she could make it another ten minutes, let alone two hours. "Maybe we should stop here tonight."

"I vote for that," Coop said. "I'm exhausted and still not comfortable going into this town you're taking us to, Adrian, no matter how small and out of the way it is."

Dashay dropped onto the boulder next to Riley. "We won't survive much longer without water, and our food rations are almost gone. We have to go, even if it means risking capture. Our other option is a permanent nap. I'm not liking that choice."

Adrian walked to the edge of the stream. "Are you sure we

can't drink this water? If our choice is this or death, what do we have to lose?"

Riley hefted herself off the rock and moved next to him. The glimmering water was so enticing that her resolve wavered, but she stood her ground. "Coop and Dashay nearly died from contaminated water. This stream may look clear and fresh, but we have no way of knowing what could be living in it. The only water sources we can trust are wells, springs, or water we've boiled. Dashay's right. We have to move on today, but we'll take a rest in the shade first."

"No argument from me," Adrian said. "I don't have the strength to get Coop into that saddle."

They gathered around Coop under the enormous oak tree to take advantage of its glorious shade. Riley estimated that the temperature was close to the nineties. She rested her head against the trunk and watched Biscuit hungrily chomp the grass and take long draughts from the stream. All her problems would have been solved if she had the immune system of a horse, but even Biscuit was showing serious signs of wear.

Riley's eyelids began to droop, so she let them close, wishing she could nap, but the baby decided it was playtime. She placed her hands on her belly, hoping to quiet him, but he kicked and tumbled even more. She gently ran her hands over the bump but stopped when she felt a tap against her palm. It was the first time she'd felt a kick from the outside. She reached for Coop's hand and placed it on the spot.

He rolled the back of his head on the trunk until he was facing her. "What are you doing?"

"Just wait," she whispered.

Two seconds later, the baby gave a firm kick. Coop's eyes flew open, and he sat up, leaving his hand on Riley. "Was that our baby?" Riley nodded with tears in her eyes. "Make him do it again."

Riley chuckled and put her hand over his. "I can't make him, but you'll be able to feel his movements more and more often as he grows."

"I'm going to laugh and laugh when he comes out as she," Dashay said.

Coop beamed at her. "He or she or three, I don't care. As long as it's healthy."

"It's unlike anything you can imagine when they're born," Adrian said. He opened his mouth to go on, then paused and spun around. He pointed across the meadow. "Did you hear that?"

Dashay climbed to her feet and squinted toward where he'd pointed. "Hear what?"

Before Adrian could answer, Biscuit lifted his head and cocked his ears. The silly horse whinnied and trotted in the direction Adrian was looking. A moment later, a man came over a small rise, riding on a horse-drawn farm wagon. The others frantically glanced at each other, but there was no point in bothering to hide. The man had seen them.

He guided the horse to within ten feet of them, with Biscuit merrily trotting along beside them.

"Daft horse," Riley mumbled as the man climbed off the cart and walked toward them.

It only took seconds to guess his community association. He wore a straw hat and had a long beard, but no mustache. His simple, homespun trousers were held up by suspenders strapped over his white button-down shirt. He looked to be about forty-five-years-old and appeared strong and fit. His face was impassive, but his blue eyes projected confidence and directness.

"I didn't know there were Amish communities in Kentucky," Riley whispered to Coop.

"Afternoon, folks," the man said in a heavy German or Scandinavian accent when he reached them. "Do you realize you are on my private property?"

All but Coop got to their feet. Riley held out her hand for him to shake, but he ignored it. His gaze flicked over her, then moved to the others.

"I'm sorry we trespassed," she said. "We didn't see a sign or fence."

He removed his hat and wiped his forehead with a white handkerchief. "Those haven't been necessary this far out. No one ever comes this way. What are *you* doing here, especially in your condition?"

"We're just passing through and got off course," Adrian said. "Can you tell how far we are from Marion?"

"By the looks of you, farther than you're going today." He turned to Biscuit, who had come up behind him and was sniffing his hair. "He looks like a friendly fellow."

"That's Biscuit. He's the best horse living," Adrian said, and grinned at his friend.

The man reached into his pocket and took out a dried apple slice, which he fed to Biscuit. *You have a new friend for life,* Riley thought.

"My name is Aaron Riehl. You look in need of help. What can I do for you?"

Dashay stepped between Riley and Mr. Riehl. "I'm Dashay Robinson. We're out of water and food. What you see is all we have. That man under the tree is recovering from an infection that almost killed him just over a week ago, and as you can see, my friend is almost five months pregnant. Anything you can offer would be welcome."

Mr. Riehl gave a curt nod, then combed his fingers through his beard. "I'm aware of what has happened to the world outside my community. Since we lead separate, plain lives, we have gone on as before, mostly. Many outsiders have come begging for help. Occasionally, we've obliged those requests, as is our Christian duty. It has not always ended up well for us, but I judge you to be sincere in your need, and I see you are unarmed."

As Dashay and Adrian went to get Coop on his feet, Riley

stepped closer to Mr. Riehl. "My name is Dr. Riley Poole," she said, using her full title, which was something she rarely did when meeting strangers, but something told her it was safe to be honest with this man. "I don't want to appear ungrateful, but can you tell me where you're taking us? We've also had offers of help not go well for us."

"I am not offended, Dr. Poole. My grandmother left this world some months ago but had lived with us for the last ten years since my grandfather died. Her cottage is on a secluded piece of my property and has been empty for years, though I maintain it and keep it clean. No one from my community will know of your presence there."

"That's very kind of you," she said. "We accept your kind offer of help, and we will do what we can to be of help to you."

His look told her he didn't believe she had much to offer, but she wasn't insulted. She'd gotten that same look from many other men in the past.

Once Coop was settled in the cart, Riley and Dashay climbed in beside him. Adrian mounted Biscuit and followed the cart. They rode for fifteen minutes through cultivated farmland and lovely, gentle hills interspersed with streams and groves of trees. They passed the occasional shed or other farm structure, but they never saw a single person. The uncultivated land was as Riley imagined it had looked when the first humans set foot on it.

As the wagon turned onto the long dirt road leading to the cottage, Riley leaned closer to Mr. Riehl so he could hear her. "Won't aiding us cause problems for you? We don't want to get you into trouble."

Keeping his eyes focused on the road, he said, "That's a misconception of many English."

"English?" Dashay said.

"What they call the non-Amish," Coop whispered.

Mr. Riehl nodded. "Your friend is correct, Miss Robinson. We're a closed community. We do not marry outside of our congregation, but we don't isolate ourselves, either. Many have friends outside our communities. Some of our people had non-Amish business partners or conducted business with the English before what they call the CME happened."

"Thank you for explaining," Riley said. "So, housing us on your property is acceptable?" Mr. Riehl turned and gave her an odd grin but kept silent. "He made a point earlier to say no one would know we're here," she whispered to Coop and Dashay. "Since we're trying to stay under the radar without starving to death, this is a godsend. I say we keep to ourselves and stay within sight of this cottage until we're ready to get back on the road."

Coop leaned his head against the back of the wooden wagon. "I won't be going for hikes anytime soon," he croaked.

Riley let her mind wander as the wagon rumbled along, trying to make sense of their bizarre experience in Madisonville and where they were headed. Despite Craig and their forced escape, she was grateful for the hospital staff who helped save Coop. Thinking of the hospital, she suddenly sat forward and said, "Knee replacement."

Dashay opened an eye and stared at her. "What are you babbling about, girl?"

"Mrs. Himes' knee replacement. It was scheduled for today. I feel terrible for that poor woman. She was in serious pain and is just another one of Craig's victims."

"She's his mother. Craig will take care of her," Dashay said. "With refugees streaming into Madisonville, there's bound to be another doctor who can perform the surgery."

"That's what I'm going to tell myself," Riley said.

The road curved slightly toward the south, and the cottage came into view. It was a simple one-story structure that would meet their needs just fine. Anything would beat sleeping on bare ground out in the open.

Mr. Riehl pulled the wagon into the circle loop in front of the cottage and stopped at the three steps leading to the door. He jumped down and came around to drop the wagon tailgate.

"Dr. Poole, open the door, please. Miss Robinson and the man riding Biscuit can help me get your sick friend inside the cottage."

Adrian dismounted and joined them at the back of the wagon. "My name is Dr. Adrian Landry. Please, call me Adrian," he said, then pointed to Coop. "That's Dr. Cooper. He's Dr. Poole's husband. He goes by Coop. They're medical doctors. I'm a scientist."

"I see," Mr. Riehl said, and cracked the faintest smile. "Now we are acquainted, let's get Coop out of this heat."

Riley took a quick look around the yard before dragging herself up the stairs and was surprised but also relieved to see a bank of solar panels sitting next to an old diesel generator. She opened the door wide, then moved aside to give them space to bring Coop into the austere, two-room cottage. While they carried him to the bedroom, she waited in the main room, feeling like she'd been transported back to the nineteenth century. Even so, it was better than most of the places she'd stay in for the past five months.

Mr. Riehl came out and gestured for her to sit on a sagging sofa with faded, light blue upholstery. Dashay took the rocking chair, and Adrian dropped into a chair at the table. Mr. Riehl remained standing.

"I understand that this isn't the type of lodging you are accustomed to, but I will do my best to see to your comfort."

"Compared to where we've been, Mr. Riehl, this is like a heavenly mansion," Dashay said.

"I'm glad to hear that and please call me Aaron. We are friends now." He gazed around the room with fondness. "This home has been a part of my life since I was born. My grandparents were very tied to the old ways, so I was updating the cottage for my daughter to live in after her marriage, but

God sent the CME. The power inverter connected to the solar panels was destroyed."

Riley's head spun as she struggled to make the strings of Aaron's words make sense. Everything since they met him had been an experience of extremes. He'd delivered them to the cottage in a horse-drawn wagon, but minutes later was discussing solar panel inverters, shattering all her assumptions about the Amish.

"I was wondering how much your community was affected by the CME," Adrian said, drawing her back to the conversation.

"Not nearly as much as the rest of the world, but we definitely noticed. I haven't replaced the inverter yet, but the generator works, so you'll have limited electricity for the lamps and the water pump. I'll show you how to use it before I go. Cooking and heating the water can be done with the wood-burning stove. There's chopped wood stacked out back. You may have to chop more, depending on how long you're here. I'll return with food and other provisions tonight."

The three of them stood when he headed for the door.

"You've saved our lives," Riley said. "I don't know how we can repay you."

"I don't expect payment. Helping you is my Christian duty and my honor." He held out his hand to her. She clasped it in both of hers and gave a slight nod. "Rest now and recover. I'll be back soon. Adrian, if you'll come with me."

As Dashay closed the door behind them, Riley ran to the sink and held her mouth under the faucet, then turned the handle, but not even a drop came out.

Dashay put her hands on her hips and shook her head. "That won't work until they get the generator running to power the pump, but I saw a hand pump in the yard."

Riley took a cast-iron pot hanging from a hook above the stove and hurried outside with Dashay right behind her. Dashay pumped the handle while Riley held the pot under the spigot. After a few pumps, the glorious clear liquid poured into the pot. Riley was tempted to bury her face in it, but restrained herself. When the bowl was full, she carried it inside and drank her fill using a mug from the cupboard, then took it into the bedroom for Coop.

He was propped against the headboard with his eyes half-open. The sight of him sparked a pang of anxiety in Riley. She knew he wouldn't have survived the night if Aaron hadn't come along. She filled the mug and sat on the bed next to him to help him drink. He took small sips at first, then gulped the water. Within minutes, he sat up straighter and grinned at her with the lifesaving liquid dripping from his chin.

"Our problems are solved, Babe," he whispered. "We've escaped the Librarian and thrown Kearns' trackers off our tail. We'll have time to recover our strength in this safe, beautiful place. It's almost as if someone's watching out for us."

Riley chuckled and scooted closer to him. "Have you gotten religious on me?"

He gave her a long, tender kiss. "Maybe it's this place or the fact that I was hours from death, again."

"I'm not saying you're wrong, but whatever it is, I agree, and I'm eternally grateful." She gave him a kiss before climbing off the bed. "You rest while we get settled. I'll wake you when the food gets here."

He laid down and rolled onto his side as she walked out and closed the door. Dashay was standing at the sink, watching a stream of water pouring from the faucet.

Dashay turned to her with tears glistening in her eyes. "Have you ever seen anything so beautiful?"

"Not sure I have," Riley said, as she set the pot under the faucet to refill it. Dashay sniffled and put her arm around Riley. She leaned against her with a sigh. "We are really and truly saved, Dashay. I expected Coop to die today, but once again, help arrived from a kind stranger just in time. Coincidence? Fate? Divine providence?"

Dashay stepped away and turned to face her. "What's gotten into you?"

Riley shook her head. "Something Coop said."

"I say stop questioning it. Accept and be grateful."

"It's hard not to question, but I am grateful, and I intend to enjoy each second while it lasts."

"Glad to hear it. Now, as your self-assigned midwife, I'm ordering you to climb into that bed with your husband and rest. Let me take charge for once."

Riley hugged her, then trudged to the room and hefted herself onto the bed. Coop was sleeping soundly, and his color was better. She watched him for a moment before closing her eyes, feeling secure for the first time in as long as she could remember.

Yeager walked to the edge of the river and squatted over the hoof prints leading toward the water. He'd followed Daybreak's tracks for two days from where he and his team had found the wheelchair in the woods, but he feared the trail had gone cold. He'd sent two of his men across the river in a raft, but they found no tracks on the opposite side. The water was too deep for the horse to walk, so they all must have swum far downstream. His team could search for days and not find the spot where they exited the water.

He strode back to the jeep for his map and spread it across the hood. Dr. Walser in Huntington had informed him that Daybreak was traveling west with his party toward Colorado Springs. They'd already been forced south by the floods. They wouldn't want to get too far off track in their condition. He studied the map for the most likely places for them to go. It was a sparsely populated farming region, so their options were limited.

He folded the map and whistled for his men. Once they were congregated around the Jeep, he said, "I was hoping to avoid this, but we need to split up." He divided them into four groups of two and gave them their assigned grids. "I'll take this area with Amish settlements. They're not likely to give refuge to outsiders, but they should know more about the area than anyone else. Return to Madisonville within a week. Remember, Kearns wants Daybreak alive. If you run into trouble, get to the closest base and use the radio. You have the frequency."

They broke for their separate vehicles while he gave directions to his driver and climbed into the Jeep. He was growing impatient but still had time and preparedness on his side. The chase was far from over, but he was as confident as ever of accomplishing his mission.

Yeager directed his driver to the largest Amish community in the area. It had taken more than a week, threats, and painstaking intel gathering to glean information in the Amish communities he'd searched so far. He'd concluded this was the one most likely to be harboring Daybreak and his associates. The smaller communities he'd visited were closed and viewed all non-Amish with suspicion, but he'd learned enough from them and non-Amish he'd come across, that this sect was more open and interacted with outsiders regularly.

He'd returned to Madisonville before searching the area to get reports from the rest of his team, but they'd failed to hunt down Daybreak just as he had. He gathered his full team and headed back to Amish country to continue his search, timing his arrival to coincide with the conclusion of their Sunday services. Yeager hoped to catch them at their after church meal.

He'd crossed paths with a member of the congregation who willingly shared the home where that week's service would be held. By the time his driver parked the Jeep next to the line of black buggies, several older men were on the porch watching them. Yeager got out and approached in his usual self-assured manner.

One of the oldest looking men with an impressive beard stepped forward with his hands clasped in front of him. The stoic men behind him followed Yeager with their eyes but remained silent.

"You are trespassing on private property, sir," the old man said, keeping his voice calm and even.

Yeager stopped at the bottom step of the porch and gave a warm smile. "I am aware, and I apologize for interrupting your Sunday worship, but I'm pursuing an urgent matter. I'm here on behalf of President Kearns. She has declared martial law, which gives me the right to enter your property." He reached into his pocket and pulled out the ID Kearns' people created for him before he left Philly. "My name is Colonel Orson Yeager. I'm searching for four dangerous fugitives and believe they may be hiding amongst your community."

Yeager signaled for his driver to get him the wanted posters. When he had them in his hand, he ascended two steps, just close enough for the old man to take them if he reached. The man didn't move.

"I assure you, no one is hiding on any of our properties. We would know and wouldn't allow it. Many have tried since God sent the sun flare and have been *encouraged* to leave."

"I mean no offense, sir, but these are skilled subversives. They could be hiding nearby, and you would never know. All I'm asking for is the chance to search your dwellings."

Yeager noticed the slightest flare of the man's nostrils but nothing more. "That is unacceptable, sir, and I won't permit it."

"Let me be clear. I'm going to search with your cooperation or not. If you attempt to stop me, your land will be confiscated, and you'll be forced to leave the area. I don't want that. You don't want that. Allow me to conduct my search and I'll be on my way."

One man behind him leaned forward and whispered in his ear. A few of the men closest to him nodded.

"We know every inch of this land and can assure you that the people you seek are not here, but we will permit your search with your word that you'll leave and not bother us again once you've finished."

Yeager extended his hand to the man. "You have my word that we'll leave and that my men and I will do our best not to interfere in your lives."

The man stared at Yeager's hand for a moment, then gave it a firm shake. "We appreciate that. I will have one of our brothers show you the locations of all dwellings in our community. Do you have a map?"

Yeager gave him a broad smile, trying not to laugh at his question. Not only did he possess an extremely detailed map, but he'd obtained a photo with an aerial view of the region taken two years earlier. "Yes, I have a map, sir. That would be helpful."

The man turned toward the open door of the large house, and said, "Aaron, come here please."

A man in his forties with an equally impressive beard came out onto the porch a few seconds later. "Yes, Thomas?"

The old man pointed to Yeager. "Colonel Yeager here is searching for four people. Have you seen strangers on any of our properties?"

"I haven't. What do they look like?"

"He has drawings. I want you to indicate every structure within the boundaries of our community to the Colonel, so he can search."

Yeager noticed the slight hesitation before Aaron nodded and put it down to the man, not wanting his team nosing around their properties.

Aaron turned to Yeager, "What do you need me to do?"

"Is there a table where we can work?"

Aaron nodded before bounding down the steps and motioning for Yeager to follow him. He took him to a picnic table behind the house. Yeager's driver followed with a folder containing the map along with other information he'd gathered. Yeager spread the map on the table and handed Aaron a red marker.

"All I need is for you to circle every structure in the area with that pen. Make sure not to overlook any because if I find them, I won't be pleased."

"I'll do my best, sir, but some barns or other buildings may have been constructed that I'm not aware of. They'd be near houses though, so you'll be able to see them."

"Do what you can."

Yeager watched over Aaron's shoulder as he circled properties for them to search. There were far more than Yeager expected. His team would have to work efficiently to search them all before Daybreak's party got word of the search.

Aaron drew one last circle encompassing the entire area and handed Yeager the pen. "I've tried to remember all the properties, but if I've missed any, they'll be inside this circle."

Yeager patted his shoulder. "Good man. Thank you." He studied the map for a moment, then folded it and slipped it inside the folder.

Aaron stood and gave a slight nod. "You're welcome. Would you and your men like some lunch? I'm sure there is extra food from our meal."

"No, but thanks for the offer. We need to get to work."

Yeager headed back to the Jeep with his goldmine of information. It was more than he'd expected. They'd been prepared to search without cooperation but having the map would simplify his job. He climbed into the Jeep and ordered the driver to take him back to the house two miles away that he was using as his base of operations. Within the hour, he and his men would be one step closer to capturing Daybreak.

Aaron ate his meal, then gave the excuse that he had a sick heifer he needed to attend to and left. It wasn't a lie, but he'd attended to the cow earlier that morning. He reminded himself that he'd need to check on her again before returning home that evening.

He drove the wagon slowly until he was outside of view of the house, then urged his horse to go as fast as he dared. He bounded off the wagon the instant he pulled in front of the cottage. He raced up the stairs and pounded on the door. He was tempted to barge in but didn't want to be rude.

Riley came to the door and gave him a worried look when she opened it. "What's wrong, Aaron?"

"There's a man named Colonel Yeager searching for you. He gave me these."

He held out the posters to her but she didn't take them. "Yes, we've seen those. Do what you want with them." She moved aside and motioned for him to enter. "There's no way we can prove it, but the information on those posters is a lie. None of it is true, but we understand if you want to throw us off your land."

Her look was open and honest compared to that of Yeager. He was certain that man was hiding something. "I have no intention of doing that, but I do need to hide you."

"We can't let you do that, Aaron," Adrian said. "You've saved our lives and given us days of rest. We'll go now."

Dashay came away from the sink and moved next to Riley. "We're grateful you believe us, but why do you?"

"It only took me moments to judge that you are decent people. This Yeager is not, in my opinion, and I do not trust the government. You've done nothing to make me doubt your story or integrity. I make my choice knowing full well the consequences if I'm caught."

The others glanced at each other, then Riley said, "I hope nothing makes you regret this, but we accept your offer of help. What do you want us to do?"

"Throw as many of your belongings in the wagon as you can and hide the rest in the chests and wardrobe. I'm taking you to an English warehouse that belonged to my friend. He and his family didn't survive the CME. The warehouse has been empty since. I'll come back for you when it's safe. It may take several days. I'll bring you food and water as usual."

Riley nodded and turned to collect her belongings. Aaron helped them pack the wagon and hide the few possessions they wouldn't need. He threw in all the quilts and blankets and some dishes. They were ready fifteen minutes later. He made them lie down in the wagon and covered them with the quilts and hay before heading to the warehouse.

During the ride to the warehouse, he questioned himself several times about what he thought he was doing. If he were caught helping Riley and the others, he could lose everything, even his family, but he couldn't get the story of the Good Samaritan out of his head. Doing the right thing was right, even sometimes at substantial risk, and the only person he had to answer to was God.

He pulled the wagon around the back of the warehouse so it couldn't be seen from the road, then helped the others out before shooing them inside the building. While he was gathering an armload of their supplies, he heard Dashay gasp. He hurried inside to find the cause. They were all staring toward the southwest corner of the warehouse. Where four partially decayed bodies lay slumped against the wall. Coop walked to them and squatted down to inspect them.

"They must have come here for shelter," he said. "Looks like they've been here for months and must have died of thirst or starvation."

"I'm sorry. I didn't know," Aaron said. "I'll get rid of them."

As he started for the back of the warehouse, Riley put a hand on his arm to stop him. "We've seen worse, Aaron, and we're doctors. We'll dispose of the bodies tonight after dark."

Aaron knew he should insist on doing it, but he needed to get back before he was missed. "Fine but be careful. I have to go now. I'll bring food tomorrow night. You should have enough to last until then. Stay out of sight."

He left without another word and went to check his heifer with his gut tied in a knot. He'd done what he could and would leave the rest to God.

Riley finished drying the last of the plates and put them back in the cupboard. She'd washed the dishes to the thunk of Coop's ax as he chopped wood in the back. She was going to miss watching him swing that ax. It was such a turn on. She'd decided it would be his new chore once they were home.

It had taken him two weeks to recover from Typhoid Fever and regain his strength. The week in that disgusting warehouse when they were hiding from Yeager hadn't helped. She was grateful every day that they'd escaped him with Aaron's help, and there'd been no consequences for him.

Riley and the others finally had a name and description to put with the person hunting them, even if that provided little comfort. Yeager was clearly determined to stop at nothing to find them. The escape from Madisonville had been a close call. They all hoped their month of hiding out on Aaron's farm had thrown him off their trail.

Coop had been slowly adding activities to rebuild his lost muscle mass. Riley kept telling him he was going at it too hard, but he ignored her. He wanted to be strong enough to get back on the road as soon as they could. Riley's growing belly was his biggest motivation. When they'd been at the farm for four weeks, he declared it was time to go. Riley agreed, though it was heartbreaking to leave their peaceful sanctuary behind. It reminded her of leaving their first camp by the river in the early days after they left the ranch. They were only there for a few days but leaving had felt the same

Aaron had gone above and beyond what they'd asked of him. He'd provided them with food and provisions they needed for the journey. He'd even found four bikes to replace the ones they'd had to abandon in Madisonville. He'd trained them to hunt small game with a shotgun, if they ever got their hands on one, and lent them his to use while they were at the cottage.

Another nugget of useful information that Aaron passed on was how to find underground springs and other ways to procure water. There would be bodies of water along most of their route, but they wouldn't always have time or means to stop and boil it. It was a comfort to know they wouldn't end up in the condition they were in when Aaron found them.

The most significant gift he'd given them was in helping to build a new cart. Besides being a farmer, he was a skilled carpenter, and the new cart was an improvement on the one they left behind. It was bigger, sturdier, and had compartments for the supplies they'd collected with his help.

They'd done their best to repay his generosity in the small ways they could but were limited in what they could offer. They had tended to the land surrounding the cottage and helped him continue to update the cabin for his daughter, whose wedding would be held the week after they left. Adrian had helped him install the new solar inverter and overhaul the generator.

Riley and Dashay spent most of their time cooking, cleaning, and tending to Coop until he was recovered. It was a simple and contented existence. Riley could see the appeal of that life but understood that they weren't living an actual Amish existence. Being on the farm also helped her understand why her father became a farmer after retiring from his medical practice. She looked forward to working alongside him when they reached home.

Dashay finished sweeping the floor and hung the broom on its hook before turning to face Riley. "Guess it's time to go. If you didn't have your children waiting for you, I'd stay here forever."

"Aaron's daughter might have something to say about that, and I don't think either of us would exactly fit in with the Amish lifestyle. Besides, get out there and find Nico."

"Nico," Dashay repeated softly. "Sometimes, I forget what he even looks like. You know as well as I do the odds of finding him are remote."

Riley took her hand and led her toward the door. "He knows where you are headed, and you know where his family is. It may take time, but you'll find each other. It definitely won't happen if you stay on a secluded farm in the middle of Kentucky." They walked out onto the stoop and took a last look around. "When we get to my dad's farm, we'll have the best of both worlds; modern conveniences and country life."

"Let's get out of here, then." She bounded down the steps to where Coop was helping Adrian organize their belongings in the cart. "Remember to leave room for Riley."

"I don't need to go in the cart," Riley said. "I've been riding my bike around here every day to get the muscle mass back since Aaron brought them."

"You're fine to ride today," Coop said, "but I give it two weeks before that bump of yours is too big for you to keep your balance on the bike."

Riley ran her hands over her belly, knowing his prediction was probably right, but she wasn't there yet.

"Is Aaron coming to say goodbye?" Adrian asked. "We're ready to go, and I'd like to get out of here as early as possible before the sun gets too high."

"He told me last night before he left that he wanted us to wait for him. Said he has another gift."

"What else could he possibly have to give us? Looks like he's already cleaned out the entire county to outfit us," Dashay said.

Coop shrugged. "No idea, but I guarantee it will be worth waiting for."

Adrian looked up at the sky. "As long as he gets here soon."

They'd held a meeting the night before to make their final plans for departing and had decided it would be best to travel from five to noon, then stop and rest until five in the evening and go on until eleven. Temperatures had continued to soar by the day, and Aaron told them it was the hottest summer he could remember. That had led Adrian to give them a detailed class on why he thought the CME had affected the weather, not that any of them had asked or cared. All they knew was that it would be too hot to travel during the middle of the day.

Riley glanced at her watch. It was almost eight, an hour later than they had hoped to leave, but they couldn't leave without thanking Aaron for all he had done for them.

They stood around fidgeting for a few more minutes until Riley said, "I'm going to use the bathroom one more time since it will be my last chance at an actual toilet in who knows how long."

She took her time walking back inside since there was no hurry. After using the toilet and flushing it a few times for good measure, she did a third check, making sure they hadn't left any belongings or forgotten to clean anything. The house was cleaner than when they'd arrived, and she didn't find any of their things. She shrugged and went to join the others. When she got to the stoop, she was relieved to see a plume of dust coming up the road.

"Here he comes," she called to the others.

They turned toward the road in unison as Aaron came into

view. He pulled his wagon next to the cart and reached behind the seat to retrieve something wrapped in a quilt. He jumped down and smiled as he offered the bundle to Coop. He took it and unwrapped the quilt to find a shotgun and a rifle.

"These are for you. I'm sure you would have found your own somewhere along the way, but I wanted to make sure you had a way to get food. We can't have the little mother going hungry. Along with the fishing poles we made, you should have plenty to eat."

"We can't take these," Coop sputtered, overcome by his generosity. "You need these to feed your own family."

Aaron dismissed his comment with a quick wave of his hand. "We have more guns than we can use, and it's easy for me to get more. Take them so I can sleep at night knowing you are fed and safe."

Riley almost forgot herself and gave him a hug, so she stepped away in time, wiping a tear from her cheek, and shook his hand. "You're truly a kindhearted man. We don't deserve all you've done for us."

He removed his straw hat and gave a bow before tapping it back on his head. "Serving you, my friends, has been an honor and has given me great satisfaction. In fact, I've decided to start going out looking for other people who need help. My daughter and her husband don't want to live isolated out here in the cottage and will stay with his parents until they can get a house closer to the community. This house is updated and just waiting for someone in dire need."

Coop put a hand on his shoulder. "It's a noble idea, Aaron, but too dangerous. You were just lucky to find people like us who had no wish to hurt you. We've seen how people can treat each other out there. It can get ugly."

"He's right," Riley said. "Most will take advantage of you or worse, cause you serious harm. Tend to your family and the others in your community. There is generosity and nobility in that, too."

"I appreciate your warnings, but I'm not completely naïve to the ways of the world. I've prayed and found this is my calling. What if someone in a situation like you were in distress and no one came? I couldn't live with myself knowing I could have helped."

"If you insist on doing this, at least don't go alone," Dashay said.

"I'll keep that in mind. Now, go before it gets too warm."

They thanked him once more, then got on their bikes and pedaled down the dirt road for the last time. Riley was anxious about leaving their protective bubble, but this place was not her home. Being protected and secure on the farm had been a tremendous relief, but if she wanted to see her children again, she had to venture out into the world. They had a thousand miles and at least eight weeks of travel ahead, but they were rested and ready after their respite. They were better outfitted than they'd been since the start of the trek. She gave a whoop, then pedaled faster, ready to take on the world. It was time to go home.

CHAPTER THIRTEEN

RILEY'S ALARM was set for one in the morning, but she'd been awake since midnight with too much adrenaline coursing through her to think about going back to sleep. The other three were dead to the world, which made sense since they'd pedaled all day in the heat while she rode in the cart. Coop's prediction had been right about her pregnant belly impeding her ability to pedal the bike. It had taken fourteen days to travel to St. Louis, but she'd only made it five before having to give up the bike.

The journey to St. Louis had been uneventful. They'd avoided populated areas but stayed close enough to sneak into towns for supplies to augment the fish and wild game they caught, and the vegetation Adrian collected. They hadn't seen copies of their wanted posters but saw occasional signs that Kearns' forces had passed through and were now ahead of them.

That night, they were in an abandoned house three blocks from where Adrian's in-laws lived in a western suburb of St. Louis. They'd arrived after dark and agreed to sleep for a few hours before going to Adrian's in-law's house on foot. The block was quiet, but several surrounding houses appeared to be occupied. It was an upscale neighborhood, but Riley guessed many of the inhabitants were probably squatters like them.

If they found Adrian's family, the other three would stay a night or two, then move on without Adrian. Riley sincerely hoped his family was well and waiting for him. She'd grown fond of Adrian and would miss him on the journey, especially his knowledge of plants and his cooking. It would be nice for one of their band to have a happy ending, and it would give her hope of reuniting with her own family.

She heard Coop stir and roll onto his side, facing her. "What are you doing awake?" he whispered.

She slid closer to him so he could hear her. "Who can sleep when we're about to go on a secret mission?"

"What secret mission? We're going to walk to Adrian's house."

"In the middle of the night to avoid Kearns' trackers."

"That's just a precaution. Adrian says Kearns couldn't know where his wife's parents lived, but wants to be prepared, just in case. I don't see why you insist on going. You should wait here with Dashay, and we'll come back for you."

Riley sat up and leaned against the headboard. "As I told you, I refuse to let you abandon me here. Dashay can go with Adrian and you stay."

He reached for her hand but she folded her arms. "Don't be melodramatic," he said. "I'm not abandoning you, and Adrian wants me along in case he runs into trouble, which is why you shouldn't be there. You don't exactly have your usual cat-like reflexes these days."

It was annoying when he was right. She would not only be putting herself in danger, but their child as well. But the thought of him never coming back frightened her more. She refused to go through that for a third time.

"If you're going, I'm going."

He was quiet in the dark for several moments before saying, "You know I love your courage and tenacity, but not so much when it spills over into stubbornness. We'll all go but promise to be uber-vigilant and stay out of the fray."

She grunted as she leaned down to kiss his forehead. "You have my word. I don't want anything to happen to me or the baby any more than you do."

There was a faint tap at the door, and Coop called out, "Come in."

Dashay pushed the door open and walked in with Adrian. "We woke up and heard you two whispering. And not very quietly," she said.

"Sorry," Riley said. "That was my fault."

"Since we're all awake, let's get this over with," Adrian said. "I can't stand not knowing any longer."

Coop and Riley climbed off the bed and followed Dashay and Adrian down the stairs. For all her insistence to go on the mission, Riley's heart pounded as they left the house and started the walk to Adrian's in-law's house. It was a hot and cloudy, but dark night. There was just enough light for them to see the sidewalk. They moved at a speed Riley could handle, which was faster than most five-and-a-half month pregnant women.

They turned a corner and Adrian ducked behind a bank of shrubs. The others squatted next to him as he pointed at a stately two-story house across the street. "That's it," he whispered. "It doesn't look like anyone is there from this vantage point."

"Only one way to find out," Coop said. "The rest of you stay here and wait for my signal."

Coop took a step toward the street, but Dashay grabbed the back of his shirt to stop him. "Stay here with Riley. I'm going. If anything goes sideways, I wouldn't want your kid to grow up without a dad."

"Wait," Adrian said, in a harsh whisper. "This is my family. I should be the one to go. If they're there, my face should be the first they see."

"Good point," Dashay said. "We both go."

They straightened and stole across the street in a crouch. It was dark enough that Riley couldn't see them after twenty feet. "We won't see their signal," she said.

"We'll give them five minutes, and if we don't hear anything, we'll follow them. That's long enough for them to know if his family is there."

Riley straightened and set the timer on her watch. She was too agitated to be still, so she paced back and forth along the sidewalk. The temperature was still in the eighties by her estimate, and it was steamy. Between the heat and fear, she was drenched in sweat after two minutes. It was something she was becoming used to after their trip from the farm to St. Louis. After growing up in cool and dry Colorado, she couldn't understand why anyone would choose to live in humid climates.

She flinched when her alarm sounded. She silenced it and Coop took her hand as they crossed the wide tree-lined street. They made it across in seconds and she let out her breath in relief to be out of the open. They hurried up the steps to the open front door. They tiptoed inside but relaxed when they found Adrian and Dashay at the kitchen table with their flashlights turned on. The looks on their faces told her the news was not good.

Even with only the light of their flashlights, Riley could tell that no one had been in the house for weeks at the least. Dust covered every surface and petrified food sat on plates left unwashed on the table.

Adrian's head was lowered, and he held several pieces of paper. Before she could ask what he had, he handed them to her, said, "Read this."

The bigger sheets she recognized without reading them. They were copies of their wanted posters. Resting on top of them was a note scribbled on a page torn from a yellow legal pad. Her hands trembled as she read.

I nearly had a heart attack when I found these stapled to a telephone pole on my way to get our daily rations. I tore them down and ran straight home. What is this about, Adrian? Knowing you as I do, I can't believe this is true, but who knows anything in this insanity we live in anymore? I'm clinging to the hope that you're the same Adrian I've known and loved all these years.

Mom and Dad were horrified, but I did my best to convince them it was all a lie. We packed up that night and snuck out of town despite the military barricades. Most of the group running our Zone aren't the brightest bulbs. We've gone to Cousin Jack's since no one would know to look for us there. If what this poster says is lies, come to us as soon as you can. If it's true, I hope to never see you again. I'll wait for you until my dying breath. If you don't come, I'll know but will always love you either way.

K.

"This is terrible, Adrian," Riley said. "I'm so sorry, but at least you know they're alive. They survived the CME."

Dashay put her hand on Adrian's shoulder. "That's what I was saying when you came in. They're alive and waiting for you."

Coop reread the note. "Where is Cousin Jack?"

Adrian pulled a napkin from the holder on the table and dried his face. "I have no idea. I don't remember K having a cousin named Jack. It must be code so Kearns' people couldn't follow them. Hope I can figure it out before you leave St. Louis."

Riley switched on her penlight and shined it around the kitchen and into the great room beyond. "Could they have left paperwork here that might have clues?"

Adrian walked to a small built-in desk in a corner of the kitchen. Opening the drawer, he said, "I wouldn't know where to begin. I didn't exactly go through my in-law's documents when I came to visit."

"Doesn't matter. There's no time for that," Coop said. "Your wife gave us two other significant bits of information. This area is within a Residential Zone and the people chasing us have been here. We need to get to the outskirts of the city tonight. We'll sleep during the day tomorrow, then travel again tomorrow night."

"If this is in a Zone," Dashay said, "how did we get into the city so easily? We didn't see a single checkpoint or fence."

Adrian scratched his head. "We stayed off the main roads and came in through a little-known route. Things also might have gotten less restrictive since my family left. Imagine the resources it would take to control a city of this size."

Riley folded the papers and handed them to Adrian. "Let's hope that holds true as we get farther west. For now, I agree with Coop. Let's get out of here," she said, then shivered. "I feel like we're at Miss Havisham's manor in *Great Expectations*."

As they all headed for the door, Adrian gave the room a last look. "It may feel that way to you, but I have years of happy memories in this place. Even though my family's gone, it's comforting to be in a familiar place after so many harrowing months."

Riley squeezed his hand, then linked her arm in his and nudged him toward the door. She understood his feelings. It was how she'd felt when she made it to the ranch, a place she'd never see again. It was tough enough that the CME had destroyed so many lives without Kearns piling on. All Riley could do was hope that one day Kearns would pay for her crimes.

Coop led them back to the house they'd stayed in to retrieve Biscuit and their belongings. The poor horse wasn't thrilled to have to pull the cart again after so little rest.

"Just a bit longer until you can rest for an entire day," Riley whispered to him and gave him an extra piece of apple as Coop and Adrian hooked up the cart. "You're doing great, old friend. You've got this."

Biscuit nodded twice as he chomped his apple. There were times Riley was convinced he understood her. Even if not, she knew they could trust him to do what they needed. She climbed onto her cushioned makeshift seat, feeling guilty that she got to relax while the others had to ride. They needed a day of rest as much as Biscuit.

Coop and Adrian agreed it was best to double back the way they entered, even though it was out of their way. They couldn't risk running into a checkpoint. They saw occasional patrols in the distance but never ran into any directly. They headed southeast until they were clear of the city limits, then turned due west. None of them knew what to expect from that point on but hoped it would be as uneventful as their journey to St. Louis had been.

They traveled roughly thirty miles and couldn't go another inch. They stopped south of the Missouri River in a forested area by a stream. As the sun rose, Riley helped the others set up their tents and put together a cold meal of the last of the bread Adrian had baked two days earlier, jerky and apple slices. After eating, they all collapsed in an exhausted stupor while she cleaned up, then took out a novel she'd found in the house they'd stayed in on one of their stops. She'd dozed some during the night and wasn't tired, so she lowered herself into a folding chair to read.

She got through a few pages of the novel but had too many thoughts racing through her brain to keep focused on it. She'd convinced herself that Adrian would find his family and stay behind and hadn't thought through what would happen if he didn't. Even though Kearns' people were searching for all four of them, she'd hoped that separating from Adrian would mean less danger for the rest of them. If he didn't figure out who Cousin Jack was, she had to accept the possibility that he could remain with them all along the way to Colorado. As fond as she was of Adrian, she'd hoped to avoid that risk.

Another new situation to contend with was that Kearns'

troops were no longer chasing them but were in front, waiting to capture them. The slightest miscalculation could mean their journey would end in an instant. Another fear lurking at the back of her brain was that the military had reached Colorado Springs and her children were already in a Residential Zone. Odds of that were slim since Kearns' reach possibly didn't extend that far yet, but it was a possibility. If that were the case, she'd not only have to find her children without being captured, but rescue them, too.

She shook her head to clear it. There was no point in planning for trouble that hadn't happened. They faced big enough challenges as it was. She turned her thoughts instead to what was working. They'd easily found the food and water they needed. The weather had cooperated, even if temperatures were higher than normal. It was the middle of July, so the heat wasn't going away soon.

As they made their way out of St. Louis, Coop suggested they travel at night to avoid the worst of the heat. Traveling in the dark presented its own set of challenges, but Aaron had provided them with a solar battery powered light for the cart, so at least they wouldn't be moving blind. They always had the option to change their minds if night travel didn't work.

Dashay sat up and stretched. She'd been riding in the cart, napping with her head in Riley's lap. "How long have I been asleep?"

"Two hours. Look at Adrian."

Dashay turned toward where Adrian was weaving back and forth across the road with his eyes half-closed.

"He needs to get off that bike before he crashes or passes out from heat stroke. It must be a hundred degrees out here," Riley said.

"Coop, hold up," Dashay called. When Coop tugged on Biscuit's reins to stop him, she climbed out and walked to Adrian. "Adrian, get in the cart. I'll bike for a while."

He didn't seem to hear and kept riding straight for her.

"Adrian!" Riley shouted.

He slowly raised his eyes and saw Dashay just in time to press the breaks. Coop got off his bike and walked back to join them while Riley got out of the cart. They started examining Adrian in tandem.

"Heat exhaustion," Riley said. "Dashay, grab three canteens. Help me get him into the shade, Coop."

They helped Adrian off his bike, then each took an arm and half dragged him to the nearest tree. Riley ordered him to strip down to his underwear. When Dashay ran up with the canteens, Riley opened two of them and doused Adrian, then handed him the third one to take a drink. He took a few sips, then lowered the canteen.

Riley squatted next to him and raised it back to his lips. "All of it. Drink it down." He scowled at her but took several gulps. "Good boy."

"I'm not Biscuit," he mumbled.

She straightened and put her hands on her hips. "You're feeling better though, aren't you?"

He nodded and took another drink.

Coop took off his cap and leaned against the tree. "I'm not feeling much better and look at Biscuit. It must be at least a hundred and ten. We've got to stop."

Riley scanned the area. "I agree, but I'm not comfortable this close to the road where anyone passing can see us."

"We haven't seen a soul since we've been on this road," Coop said. "Everyone else is too smart to be out in this heat."

Dashay said, "These trees are the only shade I can see. Looks like farms and wild fields for miles."

Riley signaled for Adrian to take a drink, then said, "We'll rest here for thirty minutes, then we can find more secluded shade."

"We need water, too," Dashay said. "We only have two full canteens. I'm fresh after my nap. I'll go scout the area for shade and water while you rest."

Riley put a hand on her arm. "No, Dashay. You're not going out there alone."

Dashay cocked her thumb at Coop and Adrian. "These two are in no shape to go, and you can't ride a bike. I'll take the rifle with me. Like Coop said, we're the only fools out here."

Coop squinted at her. "Not exactly what I said, but you're not wrong."

"I could ride Biscuit," Riley said.

Dashay burst into her deep, melodious laugh. "Even if Biscuit were in any shape to go, we'd never get you into that saddle. I'll be fine on my own, Riley. Trust me to know how to stay out of trouble."

"I vote no, but it's up to Coop. He's the boss."

"Go but be back here in thirty minutes, tops. Riley, give her your watch. Take a canteen and the rifle."

Riley wasn't happy with Coop's decision, but kept her mouth shut for once.

Dashay got the equipment she needed from the cart, then carried the other canteen to them. She held it out to Coop. "Drink, then give your stubborn wife some."

Coop saluted her before unscrewing the canteen cap. "Thirty minutes," he said as Dashay took off down the road.

Riley could feel him watching her. She looked up and said, "What?"

"Dashay is smart. She'll be fine."

"Every time you say that something goes horribly wrong."

He winked at her. "Not every time." He handed her the canteen, and said, "Sometimes we have no choice. We're pushing that horse and ourselves too hard, and I'd like a little advanced information about what we're storming into for once."

"That's true," she conceded. "Feeling better, Adrian?"

When he didn't answer, she spun around to check on him. He was sound asleep, breathing steady and deep with his mouth hanging open. She pressed the back of her hand to his forehead. He was much cooler.

"Think I'll do the same," Coop said. He sank down next to the tree and pushed his cap over his eyes.

Since Riley wasn't tired after riding in the cart, she retrieved her novel from the cart to give it another shot. Not wanting to disturb Coop and Adrian, she carried it to where Biscuit was resting in the shade of a different tree. She lowered herself to the base of the trunk, hoping she'd be able to get up again without help. That was getting more difficult the bigger her belly grew.

She settled in and flipped to the last page she read at the river. She had better luck getting into the story the second time and fifteen minutes had passed without her noticing when Dashay gave a soft whistle as she rode toward her. Riley didn't bother to get up.

Still straddling her bike, Dashay said, "I hit the jackpot. There's a village just over that rise. I wouldn't even call it a town. A couple there has a bottled water stand on the side of the road. They found a warehouse filled with cases of bottled water and now they trade for things they need."

"That's fantastic news," Riley said. "They must be doing a booming business today."

"They also pointed out a small park with a gazebo where we can rest until dark when it's cool enough to travel. Glad I went scouting?" Riley scowled at her as she tried to get up. She only made it as far as her knees. "Need help?"

She held out her hand and Dashay helped her to her feet. She dusted herself off and grabbed her book. "Mind getting Biscuit harnessed while I wake those two? I'll make room in the cart so they can both ride with me."

Once they were on their way, Riley rigged some shade with a blanket and two fishing poles. It did little to reduce the temperature, but it kept the direct sun off them.

She was relieved when they reached the water stand after twenty minutes, ready to trade whatever it took to get safe water. Coop and Adrian climbed out of the cart first, then helped her out. A couple who looked to be in their late twenties sat under a pop-up canopy at a card table covered with bottles of water. A toddler slept under another canopy behind them, and a girl of about four played with blocks on the blanket next to him. Riley looked on fondly as the baby did flips inside her. She hoped he'd never have to nap on a blanket by the side of the road.

"Here are my friends I was telling you about," Dashay told them.

"Hello," they said in unison.

Coop tipped his cap to them. "Afternoon. Dashay says you trade water for goods. What's your price?"

The man looked up at him, shading his eyes with his hand against the glaring over Coop's shoulder. "We trade for what we believe is fair. We won't gouge you, but we need to survive in these crazy times, too."

Riley stepped closer to be in the shade of their canopy. "What are you looking for today?"

"Food," the woman said. "Food is always at the top of our list."

Coop put his hand on Riley's shoulder. "For us, too. Unfortunately, we can't part with our food for obvious reasons."

The woman glanced at Riley's belly, then at her children. "I understand. Medication and medical supplies next."

Coop and Riley exchanged a look, and Riley nodded. "We can help you there. We're doctors. We have a limited stock of medical supplies we can part with. We can't give you prescription medications unless we examine you and see you have a need. We're willing to trade over-the-counter drugs you need."

The man sat up straighter. "You're doctors? Will you look at our son? He scraped his leg last week by the creek. It was just a minor scratch, but the wound is getting worse."

"Of course. We'd be happy to," Riley said. "Can you grab the med pack out of the cart, please, Dashay?"

Dashay gave Riley a knowing look as she turned toward the cart. Riley didn't like the thought of taking advantage of the child's injury but being doctors had been a clear asset and had even saved their lives on their journey. Their medical knowledge and skills were their currency, but it was also a privilege to put those skills to good use. Riley would willingly give that service and hoped it would mean not having to sacrifice their precious provisions.

"Can you lift your son up to the table?" she asked. "I have a hard time getting on my knees these days."

They removed the bottles of water from the table and the woman spread a blanket over it before her husband lifted the little boy to the table. He wasn't happy to be awakened from his nap and plunked on a table in front of strangers. He took one look at Riley and let out a wail as he reached for his mother. The woman stepped closer and whispered calming words in his ear.

As he wiggled on the table, Riley saw the angry three-inch wound on his right shin. It was tomato red, swollen and oozing pus.

"What's his name and how old is he?" Coop asked before Riley reached for his leg.

"This is Miles. He's eighteen months old."

Riley gave her a warm smile. "My nephew's name is Miles. He would have just turned one."

Her breath caught as memories of Lily's baby unexpectedly flooded over her. She took a few breaths to fight her tears and turned her attention to Miles.

"Hello, sweetheart," she said as she gently placed her hand on his foot. When he pulled his leg away, his mother put her arms around him and held him tight. Riley cocked her head for Coop to help her. "You're going to have to hold him still. He won't like this."

Coop wrapped his hand above and below the wound while Riley leaned over and shined her penlight on it. The broken skin had closed over a foreign object. That meant she'd have to open the wound to remove it.

"Dashay, do we have any more lidocaine?" she asked over the boy's whimpers. Dashay unzipped the med pack and searched through it. After a few seconds, she held up the vial and smiled. "Prefect. I'm going to have to inject your son with medication to numb him so I can open the skin. It's going to be very painful for a few seconds, then he won't feel a thing. You're going to have to hold him still and keep him distracted."

The man came up beside his wife and spoke to Miles to get his attention away from Riley. The father made funny faces and sounds while she filled the vial. She glanced at Coop and held her breath before injecting the needle. Miles let out an ear-piercing shriek, but Coop kept his leg immobilized. Mile's parents tried to calm him, but he was inconsolable. A minute later, he quieted and forgot about Riley when his father offered him some cheese crackers.

Riley let out her breath and pulled on a pair of gloves. Coop and Dashay handed her the instruments she needed so she could go to work on the wound. She opened the skin with a scalpel and Dashay dabbed at the blood and pus that poured out. Riley saw the cause of the infection as soon as the field was clear. A large, angry thorn was embedded in the opening. She plucked it out with a pair of tweezers and held it up to show Mile's parents. She dropped it on the ground and after disinfecting the wound, asked Dashay for sutures. She had the skin closed within ten minutes.

Dashay bandaged it, then Coop let go of Miles' leg. The child was oblivious to the fact he'd just had minor surgery.

As Riley pulled off her gloves, she said, "You're lucky we came along when we did. That infection could have become septic and possibly even fatal without treatment. I've put antibiotic cream over the incision, but I need to give Miles an antibiotic injection. Is he allergic to any medications you know of?"

They both shook their heads. "He's never even been sick," the father said.

"That's fortunate. It means he should recover quickly. I'll inject him and keep medicine on standby, just in case. You need to keep his incision clean and covered for a few days. We'll leave you with bandages and scissors to remove the sutures. Dashay will show you how."

The mother jumped up and gave Riley a hug. "How can we repay you?"

"I know a way," Adrian said, "with water."

The father picked up the bottles that had been on the table and carried them to the cart. "Take as much as you can carry. It's nothing compared to the price of our son's life."

"You have no idea how much that means to us," Riley said, "especially today. I'm Kate. That's Coop, my husband and the other man is Andy." Adrian raised an eyebrow at her but dipped his chin and smiled. "What are your names?"

The man put his arm around the woman's shoulder. "I'm Cody. This is my wife, Monica. Our daughter's name is Mandy. She's four."

"You have a lovely family," Riley said, again overcome with memories of home.

While Coop and Adrian helped Cody load several flats of water into the cart, Monica laid Miles back on his blanket under the canopy. Mandy continued to play with her blocks as if her brother hadn't just had an operation.

Monica gestured to the chairs, and said, "Please, both of you sit." Riley and Dashay took the seats without hesitation.

"Where do you live?" Dashay asked as they watched the men work.

"We have a small farm near here. My husband inherited land from his grandfather. We moved from St. Louis about a year ago. That's where our families are, the ones that survived. We haven't been able to get into the city since the Zone was created, but we're hoping that won't last much longer."

"Why do you say that?" Riley asked.

"Because of the war."

Dashay glanced at Riley, then said, "War?"

Monica raised her eyebrows. "Seriously, you don't know?" Dashay shrugged. "Where have you been hiding?"

"Literally in the middle of nowhere," Riley said, chuckling.

"Then you don't know about the new country?"

Dashay sighed and rubbed her forehead. "Maybe it would be quicker for you to start at the beginning."

"About a month ago, we started hearing rumors that the western states have split from the US and formed a new country because they don't agree with what Kearns is doing. We didn't believe it was possible at first, but people fleeing St. Louis said they've heard the soldiers talking about it. Kearns is sending troops to the border to take back the states that seceded."

Riley was stunned. Kearns was a despicable person, but Riley couldn't accept that part of the country would rather secede than remove her from office. Although, with the world in its current state, that wouldn't be a straightforward proposition. Nothing made sense in their insane world anymore.

"You believe it's true?" she asked softly.

"It *is* true," Monica said without hesitation. "We're sure of it."

"Which states?" Dashay asked, sounding as shocked as Riley.

Monica ticked off on her fingers as she named them. "Montana, Wyoming, Colorado, New Mexico, Texas, Arizona,

Utah, Idaho, Nevada, and California. Get this, I heard Oregon and Washington were annexed into Canada. North and South Dakota are still trying to decide which side they're on."

Riley slowly got to her feet. "You said Colorado?" Monica nodded. "That's where I'm from. We're headed there. Are you telling me my family lives in a foreign country now?"

"Yes. I've heard they don't let anyone over the border without someone to vouch for them, and you have to get past the US military to even reach the border. It might be better to find somewhere else to live, at least until after you have the baby."

The men had wandered over and the smile slid from Coop's face when he saw Riley. "What's the matter, Babe? Is it Miles?"

Riley repeated what Monica told them.

Coop gave a low whistle, then said, "Where's this border?"

"Along the boundaries of Montana, Wyoming, Colorado, New Mexico, and Texas. All the states west of there, except Oregon and Washington, are part of the new Western States of America," Cody said. "That's the name of the new country, and Kearns is sending the military out there for war."

Riley locked her hands behind her neck and began to pace. "This is absurd. I won't believe it. If these western states are in anywhere near as bad a condition as the states we've passed through, how did they mobilize and organize so quickly? How did the states' leadership communicate without technology? How did they form a new government from scratch? I can't wrap my head around it."

"How has Kearns been able to do what she has?" Adrian asked. "She controls the entire rest of the country."

"I don't know about any of that," Monica said, "but you'll be walking into a hornet's nest if you keep going west."

Riley spun around to face her. "My two youngest children are there. I've been trying to get home to them from DC since the CME hit. My oldest daughter is headed to Colorado with other members of my family. What's going to happen to her?"

Coop put his arms around her and kissed the top of her head. "Take a breath. We'll figure this out. First, we have to find out how much of it's true. You know how rumors spread."

Riley stepped away from him and took a breath. "You're right. We need to get out of this heat and rest, then we'll plan our strategy. Where's the gazebo?"

"It's a few blocks away at the park. You can't miss it," Cody said. "I'm sorry to give you bad news after you saved Miles' life. I'm sure it'll be fine."

"Thank you," Dashay said. "I hope you're right."

"We'll bring you dinner in a few hours," Monica said. "Go. Get some rest."

"We will," Coop said as he put his arm around Riley and guided her toward the cart. "And thank you again for the water. You've saved our lives, too."

After a four-hour nap in the gazebo and a delicious meal of cold chicken, bread, and salad from Monica, the four of them sat talking softly and staring up at the stars in their camp chairs. Biscuit hungrily chomped the grass after a long drink from a koi pond in the park, with fish darting about in the water and toads croaking along the edge.

They'd all agreed to spend another day in the park, resting and figuring out what to make of the bizarre and devastating news from Cody and Monica.

"My brain doesn't want to accept it's true," Riley said, "but Monica and Cody believe it. That might explain why we never ran into patrols in St. Louis."

"If it's true and we somehow make it across the border, it would solve our Kearns and Yeager problem," Adrian said.

Riley sighed and slumped in her chair. "It would, but how the hell are we going to cross the border? We already barely evaded

Yeager, and from what Aaron told us, he doesn't sound like the type of man who gives up easily. We'd have to get past him and the whole US military in the middle of a civil war."

Coop leaned forward and looked at her. "Are you saying you want to stop trying to get home?"

She pushed herself out of the chair and glared at him with her arms crossed. "Never! I refuse to let Kearns stop me from reaching my children. I'm saying this is going to take a carefully crafted plan. I'm just not sure what that is yet." Turning to Adrian, she said, "Have you figured out who Cousin Jack is? If your family is with him on this side of the border and you cross over, they'd be lost to you."

"That occurred to me," he said. "That's likely to happen anyway, but after giving it some thought, the only person I could come up with is Kenzie's cousin, John Clark, in Fort Worth. I've only seen him a few times, but I remember hearing family members call him Jack. If I'm right, I could cross the border into Colorado with you, then make my way to Texas. The hardest part will be remembering John's address. I've only been to his house once."

Dashay clicked her tongue. "That will be the hardest part? You're always going on about your eidetic memory. Isn't this a perfect time to put it to use?"

"It's been eighteen years since I was there. That's a stretch, even for me."

Coop stood and put his arm around Riley. "We have a thousand steps to consider before your trip to find Cousin Jack. What are our immediate concerns?"

"I've been thinking we should do what we can to change our appearances," Dashay said. "And Riley was right to give fake names earlier. I wasn't thinking when I told Cody and Monica my actual name."

"Yeager's people may not know Riley's pregnant, so that might work in our favor, too," Coop said.

Adrian shook his head. "I'm sure librarian boy gave Yeager detailed descriptions. He probably wanted us caught as much Yeager."

"Either way, Dashay's right," Riley said. "I could cut my hair. I was thinking about doing it since it would be cooler in this heat."

Dashay got up and ran her fingers through Riley's hair. "I hate to see you lose your lovely curls, but you're right. You should dye it black, too."

Coop made a face. "Not looking forward to seeing that. Is it safe to dye your hair when you're pregnant?"

She nodded. "Yes, as long as I'm careful about the type I use. I should only need to do it once if we make it over the border in four weeks. I can look for root touch-up in the meantime."

"What about you, Dashay?" Adrian asked.

"I'll lose the braids, then straighten and bleach it. My friends and I used to do that all the time when I was a teenager. What about you two?"

Coop rubbed his chin. "We don't have beards in the sketches, so we'll let them grow and our hair. Even my baseball cap and Adrian's straw hat might be enough to fool people."

"Zach used to talk about how even minor changes are enough to keep people from recognizing you," Riley said. "We should have thought of it sooner."

"That's one box checked," Coop said. "We'll look for the materials to carry out our disguises tomorrow, but we should wait until we're away from Cody and Monica to make the changes. What's next on the list?"

Riley held out her sandaled foot. "Boots and clothes for me. We need to replenish the medical supplies, and as Monica says, food. Always food."

Adrian gave a sniff. "They're not hurting too bad in that department, evidenced by that feast they gave us."

"That could have been nothing more than gratitude," Riley said. "They might share more or direct us to where we can find our own. I was thinking earlier that as we continue to move west, we should see corn fields like Aaron's if farmers have been able to cultivate them. That's a versatile and filling nutrition source."

Dashay yawned and stretched. "I'm having a hard time putting two thoughts together, so my first order of business is sleep."

"I agree," Adrian said. "I know we've gotten off our daytime sleep schedule, but I'm exhausted after my brush with death today."

Coop nodded. "I'll stand the first watch and we'll pick this up in the morning."

Adrian and Dashay made their way to their tents, but Riley sat next to Coop to keep him company while he stood guard. They hadn't run across anyone but Andy and Monica since they'd been in the village, but they still had to be vigilant.

Coop rested the rifle against his chair, then reached over and twisted a curl of Riley's hair around his finger. "I'm going to miss your fiery locks."

She pulled his hand to her lips and kissed it. "It's only temporary. You might like my new look."

He gave a warm smile, and she melted at the sight of his dimples, as always. She hadn't seen them since leaving the cottage.

"Doubtful," he said. "You're taking the news about this new country better than I expected. It's a blow when we all thought we were home free from here on."

Riley gave a soft laugh. "I haven't thought I was home free since five-seconds after the CME struck. This latest obstacle is a kick in the gut, but we'll figure it out. We have weeks before we'll be close enough to know if the reports are true. I'll save my meltdown for later. Until then, we'll have smaller obstacles to face, like finding safe water and food on the plains in record-breaking heat."

He leaned closer and gave her a lingering kiss. "Have I told you how incredible you are?"

Keeping her eyes closed, she whispered, "Not for the past hour. You're falling down on the job."

"I promise to step it up."

She wove her fingers into his tangled hair and pressed her lips hard to his. At that moment, she felt that even if the world was crashing down around them, as long as she had Coop, there was nothing to fear.

CHAPTER FOURTEEN

RILEY HIT snooze on her watch alarm, hoping for ten more precious minutes of sleep.

She felt Coop roll over to face her. "You're wasting your time with that snooze function. You never fall back to sleep."

"You know what they say, never give up. Today might be my lucky day," she mumbled. "It's getting harder to get up every day, especially with this kid kicking me every two minutes all night. I remember why I never camped when I was almost seven months pregnant." She watched him in the faint moonlight that was shining in through the tent window. "Why are you smiling?"

"I'm still not used to that short black hair of yours. I wake every night thinking a strange woman is in my bed."

She kissed the end of his nose. "Isn't that every man's fantasy?"

He rolled onto his back and tucked his hands behind his head. "Not this man's, and it's tough to fantasize about a woman who looks like she swallowed a basketball."

Riley groaned as she pushed herself to a sitting position. "It's been more than a month since I dyed my hair. If you're not used to it by now, you never will be. I'll grow it out and change the color back once we're safely over the border."

Coop climbed out of his sleeping bag and pulled on his jeans. "Speaking of the border, we're roughly a week away from it and still we have absolutely no plan for crossing. I climbed to the top of that grain silo in the field just after sundown to have a look. Military encampments fill the plains west of us."

"It's what we expected with the number of convoys heading west these past few weeks. We'll know more when we're closer to the border."

He helped her to her feet, then kissed the back of her hand. "I'm not happy going into this blind."

"Our disguises have kept Yeager off our tails despite those posters being plastered on the walls of every town we pass. As bad as it is, I have to admire their determination. Don't worry about the border. I'll convince the guards I'm from Colorado Springs. They'll welcome us with open arms."

Coop grabbed his dirty clothes scattered on the tent floor and shoved them into his pack. "Sure, you're awake? Sounds like you're dreaming to me. They'll most likely arrest you as soon as they get a look at your face."

Riley shrugged and reached for her pack. "What's with the gloom this morning? We've been making great time and haven't run into trouble in weeks."

Coop stopped packing and stared at her. "Now you've jinxed it." He spit on his knuckles three times, copying Riley's ritual. "Let's eat and get going. We're losing moonlight."

Riley watched him leave the tent, wondering what had brought on his foul mood. Their trek had been uneventful for the past month. They'd been fortunate to find nature trails that kept them off major highways but provided cleared tracks wide enough for the cart. They'd had plenty of clean water through occasional thunderstorms and Adrian's ability to locate underground springs.

Getting food had been the bigger challenge and had taken a toll. Riley was growing concerned at how thin Coop was. He'd worked to maintain the muscle mass he built on the farm but diminishing protein consumption was eating away at him. Dashay and Adrian were facing the same situation. Riley was the only one carrying a healthy amount of weight because the others refused to let her do strenuous chores and insisted on giving her the biggest food portions. She felt guilty eating in front of them but needed the calories and nutrients to keep the baby healthy and growing.

Coop hunted for small game, but ammo was running low and animal sightings were growing infrequent. Adrian and Dashay caught fish when they could, but water sources became scarcer the farther they progressed into the plains. Their only other animal protein came from the occasional wild boar or deer Coop shot. Corn was the one staple they never seemed to lack. Though Riley was pleased to see survivors cultivating crops, she swore to herself that once they reached home, she'd never eat another kernel of corn in her life.

Adrian continued to augment their food supply with a variety of plants, wild fruits and nuts he gathered along the way. Overall, they'd rarely gone hungry or thirsty and had become proficient at living off the land. She'd considered herself a skilled outdoorswoman before her ill-fated trip to DC but had been little more than a novice. She'd realized her modern conveniences had spoiled her. She'd since grown confident that she could do more than just survive in their bizarre meld of nineteenth and twenty-first century worlds.

"You're far away," Dashay said, as she came into the tent carrying two bowls of corn mash and field onions with chunks of fish.

Riley sank onto the folding chair Coop had found for her since it had gotten too hard for her to use the camp chairs. "I was thinking how much this experience has changed us. You and I aren't the same people we were when we met in Branson's compound." She took a bite of the corn mash and was surprised at how much better it tasted than it smelled or looked.

Dashay took a spoonful from her own bowl. "What's got you in such a philosophical mood?"

Riley shook her head. "Coop and pregnancy hormones, maybe. I'm so close to home I can taste it, but there's this enormous wall blocking my way. I miss my babies, Dashay. Will I ever hold any of them in my arms again, especially Julia?"

Dashay squeezed her hand. "I won't give you false assurances and say everything will be fine. I can't predict the future, but if those children have even a fraction of their mother's courage and determination, they'll be waiting for you on the doorstep."

"You two about ready?" Adrian called from across the camp. "Coop's champing at the bit to get going."

Riley finished her last few bites of mash, then wiped the bowl and held out her hand for Dashay's. She rested her hand on Dashay's arm, and said, "Thank you, friend. You said just what I needed to hear."

"Good, then let's get you home."

"It's time we chose a name for this baby," Coop said as he rode next to Riley in the cart.

They'd created a system of the three riders rotating two-hour breaks of riding in the cart so they wouldn't get too fatigued on the bikes. They were becoming experts at repairing tires, which was usually required a couple of times a day especially when traveling on the rougher surfaces. That day, they'd been traveling for just over six hours, and Coop was on his second break. He'd brought up the baby's name earlier and had given such ridiculous suggestions that Riley laughed so hard she had to beg him to stop. But she was relieved to see he'd returned to his usual jovial mood.

"I'll only discuss this if you promise to be serious. If it's a boy, the name is decided. Neal Xavier Cooper, IV. To avoid confusion, we'll call him Neal since you go by Coop."

He pulled off his cap and ran his hand through his tangled hair. "I never liked the name Neal, hence Coop."

"What's wrong with Neal? It was your father's name."

"He went by Junior with family."

"We're not calling our son that. What about Xavier? Xav for short."

Coop put his cap back on and sat back to consider the name. "That's unique and kind of cool, like Dr. Xavier in the comic books."

Riley chuckled. "I don't know about that, but if you're happy, Xav it is."

"What if on the off chance it's a girl?"

Before Riley could answer, Adrian cried, "Whoa, Biscuit," and brought the cart to an abrupt stop. Dashay had to slam on her brakes to avoid slamming into them.

She pedaled to the front of the cart, and said, "What the hell, Adrian?"

"Look," Riley heard him say.

Coop helped Riley out, and they rushed to where Dashay and Adrian were staring at a truck on its side in a ditch. The motor was running, and the lights were on.

"Grab the med pack, Dashay," Riley said over her shoulder as she hurried with Coop to the truck.

Coop peered in the window and tapped on the glass. "Anyone in there?"

"Yes. Three of us," a faint voice said.

Coop waved to Adrian. "Find something we can use to pry the door open."

Riley carefully climbed down next to Coop and pressed her

forehead to the window. There was a man behind the wheel and two women on the seat beside him.

"We're going to get you out," she called through the glass. "Can you turn off the engine?"

The man stared at her in a daze, then lifted his free arm and let out a yelp. "I think my arm's broken."

The woman next to him reached down and turned the key. The engine went quiet, but the lights stayed on.

"Can you open the door?" Coop asked the woman closest to the passenger door.

She grabbed the handle and shoved on the door, but it was too heavy for her to push open. Adrian returned with a shovel and slipped it into the opening while Coop pulled on the outside handle. They got the door open on the first try, then kept it propped open with the shovel.

Riley pulled her penlight from her pocket and shined it into the car. The three occupants were covered with cuts and bruises, but the windshield was intact and none of them looked to be bleeding excessively.

"We're surgeons and our friend's a nurse," Coop said. "We're going to examine each of you before we lift you out. Tell us how this happened and what hurts."

"What's your name?" Riley asked the woman on the passenger side as she shined the light in her eyes.

"Michelle," she said, weakly.

"Nice to meet you, Michelle. I'm Katie. This is Xav and Chante is holding the backpack. How did this happen?"

"My name is Dale," the driver said. "I swerved to miss a coyote. At least, I think it was a coyote."

"You did your best, Dale," Coop said. "Don't blame yourself. Who is your friend sitting in the middle?"

"Faith," the woman answered. "I think I broke Dale's arm when I smashed into him, but I'm not hurt other than bruises and a cut on my leg."

"Good to hear, Faith," Coop said. "We're going to take good care of all of you."

Riley and Coop triaged them in a hurry, then Coop, Adrian, and Dashay worked carefully to remove them from the wrecked truck while Riley spread quilts over the dirt on the side of the road. Once their patients were arranged on the blankets, Riley and Coop got to work treating them.

Riley looked up from stitching Michelle's head laceration when she heard the loud hum of car engines. Adrian stepped into the middle of the road and waved his arms to stop them. Three black, dusty SUVs came to a stop ten yards from the accident. Riley turned her focus back to Michelle, trying to ignore the panic rising from her gut. If these were Kearns' people, there would be no chance of escape.

She caught snippets of Adrian's mumbled conversation with three men dressed in worn civilian clothes but couldn't make out the words. She glanced up when the exchange became heated and saw Adrian backing away from them, shaking his head. Could it be possible her journey was over so close to the end?

She finished with Michelle and asked Dashay to bandage and clean her up while she moved to Faith. Her injuries were less serious than the other two. When Riley passed where Coop was splinting Dale's arm, she gave him a knowing look as her panic neared a crescendo.

Coop winked and smiled. "Take a breath. You've got this. We'll be fine."

He didn't believe that any more than she did, but she appreciated the gesture. She'd overcome her crippling anxiety in the months since the CME and had even been fearless, but if she failed before achieving her goal, what did it matter?

Adrian leaned over her shoulder and whispered, "It's not good, Riley. They say they're taking us with them. If we resist, they'll use force."

"Are they military? Is it Yeager?" Adrian shrugged. "They can't just haul us away with no explanation. This is still the United States. We have rights."

"They seem like types who do whatever they damn well please." He straightened and stepped toward Coop. "Look out. Here they come."

Riley turned to Faith and said, "That should do it. Your injuries should heal within a week, but you might be sore for the next few days. If your neck becomes painful, find a doctor if you can. I'll have my friend get a chair from the cart for you."

Faith nodded and slowly stood while Riley struggled to get to her feet. A man from the SUVs stuck out his hand to help her. She stared at it for a moment before taking hold of it. When she was upright, she stripped off her gloves and stared at him with her hands on her hips. He was over six feet tall and broad shouldered. His jeans and T-shirt were stained and worn, but he was clean shaven, and his sandy hair was short and well groomed. His bearing and facial features reminded her of her first husband, Zach. This man clearly hadn't been scraping out an existence on the road as they had.

Making herself look as threatening as her five-foot and pregnant stature would allow, she said, "My friend tells me you're expecting us to go with you, but you have no right to just drag us off. Who do you think you are?"

He watched her for a moment with a hint of a smile, then reached into his pocket and took out four copies of their wanted posters. He deliberately unfolded them and held them up for her to see.

"You may have disguised your appearance, but you are Dr. Riley Poole," he said in a deep, smooth voice. "No one on my team will do anything to harm you, Doctor, but you and your companions are coming with us." He refolded the papers and put them back in his pocket, making sure she saw the gun holstered at his hip.

Admitting to herself that it was futile to resist, she lowered her shoulders in defeat. She'd made the conscious choice to shelter and protect Adrian with full knowledge of what the consequences could be. There would be time later to question whether that decision had been worth the price, but her first thought was that given the chance, she would do the same again.

She took a breath and raised her eyes to meet his. "We need to finish treating the accident victims. We can't just abandon them here."

"Do what you need to. You have my word that your patients will be taken to a place where they'll be well cared for."

"Thank you," Riley said, stunned at his willingness to assist the injured strangers. "I won't leave my horse either. He's part of our family."

Riley could see he was struggling not to roll his eyes. "I'll arrange a horse trailer to transport him. Those are easy enough to come by around here."

Riley took a chance to test the boundaries of his cooperation. "And the cart?"

"Is it part of the family, too?" he said, mocking her. "You won't need the cart."

With nothing to lose, she crossed her arms and stood a little taller. "I insist on the cart."

Coop came up behind her and rested his hand on her shoulder. "Evening," he said in that jaunty way she loved. "I'm her husband. Trust me when I say you don't want to cross horns with her."

The faint smile returned, and he said, "I'll get another trailer for the cart."

Riley nodded her thanks, wondering how he could call for whatever he needed at a snap of his fingers. To have that kind of pull in their post-apocalyptic world meant he had to be one of Kearns' people, but he didn't fit Yeager's description.

"Kind of you," Coop said. "Are you going to tell us who you are before you carry us away into the night?"

"No. Are you finished treating these people?" Riley glanced at Coop, who gave a quick nod. "Good. Wait here."

He walked to the other men standing ten feet behind him and began issuing orders. Adrian and Dashay joined Coop and Riley, and the four of them watched the men speaking too quietly for them to hear what they were saying.

"Are they Yeager's men?" Dashay asked, keeping her voice low.

Riley turned to face her and whispered, "Hard to say, but I'd guess not. If they were, we'd be handcuffed in the back seats of those SUVs by now, but I don't know who else they could be."

"Someone wanting a hefty reward?" Adrian said.

Riley glanced back at the SUVs. "Likely, but they seem pretty connected. Hope this doesn't mean there's a third group hunting us."

"No time to speculate," Coop said. "Grab what you can carry from the cart before they come for us."

Riley grabbed her backpack and threw it over her shoulder, then took the smaller med pack. Dashay and Coop each reached for the guns, but the tall man strode up before they had their hands on them.

"No, you don't," he said. "We'll take care of those. Get in that lead vehicle, now."

As Riley slowly shuffled to the SUV, she felt that familiar knot of panic tightening in her gut. They were surrendering to these men, not knowing who they were or where they were taking them. Would they take them to a camp or facility where they'd live out the rest of their lives? Or was this their last day on earth?

The man that spoke to them didn't seem violent, but his calm demeanor could have been a cover. From the window she saw members of his team escorting the accident victims to another vehicle. Their captor had been true to his word unless he was merely transporting them to the same prison.

Their captor climbed into the front passenger seat and the

driver got behind the wheel. As they drove away, leaving Biscuit and the cart Aaron built behind, the thought *you failed your children* looped in her brain. She'd fought so hard for so long, all for nothing. The enormity of it pressed down on her until she feared she'd be crushed under its weight. She slumped against Coop, struggling to hold back her tears, not wanting to show her weakness to the man who held their fates in his hands.

The journey to their mystery destination took three hours. As afraid as she was, Riley marveled at the feel of traveling so far, so fast. The ground they'd covered in that time would have taken them a week to cover in the cart.

As the sun rose behind them, the driver turned off the highway onto a dusty, unpaved road. Riley sat forward to take in their surroundings. They rode for another fifteen minutes through what looked like an abandoned cattle ranch in the middle of nowhere. It was the type of place where no one would ever hear from them again.

The driver finally pulled up to a house as big as Uncle Mitch's ranch house. Riley had expected a camp surrounded by barbed wire or a concrete box prison. The sight of white lace curtains in the windows was comforting, even though they might have already been there when these people murdered the occupants and took over the house.

"Here we go," Coop whispered when the tall man opened his door and the driver opened Riley's.

The driver stepped aside for her to pass and motioned toward the front steps of the house. She put a pack on each shoulder and trudged up the steps to meet her fate. As she reached for the handle, the door swung open and a perfectly tanned and toned woman in her mid-thirties with long, shining brown hair smiled down at her. She waved Riley and the others inside, then stopped in the middle of the tastefully decorated great room.

"Please, take a seat," she said, then waited for them to comply. They arranged themselves on the two couches, waiting for her to speak. "My name is Bailey Jackson. I want to assure you you're in no danger, but you are not free to leave."

Adrian crossed his arms in a huff. "Where would we go?"

Bailey ignored him. "You have hot and cold running water, clean, soft beds, and fresh food at your disposal. Help yourselves to whatever you'd like."

Dashay got to her feet. "Sounds great but when are you going to tell us who in the hell you people are and why you've kidnapped us?"

Bailey looked shocked. "Kidnapped? Excuse me for a moment."

She hurried out the front door and bounded down the steps.

Coop took his cap off and rubbed his face. "Did you see her reaction when you said, 'kidnapped,' Dashay?"

"I've had enough," Riley said, and heaved herself off the couch. As she reached the door, Bailey returned with the driver and the tall man. Riley planted herself in their way. "We're done with this cryptic game of yours. Who are you people and what do you want with us?"

"We'll explain, Dr. Poole, but please take your seat," the tall man said. Riley didn't move. "Very well. If you prefer to stand. I'm Conrad Elliot," he gestured to the driver with dark, short hair and even darker eyes standing behind him, "and this is Paul Kinlaw. I promise to tell you who we are and why we brought you here, but not until you answer our questions."

Dashay gave him her fiercest stare. "Why should we?"

"Because if you don't, Ms. Robinson," Paul Kinlaw said, "We'll hold you here until you do."

"Paul," Bailey snapped. He sheepishly took a step back. "What my colleague means is, the information we share with you depends upon the answers you give us."

"In other words, we're at a stalemate until you tell us what we need to know," Conrad said. "We can't let you go, so our only other option is to keep you here."

"So, we're hostages until we spill our guts?" Coop said.

"Hostage is a strong word," Bailey said. "We prefer the phrase *long-term guests*."

"Call it whatever helps you sleep at night, but we've been down this road," Dashay said as she dropped back onto the couch. "We're your prisoners."

"Ask your questions," Riley said, to the surprise of everyone in the room. "We'll tell you anything you want to know."

"What are you doing, Riley?" Coop said behind her.

Without turning to face him, she said, "I'm tired and want to go home. That can't happen until they set us free. The way I see it, we have nothing to lose by answering their questions." She locked her eyes on Conrad. "So, ask."

"Smart choice, Dr. Poole," he said. He gestured toward the couch. "Please."

Riley hesitated for a second before lowering herself onto the couch next to Coop. Their three interrogators took chairs from the dining room table and sat facing them.

Conrad pulled the Wanted posters from his pocket again and held them up. "Tell us the cause of this."

Riley was shocked by his question. "You don't know?"

"You're not with Yeager?" Adrian asked.

The interrogators glanced at each other. Bailey shook her head. "Who's Yeager?"

Riley felt the weight lighten from her shoulders. If these people weren't with Yeager, they might still have a chance. "Colonel Yeager is the man hunting us. He's one of Kearns' hounds. We thought you were with them."

"We are not," Paul said, emphatically.

Riley turned to Adrian. "Tell them. All of it"

Adrian looked stunned. "Have you lost your mind, Riley? Without knowing who they are or if we can trust them?"

"My substantial gut is telling me it's safe. Tell your story, Adrian."

He glanced at Coop, who just shrugged. Adrian took a breath and locked his hands in his lap. "If you promise to protect me when they hear what I have to say."

Riley gave him an encouraging smile. "You have our word."

"I didn't mean you, Riley, but fine. I hope you know what you're doing." He slid to the edge of the cushion and straightened his shoulders. "I'm an astrophysicist. I was a solar specialist at Goddard Space Flight Center in Maryland. I was the first scientist to spot the CMEs."

"CMEs?" Conrad said. "Plural?"

Adrian gave a slight nod. "Yes. The CME that was predicted to hit earth thirty-six hours after the public service announcement was a second CME. It hit us, but by then, no one noticed."

"We weren't too concerned because the biggest impact was supposed to be in the eastern US," Paul said. "Everyone west of the Mississippi was blindsided."

"The entire world was blindsided," Dashay said.

Adrian sighed and rubbed his forehead. "She's right. I discovered a second CME, far larger than the one that was announced, that was going to hit Earth hours earlier and have a much more devastating impact. I confirmed it with scientists at the Space Weather Prediction Center in Colorado, then reported it to my superiors. The President was traveling home from a summit, so my superiors reported the information to Kearns. She summoned me to the White House."

Bailey's eyes widened. "You met with Kearns before the CME?"

"I did, seven hours before it hit. The short version is, I told her to warn the world of what was coming. She refused, saying it would only cause mass panic. To my everlasting shame, I did nothing to get the word out. A warning may have saved hundreds of thousands, if not millions, of lives. Kearns shipped me off to Andrews. I escaped in the chaos after the CME. I'm the only person alive who knows Kearns' dirty secret. I'm sure she wishes she'd kept me closer. If she had, I'm certain I'd be dead by now."

The three of them stared at him in stunned silence.

"Yeager is her hunter," Riley said, softly. "He's been chasing us across the country, though we've seen no sign of him in weeks. We've been doing our best to avoid military convoys."

Bailey cleared her throat. She took a moment to gather her thoughts. "If true, this is shocking news. We assumed you tried to assassinate Kearns. How did the four of you end up together?"

"Simple," Dashay said. "We were taken hostage by the same madmen."

"I see," Conrad said. "Are you trying to cross the border to escape Kearns?"

"Yes, and no," Riley said. "Dr. Cooper and I got stranded at a medical conference in DC. I'm from Colorado Springs. We've been heading there since the CME struck. My two youngest children are with my parents there. My oldest daughter was with me at the conference. She's fourteen." Her voice caught, and she had to take a few breaths to continue. "We got separated."

Bailey gave her a sympathetic look. "That's rough."

Conrad got up and ran his hand through his hair, just the way Coop always did. "This is unbelievable," he said. "Crossing paths with you was a one in a million chance."

"You weren't searching for us?" Adrian asked.

"No. We saw the truck off the road and stopped to help. We were shocked when we saw it was you treating the victims. To us, you looked like assassins trying to save the lives of strangers. It didn't compute."

"Then why did you bring us here?" Coop asked. "Tell us who you are."

Conrad turned to Bailey, and she gave a quick nod. "We're members of a task force for President John Purnell of the Western States of America. We cross the border covertly and recruit people who would be assets to our new country. This is our most forward staging area."

Riley wanted to shout for joy but restrained herself. She reached for Coop's hand and held it between both of hers. "This is the best news we've had in longer than I can remember."

Conrad faced them, looking like he'd just won the lottery. "For us, too. Not only are you trying to cross the border, but you have valuable intel on Kearns that must get to the President. We hit the jackpot with you."

Coop held up his hands to quell Conrad's enthusiasm. "It's not that we don't appreciate the help, but why not just remove Kearns and get your president elected in her place?"

"That's our end goal, but for now there's a continent and Kearns' forces between us, and she still has powerful allies," Bailey said. "It was more expedient to create our new country and work from there."

Coop nodded, but his question got Riley thinking, so she said, "What guarantee do we have that conditions are any better over your border? We could be running headlong into a worse situation than the one we're fleeing."

Bailey said, "I would ask that question in your position. All I can do is assure you conditions are far better in the WSA. Kearns' border guards stop anyone from crossing the border to get out. Our president's guards don't do the same. Anyone who would like to go back is free to do so. No one does. If you get to the WSA and find it's not what you'd hoped for, you can head right back to the USA."

Adrian said, "I'm all for crossing the border with you, but I don't remember volunteering to take my story to your president. That hasn't gone well for me in the past."

Paul locked his eyes on Adrian. "We won't force you, Dr.

Landry, but don't you have an obligation? You said you regret not taking action to warn people about the CME. Isn't this a chance to redeem yourself?"

Adrian stared at the floor and stroked his beard while he considered Paul's point. Finally raising his eyes, he said, "I can't prove it. Kearns and I were alone in the Oval Office. What good would it do?"

"You don't need to prove it," Conrad said. "All it takes is an idea. We have undercover officers infiltrating Kearns' military and traveling east, fueling unrest against her. Not that it takes much to do that. If we spread the truth about her refusal to warn the country, we would win a huge propaganda victory. We won't need to force her out. Her own citizens will do it for us."

Adrian looked like he was going to be sick. "I'm a nobody. I'm not prepared to take down the government of the most powerful country in the world."

Riley reached over and patted his shoulder. "Remember the millions that may have died due to her actions. Think of those who gave their lives in Charleston rather than succumb to her rule. What about all the people she forced into her Residential Zones? She ran my family off the ranch they've owned for generations. That's just some of the havoc she's inflicted. Why wouldn't you want to stop her?"

"Listen to Dr. Poole," Paul said. "You have the chance to be a hero and save countless more lives."

Riley felt pity for Adrian as she watched his shoulders slump under the weight of the decision he had to make. It was hard to believe he was the same man that not so many months earlier she would have gladly abandoned him on the side of the road.

"You don't have to decide today," Bailey said. "Our more pressing priority is getting you over the border."

"You're not taking us?" Dashay asked.

Conrad shook his head. "We need to maintain our cover and

can't risk crossing, but we'll do what's necessary to get you to the other side."

Coop stood and helped Riley to her feet. "First, we need rest and food, especially Riley."

"Of course," Bailey said. "Come with me."

As they all started for the stairs, two trucks pulled in front of the house. One pulled a horse trailer and the other a flatbed carrying their cart. Riley rushed to the doorway and watched as two men led Biscuit out of the trailer. She ambled down the steps and hugged her friend. He seemed overjoyed to see her.

"Hello, boy," she said, as she scratched behind his ears. "You didn't think I'd leave you behind, did you?"

She heard Conrad's booming laugh from the porch. Riley couldn't predict what awaited her on the other side of the border, but any organization that would spend valuable resources to bring her that silly horse and rickety cart couldn't be all bad.

———

A delicious meal of ribeye steaks, a luxurious hot shower, and a four-hour nap in an actual bed restored Riley to an almost human state. She was the last one downstairs and found the others seated around a kitchen table covered with papers. Coop pulled out the chair next to him and she lowered herself into it.

After glancing over the papers, she said, "What's all this?"

"In four days, just after sundown," Conrad said, "we'll drive you to a small, remote town north of the last outpost of Kearns' troops. The town sits a few miles from the two-hundred yard 'no-man's-land' at the border. You'll go three miles on foot after we drop you to meet your guide."

Riley frowned. "We can't take Biscuit?"

"Sorry, but no," Bailey said. "He's too conspicuous and the terrain is too rough for a horse."

"I have an idea how Biscuit can play a role, but we'll get to that later," Conrad said. "When you reach the town, you'll proceed to a bar called the *Dancing Gecko* and look for Bailey's cousin, Jax. He'll escort you through no-man's-land. We'll provide his description and code words to give him."

Dashay chuckled and said, "Seriously? Code words. Can't we just walk up to him and say, 'hey, Jax?'"

Paul glared at her. "This is no joke, Dashay. Kearns does not want her citizens leaving the country. She has her spies posing as residents of western states desperate to get home. She'll stop at nothing."

"I apologize," she said. "Continue."

Conrad nodded and went on. "Jax will get you over the border, then you'll walk two miles to another staging area. A driver will meet you and take you to Denver. He'll explain what happens from there. Adrian, if you decide to meet with President Purnell, and I strongly encourage you to do so, I'll send a note for you to give the driver. He'll know how to arrange it."

Riley got up and walked to the window. Biscuit was munching on hay in the shade of the only stand of trees near the house. "And Biscuit?" she asked.

"We'll use him as a decoy. We'll have a team disguised as the four of you ride Biscuit and the cart south to deflect attention from you. If anyone is tracking you, it'll throw them off course. By the time they discover the mistake, you'll be safe in the WSA. It could help us get our hands on this Yeager character. If he's in direct contact with Kearns, we can pump him for information."

"I've got to ask. How are you conducting these operations without phones or other electronic communications?" Adrian asked. "You can't be doing it all with radios."

"Hams, short range radio relay stations, good old-fashioned letter carriers," Bailey said. "There's even talk of resurrecting telegraph lines."

Adrian scratched his head. "Fascinating."

"Yes, fascinating," Riley said, short on patience. "What happens to Biscuit after the mission?"

"I'll return him to you somehow," Conrad said.

Riley said, "Keep the cart. Just take care of my horse and bring him home to me."

Bailey stood and gathered the maps and papers. "We'll go through the plan in more detail over the next few days. In the meantime, rest and recover your strength."

Coop stood and stretched. "Don't have to tell me twice. Too bad we can't take that bed with us."

Riley took one last peek at Biscuit before letting Coop lead her up the stairs. The plan for getting them into the WSA was solid, but not without risk. They'd been through worse. Her thoughts flashed to the night they escaped Branson's compound, hoping that was far more harrowing than the border crossing would be. This time they had an entire task force backing them up, and no matter how they felt about the rest of them, they'd do whatever it took to get Adrian to the president alive.

Nico finished patching his last patient from a border patrol gone bad just as the sun was setting. He cleaned up and grabbed a quick dinner in the mess before going on his nightly walk into the desert. That evening, he headed toward the far northwestern edge of the encampment. His commanding officer had ordered everyone to stay within the camp boundaries, but he was off duty and needed time away from the crowds and noise.

He walked for an hour past the last tents in camp, then turned west for the border. When he reached the barbed wire fence, he sat on a boulder and stared into no-man's-land, reflecting on his long trek to reach that point. It hadn't been the journey he'd started out to make but had ended up as the one he was meant to take. Part of him longed to cross the wire and head to New

Mexico. It was a cruel fate that he'd made it that far and was stuck on the other side of the border.

If Dashay had survived, she was likely on the opposite side of the border, too. A day hadn't passed since Yeager captured him that he hadn't thought of her. As much as he missed her and would love to spend the rest of their lives together, their fates had sent them on different paths.

Over the months of transfers to units heading west and stops at bases along the way, he'd had nothing but time to consider what he'd do when he reached the border. The news that the western states had seceded and formed a new country was a shocking blow. Even though his family and the love of his life were in the new country, crossing would make him a deserter. That was something he couldn't consider. He had no love for Kearns and her rogue government, but he still felt fealty for his country.

He pulled the four wanted posters from his pocket and studied each one. He'd never questioned that Dashay, Riley and Coop were innocent. Theirs was guilt by association. His feelings toward Adrian weren't so black and white. He'd asked himself a hundred times during his trip to the border if he could trust the story Adrian had given them. He wasn't a malicious or violent person, but he certainly was odd. He'd been alone in that room with Kearns before the CME and only the two of them knew the truth. Nico hoped with all his soul that Adrian was the one in the right.

Odds were that he would never know. Those people had passed out of his life, and he was alone to make his way. With civil war looming on the horizon, no one could predict what their futures would hold. He just hoped that one day, his would bring him the answers he sought.

Riley stood on the front steps watching Biscuit ride away, sure it was for the last time. For all Conrad's assurances, if it was so difficult to get people across the border, how did he plan to do it with a horse? It just wouldn't be worth the risk. She'd spent extra time brushing him and feeding him apple slices before the decoy dressed as Coop hitched him to the cart. The draft horse had trotted away with no clue what awaited him.

When the cart was out of sight, Riley went upstairs to finish packing. Bailey had assured them all they needed was one change of clothes and basic first aid supplies, but she'd persuaded her to let Coop carry an extra med pack. The one thing she'd learned on their harebrained field trip, as Coop had taken to calling it, was that their adventures never went according to plan.

Coop came in and pulled her into his arms. "We made it, Babe. Only ten miles to freedom."

She pulled away and spit three times on her knuckles. "Remember when we were trying to reach the ranch, and we kept saying, 'we'll be there tomorrow,' or 'we'll be there in a few hours?' It took weeks and weeks and almost dying multiple times to make it."

"We were alone and clueless then. We're veterans now and have experienced people helping us. How are you feeling?"

"Excited. Anxious. Wishing we were already home."

Coop looked over her head to the window. "Turn around." They faced the window together and watched the sun slip below the horizon. "What a sunset."

"You can't know how I've missed that," Riley whispered. "The Rockies are just beyond that horizon. Can you imagine how many times on those flat, dusty plains I wondered if I'd live to see my beloved mountains?"

"I knew. Every day, I knew."

She put her arms around him and gave him a tender kiss. "None of it would have been possible without you. Julia and I would have been dead within a week."

Coop let out his glorious laugh. "Not the Warrior Princess and Red Queen."

Dashay tapped on the open door. "You two lovebirds coming? Conrad's already pacing in the front yard."

"On our way," Coop said. He helped Riley with her pack, then threw his two packs over his shoulders. "Showtime."

They were on their way fifteen minutes later. She watched out the back window of the vehicle as the house receded. Once again, she was saying goodbye to her sanctuary, but for the first time, she was eager to go.

The drive to the drop point took longer than she'd expected, but soon, Paul pulled off the road and killed the engine. Her heart pounded as they climbed out of the car. She looked around and was confused to see they were surrounded by nothing but dusty plains and tumbleweeds.

Conrad hugged Dashay, then kissed each of her cheeks. Riley noticed a look that passed between them as they stepped apart and couldn't wait to ask her what it meant. Conrad moved to Riley and gave her the same hug and kisses, but not the look.

"I'll deliver Biscuit personally, so keep an eye out for me and take care of that little one." He shook Coop's hand, then walked to Adrian. Putting a hand on his shoulder, he said, "You have the note for the driver on the other side. I hope you'll put it to use. Your country needs you."

He shook Arian's hand. Then he and Paul got back in the car and drove off without another word.

Dashay faced west, and whispered, "I thought I knew the meaning of middle of nowhere, but I was wrong."

"Three miles," Coop said. "Piece of cake."

He took Riley's hand and whistled, *Heigh Ho,* as they started for the town. Though Riley felt the weight of her pregnant belly, it was good to walk. She'd grown soft riding in the cart and sitting around at the safe house.

To take her mind off what was coming, she let go of Coop's

hand and slowed to walk beside Adrian. "Have you made up your mind?"

Adrian took his time answering. "I haven't. I don't understand why someone else can't tell President Purnell about Kearns."

"He needs to hear it firsthand from you. Deep down, you know that. He'll want to question you about the details."

"I suppose that makes sense." Adrian was quiet for a moment, then said, "It was nice in those early days after we left the compound. No one knew who I was or what I'd done. Until we found out about Yeager, I thought I'd put it behind me. Now, I've lost my family because of it and these people want to use me to take down Kearns. It's worse than ever."

"Don't forget what Paul said. This is a chance to redeem yourself. Think of the lives you can save. It could prevent a war."

"I still have time. Let me give it more thought."

Riley stepped in front of him, making him stop. "I will, Adrian, but remember that once you've performed your duty, the new government will be grateful. They could help you find your family."

He looked her in the eye. "I hadn't considered that. Thank you, Riley."

She patted his shoulder, then motioned for him to continue as she waited for Dashay to catch up to her.

"Adrian doesn't respond well to pressure, Riley," she said. "You know he mulls things forever before he decides."

Riley smiled. "I do. I was just adding fodder to the mix. On a different subject, I know it's none of my business, but what's the deal with Conrad?"

"I don't even need to look at you to feel you judging me, but I've been lonely these last months, and it was something to pass the time. He's an impressive man, though. As unlikely as it is, I wouldn't mind crossing paths with him again."

Riley chuckled. "Who am I to judge? I'd known Coop for a few days before we were making out in the hotel lounge. But what about Nico?" When Dashay kept her eyes straight ahead and didn't answer, Riley said, "None of my business."

"Of course, it is, Riley. I just wasn't sure how to answer. Nico feels like a different lifetime, and you know what the odds are of us finding each other. Nil."

"Do you plan to go to New Mexico and look for him?"

"Impossible to say. Right now, I just want to get you home. Who knows what our futures hold?"

Riley squeezed her hand. "Excellent point." She glanced up and saw pinpricks of light in the distance. "That must be the town."

The four of them picked up the pace and reached the edge of what Conrad had called a town in thirty minutes. What Riley saw was more a collection of buildings.

"Conrad and I have differing ideas of what a town is," she said.

Coop pointed to a sign twenty yards ahead. "Made it easy to find the bar."

They made their way to the bar, not knowing what to expect. A few patrons looked up when they entered, but most ignored them. They were mostly cowboy types with a few bikers thrown in. The bar was dark, lit only by candles and lanterns, but there was an actual jukebox playing in the corner. The bartender stared for a moment, then went back to setting bottles on the sparsely stocked shelves behind the bar. Riley felt like she'd stepped onto the set of a bad seventies' movie.

They found a table in the corner to not appear so conspicuous. A girl wearing a leather miniskirt who looked no more than eighteen approached their table.

She took a tablet and pen from her apron pocket. "What can I get you?"

"I'll have a beer and she'll have a club soda," Coop said, pointing to Riley.

"Beer for me, too," Dashay said.

Adrian squinted at the girl in the darkness, looking totally out of his element. "Do you have iced tea?"

The girl stared at him like he'd asked for a glass of blood. "We have a few Diet Cokes left."

"That'll be fine."

As she sauntered off, Coop said, "I don't see anyone matching Jax's description."

Dashay gave one more look around. "Me, either, but those two in the corner have been watching us since we came in."

Riley gave them a quick glance. One was a man in his fifties with a long bushy beard and hair to match. He was with a woman at least twenty years his junior, wearing a cowboy hat over her two braids.

Adrian let out a gasp. "The woman just smiled at me and she's coming over."

"Relax," Dashay said. "Maybe mousy scientist is her type."

As she approached their table, she said, "Is that you, Cousin Louis? I wasn't sure if you made it. How long has it been?" Adrian froze, staring at her with eyes as big as saucers. "You're acting like you don't recognize me. It hasn't been that long. Didn't we dance at Mildred's wedding?"

Mildred's wedding was one of the code words Conrad had told them to expect from Jax, but he was supposed to have the exchange with Dashay.

Adrian recovered enough to say, "I think we did. It was *Achy Breaky Heart*, wasn't it?"

The woman gave him a playful slap on the shoulder. "No silly, it was *Cotton Eye Joe*."

She'd given all the right words, but she most definitely was not Jax.

"You're right," Adrian said. "So much has happened since then, I'd forgotten."

"Are you going to introduce us to your cousin, Louis?" Dashay said.

The woman extended her hand. "I'm Jaxi." Dashay took her hand and flashed a smile. "Come meet my friend," she said, waving them to her table.

Adrian looked to Riley and Coop in a panic. Riley gave a slight nod and stood to follow "Jaxi." Adrian jumped up so fast he nearly knocked his chair over. Improvisation clearly wasn't his strong suit.

When they reached Jaxi's table, she made a flourish with her arm, and said, "Everyone, this is Buck. Buck, this is my cousin, Louis and his friends."

The man looked up from under his bushy eyebrows, and mumbled, "Howdy," in a gravelly voice.

"This place is too dark and stuffy," Jaxi said. She leaned closer to them and put her hand to her mouth. "I have beer in my wagon. Let's take it to your trailer, Buck."

He got up without a word and lumbered toward the door. As Riley and the others followed, she prayed they weren't walking into a trap. Jaxi had a horse and wagon parked on the side of the bar. She motioned for the others to get in the back while she rode on the seat with Buck. He took them to a trailer park a mile west of the bar and stopped in front of the most dilapidated trailer Riley had ever seen. Buck climbed off the wagon seat and grunted for them to go with him inside the trailer. She wondered if they'd ever come out again.

What she saw inside was her biggest surprise of the week. The trailer was clean and looked newly refurbished and decorated. Buck pointed to the two couches while Jaxi sat at the small wooden table. Buck remained standing.

"Where's Jax?" Adrian blurted out. "What did you do to him?"

Buck let out a booming laugh. "Jax works for me. I sent him on another assignment since Conrad kept insisting that you were priority assets. You're not what I expected."

"Likewise," Coop said.

"Sorry about that. We didn't have time to get word to you." He dropped onto a bench with a grunt. "Now that I see you, I'm not sure we should go ahead with the mission."

Riley shifted forward on the cushion. "What do you mean? We've come this far."

Buck pointed to Coop and Dashay. "Those two are fine, but a pregnant woman and him? He looked like he was going to have kittens when he caught sight of Missy here."

Dashay pointed at Adrian. "He's the priority asset."

When Buck raised his eyebrows in disbelief, Adrian reached into his pocket and pulled out the note for the driver. Buck read twice, then folded it and handed it back to Adrian.

"I see," he said, then sat staring at them and stroking his beard.

"I'm crossing that border with or without you," Riley said.

"You wouldn't make it ten yards without me."

"She's tougher than she looks," Dashay said.

"Not the problem. The situation has escalated in no-man's-land. The enemy patrols have started shooting people crossing the area instead of taking them prisoner. I don't know where they get these morons. If Kearns knew, she'd be the one having kittens. What good are a bunch of dead citizens to her?"

Coop glanced at Riley, the fear obvious in his eyes. "You know how to get past these patrols?"

Buck gave a quick nod. "I do it every day, but now you understand my hesitation."

Riley got up and stepped in front of him. She was as tall standing as he was sitting. "You've made the risks clear, but we have to get across that border. We won't hold you responsible for what might happen."

Buck stood and extended his hand. "It's your life, Mrs..."

Riley shook his hand and said, "It's Doctor. Dr. Poole but call me Riley. That's my husband, Dr. Cooper. Goes by Coop. That's Dashay. She's a nurse, and the star of the show is Dr. Adrian Landry."

"No wonder they want you over there," Missy said. "Let's do it, Buck. Conrad and Bailey are counting on us."

Buck gave an almost imperceptible nod.

Riley stretched to her full five feet. "What do you need us to do?"

Yeager lifted the binoculars to his eyes. When he recognized the horse and cart, a smile crept up his face. After months of being one day behind or one town away, he finally had Daybreak. He climbed into the van and pounded on the side for his driver to go.

They caught up to the cart within five minutes, and the driver blared the horn for them to stop. The man on the seat driving the cart matched Daybreak's description. He pulled on the reins and the horse came to a halt, but the man didn't move. Yeager jumped out of the Jeep and strode up to him, psyching himself up to take control of the situation. The cart driver was wearing a straw hat and kept his head lowered so Yeager couldn't see his face.

"Get down from there, now," Yeager ordered.

Without raising his head, the man said, "Why should I?"

Yeager reached up and yanked the hat off his head. "Because I'm taking you into custody in the name of President Kearns, Dr. Landry!"

The man raised his eyes to Yeager, then smiled and said, "Who?"

He wasn't Daybreak. Against his best efforts to stop it, Yeager felt a twinge of panic spark in his gut. He'd taken the bait.

The man pulled the piece of hay from between his lips, and said, "You must be Colonel Yeager." On cue, the three people in the back of the cart stood and removed their hats. They were decoys, too. "Looks like we're taking you into custody."

Yeager and his driver turned and raced toward the Jeep. The

decoys in the cart raised their weapons and fired. The driver went down, but Yeager dove behind the steering wheel just in time. The Jeep was running, so he ducked and threw the gearshift into reverse. The imposter driving the cart urged the horse to turn the cart, but he got confused and was too slow. Yeager spun the Jeep around and sped off, leaving the cart in his dust.

He felt guilty for leaving his driver behind. They'd become as close to being friends as Yeager ever was with anyone, but he couldn't risk going back for him. As he raced back to his camp, he chided himself for not bringing backup. With his years of experience, he knew better but thought he'd have nothing to fear from Daybreak and his associates.

He also wondered who those people helping Daybreak could have been. From intel he'd gathered in the long chase, they always traveled alone. That they now had supporters trained in military tactics was a new cause for concern. They were up against the border and if Daybreak crossed, he'd be out of Yeager's reach permanently. He'd have to come up with a new strategy to do whatever was necessary to prevent that. No matter if it took the rest of his life, he could not let Daybreak slip through his fingers.

Riley and the others had trudged through sage brush for over an hour when she began to question her insistence in crossing the border that night. She'd made the mistake of wearing shorts because of the heat, and now her legs were covered with scratches. *This is the easy part,* she thought as she hopped to the side to avoid a tumbleweed.

Coop was behind her and tapped her shoulder. "Look at your legs. Buck told you to wear pants."

Not needing to hear the obvious, she said, "Ask him to stop so I can change."

She pulled her pack off her shoulder as Coop ran ahead to catch up with Buck. She had just opened the zipper when he ran back, shaking his head.

"He says there's no time. We're already behind schedule. We only have a few hundred more yards."

She scrambled to her feet and dusted off her shorts. "I can make that."

"I'll go in front of you and pick out the clear spots."

She got into step behind him, keeping her eyes focused on the ground to avoid the stickers. There was no point in looking up. Buck and the others were so far ahead, she couldn't see them in the darkness. She trudged on, reminding herself that her children were the prize at the end of the nightmare. Emily and Jared were only a few days away. It had been nearly eight months since she'd held them, but it felt like a lifetime.

She was absorbed in imagining her reunion with her children when she bumped into Coop. When she looked up, he said, "We're here, Babe. No going back."

Ignoring her stinging legs, she straightened her shoulders and said, "I'm ready."

Buck put on his pair of Night Vision Goggles, then waved them over to him. "Wish I had NVGs for all of you, but I was lucky to get my hands on these. This is my first trip crossing this far north, so the ground will be as new to me as it is to you. Follow my orders without question, no matter what I tell you to do, and we'll get you across alive. Ready, Missy?"

She nodded and followed him to the barbed wire fence. He pulled a pair of wire cutters from his pocket and cut the strands. Missy put on a pair of heavy work gloves and peeled the wire out of the way.

When the opening was ready, Buck stepped through but held up his hand to stop them. "Wait for my signal."

Riley's heartbeat quickened, and it was getting harder to take a deep breath. Coop reached for one hand and Adrian for the other. She felt their strength flow into her. Dashay danced around like she was warming up for a marathon.

"I'm pumped," she whispered.

A second later, Missy said, "There's the signal."

She moved to the post by the opening in the fence and waved them into no-man's-land. Dashay went first, then Adrian. Riley was impressed with his bravery. He'd come a long way since she found him tied to a tree and dying in Branson's compound.

Coop gestured for Riley to go next. When she passed him, he put his fingers through a loop on her pack and followed her. Missy brought up the rear and re-wrapped the barbed wire behind them to conceal the opening. Riley refused to let herself think about where she was and concentrated on the border fence on the far side, just visible in the moonlight. Her muscles ached, her mouth was parched, but the surge of adrenalin propelled her toward entrance to freedom and home.

They had just reached the halfway point when Riley heard the rumble of an engine in the distance. Before she figured out what it meant, Buck shouted, "Hit the deck."

Riley dropped to the ground and curled into a ball. She turned her head just in time to see a patrol Jeep with two occupants slowly heading north past the spot where they'd entered no-man's-land minutes earlier. They drove by without noticing.

"Stay put," Buck said, just loud enough for her to hear.

His warning was unnecessary. She had no intention of moving until that Jeep was long gone. They all waited, hidden in the sage brush until silence returned. It felt like hours to Riley but couldn't have been more than five minutes.

"Clear," Buck finally said.

Riley got to her feet and was surprised to find Missy only two feet away from her. "That was too close," she said.

They were facing the US side of the border. Missy leaned forward and squinted at the fence, then spun around to face

Buck, and said, "Check the fence. I think the barbed wire came loose. They'll see the opening in the fence."

Buck stared at the fence through his NVG's. "You're right. Nothing we can do about it. Let's book it." They started for the far border again, but only made it five yards before they heard the Jeep returning. "Run," he bellowed, waving them forward.

Coop pulled Riley's pack from her shoulder and tossed it into the brush. She stared at him in shock for a second, then grabbed her belly and took off after Missy. She was huffing and puffing but knew she had to reach the far side or die.

She looked back over her shoulder to see what was happening when the Jeep stopped. It was parked with the headlights shining on the opening in the barbed wire. She faced forward and ran with all her might, but it was too late. The men began sweeping the area with searchlights.

Buck rushed past her, heading toward the Jeep, yelling, "Don't stop. I'll cover you."

The gun shots started seconds later. Riley heard the thunk of rounds hitting the dirt near her feet. Coop grunted and went down with a thud.

"Coop's hit," she screamed and dropped to her knees beside him.

"Adrian, too," Dashay yelled back.

"Where are you shot?" she asked Coop.

Before he could answer, she saw the blood stain spreading under his T-shirt sleeve.

"My arm," he gasped. "Get out of here, Riley. Are you insane?"

"Clearly, or I wouldn't be here," she said. She glanced up and saw Buck firing at the men. One of them went down, but the other was still on his feet. "Why is it always you?" Riley hissed at Coop through her teeth.

Coop yanked off his shirt and held it out for her to tie around his arm. "Don't waste time on me. I can't even feel it. The broken rib and collapsed lung were much worse."

"Shut up," she barked as she tied the shirt on his arm. He pantomimed locking his lips and watched her work. "Adrian got shot, too. This might have all been for nothing. Why do you ever listen to me?"

A round hit the dirt five inches from Riley's knee. "Because you're usually right." He grasped her hand to get her to stop and listen. "Don't blame yourself for this. Please, Riley, leave me and get the hell out of here."

She pulled her hand free as another round hit the dirt, and Missy screamed. Riley looked up just as Buck crumpled in a heap. She turned to find Missy, but she must have gone to help Dashay with Adrian and was behind her.

"Don't move," she told Coop and got up, running in a crouch to Buck. Blood was seeping through his shirt at his abdomen, but he was alive and conscious.

"What are you still doing here?" he gasped.

"Saving all your lives." She cut off his pant leg and pressed it to his stomach. "Hold this. Press down." He put his hand over the cloth and did as she ordered. "Are there rounds in the rifle?"

"I think so. Don't know how many," he whispered.

Riley crawled to Buck's weapon and stared at it for a moment, trying not to freak out over what she was about to do. What she had to do. Forcing herself to pick it up, she raised her head just enough to get a look at the other border guard, but she couldn't find him in the darkness. She picked up Buck's NVGs and slid them over her head. Keeping as low as she could, she scanned the area again and spotted the guard crouching next to the Jeep, reloading his weapon.

Riley took three deep breaths to steady herself, then stood and aimed. He stood just as she pulled the trigger and the round hit his thigh. He yelped and dropped his weapon, then slid to the ground next to the Jeep.

Missy flew past Riley. When she saw the guard was still alive, she aimed her handgun and fired. The guard slumped over.

Missy stood above him for a moment, then rushed to Buck's side. Riley shoved her shock at what had just happened aside and crawled back to her patient. He was still conscious, but only just.

Missy was holding his head and rocking back and forth, sobbing. Riley touched her arm to get her attention. "I'm going to do everything in my power to save him, but you need to let me work. My supplies are in the pack next to Coop. Bring them to me." Missy nodded and lovingly laid Buck's head on the ground. As she got to her feet, Riley said, "Great job taking out that guard."

"Not nearly as great as what you did."

As Riley removed the cloth from Buck's wound, she said, "I was aiming for his head."

"You disarmed him. That's what matters."

"How's Adrian?"

"Got hit in the foot. He'll live."

When Missy hurried for the med pack, Riley examined Buck. The round had entered on the left below his navel, hopefully low enough to miss his kidneys and bladder. There was no chance it missed his intestines. They had to get him into surgery as quickly as possible.

When Missy returned with the med pack, Riley said, "Get that Jeep down here and we'll load our patients into it. I'll do what I can for Buck on the way, but he needs surgery. How far are we from Denver?"

Missy shook her head. "Three hours, minimum, and there's nothing between here and there. We'll meet our contact over the border and convoy. He may have more medical supplies in his SUV."

"It'll have to do. Get the Jeep."

The three women loaded the injured men into the Jeep, then Missy drove to the far border and blew through the barbed wire without slowing down.

"I'll fix that later," she said as Riley and Dashay stared at her in shock.

Riley did what she could to stabilize Buck, but he needed far more work than she could give. She'd injected him with the last of the morphine, so at least he wasn't feeling pain.

Coop was out cold and missed all the excitement. Adrian had been shot between his big and second toes. The bones were shattered, but Riley convinced him he'd have a rough but complete recovery.

Their contact was waiting three miles from the border. Riley and company went with him while Missy shot out of there in the Jeep to get Buck to a hospital in Denver. She promised to let them know how he did.

As they made their own way to Denver, Riley fought off the post-trauma panic threatening to overtake her and reminded herself that Colorado Springs was only hours away by car. Their escape had been a harrowing close call, but they'd made it. As they neared Denver and her beloved mountains came into view, she knew it had all been worth it.

CHAPTER FIFTEEN

RILEY AND COOP sat beside Adrian's bed in the recovery room at a Denver hospital, waiting for him to come out of the anesthesia. Adrian had begged Riley to perform the surgery to repair the shattered bones in his foot since there wasn't another orthopedic surgeon available. She was exhausted and had been reluctant but relented for his sake. Now, she was eager for him to wake up so they could get him back to their quarters and prepare for their meeting with President Purnell the following day.

After their ordeal at the border, Adrian had decided to tell the President his story, believing he owed it to Buck and everyone else who'd risked their lives for him. Ian Cole, the contact who'd met them on the western side of the border, had driven them directly to the hospital so Coop and Adrian could receive treatment and promised to arrange an interview with the president. He'd returned that morning to give them the details and take Dashay to their quarters. Coop had insisted on staying with Riley and dozed in the waiting room during Adrian's operation.

The hospital and parts of Denver Riley had seen reminded her of Charleston minus the impending war, though the nurses assured her that once outside the city limits it was a different story. That news disappointed her, making her wonder what it meant for her children and family. She'd learn the answer soon enough when Ian drove them to Colorado Springs after their meeting with Purnell.

Adrian's eyes fluttered open, drawing her from her thoughts. Coop leaned over and said, "It's about time, Sleeping Beauty."

Adrian gave him a silly grin, still under the effects of the anesthesia. "Where am I?"

"Tell him whatever you want," Riley told Coop. "He won't remember."

"I never get to see patients in recovery. I could have some fun with him."

The post-op nurse came in, so Riley got up and motioned for Coop to follow, sparing Adrian. "Let's let her work. I need to check your sutures."

As they left the room, he said, "You're not the only doctor who knows how to suture an arm. Mine did an excellent job. You need to eat."

"I won't argue with that." They went to the cafeteria, and while they ate egg salad sandwiches and field greens that Adrian would have been proud of, Riley said, "I spent time in this hospital years ago for seminars and training, but it feels different. Like I'm looking at it through someone else's eyes."

"Could it be seeing it for the first time since an apocalypse?"

She shook her head. "More than that. I'm not the same woman from the one who stepped on that plane in January. I remember how terrified I was when the plane took off. If only I'd known what was coming." She grew quiet and stared at her plate. "Coop, I shot a man."

He reached across the table and covered her hands with his. "You did, and it was the most impressive act of bravery I've ever seen. You saved all our lives."

"I stood there and watched that man die. Have I become so hardened?"

"There was nothing you could do, and you weren't the one who killed him."

"I tried to. I would have."

"Do you remember our conversation in the DC hotel, a hundred years ago? You asked if I could shoot someone to protect you. I said yes without a second thought. You didn't think you could because of the healer in you. That sets you apart but taking that shot came from the healer in you, too. That part wanted to protect us."

"I hadn't thought of it that way. That helps." She allowed herself to picture that moment at the border. "Did you see Missy shoot him? She didn't hesitate."

"Buck is Missy's father, Riley. Dashay told me." Riley was stunned. She'd imagined a different relationship between them. "Buck didn't like her joining him on missions, but she insisted. I hope he survives. If he does, that will be because of you, too."

She got up and walked to a southern facing window. When Coop came up behind her, she said, "My father is a ninety-minute drive in that direction. My mother, my children, my sister. I'm almost there, Coop. What will I find?"

He wrapped his arms around her and their child. "Your children are waiting to welcome their mother with open arms. I've never been so sure of anything in my life."

Adrian sat with his injured foot elevated on a stool as he waited with Riley, Coop, and Dashay outside the President's office in the Colorado capitol building, doing his best to appear calm. Riley saw through his façade.

She put a hand on his arm to calm him. "Stop fidgeting. The President just wants to talk to you. He's not Yeager."

"I don't know how I let you pressure me into this. I'm about to confess my most shameful secret to the president of a country."

"Picture him as a plant," Dashay said, and burst out laughing.

"Not helpful," he said, and crossed his arms. "Telling the truth about Kearns won't make the slightest difference and you know it. We're wasting time. I just want to find my family, get a nice piece of land with a garden, and peacefully live out the rest of my life."

"That's for tomorrow, and we didn't pressure you," Riley said. "Meeting with President Purnell was your decision, but you owe this to us and the rest of humanity. You just have cold feet." She reached down and adjusted the wrap on his splint to distract him. "How's the pain?"

"Throbbing. The pain meds haven't kicked in yet."

She patted his shoulder. "They'll take effect about the time your interview starts. You won't care about anything then."

"Aren't you going to ask about my pain?" Coop asked, rubbing his arm through the sling.

Riley shook her head. "You told me in the car it doesn't hurt."

He winked at her. "I lied."

The door to the President's office opened and his chief-of-staff walked out. "Come with me, please," she said.

Riley helped Adrian with his crutches, then followed the others into the President's office.

He stood when they entered, and said, "Welcome to the Western States of America. We're honored you've joined our great nation."

He was a distinguished looking African American man of about fifty-five. Buck's age. Riley smiled at picturing the contrast between them. But though she still hadn't come to terms with the secession, she considered this man was every bit as courageous as Buck.

"Thank you for taking the time to see us," Coop said, and extended his good hand. The President shook it and motioned for them to sit. After returning to his seat, he said, "I'm sure you have questions, but unfortunately, my time is limited today. I've been informed of your heroic sacrifice to get here, and I'm eager for the information you have. Dr. Landry, tell me about your encounter with Aileen Kearns."

Riley noted that he didn't call her President Kearns. Adrian sputtered a few times, then settled in and recounted his story in more detail than Riley had heard the three previous times.

"This is astounding," the President said. "When the US citizens hear of this, they'll rise against Kearns and solve our problem for us."

"I'm not sure I'd agree, Mr. President," Adrian said. "While there isn't much love for Kearns, most people are afraid and just doing their best to survive. I'm not sure those living in the eastern US are even aware of your country."

"They are," the President said. "We began sending teams east to disperse leaflets to get the word out over two months ago. That's just the tip of the iceberg. That's partly the reason more people are attempting to cross the border. At least, the ones not being held in Kearns' internment camps."

"Internment camps?" Dashay asked.

"Our term for her 'Residential Zones.' Reports of what goes on in those camps from people who have escaped are disturbing."

"We've heard some of those stories, too," Riley said, "but you clearly have more updated information than we do."

"In some respects, but I'd like to hear of your ordeal getting here when I have more time. My aid will schedule it. In the meantime, I'd like you to remain in the capital as our guests. I have a proposition I need to discuss with you, Dr. Landry."

"I'm flattered by the invitation, but I need to search for my family," Adrian said. "I believe they're in Texas, so I have a long way to go."

The President stood, signaling the meeting was over, so the others followed. "You can't travel until that foot is healed. Stay in

Denver and hear my proposal, then I'll provide you with transportation and resources to locate your family and bring them here."

Adrian reached out to shake his hand. "Thank you. That's a generous offer. I accept."

The President turned to the others. "And the rest of you?"

"Thank you, but we can't stay," Riley said. "I have two children and my parents waiting in Colorado Springs. I haven't seen them since the first of the year." She put her hands on her belly. "And I need to get home before this one arrives."

"Then, I won't keep you. Ian Cole will arrange your transportation home. Best of luck to all of you and go with our deepest thanks."

The door opened as if by magic and the president's aide entered. "I'll escort you to your driver," he said.

None of them spoke as they followed the aid to the main entrance to the capitol where Ian was waiting for them.

As soon as they were all seated in the car, Riley said, "Excellent job, Adrian. That wasn't so terrible, was it?"

Adrian grinned at her. "Not at all, but I'm glad it's over. That was a far cry better than my encounter with Kearns."

Dashay tapped him on the shoulder. "I wonder what this proposal of his is?"

Adrian shrugged. "He probably expects me to parade around spouting propaganda. I refuse to do that."

"He's got people for that," Coop said from the front seat. "He probably wants you as a scientific advisor."

Adrian rubbed his clean-shaven chin. "I hope that's what it is. I'd gladly do that. I could bring my family here and settle on the outskirts of the city. It would be a pleasant life."

"Whatever Purnell wants," Riley said, "this better not be goodbye. We're family now, and Colorado Springs isn't far. My father would love your advice for his little farm."

Adrian squeezed her hand. "Of course. I'd never abandon my little sister."

Riley turned to Dashay. "And you? What are your plans?"

Dashay looked at her without those striking dark eyes. "I was hoping to go with you and Coop, if you'll have me."

Riley squealed in delight and threw her arms around Dashay. Ian glanced at her in the rearview mirror. "I'm so glad. You're family, too, and I'll need you when the baby comes. Emily's going to love you."

Dashay kissed her cheek. "We're going to have some fun, girl."

"I'll get you a job as my surgical nurse, if the hospital is still standing."

Coop turned toward her and smiled. "If not, we'll build a new one."

As Ian pulled in front of the apartment complex where they were staying, Riley said, "Is this real or just a dream?"

Ian got out and opened her door. "As real as I am, Dr. Poole. This is the part of my job I love, reuniting families. I'll be here at eight in the morning to take you home."

Riley's gut tightened as familiar sights sped past her window on the way to Colorado Springs. She'd fought to reach this moment for so long, but now that it was here, she was riddled with fear and doubt. What if her family hadn't survived? She and Uncle Mitch hadn't ever been able to reach them on the ham radio. A hundred things could have caused that, but Riley feared it was because no one was alive to answer their call.

Coop took hold of her hand. "I can see the thoughts spinning in your brain. Your family is fine. Your children love you and will be overjoyed to see you alive and safe."

"Listen to your man," Dashay said, then turned toward the

window. "This area looks pretty much untouched. This is what you've survived for. It's going to be brilliant."

"Dashay's right," Ian said. "I haven't been to Colorado Springs since the CME, but I've heard reports that they weathered it well, in large part because of the strong military presence."

Riley wiped her cheek with the back of her hand. "Thank you. That helps. I have a terrible habit of always expecting the worst."

She gave Ian the last few directions to reach her father's farm, and when they finally turned onto the long driveway, she stared out the window in amazement. Nothing had changed, and she was tempted to jump out and run the last hundred feet to the house.

As Ian pulled the car into the space beside her father's truck, Emily came around the corner of the barn carrying a compost bucket in each hand. She dropped the buckets when she saw the car and stared at it in alarm. Riley froze, unable to tear her eyes from her beautiful daughter. She'd grown six inches, and her fiery red hair curls nearly reached her waist, but she was still her Emily.

Riley's hands trembled as she released the seatbelt and reached for the door handle. She was on the far side of the car from Emily, so she couldn't see Riley when she climbed out and started for her. When she emerged from behind the car, Emily's eyes widened, and she took a few steps toward Riley.

"Mom," she said, just loud enough for Riley to hear.

Riley managed a slight nod. Emily screamed and started for her. When she reached her, they threw their arms around each other and sank to their knees, sobbing on each other's shoulders.

Riley heard the screen door slam and looked up to see her mother racing down the steps. "What's going on out here, Emily?"

Emily looked up at her grandmother. "It's Mom, and she's fat."

Emily helped Riley to her feet, then stepped out of her way.

"Hello, Mom. I'm home."

Marjory studied her in confusion. "Home, but not fat. Pregnant."

Riley held up her hand to show her wedding ring. "And married."

Marjory moved to her in three strides and pulled Riley into her arms. Through her tears, she said, "I don't understand any of this, but you are the most beautiful sight I've seen since January."

Riley clung to her mother, feeling her strength and love pour into her. When she could pull herself away, she said, "Didn't Julia tell you about Coop and the baby?"

Marjory raised her eyebrows. "Julia? She's not with you?"

Riley put her hands to her face. "We got separated. She's with Uncle Mitch and his family. We got delayed. They should have gotten here long before us. This is terrible news."

Riley heard the car door close and Coop came up behind her. He held his good hand out to Marjory. She hesitated a moment before shaking it.

"I'm Riley's husband, Dr. Neal Xavier Cooper III. I go by Coop." He let go of Marjory and rested his hand on Riley's shoulder. "What's wrong, babe?"

"Julia's not here. They never made it."

"Don't panic yet," he said. "We got held up. They could have, too."

Riley turned away, shaking her head. "You know where they are. Kearns' people got them. We have to go back. I have to find Julia."

Emily stepped next to Coop and Riley, then crossed her arms and stomped her foot. "Someone tell me what's going on, right now! You lost Julia and you're married, Mom? You're having a baby?"

Coop turned and grinned at her. "Right on all counts. You must be Emily. I'm Coop."

Emily eyed him for a moment. "Yeah, I heard. Where's my sister?"

The screen door slammed again before Coop could answer, and Jared stepped onto the porch. He was taller, too. Tanned and confident. Not her baby anymore. He stared at her in stunned silence. Riley started for him, but he did the last thing she expected. He turned and went into the house. Riley quickened her step, but Marjory caught up to her and put a hand on her shoulder to stop her.

"He needs a minute. Let me go and I'll get you when he's ready. We'll straighten this mess out."

She gave Riley another hug before hurrying into the house.

"He's been pretty mad at you," Emily said. "We tried to explain, but he's too much of a baby to understand."

"Come here," Riley said, then put her arm around Emily's shoulder. "I'll need your help to get him to forgive me."

"You know Jared. He comes around eventually." She stepped out from under Riley's arm and turned to face Coop. "So, you're my new dad?"

"Looks that way," Coop said, and flashed his biggest smile.

"I guess that's cool." She turned and put her hands on Riley's belly. "I'm going to have another brother or sister? When?" The baby gave a big kick under her hand before Riley could answer, and Emily giggled.

"Isn't that awesome?" Coop said. "I love it when he does that."

Emily made a face. "It's a boy?"

"We don't know for sure, but I've decided it is. He'll be born in about seven weeks."

"Jared's going to hate not being the baby anymore. Who's that in the car?"

Riley had forgotten Emily's way of changing topics with dizzying speed, but she turned toward the car and waved for Dashay. She got out and walked toward them, smiling.

Riley took her hand and said, "This is Dashay, my best friend and new sister. Dashay, meet Emily."

Dashay picked Emily up and swung her around. Riley laughed at her shocked look.

When Dashay put her down, she said, "I've heard endless stories about you for months and couldn't wait to meet you. Your mom talked about you every day."

Emily looked even more shocked at that. "You did, Mom?"

Riley nodded enthusiastically. "I've been counting the seconds until I got home to you. Dashay is family now, and she's going to live with us. Speaking of family, where's your Papa?"

A cloud passed over Emily's eyes. Riley feared the worst, but Emily took her hand and said, "Come on. He's in the house." When they'd gone a few steps, she turned to Coop and Dashay. "You, too, Dad and Aunt Dashay."

As they started for the house, Ian got out and opened the trunk. "I'll leave your bags on the porch. Best of luck to all of you."

"Thank you, Ian," Riley said. "Take care of Adrian."

Ian gave a slight bow, then went back to unloading the car.

"Who's that?" Emily asked.

"Someone we just met who drove us from Denver," Riley said. "We'll tell you about our whole adventure later."

"It's a wild one," Coop said. "Your mom and sister are quite the badasses."

Emily giggled again and cocked her thumb at Coop. "I like him."

"Yes, we all do," Dashay said, her voice dripping with sarcasm.

Once they were in the house, Riley heard the soft mumble of Jared and her mother drifting out from the kitchen. She was dying to go to her boy and pull him into her arms, but she trusted her mother to tell her when the time was right. In the meantime, she needed to see her father.

Emily led them to his study on the first floor. When they reached his closed door, she said, "Papa's sick. Nana says it's because he worked too hard saving people after the CME, but I think it's something else she's not telling us. Now that you two doctors are here, you can fix him."

"I promise we'll do our best," Coop said. "And Dashay's a nurse. She'll help too."

Dashay nodded. "Definitely. The two of you go in first. Coop and I will wait in the front room."

Coop squeezed Riley's hand before they turned and went back to the front of the house. Riley let out her breath, then turned the knob to her father's office. What she saw shocked her, but she hid her reaction. The man in the bed looked half the size of the robust father she'd left behind, and she wondered what could have caused him to waste away so much in such a short time. Her doctor brain began flipping through potential causes, but they were too dire for Riley to accept.

They had converted his office into a bedroom and the bed was against the far wall.

Thomas stirred and opened his eyes when he heard their footsteps. He stared at Riley, uncomprehending for a moment, then gave her a weak smile. "Is that my Riley Kate?" he asked in a raspy voice.

Riley sat on the edge of the bed and took her father's hands in hers, disturbed at the feel of his bones through the skin. "I'm home, Dad. I've missed you every day."

"I never doubted that you'd be back, but no one would listen."

Emily moved to the end of the bed. "It's true. Papa kept telling us. But we didn't believe him. I'm glad you were right, Papa."

His voice caught when he said, "Me, too." He glanced at Riley's belly, and said, "What's going on there?"

"Mom got married. His name's Coop. I like him. She's going to have a baby, Papa."

He gave a faint chuckle. "That was my diagnosis, too. You got married?"

"It's a long story, Dad. There's time for that later, but I can't wait for you to meet my husband. We met at the conference. You may have heard of him. Dr. Neal Xavier Cooper III."

"*The* Dr. Cooper, inventor of the Xavier procedure?"

"Yes, Dad. He's incredible. I wouldn't be here without him."

"And my Julia?"

"She's traveling with Uncle Mitch and Aunt Beth. I expect to see them show up any day. They're bringing the whole crew. Fifty people."

"We'll need a bigger house."

Riley laughed at his joke, then grew serious. "What's going on with you, Dad? The truth."

"I honestly don't know, but I have a few theories. Maybe your famous husband can diagnose me."

"If anyone can, it's Coop." Riley leaned down and kissed his cheek. "I'll bring him to meet you in a minute, but I need to see Jared first. Mom's talking him into not hating me."

"That boy loves you with all his heart. It just takes him a little longer. Go to him."

Riley left her father, hoping she was right about Coop's ability to diagnose him. She hated seeing him that way and was determined to do whatever it took to get him well. She just hoped it wasn't too late.

Riley walked down the hall with Emily but stopped just outside the kitchen. "I better do this on my own. Why don't you go get to know Coop and Dashay?"

Emily left without arguing, and Riley was pleased to see some things had changed for the better. She tiptoed into the kitchen and stopped a few feet from where her mom and Jared sat at the table.

Marjory stood and lifted Jared's chin until his eyes met hers. "It's time to welcome your mom home."

Marjory left the room, giving Riley's hand a squeeze as she passed. Riley gazed at her precious son staring down at his hands resting on the table.

"I'm sorry I took so long to come home, Jared. I didn't mean to, and I hope you'll forgive me. I've missed my special buddy every day. You wouldn't believe what I went through to get back to you."

Jared didn't move, and Riley was afraid she'd failed to reach him. Not knowing what else to do, she stood still and waited. In a flash, he jumped out of his chair, knocking it over with a crash, and ran into her arms.

She mouthed a prayer of thanks and stroked his hair while he had his cry.

Finally pulling away, he said, "I'm sorry, Mommy. I was just so mad when you didn't come back. At first, I thought you stayed away on purpose, but later, I knew it wasn't your fault. So many bad things happened to everyone, even my friends. Some of them died."

Riley took his hand and led him back to the table, aching at the pain he'd known in his short life. He righted his chair and sat next to her. "Then why did you run when you saw me?"

"I was just so surprised to see you, and you look so different with your black hair and that huge stomach. Nana says there's a baby in there."

Riley ignored the tears streaming down her face. "It's true. You'll have a baby brother or sister soon."

"I'm going to be a big brother?"

Riley nodded. "You'll be an excellent big brother. You want to feel it move?"

He made a face, then said, "I guess." Riley guided his hand to where the baby was turning cartwheels. His eyes widened when he felt it move. He held his hand on her belly for a moment longer, then pulled it back. "That's weird."

Riley laughed. "I guess it is. Do you want to meet my husband, Coop?"

"My new dad?"

"He'd love to be your new dad, but that's for you to decide. Get to know him first. I think you'll love him."

Jared got to his feet and took a breath. "Let's go."

Riley held his hand as they walked to the living room. Coop got up from the sofa when they came in.

He put his hand out to Jared, and said, "Hey, big guy, I'm Coop. You're much taller than your mom described you." Jared took Coop's hand and gave it an exaggerated shake. "That's a firm grip. Just what I like in a man."

Jared turned to Riley, beaming at her. Coop had won him over in ten seconds.

Riley took a moment to take in the sight before her. It had been a dream for so long that it was a feat for her mind to accept what she saw was real. Once Julia was safely under their roof and her father recovered, she'd possess everything she could wish from life.

———

Julia sat at her desk in their house in their third internment camp. She still blamed herself for letting the guard in Memphis overhear her say her mom was on the wanted poster. They'd questioned the entire family for days, then moved them to Kansas City for two months and finally to this dinky little town in the middle of nowhere called Woodward, Oklahoma. She liked the house better than the one in Kansas City, and it wasn't too far from home.

There had been talk at one point of using the family as bait to catch her mom. Nothing ever came of that, but it proved to Julia that her mom was still free, and it gave Julia an idea. She finished writing her tenth letter for the day and folded it into an envelope with one of the wanted posters of her mom she'd torn down. She wrote Dr. Katie Cooper on the envelope and dropped it on top of the other letters.

Holly was watching from her bed on the other side of the room. "I don't know why you bother with those letters. What are the odds that any of them will ever get to your mom?"

Julia turned her chair to face her. "I don't know the odds, but what does it hurt? Lightning might strike one day, and Mom will find out where I am. She's probably been in Colorado Springs for months now. I hate to think what it was like for her when she got home, and I wasn't there. You know she's blaming herself, but she shouldn't. If she and Coop didn't leave when they did, they'd be stuck in Oklahoma City with us, and we're never getting out of here."

Holly slumped against her pillows and crossed her arms. "I told you to stop saying that. Grandpa heard that people in the WSA are going to fight to stop Kearns. If they win, we'll get out of this hellhole compound."

"I hope he's right, but that could take years. What do we do in the meantime? Sit around crying? I'm going to write my letters and sneak them to people the guards are moving to other camps. Someone will escape and give my letter to Mom."

"You're delusional."

Holly's words stung. Julia got up and dropped onto her bed. "I don't know why you care, and what would you do if it were your mom? Besides, it's not like we have anything else to do but go to that joke of a school. I'm smarter than our moron teachers."

Holly was quiet for a minute before saying, "I'm sorry, Julia. Don't listen to me. I'm just so sick of this place and the guards and all the people." She moved to Julia's bed and put an arm around her. "Keep writing your letters. One day, your mom and Coop will find out where we are and come to the rescue."

"Thanks, Holly. I'm sick of this place, too, but Mom always taught me to find the good in any situation. Maybe we can figure out a way to make things better for the younger kids. It would take our minds off our problems."

Holly jumped and grabbed Julia's notepad and pen from their desk. "Excellent idea. Where do we start?"

Julia sat up and smiled at her cousin, glad for something to take their minds off their problems. She imagined what would make Jared and Emily happier if they were in the camp. Whenever she thought of them, she saw them the same as they were the day that she and her mom left for DC. She'd changed so much since then but hoped her brother and sister wouldn't change too much before she made it back to Colorado, however long that would be.

Yeager parked his bike in front of the Dancing Gecko and made his way into the darkened bar. After the cart incident, he'd struck out on his own to find Daybreak, no longer trusting anyone else. The track had gone cold for weeks, but he'd had a breakthrough when someone had seen a group matching Daybreak and his companions. He'd followed their trail to this bar, certain he was close on their heels.

He lowered his cowboy hat over his forehead and walked to the bar. "Someone sent me here to ask for Jax," he told the bartender. "Is he here?" The bartender cocked his head toward a table in the far corner where a young, dark-haired man sat alone. Yeager touched the rim of his hat. "Obliged."

He strode to the table and sat across from Jax without being invited to do so.

Jax studied him for a moment, then said, "Do I know you?"

Yeager sat back and folded his arms. Keeping his voice low, he said, "My sources tell me you're the person to see for crossing the border."

Jax chuckled. "Your sources? I don't know what you're talking about. I'm just here enjoying my beer."

Yeager pulled a folded piece of paper from his pocket and slid it across the table. "That will explain why I'm here."

Jax ignored the paper and took a sip of his beer, so Yeager unfolded it for him.

Jax glanced at it. "That you?" Yeager lifted his hat for Jax to get a look at him, then lowered it again. "I see new wanted posters every day. Half the country is wanted by Kearns."

"But not on her top ten list."

Jax gave the wanted poster another glance. "How do I know you don't deserve it?"

"I can't prove it. Listen to what I have to say."

"How do you know you can trust me?"

Yeager leaned closer to him. "I don't but I'm out of options. Kearns' people are closing in on me. I was one of her top military commanders from the beginning, but I became disillusioned when I saw the atrocious way she was treating her own citizens. She's power hungry and insane, if you ask me. So, I deserted. She's desperate to find me because I possess vital information she doesn't want shared with the enemy, but that's exactly what I plan to do."

"Who told you to come to me?"

"I came upon a group of people who said there's a faction helping people cross. They mentioned you."

Jax eyed Yeager as he toyed with his beer. "This isn't usually how this works."

"I understand but look at it this way. If I'm not who I say I am, I'm just one guy. How much trouble could I cause?"

"Good point. You know how to ride a dirt bike?"

"I'm a fast learner."

Jax got up without a word and started for the door. Yeager followed, not knowing if he was getting help to cross the border or if he was walking into another trap. But one thing he'd told Jax was true. He was out of options.

Once they were outside, Jax ducked around the side of the

building and motioned for Yeager to follow. He led him to a shed, then unlocked the chain holding it closed and waved Yeager inside. Two dirt bikes stood at the back of the shed.

"You're lucky you caught me on a slow night. I'll get you as far as the border fence, but you're on your own to cross to the other side. I know when to expect patrols, but we need to time it exactly right. We've had some botched crossings lately and they've stepped up surveillance. Once you're in no-man's-land, it's your neck."

Yeager tried not to smile while Jax explained how to operate the dirt bike, as if that was something he didn't know. He listened intently, then nodded politely when the other man finished. Jax handed him a pair of wire cutters for the fence on the other side and warned him to make sure he rewired the strands once he crossed over.

They were on their way five minutes later. He rode behind Jax along a trail through a field covered in sage brush. Not only was he getting one step closer to Daybreak, but he was gathering valuable intel to share when he returned.

Jax stopped thirty minutes later and got off his bike to cut the fence. He held it open until Yeager had pushed his bike through the opening.

"Good luck, man," he said. "You're a true patriot."

He rewove the fence, then took off back towards the bar. Yeager mounted his bike and reached the far side with no trouble three minutes later. He cut the fence, rolled his bike through, then rewired the fence. It was all too easy. No wonder Daybreak made it to the pretend country. He'd have to have a word with the border patrol commander when he returned.

Riley stood at the kitchen window watching Emily and Jared play with their fifteen-month-old cousin, Miles. Riley had been delighted to learn her sister, Lily, and her husband, Kevin, had moved into their parents' home with Miles when their apartment became unlivable after the CME. They'd had a wonderful time getting reacquainted the past three weeks, and Coop and Kevin had hit it off from day one. An added perk was Coop spending time with Miles was helping prepare him for fatherhood.

Riley was also grateful that Lily and Kevin had taken over working the farm when Thomas fell ill and didn't know how they would have managed without them. Dashay and Coop had gone to work at Riley's old hospital a week after their arrival, and Riley wasn't much help with heavy work in her condition, so having Lily and Kevin picking up the slack was a blessing.

Their small farm was in better condition than many of the surrounding ones, thanks to Thomas' foresight. He'd had solar panels installed five months before the CME hit and had been smart enough to have his generator and inverter hardened. Adrian would have been impressed. They had limited electricity but had to be careful to regulate their usage. After what Riley, Coop and Dashay had been through, even three-minute showers and hot meals were a luxury.

The farm had a large garden, chickens for eggs and meat, and even a milk cow. Kevin had arranged with a local cattle farmer to breed her, so they were expecting a calf any day. Coop shared his idea with Kevin and Thomas about adding horses, and they were already well into the planning stages. Once Uncle Mitch showed up with his horses and know-how, they'd be set.

Marjory and Riley took care of the household chores and tended to Thomas, who was improving rapidly after his open-heart surgery. Coop had diagnosed a failed aortic valve that had caused further damage to his heart. They'd taken him to Denver for Coop to perform the surgery It had been nothing short of miraculous that Coop had found the replacement valve and medical equipment he needed for the surgery. Thomas had been home for a week and would be ready to return to work on the farm and treating the occasional patient before winter.

One dark spot in her return was the news that the home she and Zach had shared was destroyed in the CME. She'd insisted on Lily taking her to see it two weeks after she arrived home. Lily warned her it was a shocking sight, but Riley assured her after what she'd witnessed on her trek across the country, nothing could shock her. She'd been wrong. Natural gas explosions had decimated the entire neighborhood. Residents who survived had abandoned their homes and left the area desolate.

When Lily pulled into the driveway in front of what had been Riley's home, she stared in stunned disbelief. Nothing remained but the charred foundation with weeds growing through the cracks.

She opened her car door, hoping to go search the rubble for anything of her former life that may have survived, but Lily put a hand on her arm to stop her.

"Don't, Riley. Mom and I already tried. There's nothing left." Riley fell back against her seat filled with anger, loss, confusion. "I understand," Lily said. "We've all lost so much, but they were just material possessions. We all still have what matters."

"No, you don't understand," Riley whispered. "That house and everything in it were all I had left of Zach. It's like he was just erased."

"How can you say that? You have Julia, Emily, and Jared, the most important possessions Zach gave you."

Riley squeezed Lily's hand. "True. I was just hoping to salvage other reminders of our life together."

"Mom has pictures, souvenirs you brought home for her and Dad from your travels. Zach isn't erased. Leave this behind. You have Coop now and the baby coming. Focus on your future."

"When did you become so wise?"

"It was bound to happen eventually," Lily had said as she backed out of the driveway of Riley's past to drive her home.

It had taken a few days for Riley to put the disturbing experience behind her, but her life was so full. She had little time to dwell on it.

As she continued to watch the children that afternoon, Emily spun Miles around, producing a round of giggles. Riley smiled to see the change in Emily. Marjory told Riley one day that Emily had gone from bossy and whiny lazybones to a take-charge, right hand young woman. She'd discovered that she loved gardening and tending to the chickens. She was working her way up to helping with the pigs. Lily commented more than once on how Emily stepped up when Thomas became ill.

Riley had misjudged Emily just as she had Julia and couldn't have been prouder of her daughters. Jared was only seven, but even he had grown in more than just height. Riley hoped that now she was home, he could stop worrying about her and enjoy his childhood. Coop was going out of his way to make that happen.

Riley finished wiping the counters, then went out to join in the play while she could. All her time would be commandeered once the baby came. As she came out on the porch, she spotted movement on the far end of the drive coming up to the house. She gave a second look and realized it was a man riding a horse. She recognized the horse's color and gait immediately and hurried down the steps as fast as she was able.

Conrad tugged on Biscuit's reins to stop him, then climbed down from the saddle and gave Riley a hug. Not to be ignored, Biscuit gave a whiny of welcome and bobbed his head. Riley pressed her cheek against his and rubbed his neck. Emily picked Miles up and she and Jared ran to see what was happening.

Riley herded the children in front of Conrad, and said, "This is Mr. Elliot, and the horse is my good friend, Biscuit. He was one of Uncle Mitch's horses. I never expected to see either of you again, especially after so long. How did you manage this?"

"Wasn't easy," Conrad said, "but I'm a man of my word."

Emily stared wide-eyed at Biscuit. "You have a horse? We get to keep him?"

"You do," Conrad said, "and he's not just any horse. He's a hero."

"Hard to believe," Riley said, "but I can't wait to hear that story."

Jared walked to Biscuit and patted his side. "Can I ride him?"

"Biscuit has come a long way and needs to rest now," Conrad said, "but I'm sure your mom will let you ride him later."

"First thing tomorrow," Riley said. "I'm sure you need a rest, too, Conrad. Are you staying?"

"Just overnight if I may. Ian and Bailey are coming for me in the morning."

"I know someone else who will be happy to see you. Dashay should be home from the hospital with Coop soon."

"And I'm looking forward to seeing them, but first, Biscuit needs water and shade."

Jared took hold of the reins, and said, "We have a pond by some trees. Can I take him, Mom?"

"Of course," Riley said, surprised to see Jared so comfortable around Biscuit. "Emily, go with him."

The children walked off with Biscuit, and Riley led Conrad to the house.

"You have a nice setup here," he said. "I noticed the solar panels and can hear the generator."

"We're fortunate. Most of the families on surrounding farms weren't as prepared, but they're adjusting to nineteenth century life. We share what we can."

Riley led him to the kitchen and motioned for him to sit at the table. She poured him a glass of water, then sat across from him.

He gulped the water down, then said, "Was this your home before the CME?"

She shook her head. "My parents bought this farm after my father retired from his medical practice. He says it was the smartest thing he ever did. We're living here with them, my sister's family, and of course, Dashay." She was quiet for a moment. Gathering her courage to ask her question. "How's Buck? Did he make it?"

Conrad's face creased into a smile. "He's too stubborn to die. He's completely recovered, but he's given up his border missions. He and Missy are supporting our efforts from this side of the fence, now. In fact, I heard they're taking Adrian to Texas to find his family."

Riley left out her breath. "Best news I've had in a while. Coop and Dashay will be thrilled to hear that. Can I ask why the president wanted to see Adrian when we arrived in Denver?"

"He's given him a position as Chief National Scientific Advisor. Adrian's in heaven, as I'm sure you can imagine. He's planning to bring his family back to Denver once he finds them."

"That's wonderful. I hope he does. I saved the toughest question for last. Any progress on finding my daughter?"

Conrad lowered his head, which told Riley all she needed to know. "We're not giving up. We have people searching for them and infiltrating internment camps all over the Midwest. It's just a matter of time."

"I have complete faith in you, especially after you got Biscuit back to me."

Conrad nodded as Coop burst into the room. When Conrad got to his feet, Coop threw his arms around him, pounding him on the back.

"Great to see you," Coop said. "And Biscuit's back. You just made Riley's year and our horse ranch is now off to a promising start."

Dashay came in and shoved Coop out of her way. She grabbed

Conrad and planted a kiss on him. "You're a welcome sight. Please, tell me you're staying."

"How could I refuse after a welcome like that?"

Conrad joined the family at the firepit after Lily put Miles to bed. Riley consented to let Emily and Jared stay up late since it was a special occasion. She thought she was the last one down from the house and was surprised that Coop was missing when she got there.

"Has anyone seen my husband?" she asked, before bothering to sit.

"He went to say goodnight to Biscuit," Dashay said.

"Wonderful idea," Riley said, and walked off to join Coop. She found him in the empty pen near the barn. She gave Biscuit a slice of apple and scratched behind his ears. "He needs a proper stable."

Coop kissed her cheek, and said, "We weren't planning on it this soon, but Kevin and I are drawing up the plans. He knows some builders that can help. I've missed this guy. Nice to have him home."

Riley reached for Biscuit's brush when she felt a trickle of water at her feet. "We have a problem, Coop. My water just broke."

Coop put his hands on her shoulders. "Great! You're sure?" When she nodded, he said, "Why is that a problem?"

"It's too soon. My due date isn't for another three weeks, minimum."

She doubled over as the first contraction hit.

"Too soon or not, this baby's coming. Can you get back to the house on your own while I let everyone know?"

She straightened when the pain subsided and started for the house. "Hurry," she called over her shoulder.

They were racing to the hospital in Thomas' old farm truck with Dashay fifteen minutes later. Riley had to remind Coop repeatedly between gasps to slow down. "I want to make it there in one piece. We have plenty of time."

"We don't know that. Your C-section isn't scheduled for three weeks. I'll need to send someone for Dr. Whitney and hope she's had time to find what she needs for the surgery."

"I'm not the only woman having a baby around here," Riley said. "They'll be ready. I'm just grateful we're not doing this in some field in the middle of nowhere."

When Coop pulled into the circle drive in front of the ER, Riley was concerned to see that the only parts of the hospital with lights were the ER and ICU. Coop got out and grabbed a wheelchair for her, then pushed her to the reception desk.

"Why's the power out, Mindy?" Coop asked the receptionist before she had a chance to greet them.

"Two of the generators went down just after sunset, Dr. Cooper. The mechanics are on it."

Riley grabbed her belly and groaned. "What about the OB wing?"

"Also down, Dr. Poole, but we've got an OR setup next to the ICU."

Coop rubbed his forehead and sighed. "Is Dr. Whitney on duty?" Mindy shook her head. "Is anyone in OB?"

She stared at him for a moment, looking too scared to answer. "Dr. Whitney was on a twenty-hour shift and just left. Dr. Morton, our only other OB/GYN hasn't shown yet. Like I said, power's out over there, but we don't have any OB, anyway."

"Let's go at it this way. Which other surgeons are here?"

"Dr. Cameron."

"Who's Dr. Cameron?" Riley asked.

"No one you want delivering this baby," Dashay said. "Looks like it's us, Coop."

Riley felt another contraction coming on. She squeezed

Dashay's hand and breathed through it. When it passed, she said, "I don't care who delivers this child, just get me an epidural."

"Go to the temp OR, Dashay, and tell whoever you can find to get ready for an emergency C-section. I'll find a room to prep Riley. Mindy, please tell me there are nurses on duty who can assist us."

"Yes, Dr. Cooper. I'll send them to you."

Mindy got up and pushed her way through the ER doors while Coop wheeled Riley to an empty room near the ICU and Dashay ran to the OR. When they reached Riley's room, Coop helped her undress and get into a gown. He got her situated on the bed and began going through storage drawers to find supplies he needed.

As Riley watched him rushing around the room, she said, "Have you ever performed a C-section, Coop?"

"Once, on an OB rotation, but I've assisted in a few, too. It's a simple surgery."

Riley was grateful for his confidence and the fact that he was one of the most skilled surgeons in the world. Three nurses rushed in and began poking her with needles and hooking her up to machines.

"Go scrub, Dr. Cooper," one nurse said. "We'll take care of your wife and baby."

Coop stayed where he was, studying every move the nurses made.

She held her hand out to Coop. "Come here." He stepped next to the bed and took her hand. "They know their jobs. Trust them and get ready to deliver your son. I'll see you in a few minutes." He kissed the back of her hand, but as he turned to leave, Riley felt a searing pain in her head and the room started spinning. "Something's wrong, Coop. I don't feel right. Take my pressure."

The last thing she remembered before the room went dark was the look of fear in his eyes.

"Wake up," Riley heard Coop say from what sounded like the far side of a tunnel. "You can't hold your son until you wake up."

A son. She'd been right. She had another son. She concentrated all her effort and forced her eyes to open. Coop stood above her with the goofiest grin she'd ever seen.

"Where's my Xav?" she croaked.

He dropped into the chair beside her bed and wrapped her hand in his. "Dashay's getting him ready to meet his mother, but we need to talk first."

Riley tried to sit up, then remembered the C-section. "Is it the baby? Is he healthy?"

Coop's voice caught before he could answer, and Riley grew more concerned. "He's perfect. He's tiny, but healthy and perfect. He has fiery red hair like his mommy."

Riley relaxed and let out her breath. "What is it, then?"

"It's about you. You had sudden onset eclampsia. Your pressure went through the roof." His voice trembled when he said, "We almost lost you, Babe. Most terrifying moments of my life. Now I understand why doctors should not operate on family members."

That explains the blinding headache, she thought. "What's my condition and prognosis?"

Coop ran his hand through his hair. "I had to perform a complete hysterectomy. I'm sorry, Riley, no more babies."

Riley gave a quiet chuckle. "I have news for you. There never were going to be more babies. What else?"

"That was the worst of it, so I'm glad you took it so well. You'll need time to recover. We've got your pressure down, so that's good. You'll be weak but back to normal in two months. Promise you'll rest."

"That's not a problem. More time to spend with Xav."

Dashay tapped on the door and came in carrying a little

bundle swaddled in a green blanket. "Here's your tiny little bruiser." Coop took the baby and helped Riley settle him on her chest. "I'll let you three get acquainted," she said and left them alone.

Riley peeled the blanket aside and peered into the face of her son. Coop had been right. He was tiny and perfect. She removed his knitted cap and smiled at his curly red hair. "He may be a redhead like me, but he's an exact replica of his daddy."

Coop leaned closer and gently brushed his finger on Xav's cheek. "There's nothing better than this. We have everything we need in the world."

"Falling in love with you and having your son are more than I could have dreamed possible a year ago, but we don't quite have everything. She's out there, Coop. My Warrior Princess is still out there."

"You know I love Julia like she's my own daughter. When the time is right, we'll do whatever it takes to bring her home. You have my promise. For now, we'll rely on Mitch to keep her safe."

Riley kissed the back of Coop's hand, trusting his word. Xav gave a little squeak and opened his bright blue eyes. As hard as it was to be separated from Julia, not even knowing where she was, she had others counting on her more. She held Xav tighter and closed her eyes, ready to face whatever this new life had to bring.

END

The story continues!
HOPE IGNITES

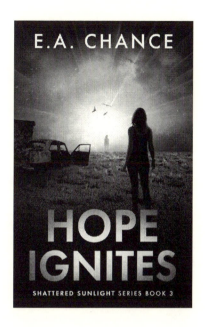

Enjoy reading Hunting Daybreak?
Please leave a review at your favorite retailer. Thanks!

* * *

ABOUT THE AUTHOR

E.A. Chance is a writer of award-winning suspense, historical and post-apocalyptic women's fiction who thrives on crafting tales of everyday superheroes.

She has traveled the world and lived in five different countries. She currently resides in the Williamsburg, Virginia area with her husband and is the proud mother of four grown sons and Nana to one amazing grand-darling.

She loves hearing from readers. Connect with her at:

https://eachancebooks.com
e.a.chance@eachancebooks.com

Made in United States
Troutdale, OR
09/13/2025

34479947R00229